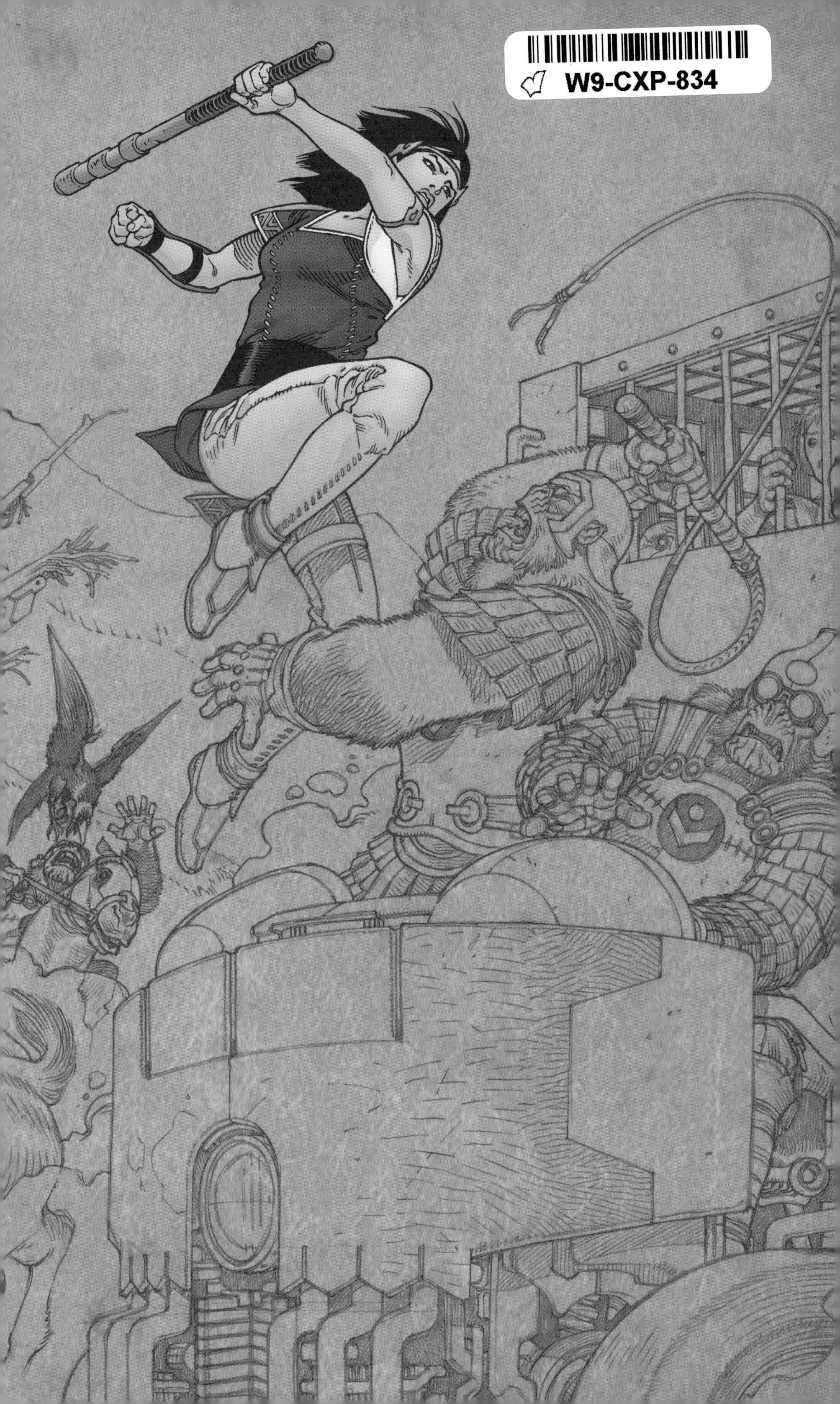

GABRIEL RODRÍGUEZ

SWORD OF AGES

BOOK 1 : AVALON

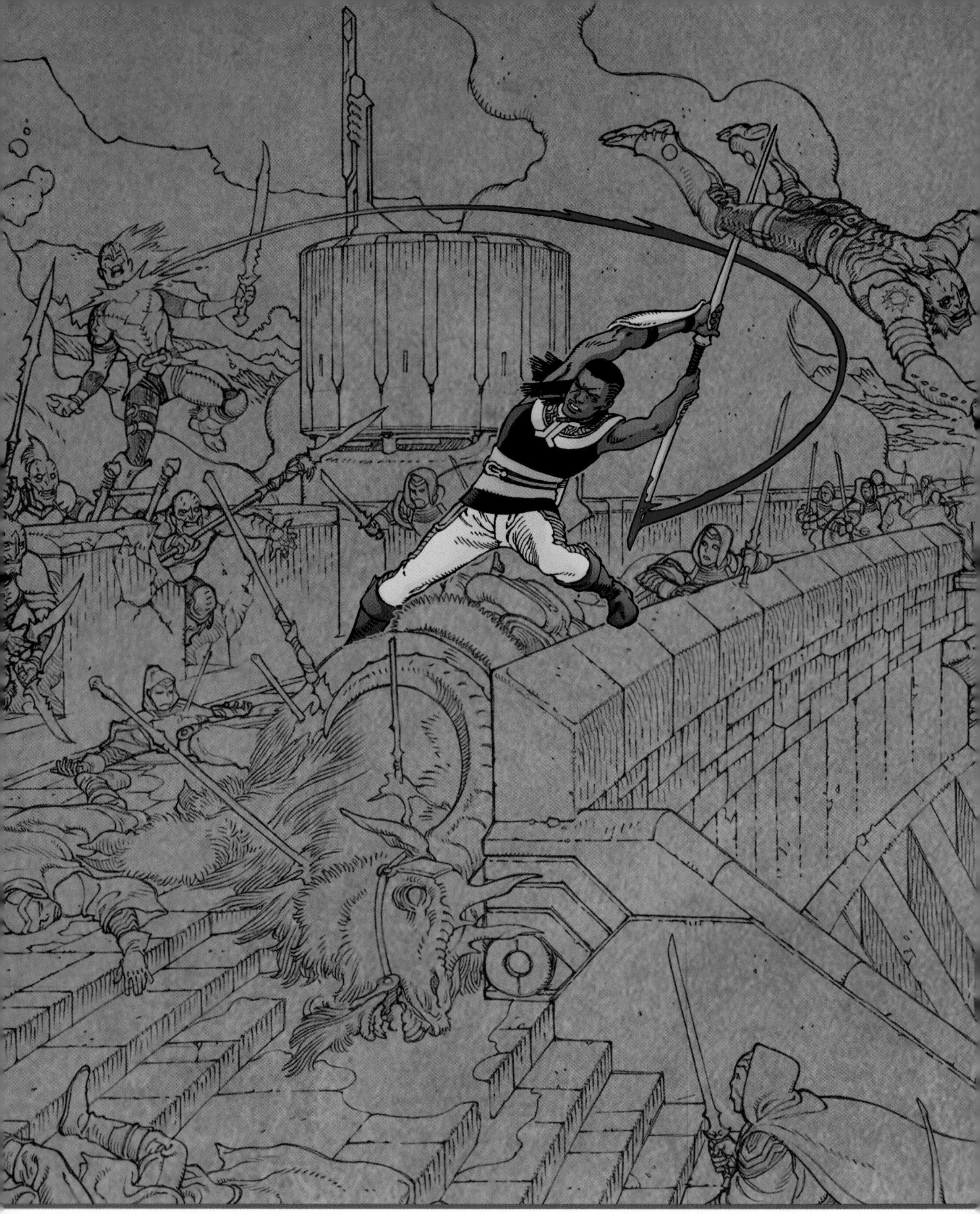

Series Assistant Edits by **Peter Adrian Behravesh**
Series Edits by **Chris Ryall** and **Ted Adams**
Cover Art by **Gabriel Rodríguez**

Collection Edits by **Justin Eisinger** and **Alonzo Simon**
Collection Design by **Gabriel Rodríguez** and **Robbie Robbins**
Publisher **Greg Goldstein**

For international rights, contact **licensing@idwpublishing.com**

ISBN: 978-1-68405-267-7

21 20 19 18   1 2 3 4

IDW®
www.IDWPUBLISHING.com

Greg Goldstein, President & Publisher • **John Barber**, Editor-in-Chief • **Robbie Robbins**, EVP/Sr. Art Director • **Cara Morrison**, Chief Financial Officer • **Matthew Ruzicka**, Chief Accounting Officer • **Anita Frazier**, SVP of Sales and Marketing • **David Hedgecock**, Associate Publisher • **Jerry Bennington**, VP of New Product Development • **Lorelei Bunjes**, VP of Digital Services • **Justin Eisinger**, Editorial Director, Graphic Novels & Collections • **Eric Moss**, Sr. Director, Licensing & Business Development

Ted Adams, IDW Founder

Facebook: **facebook.com/idwpublishing** • Twitter: **@idwpublishing** • YouTube: **youtube.com/idwpublishing**
Tumblr: **tumblr.idwpublishing.com** • Instagram: **instagram.com/idwpublishing**

Originally published as SWORD OF AGES issues #1–5.

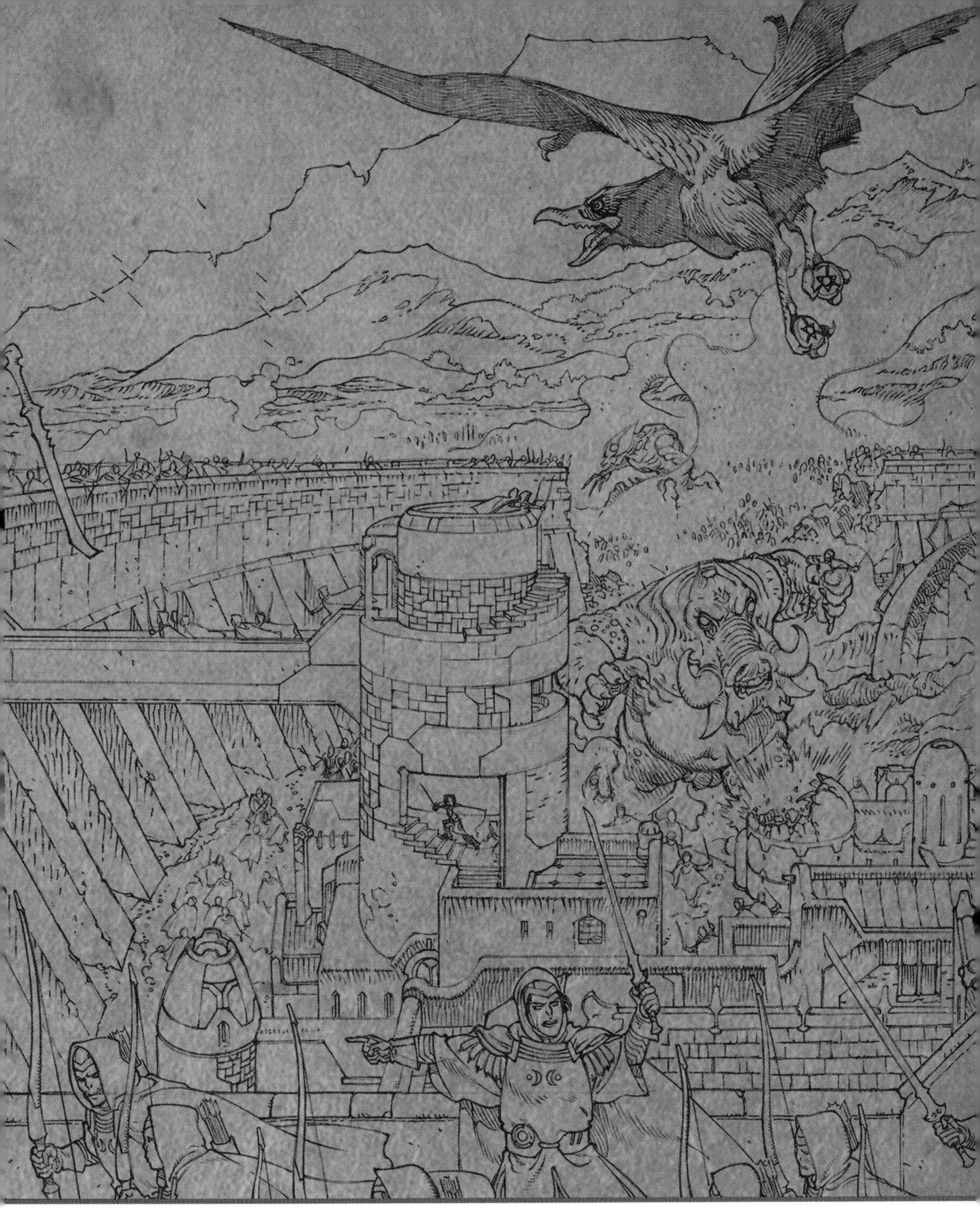

CREATED, WRITTEN & ILLUSTRATED BY
GABRIEL RODRÍGUEZ

COLORED BY
LOVERN KINDZIERSKI

LETTERED BY
ROBBIE ROBBINS

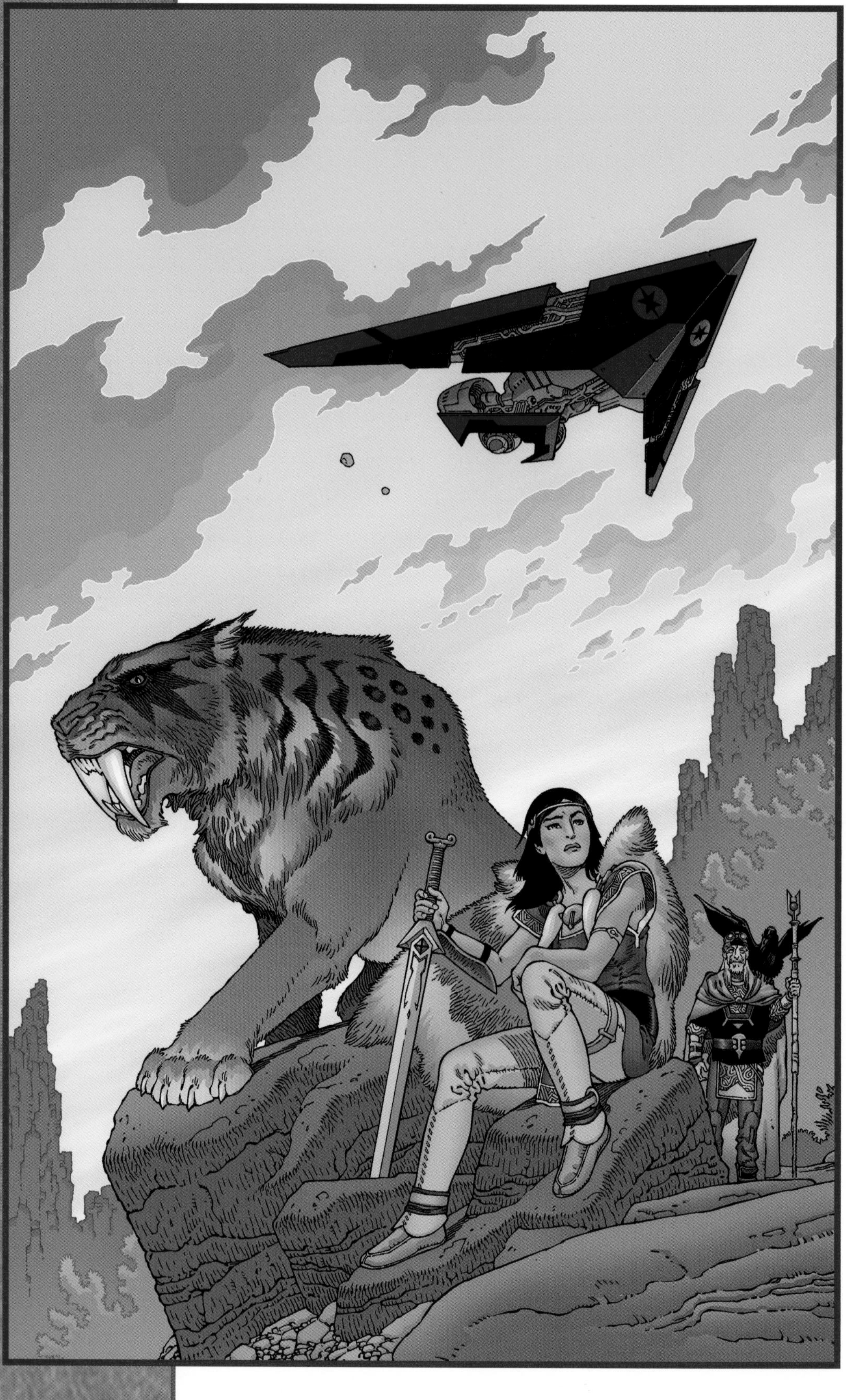

One for the *Ages*:
The Sorcery of Gabriel Rodríguez

BY
JOE HILL

So, it's 2010, and I'm in Pennsylvania with my comic-book soul brother, Gabriel Rodríguez, and outside the hotel bar the snow is falling in heavy white flakes. We're in a happy, almost-giddy mood, because FOX is filming the pilot episode of a television series based on our long-running comic, *Locke & Key*, and, as the song goes, everything is awesome. We don't know that the blizzard outside is burying any chance our TV show has of making it to the air. A hard blast of Pittsburgh winter will send production grinding to a standstill, leaving almost 30% of the screenplay unshot, and in a few months FOX will take their money and move on, without putting *Locke & Key* on the air.

Gabe and I have had all kinds of fun today: We met the actors standing in for our characters and talked at length with TV scribe Josh Friedman about the Locke family's backstory. We wandered the stone mansion standing in for Keyhouse… the ancient New England abode filled with reality-bending keys that is the setting for our comic. We shouted into a sinister well that will contain a demonic revenant hell-bent on using those keys to destroy lives.

But this is the best part of the day: settling into deep leather chairs in a bar that looks like a London gentleman's club and talking about our comic. We've only finished half—there are another 18 issues to go—and we're tossing around wild, outrageous ideas for storylines yet to come. The only subject we avoid is how this sonovabitch is going to end, because I have no fucking clue, and thinking about it scares me. *Locke & Key* has become more popular than either of us expected. People have tattoos. It's terrifying. If we don't stick the landing, I'm gonna regret it for the rest of my life.

"Hey," Gabe says, out of the blue. I think he's drinking a Fresca. You never met such a boy scout. "Wouldn't it be funny if—"

He cracks a joke about the keys. My eyes half pop out of my head. He has, off the cuff, solved the ending.

"Oh my God. Ohmigod. OH. *My*. **God!**" I reply, or words to that effect.

Gabe smiles his slight, enigmatic smile and chuckles. Coming up with wild, knuckleball notions is no big deal to *him*.

He does it every panel.

I want you to keep this little anecdote in mind. We'll come back to it.

•   •   •

There's a reason we keep returning to tales of Arthur. The legend of Camelot is a cornerstone narrative… a foundational story on which other stories are built. More than that: Malory's *Le Morte d'Arthur* is one of those stories that shaped our idea of how stories are supposed to operate.

(Other cornerstone narratives include *The Iliad*, *The Divine Comedy*, *The Tempest*, and a relative newcomer, *The Adventures of Sherlock Holmes*. By nature, foundational stories are old… pillars sunk deep into the sediment of the collective unconscious.)

The first part of the story, Arthur's magical education and the drawing of the sword from the stone, became the template for a thousand stories of a young hero discovering his or her destiny, from *Star Wars* to *Harry Potter*. If Arthur's knights hadn't sought the Holy Grail, Indiana Jones never would've looked for it. And the brutal downfall of King Arthur's reign sketched the basic outline for almost every story to follow about the passing of a golden age. There's a reason the Kennedy assassinations are so frequently described as the end of Camelot.

A cornerstone offers an artist something solid on which to build. *What* a creator builds, though, is entirely defined by the particular qualities of his imaginations and beliefs. John Boorman's Camelot is a sorrowing place of mists, doom, and stoic last stands. Guy Ritchie's Camelot is a boy's club of brawling lads, brash talk, and outrageous spectacle. Each new take on the Round Table reveals as much about the artist crafting the work as it does about Lancelot, Gawain & Co. When a retelling works, it's because an artist has found a way to tell the story that is entirely their own and so entirely fresh.

Is that all a little esoteric? Think of "Respect." Otis Redding wrote the song, and his version is three perfect minutes of soul, from the melody, to the lyric, to the defiant hurt in his voice. But in Aretha Franklin's creative hands, "Respect" went off like a grenade: It became a feminist anthem and one of the best-known pop songs in the world, powered by a new driving beat and lifted into the stratosphere by her unmatchable voice.

I kind of think *Sword of Ages* goes off like a grenade, too.

•   •   •

The work of a comic-book illustrator is not well understood. At minimum, he requires gifted hands, a sophisticated spatial sense, a vivid imagination, and the energy to complete about one page of comic-book storytelling every 48 hours for chump change. Most casual comic readers do know that much.

What they *don't* know is that the very best artists—talents like Fiona Staples, Mike Allred, Zach Howard, and Gabe—are in the ideas business. Every single panel is a high-wire act of invention. When I talk about *Locke & Key*, I am quick to note that I learned as much about the characters in the story from the way Gabe drew them as he ever learned about them from the way I wrote them. I did not know them until Gabe showed them to me.

I would script a page, filled with daydreams about what Gabe might draw—but whatever I was imagining, he routinely surpassed it, showing me a much richer, deeper, *weirder* world. Flowers with screaming faces. Shadows with fully fledged personalities.

A house in which the most casual ornaments—a window, a tapestry, a banister—whispered three-hundred-year-old secrets. FOX may have passed on *Locke & Key*, but Netflix didn't, and if we do wind up with a TV series (at the time of this writing it looks like we might), it will be in large part because the television folks simply couldn't help themselves. Gabe's ability to craft a harrowing, cinematic sequence is tempting; but his tireless whir of invention and wonder is damn near irresistible.

In *Sword of Ages*, Gabriel has thrown open the toy chest of his imagination and brought out all the goodies at last. Every page tells the story… and at the same time every page *is* a story, a kaleidoscope of dazzling possibilities and ideas. Here is Merlin in aviator goggles, hauling around on a motorcycle too cool for *Mad Max*, a badass ride that also looks like a weapon. Here is a towering, faceless Black Knight, sleek as a warrior from *Tron*, relentless as the T-1000 in *Terminator 2*. Here is Nikola, who might best be described as Han Solo in the form of a red-eyed raven (among the bad guys is a supercilious cyborg hawk named Gorice, and I am SO glad Gorice and Nikola didn't battle in this first storyline… when they do finally go at it talon-to-talon, it's going to be an instant series high). Here is a vast, beautifully crafted world, with sprawling Martian deserts, ancient monasteries, and a hundred warring alien tribes. *Sword of Ages* contains multitudes. Gabe has forcefully dreamt into existence an expansive universe—as big as the Marvel or DC universes—and somehow miniaturized it all to fit into a single book. *And made it look easy.* In issue after issue, Gabe sets artistic challenges bordering on the impossible and then solves his insoluble puzzles with a gleeful, anarchic creativity… which is both how *Sword of Ages* came to be and also sort of what *Sword of Ages* is about.

I shouldn't be surprised. I haven't forgotten what he did in Pittsburgh, the way he closed in on the perfect ending for *Locke & Key* with a laugh and a shy, knowing smile. Maybe I should start drinking Fresca.

Gabriel is a giant among comic-book storytellers, but the man himself is compact, unassuming. He has the blunt fingers of a stonemason and the temperament of a humorous but humble craftsman. He believes in God, and he believes God loves comics. I believe that, too. *Sword of Ages* is a prayer for us all to be brave, stay curious, and imagine better. I say amen to that.

There have been a thousand Camelot stories, some good, some bad. But every once in a while, a creator draws the sword ringing from the stone and shows us this world as we have never seen it before. An old myth is renewed, and we are renewed with it, led on an unforgettable adventure and returned safely home, breathless and grateful.

Saddle up and get ready to ride—your king commands it.

Joe Hill
Exeter, NH
October 2018

Thanks to my friends,
Chris and Ted, for your support
and years-long encouragement
to try writing, and to Joe, who
taught me how cats talk.

Thanks to my beloved Catalina,
inspiration and companion in
every impossible adventure.

Dedicated to
Alejandro Jodorowsky,
Jean "Moebius" Giraud,
and Harold Foster.

SWORD OF AGES

BOOK 1 : AVALON

  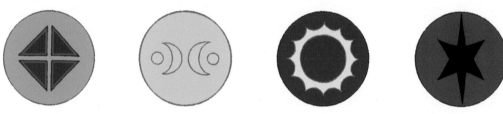 

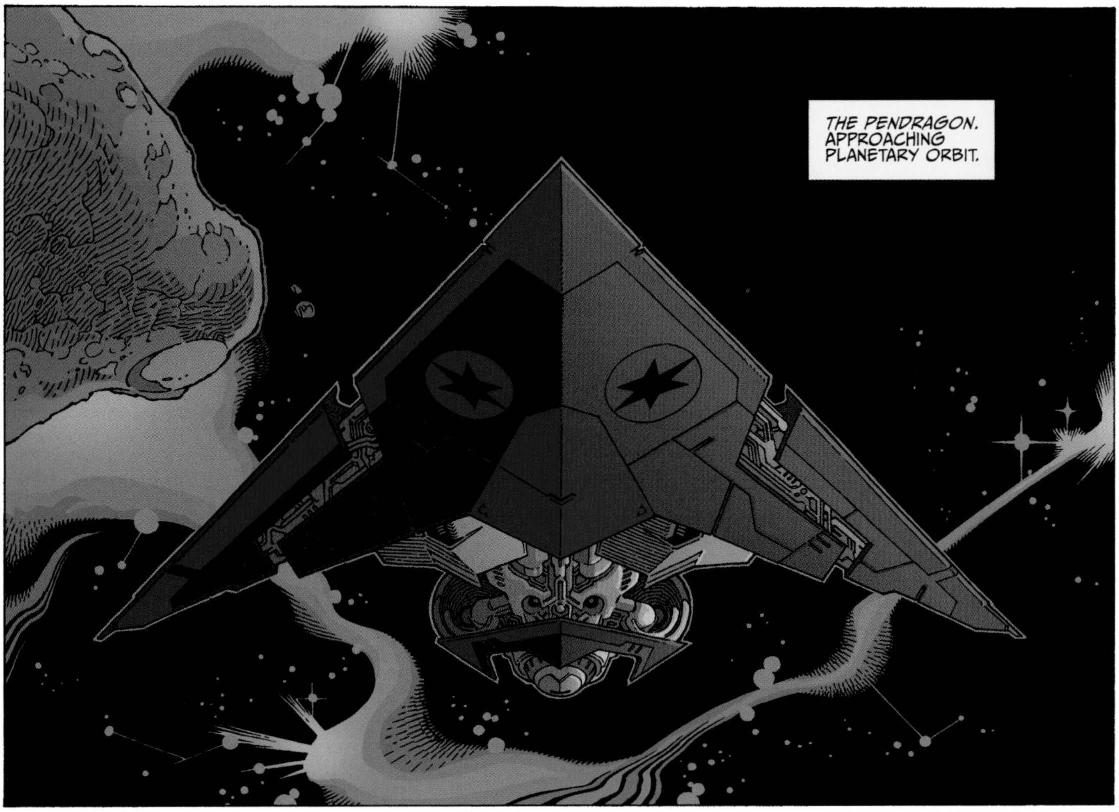
THE PENDRAGON. APPROACHING PLANETARY ORBIT.

PRELUDE: CASTAWAYS

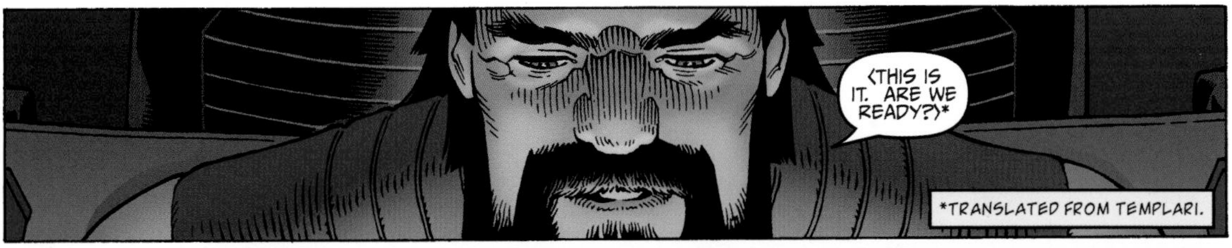
‹THIS IS IT. ARE WE READY?›*
*TRANSLATED FROM TEMPLARI.

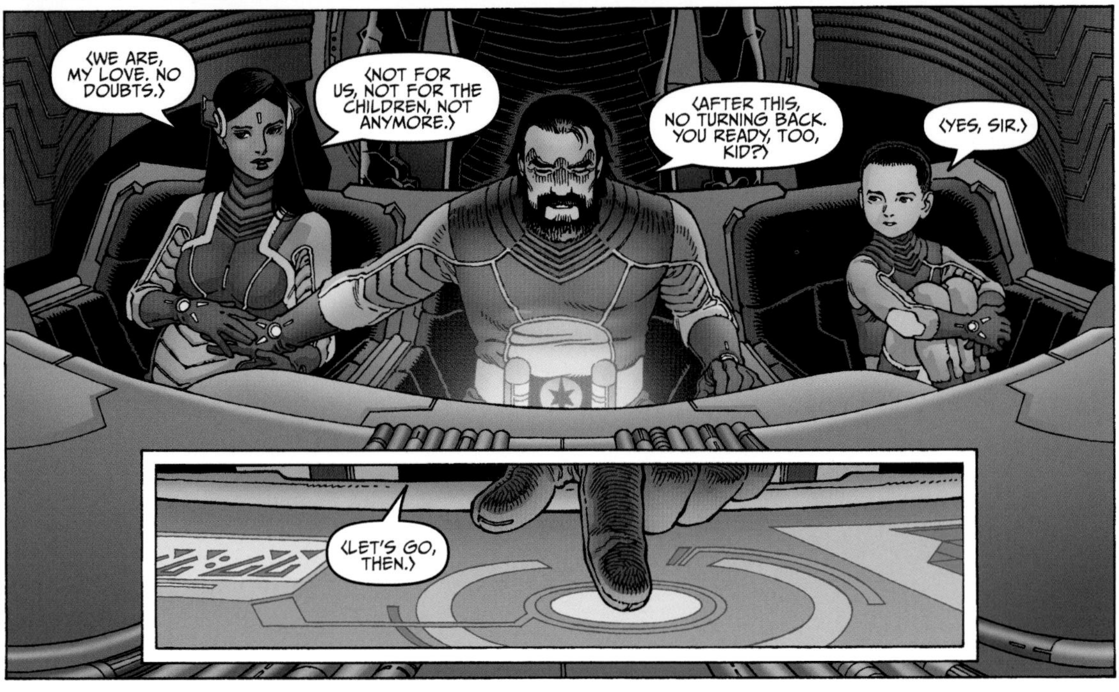
‹WE ARE, MY LOVE. NO DOUBTS.›
‹NOT FOR US, NOT FOR THE CHILDREN, NOT ANYMORE.›
‹AFTER THIS, NO TURNING BACK. YOU READY, TOO, KID?›
‹YES, SIR.›
‹LET'S GO, THEN.›

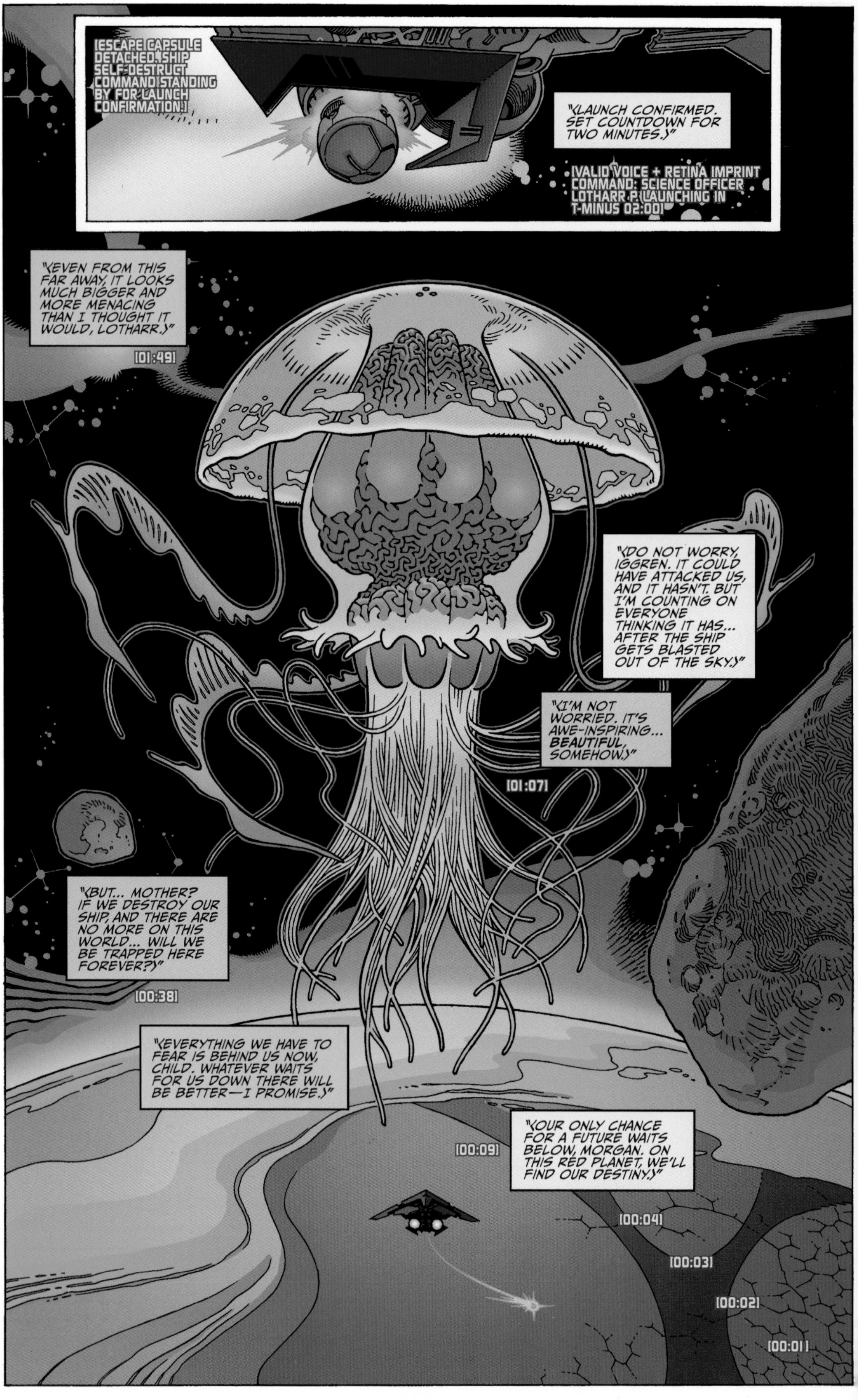
[ESCAPE CAPSULE DETACHED. SHIP SELF-DESTRUCT COMMAND STANDING BY FOR LAUNCH CONFIRMATION.]
"‹LAUNCH CONFIRMED. SET COUNTDOWN FOR TWO MINUTES.›"
[VALID VOICE + RETINA IMPRINT COMMAND: SCIENCE OFFICER LOTHARR P. LAUNCHING IN T-MINUS 02:00]
"‹EVEN FROM THIS FAR AWAY, IT LOOKS MUCH BIGGER AND MORE MENACING THAN I THOUGHT IT WOULD, LOTHARR.›"
[01:49]
"‹DO NOT WORRY, IGGREN. IT COULD HAVE ATTACKED US, AND IT HASN'T. BUT I'M COUNTING ON EVERYONE THINKING IT HAS... AFTER THE SHIP GETS BLASTED OUT OF THE SKY.›"
"‹I'M NOT WORRIED. IT'S AWE-INSPIRING... BEAUTIFUL, SOMEHOW.›"
[01:07]
"‹BUT... MOTHER? IF WE DESTROY OUR SHIP, AND THERE ARE NO MORE ON THIS WORLD... WILL WE BE TRAPPED HERE FOREVER?›"
[00:38]
"‹EVERYTHING WE HAVE TO FEAR IS BEHIND US NOW, CHILD. WHATEVER WAITS FOR US DOWN THERE WILL BE BETTER—I PROMISE.›"
[00:09]
"‹OUR ONLY CHANCE FOR A FUTURE WAITS BELOW, MORGAN. ON THIS RED PLANET, WE'LL FIND OUR DESTINY.›"
[00:04]
[00:03]
[00:02]
[00:01]

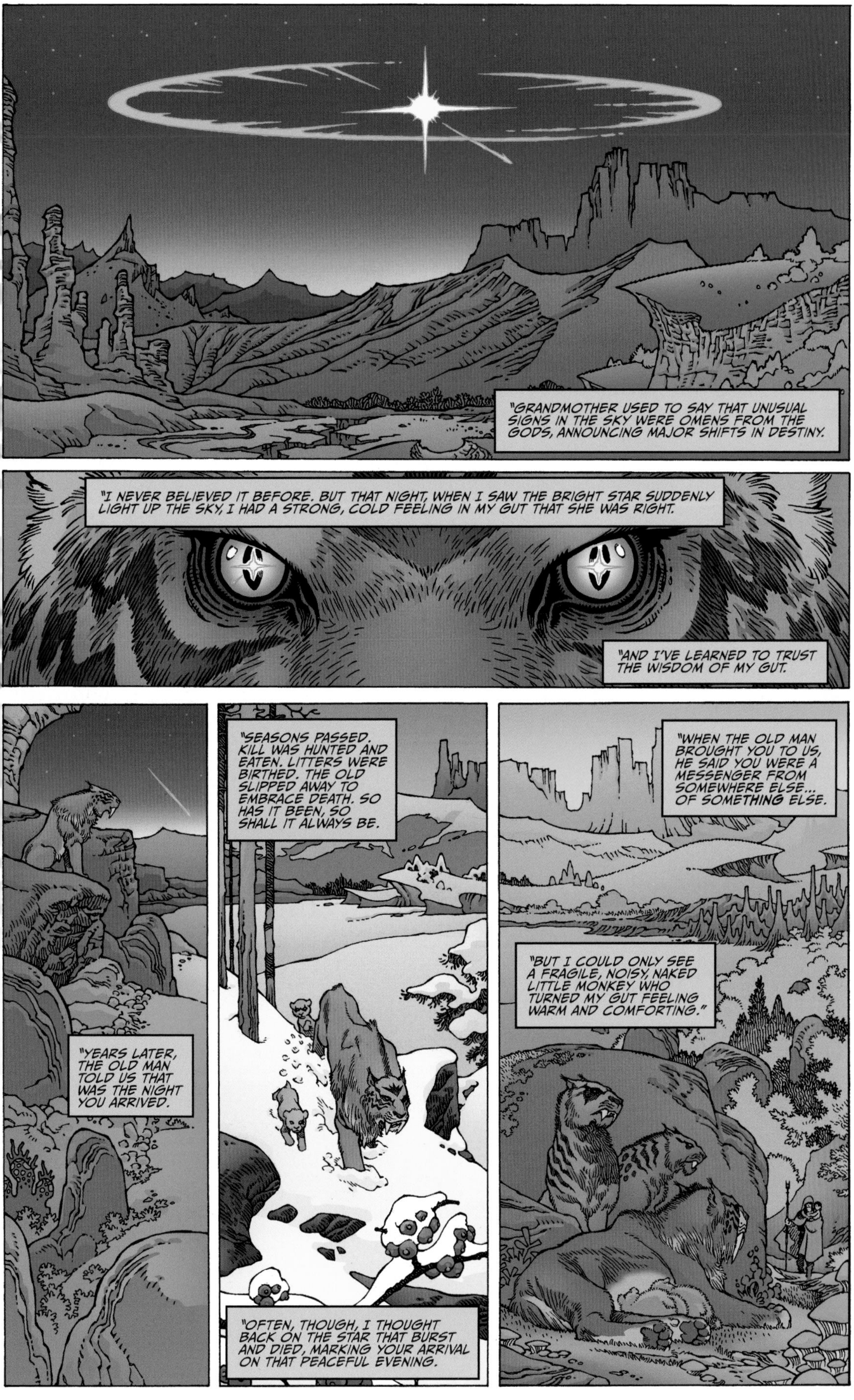

"GRANDMOTHER USED TO SAY THAT UNUSUAL SIGNS IN THE SKY WERE OMENS FROM THE GODS, ANNOUNCING MAJOR SHIFTS IN DESTINY.
"I NEVER BELIEVED IT BEFORE. BUT THAT NIGHT, WHEN I SAW THE BRIGHT STAR SUDDENLY LIGHT UP THE SKY, I HAD A STRONG, COLD FEELING IN MY GUT THAT SHE WAS RIGHT.
"AND I'VE LEARNED TO TRUST THE WISDOM OF MY GUT.
"YEARS LATER, THE OLD MAN TOLD US THAT WAS THE NIGHT YOU ARRIVED.
"SEASONS PASSED. KILL WAS HUNTED AND EATEN. LITTERS WERE BIRTHED. THE OLD SLIPPED AWAY TO EMBRACE DEATH. SO HAS IT BEEN, SO SHALL IT ALWAYS BE.
"OFTEN, THOUGH, I THOUGHT BACK ON THE STAR THAT BURST AND DIED, MARKING YOUR ARRIVAL ON THAT PEACEFUL EVENING.
"WHEN THE OLD MAN BROUGHT YOU TO US, HE SAID YOU WERE A MESSENGER FROM SOMEWHERE ELSE... OF SOMETHING ELSE.
"BUT I COULD ONLY SEE A FRAGILE, NOISY, NAKED LITTLE MONKEY WHO TURNED MY GUT FEELING WARM AND COMFORTING."

CHILDREN OF THE MOUNTAIN FORESTS

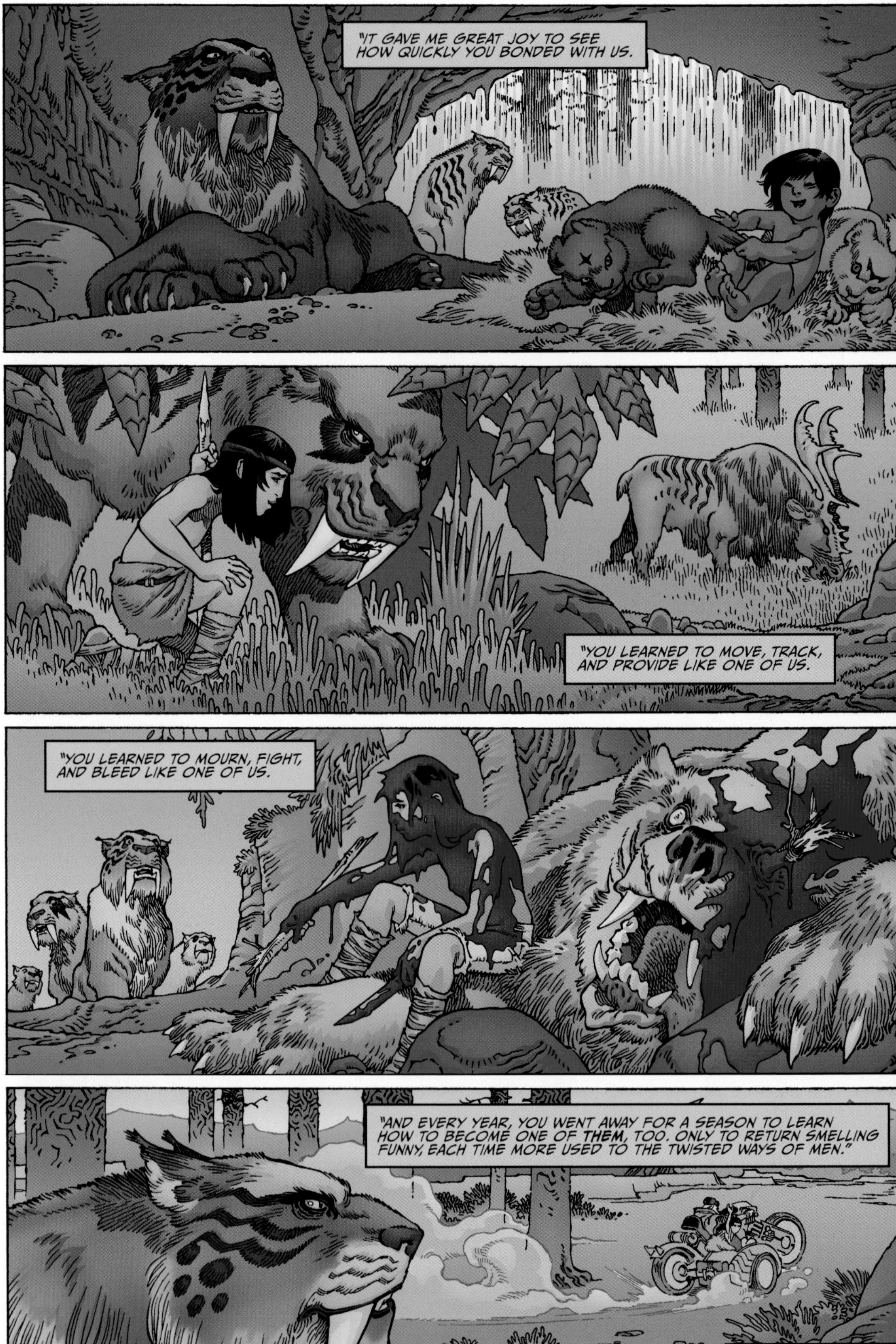

"IT GAVE ME GREAT JOY TO SEE HOW QUICKLY YOU BONDED WITH US.
"YOU LEARNED TO MOVE, TRACK, AND PROVIDE LIKE ONE OF US.
"YOU LEARNED TO MOURN, FIGHT, AND BLEED LIKE ONE OF US.
"AND EVERY YEAR, YOU WENT AWAY FOR A SEASON TO LEARN HOW TO BECOME ONE OF THEM, TOO. ONLY TO RETURN SMELLING FUNNY, EACH TIME MORE USED TO THE TWISTED WAYS OF MEN."
"C'MON, MOTHER. HUMANS KNOW HOW TO BE GOOD."

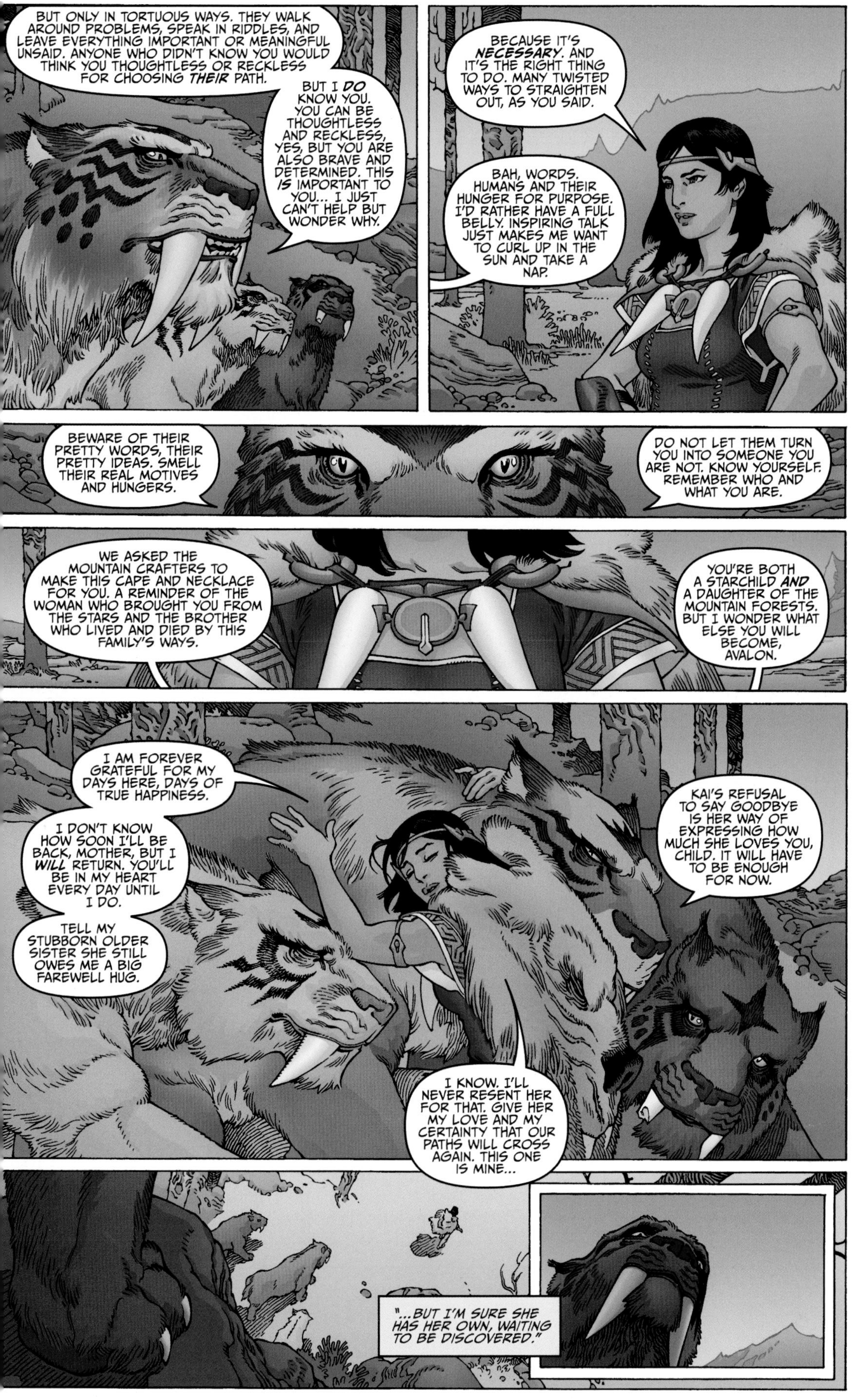
BUT ONLY IN TORTUOUS WAYS. THEY WALK AROUND PROBLEMS, SPEAK IN RIDDLES, AND LEAVE EVERYTHING IMPORTANT OR MEANINGFUL UNSAID. ANYONE WHO DIDN'T KNOW YOU WOULD THINK YOU THOUGHTLESS OR RECKLESS FOR CHOOSING *THEIR* PATH.
BUT I *DO* KNOW YOU. YOU CAN BE THOUGHTLESS AND RECKLESS, YES, BUT YOU ARE ALSO BRAVE AND DETERMINED. THIS *IS* IMPORTANT TO YOU... I JUST CAN'T HELP BUT WONDER WHY.
BECAUSE IT'S ***NECESSARY***. AND IT'S THE RIGHT THING TO DO. MANY TWISTED WAYS TO STRAIGHTEN OUT, AS YOU SAID.
BAH, WORDS. HUMANS AND THEIR HUNGER FOR PURPOSE. I'D RATHER HAVE A FULL BELLY. INSPIRING TALK JUST MAKES ME WANT TO CURL UP IN THE SUN AND TAKE A NAP.
BEWARE OF THEIR PRETTY WORDS, THEIR PRETTY IDEAS. SMELL THEIR REAL MOTIVES AND HUNGERS.
DO NOT LET THEM TURN YOU INTO SOMEONE YOU ARE NOT. KNOW YOURSELF. REMEMBER WHO AND WHAT YOU ARE.
WE ASKED THE MOUNTAIN CRAFTERS TO MAKE THIS CAPE AND NECKLACE FOR YOU. A REMINDER OF THE WOMAN WHO BROUGHT YOU FROM THE STARS AND THE BROTHER WHO LIVED AND DIED BY THIS FAMILY'S WAYS.
YOU'RE BOTH A STARCHILD ***AND*** A DAUGHTER OF THE MOUNTAIN FORESTS. BUT I WONDER WHAT ELSE YOU WILL BECOME, AVALON.
I AM FOREVER GRATEFUL FOR MY DAYS HERE, DAYS OF TRUE HAPPINESS.
I DON'T KNOW HOW SOON I'LL BE BACK, MOTHER, BUT I *WILL* RETURN. YOU'LL BE IN MY HEART EVERY DAY UNTIL I DO.
TELL MY STUBBORN OLDER SISTER SHE STILL OWES ME A BIG FAREWELL HUG.
KAI'S REFUSAL TO SAY GOODBYE IS HER WAY OF EXPRESSING HOW MUCH SHE LOVES YOU, CHILD. IT WILL HAVE TO BE ENOUGH FOR NOW.
I KNOW. I'LL NEVER RESENT HER FOR THAT. GIVE HER MY LOVE AND MY CERTAINTY THAT OUR PATHS WILL CROSS AGAIN. THIS ONE IS MINE...
"...BUT I'M SURE SHE HAS HER OWN, WAITING TO BE DISCOVERED."

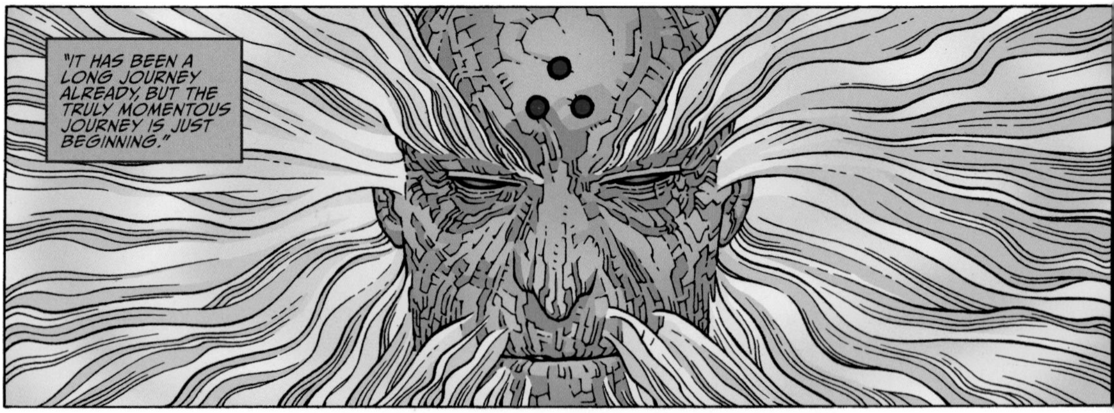
"IT HAS BEEN A LONG JOURNEY ALREADY, BUT THE TRULY MOMENTOUS JOURNEY IS JUST BEGINNING."

THE ELDER GUARDIANS

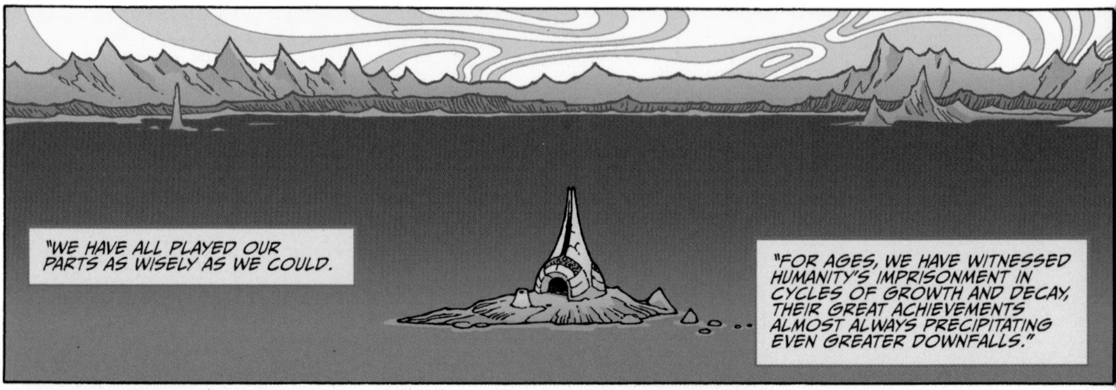
"WE HAVE ALL PLAYED OUR PARTS AS WISELY AS WE COULD.
"FOR AGES, WE HAVE WITNESSED HUMANITY'S IMPRISONMENT IN CYCLES OF GROWTH AND DECAY, THEIR GREAT ACHIEVEMENTS ALMOST ALWAYS PRECIPITATING EVEN GREATER DOWNFALLS."

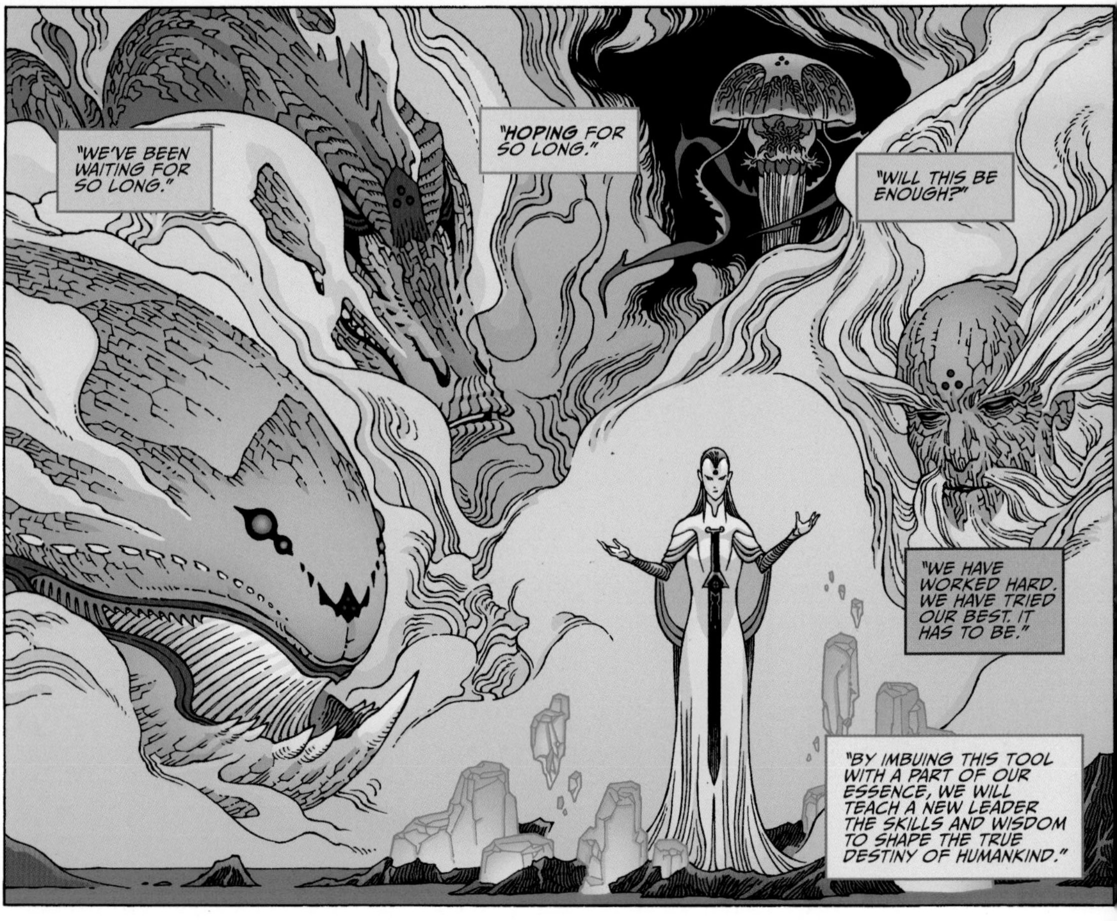
"WE'VE BEEN WAITING FOR SO LONG."
"HOPING FOR SO LONG."
"WILL THIS BE ENOUGH?"
"WE HAVE WORKED HARD. WE HAVE TRIED OUR BEST. IT HAS TO BE."
"BY IMBUING THIS TOOL WITH A PART OF OUR ESSENCE, WE WILL TEACH A NEW LEADER THE SKILLS AND WISDOM TO SHAPE THE TRUE DESTINY OF HUMANKIND."

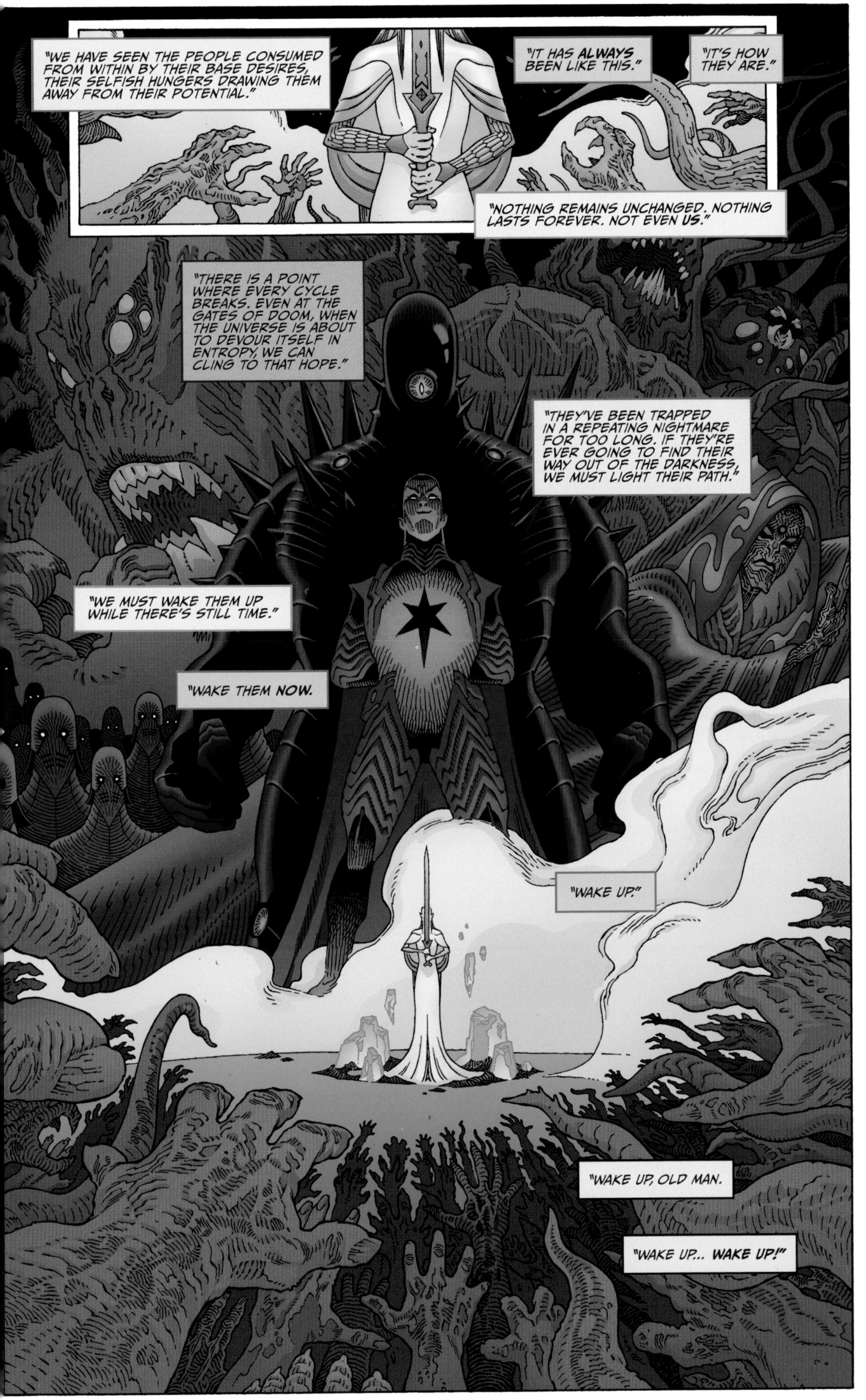

"WE HAVE SEEN THE PEOPLE CONSUMED FROM WITHIN BY THEIR BASE DESIRES, THEIR SELFISH HUNGERS DRAWING THEM AWAY FROM THEIR POTENTIAL."
"IT HAS ALWAYS BEEN LIKE THIS."
"IT'S HOW THEY ARE."
"NOTHING REMAINS UNCHANGED. NOTHING LASTS FOREVER. NOT EVEN US."
"THERE IS A POINT WHERE EVERY CYCLE BREAKS. EVEN AT THE GATES OF DOOM, WHEN THE UNIVERSE IS ABOUT TO DEVOUR ITSELF IN ENTROPY, WE CAN CLING TO THAT HOPE."
"THEY'VE BEEN TRAPPED IN A REPEATING NIGHTMARE FOR TOO LONG. IF THEY'RE EVER GOING TO FIND THEIR WAY OUT OF THE DARKNESS, WE MUST LIGHT THEIR PATH."
"WE MUST WAKE THEM UP WHILE THERE'S STILL TIME."
"WAKE THEM NOW.
"WAKE UP."
"WAKE UP, OLD MAN.
"WAKE UP... WAKE UP!"

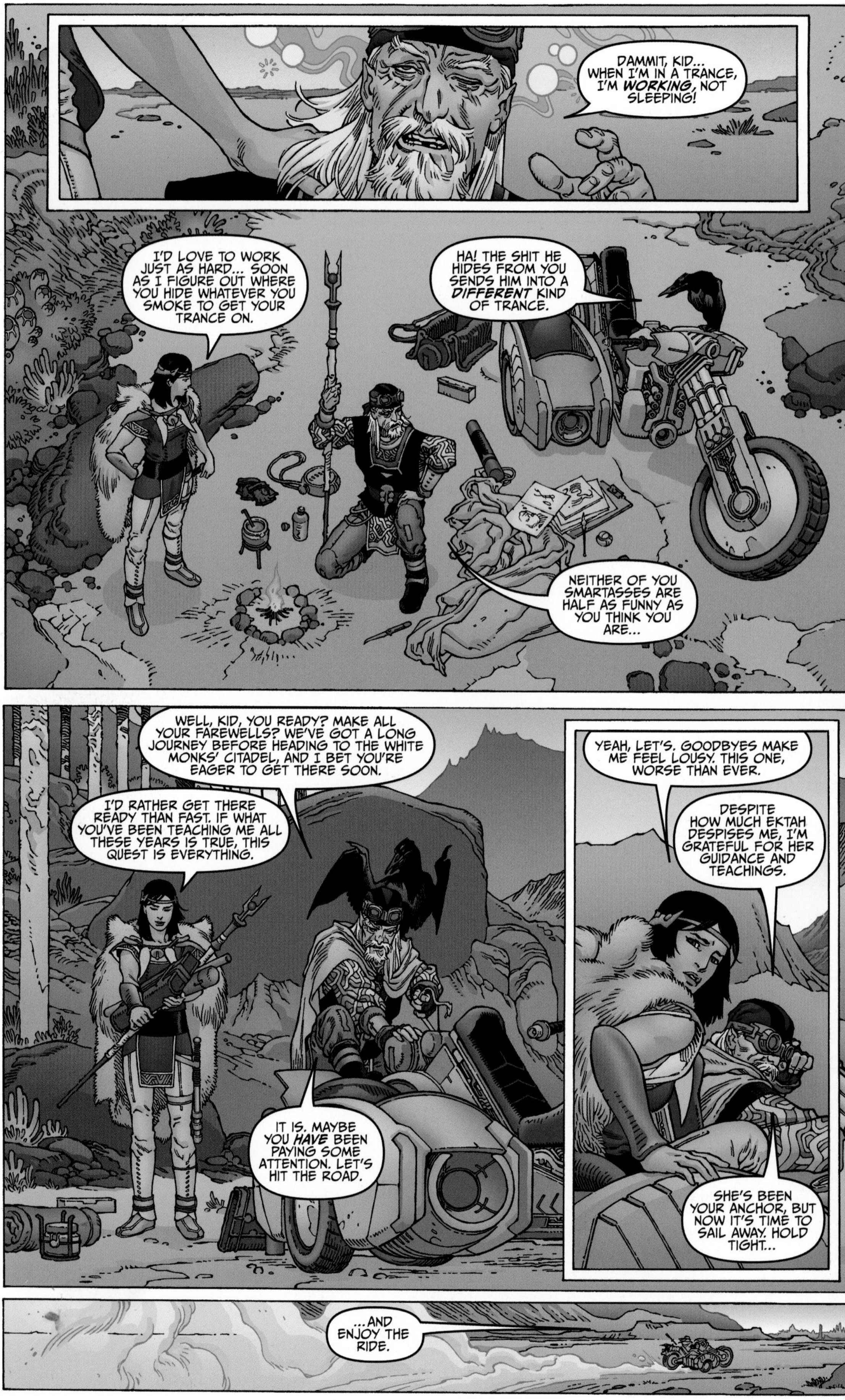
DAMMIT, KID... WHEN I'M IN A TRANCE, I'M WORKING, NOT SLEEPING!
I'D LOVE TO WORK JUST AS HARD... SOON AS I FIGURE OUT WHERE YOU HIDE WHATEVER YOU SMOKE TO GET YOUR TRANCE ON.
HA! THE SHIT HE HIDES FROM YOU SENDS HIM INTO A DIFFERENT KIND OF TRANCE.
NEITHER OF YOU SMARTASSES ARE HALF AS FUNNY AS YOU THINK YOU ARE...
WELL, KID, YOU READY? MAKE ALL YOUR FAREWELLS? WE'VE GOT A LONG JOURNEY BEFORE HEADING TO THE WHITE MONKS' CITADEL, AND I BET YOU'RE EAGER TO GET THERE SOON.
I'D RATHER GET THERE READY THAN FAST. IF WHAT YOU'VE BEEN TEACHING ME ALL THESE YEARS IS TRUE, THIS QUEST IS EVERYTHING.
IT IS. MAYBE YOU HAVE BEEN PAYING SOME ATTENTION. LET'S HIT THE ROAD.
YEAH, LET'S. GOODBYES MAKE ME FEEL LOUSY. THIS ONE, WORSE THAN EVER.
DESPITE HOW MUCH EKTAH DESPISES ME, I'M GRATEFUL FOR HER GUIDANCE AND TEACHINGS.
SHE'S BEEN YOUR ANCHOR, BUT NOW IT'S TIME TO SAIL AWAY. HOLD TIGHT...
...AND ENJOY THE RIDE.

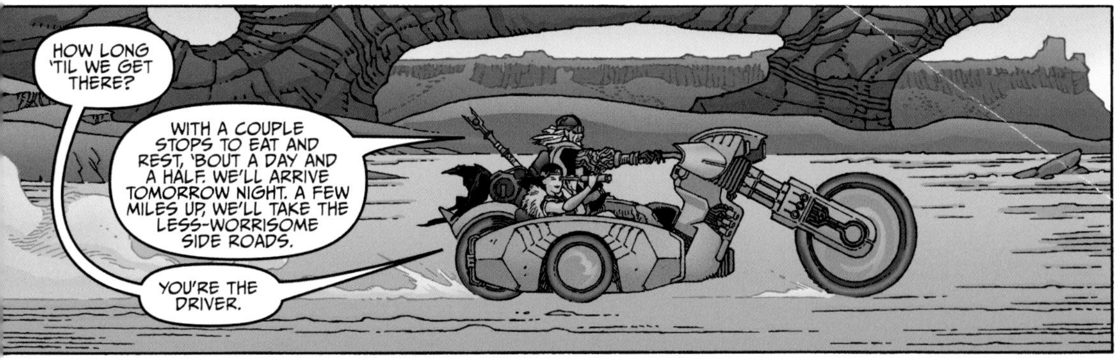
HOW LONG 'TIL WE GET THERE?
WITH A COUPLE STOPS TO EAT AND REST, 'BOUT A DAY AND A HALF. WE'LL ARRIVE TOMORROW NIGHT. A FEW MILES UP, WE'LL TAKE THE LESS-WORRISOME SIDE ROADS.
YOU'RE THE DRIVER.

ON THE ROAD

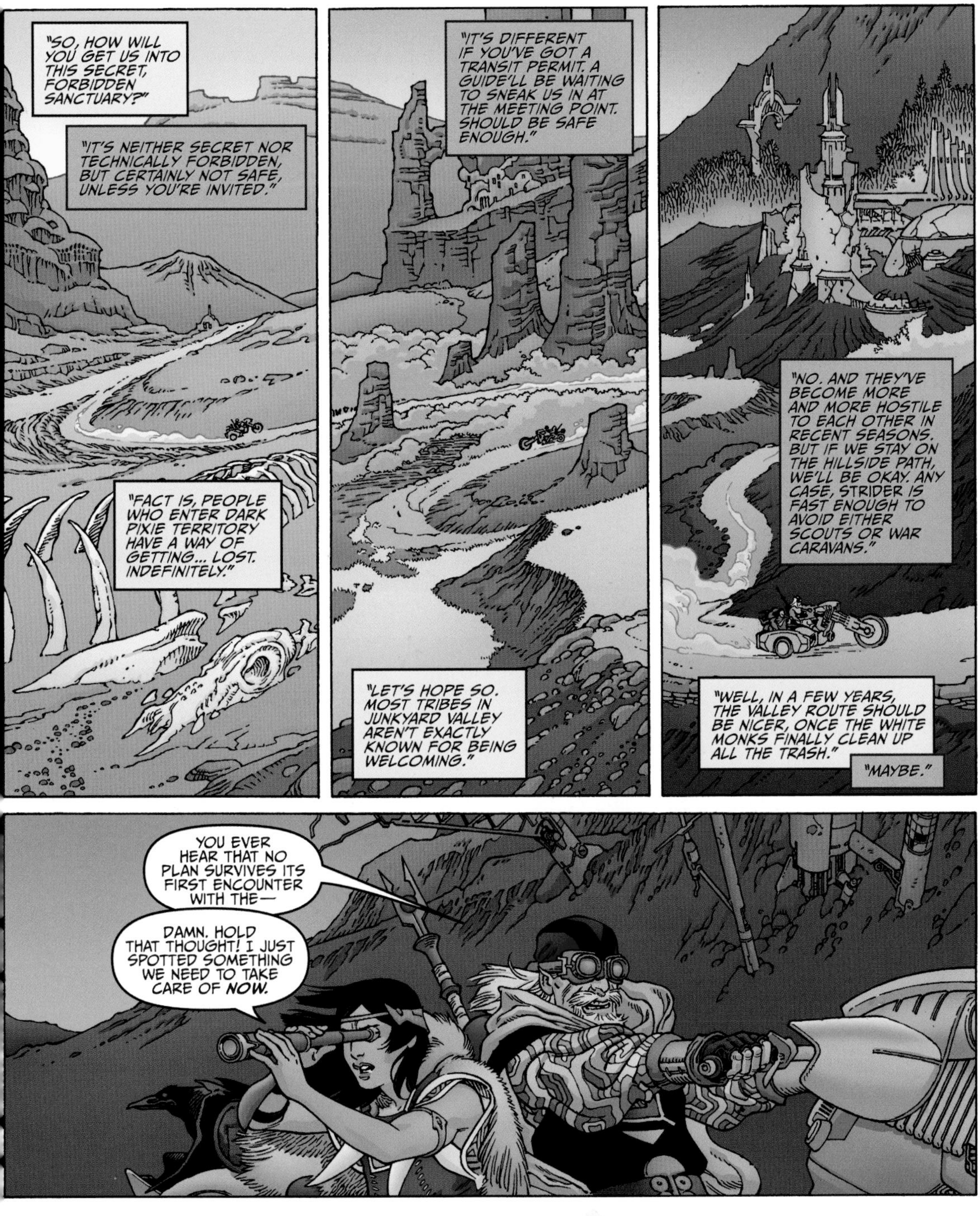
"SO, HOW WILL YOU GET US INTO THIS SECRET, FORBIDDEN SANCTUARY?"
"IT'S NEITHER SECRET NOR TECHNICALLY FORBIDDEN, BUT CERTAINLY NOT SAFE, UNLESS YOU'RE INVITED."
"FACT IS, PEOPLE WHO ENTER DARK PIXIE TERRITORY HAVE A WAY OF GETTING... LOST. INDEFINITELY."
"IT'S DIFFERENT IF YOU'VE GOT A TRANSIT PERMIT. A GUIDE'LL BE WAITING TO SNEAK US IN AT THE MEETING POINT. SHOULD BE SAFE ENOUGH."
"LET'S HOPE SO. MOST TRIBES IN JUNKYARD VALLEY AREN'T EXACTLY KNOWN FOR BEING WELCOMING."
"NO. AND THEY'VE BECOME MORE AND MORE HOSTILE TO EACH OTHER IN RECENT SEASONS. BUT IF WE STAY ON THE HILLSIDE PATH, WE'LL BE OKAY. ANY CASE, STRIDER IS FAST ENOUGH TO AVOID EITHER SCOUTS OR WAR CARAVANS."
"WELL, IN A FEW YEARS, THE VALLEY ROUTE SHOULD BE NICER, ONCE THE WHITE MONKS FINALLY CLEAN UP ALL THE TRASH."
"MAYBE."
YOU EVER HEAR THAT NO PLAN SURVIVES ITS FIRST ENCOUNTER WITH THE—
DAMN. HOLD THAT THOUGHT! I JUST SPOTTED SOMETHING WE NEED TO TAKE CARE OF *NOW*.

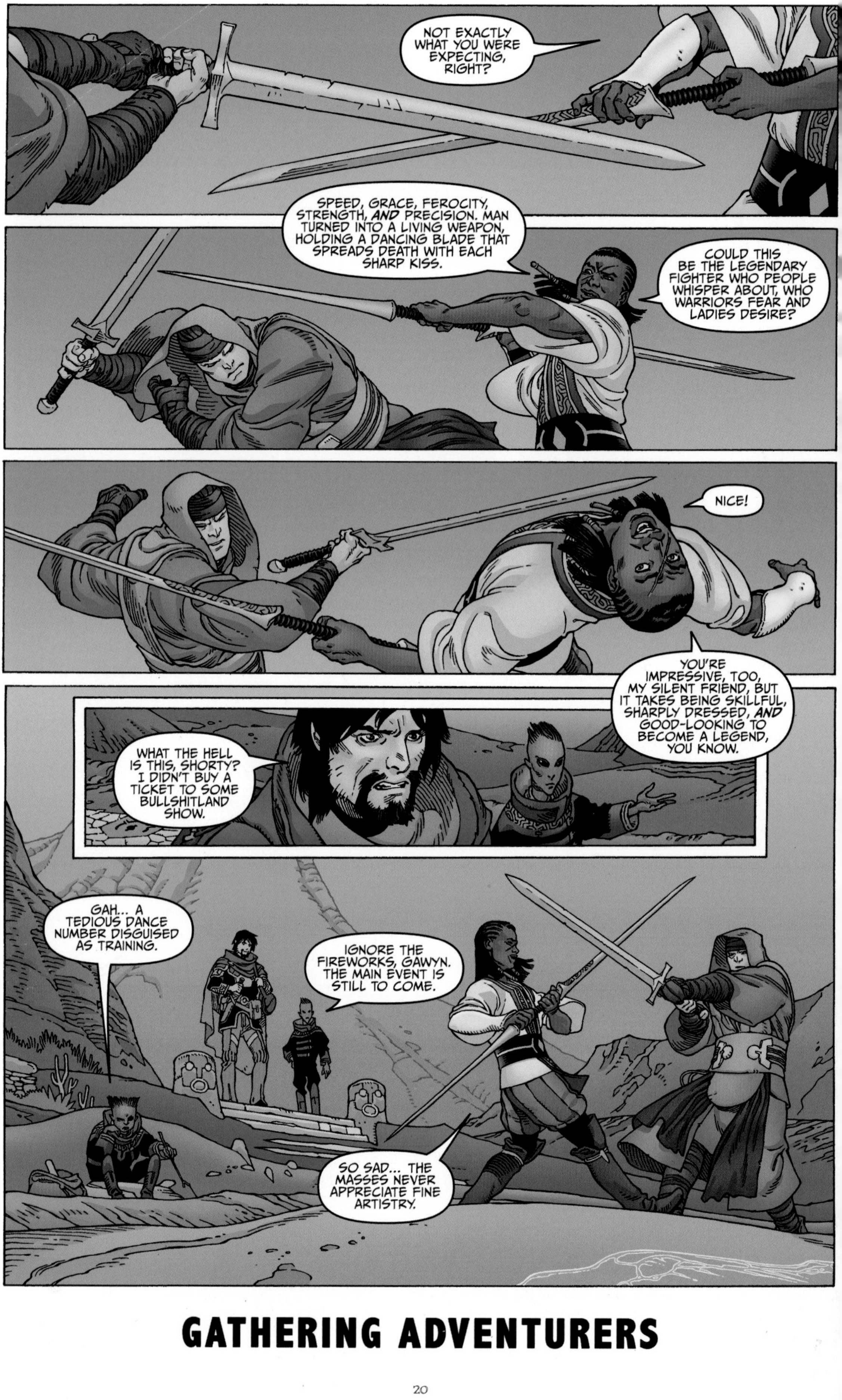
NOT EXACTLY WHAT YOU WERE EXPECTING, RIGHT?
SPEED, GRACE, FEROCITY, STRENGTH, **AND** PRECISION. MAN TURNED INTO A LIVING WEAPON, HOLDING A DANCING BLADE THAT SPREADS DEATH WITH EACH SHARP KISS.
COULD THIS BE THE LEGENDARY FIGHTER WHO PEOPLE WHISPER ABOUT, WHO WARRIORS FEAR AND LADIES DESIRE?
NICE!
YOU'RE IMPRESSIVE, TOO, MY SILENT FRIEND, BUT IT TAKES BEING SKILLFUL, SHARPLY DRESSED, **AND** GOOD-LOOKING TO BECOME A LEGEND, YOU KNOW.
WHAT THE HELL IS THIS, SHORTY? I DIDN'T BUY A TICKET TO SOME BULLSHITLAND SHOW.
GAH... A TEDIOUS DANCE NUMBER DISGUISED AS TRAINING.
IGNORE THE FIREWORKS, GAWYN. THE MAIN EVENT IS STILL TO COME.
SO SAD... THE MASSES NEVER APPRECIATE FINE ARTISTRY.

GATHERING ADVENTURERS

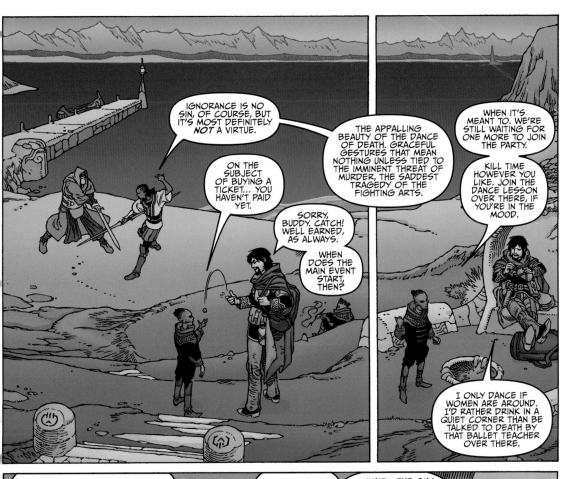

IGNORANCE IS NO SIN, OF COURSE, BUT IT'S MOST DEFINITELY *NOT* A VIRTUE.

ON THE SUBJECT OF BUYING A TICKET... YOU HAVEN'T PAID YET.

THE APPALLING BEAUTY OF THE DANCE OF DEATH. GRACEFUL GESTURES THAT MEAN NOTHING UNLESS TIED TO THE IMMINENT THREAT OF MURDER, THE SADDEST TRAGEDY OF THE FIGHTING ARTS.

SORRY, BUDDY. CATCH! WELL EARNED, AS ALWAYS. WHEN DOES THE MAIN EVENT START, THEN?

WHEN IT'S MEANT TO. WE'RE STILL WAITING FOR ONE MORE TO JOIN THE PARTY.

KILL TIME HOWEVER YOU LIKE. JOIN THE DANCE LESSON OVER THERE, IF YOU'RE IN THE MOOD.

I ONLY DANCE IF WOMEN ARE AROUND. I'D RATHER DRINK IN A QUIET CORNER THAN BE TALKED TO DEATH BY THAT BALLET TEACHER OVER THERE.

COMPLAINTS STILL SOUND BETTER THAN HOURS OF SILENCE FROM MY COUNTERPART HERE.

WHO ARE YOU, COMPLAINER? I'M THE FAMOUS *LANCER BENVEEK* OF THE RIVERLANDS.

WHY THE HELLS SHOULD I CARE ABOUT—

—WAIT—THE GUY WHO RESCUED THE DAUGHTERS OF FEMBERG DENAYAN FROM THE CANNIBALS OF TULLAT? *THAT* LANCER BENVEEK?

IN THE FLESH! YOU KNOW THOSE GRACEFUL LADIES? ANY NEWS FROM THEM? HOW ARE THEY?

DEAD, I BET. THEIR FATHER SOLD THEM TO A SLAVER CLAN FROM THE SOUTHERN VALLEYS, AND NO ONE SURVIVES MORE THAN A YEAR OR TWO WITH THEM.

...

DAMN. WHAT A WASTE.

CHEERS.

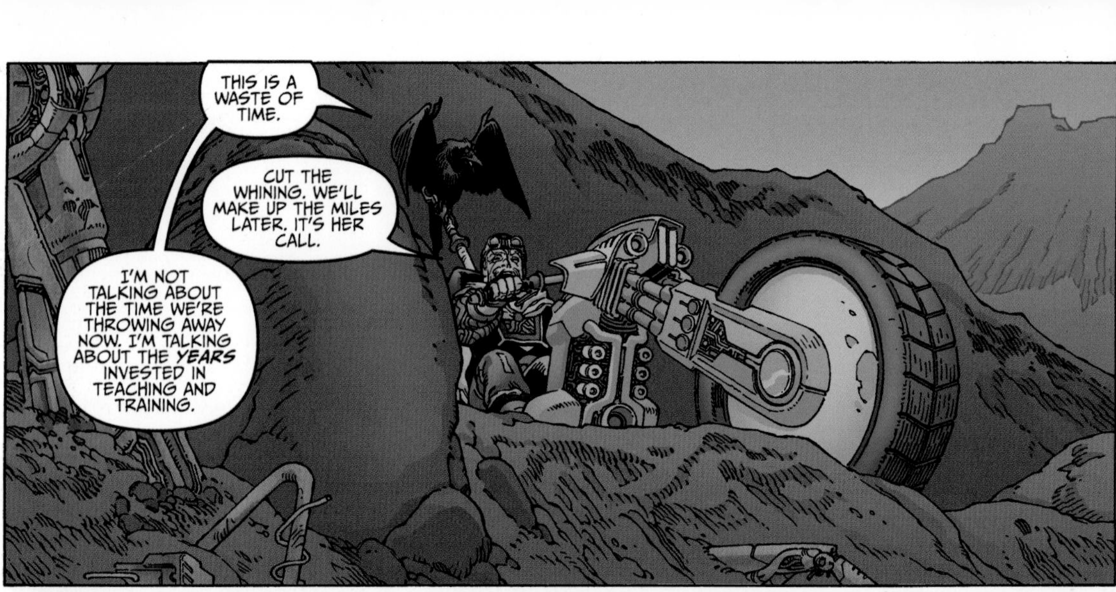
THIS IS A WASTE OF TIME.
CUT THE WHINING. WE'LL MAKE UP THE MILES LATER. IT'S HER CALL.
I'M NOT TALKING ABOUT THE TIME WE'RE THROWING AWAY NOW. I'M TALKING ABOUT THE *YEARS* INVESTED IN TEACHING AND TRAINING.

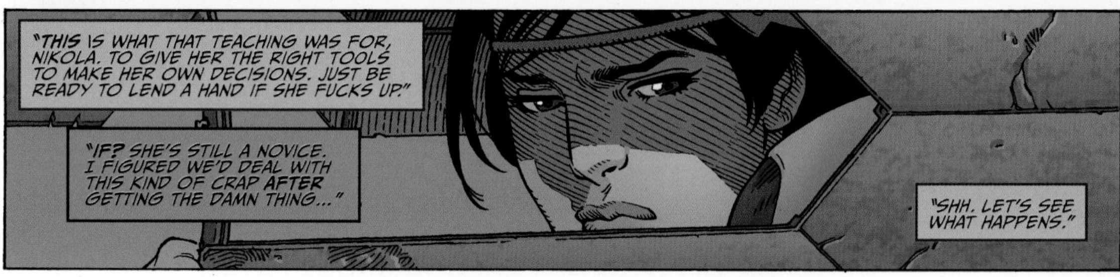
"*THIS* IS WHAT THAT TEACHING WAS FOR, NIKOLA. TO GIVE HER THE RIGHT TOOLS TO MAKE HER OWN DECISIONS. JUST BE READY TO LEND A HAND IF SHE FUCKS UP."
"*IF?* SHE'S STILL A NOVICE. I FIGURED WE'D DEAL WITH THIS KIND OF CRAP **AFTER** GETTING THE DAMN THING..."
"SHH. LET'S SEE WHAT HAPPENS."

SLAVERS CARAVAN

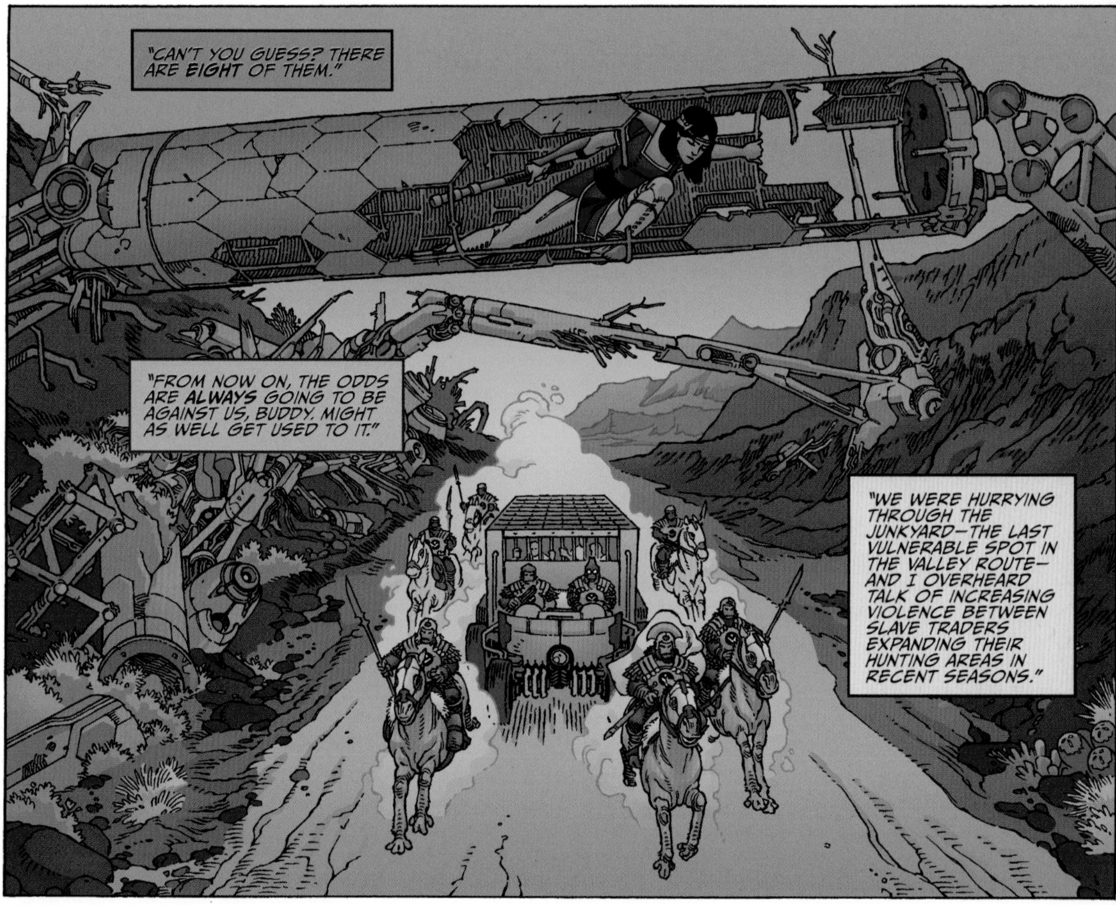
"CAN'T YOU GUESS? THERE ARE **EIGHT** OF THEM."
"FROM NOW ON, THE ODDS ARE **ALWAYS** GOING TO BE AGAINST US, BUDDY. MIGHT AS WELL GET USED TO IT."
"WE WERE HURRYING THROUGH THE JUNKYARD—THE LAST VULNERABLE SPOT IN THE VALLEY ROUTE—AND I OVERHEARD TALK OF INCREASING VIOLENCE BETWEEN SLAVE TRADERS EXPANDING THEIR HUNTING AREAS IN RECENT SEASONS."

BOSS, WATCH OUT!

WHA—?!

"BUT THIS AMBUSH WAS DIFFERENT FROM ANYTHING THEY COULD HAVE EXPECTED."

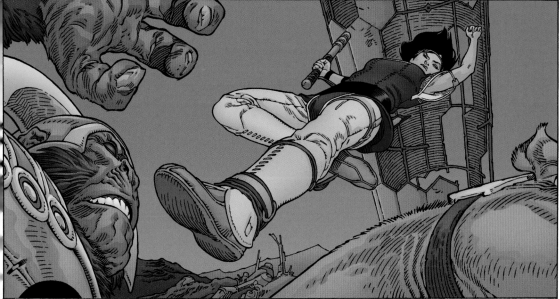

HERE WE GO.

"SHE WAS AS FAST AS SHE WAS SILENT, MOVING LIKE A CAT. YOU COULDN'T HEAR HER AT ALL OVER THE ENGINE NOISE, SLAVERS' SCREAMS..."

KRUNK!

"...AND BREAKING BONES."

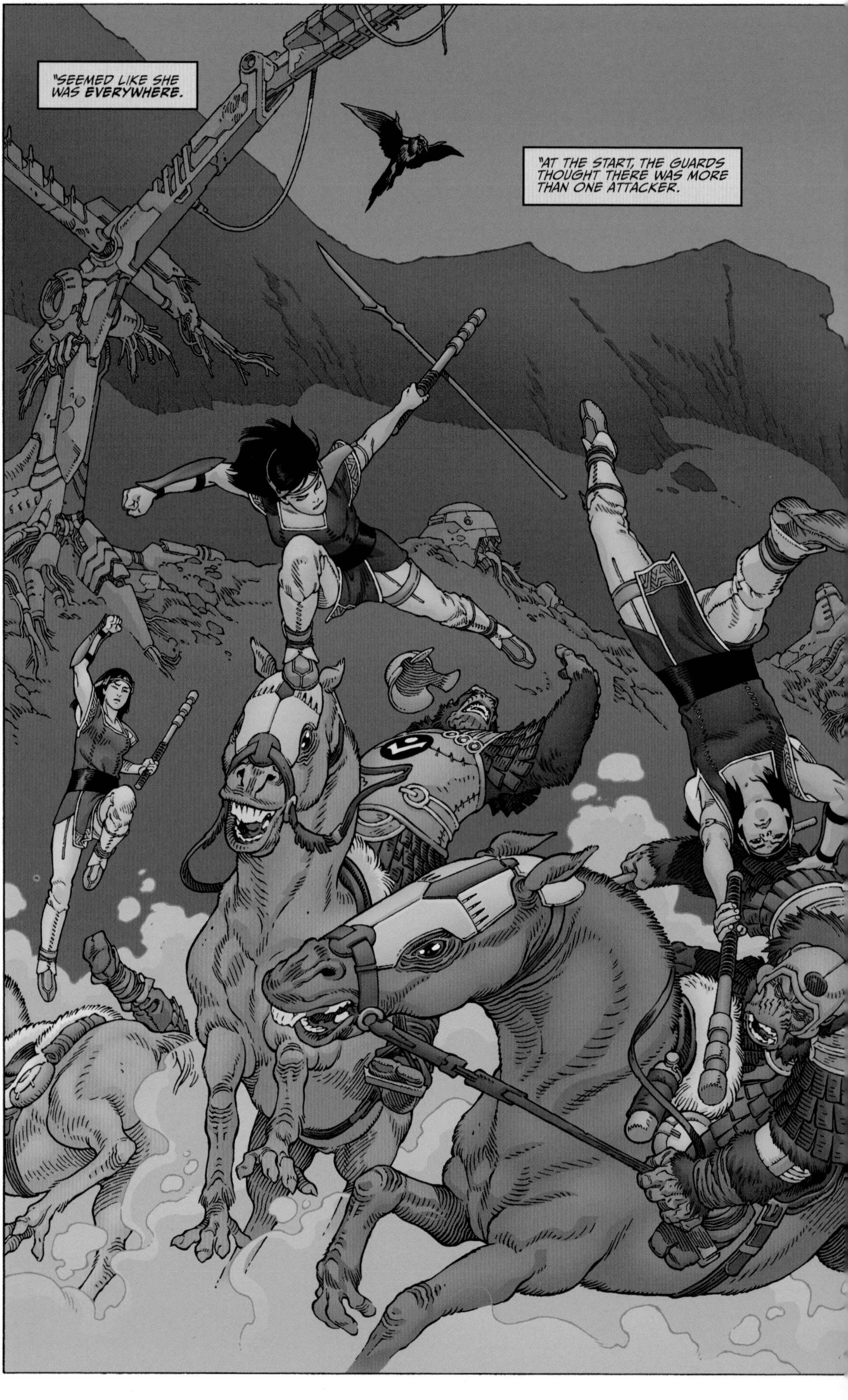
"SEEMED LIKE SHE WAS EVERYWHERE.
"AT THE START, THE GUARDS THOUGHT THERE WAS MORE THAN ONE ATTACKER.

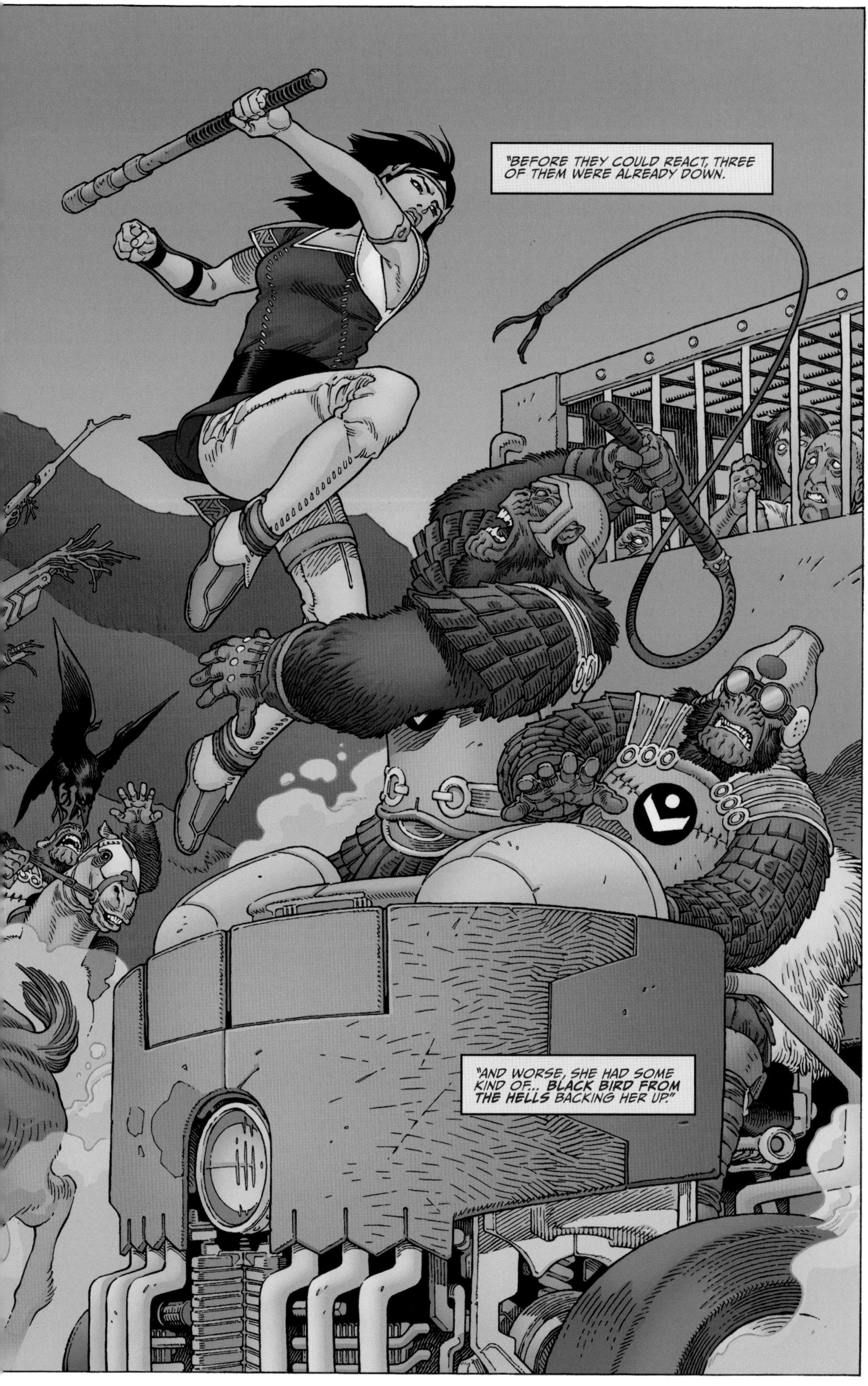
"BEFORE THEY COULD REACT, THREE OF THEM WERE ALREADY DOWN.
"AND WORSE, SHE HAD SOME KIND OF... BLACK BIRD FROM THE HELLS BACKING HER UP."

"A GUARD SPOTTED AN OPENING WHEN SHE PAUSED TO TAKE DOWN THE CHARIOT DRIVER."

DAMN, KID, WATCH YOUR BACK!

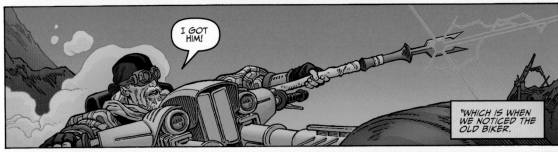

I GOT HIM!

"WHICH IS WHEN WE NOTICED THE OLD BIKER."

"NOT SURE IF THE BLAST CAME FROM HIS HAND OR FROM SOME WEAPON. NEVER SAW A BURST OF ENERGY LIKE THAT ONE BEFORE...

BZZZ
AP
-KR
AK

WHACK

"...NOR DID THE GUY WHO GOT SMASHED BY THE BROKEN BEAM."

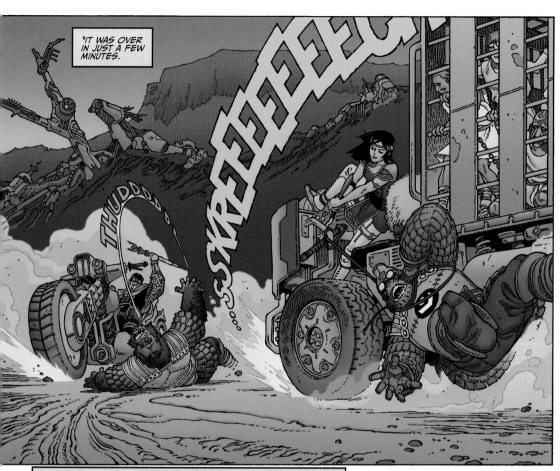

"IT WAS OVER IN JUST A FEW MINUTES.

THUDDDD

SKRREEEEEEE

"THE GIRL FOUND THE KEYS THAT UNLOCKED THE CAGE AND OUR BONDS. SHE TIED UP ALL THE SLAVERS WITH OUR RESTRAINTS.

"THEN IT GOT WEIRDER. SHE WASN'T TAKING US WITH HER.

"SHE FREED US, ONLY TO SEND US AWAY.

"SHE TOLD US TO TAKE THE SLAVERS' MOUNTS AND TRAVEL EAST TO A CITADEL OF MONKS, WHERE WE WOULDN'T BE SLAVES ANYMORE.

"I TOLD HER HOW VULNERABLE WE'D BE TO MAN-EATING BEASTS ON THE ROAD THROUGH THE WILDERNESS, BUT IT DIDN'T SEEM TO MATTER TO HER. OR THE YOUNGER PRISONERS."

CLAC

WE'LL BE BACK THIS WAY IN A COUPLE DAYS. ENJOY A TASTE OF WHAT YOU'VE DONE TO SO MANY, AND LET'S SEE IF HUNGER AND HOPELESSNESS TEACH YOU A LESSON.

"WHILE RIDING AWAY WITH THE OTHERS, I SAW HER LOCKING THE SLAVERS IN THEIR OWN CAGE."

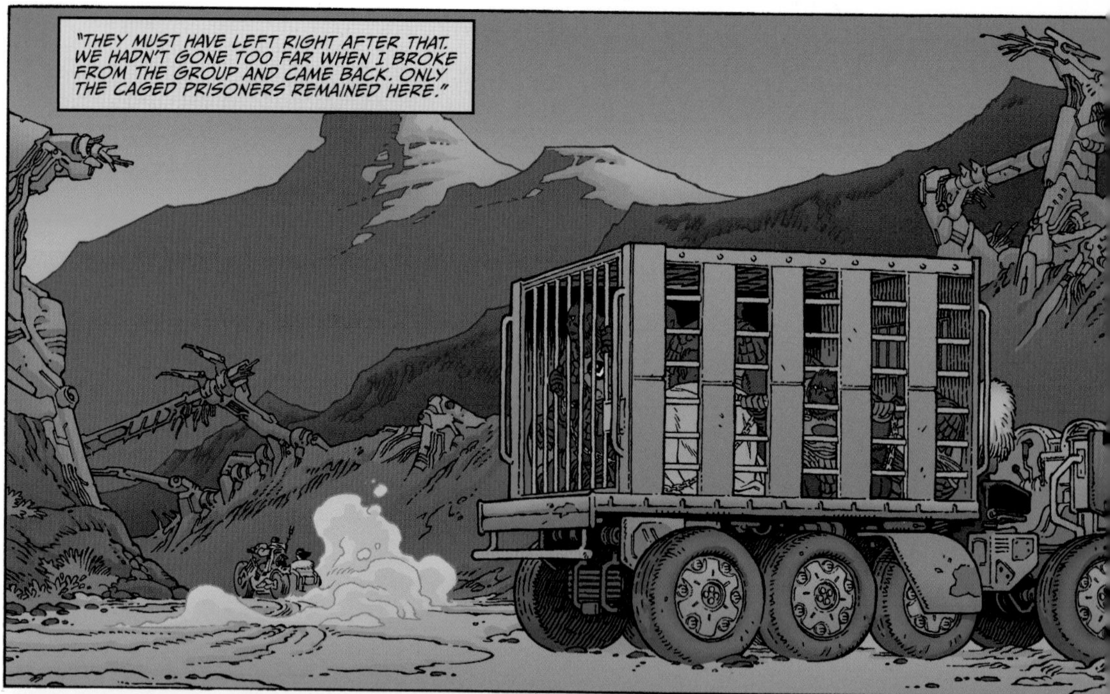
"THEY MUST HAVE LEFT RIGHT AFTER THAT. WE HADN'T GONE TOO FAR WHEN I BROKE FROM THE GROUP AND CAME BACK. ONLY THE CAGED PRISONERS REMAINED HERE."

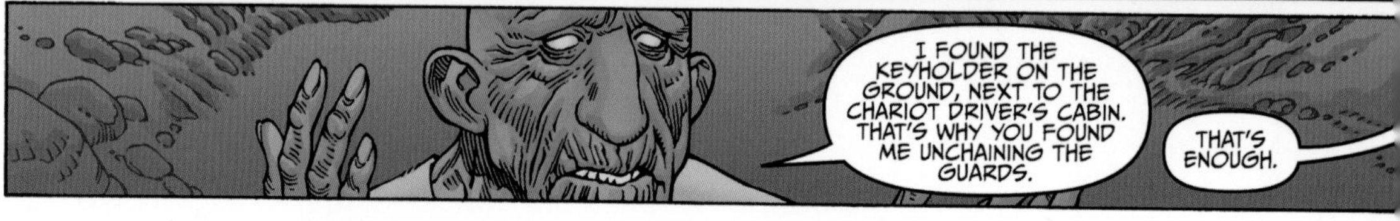
I FOUND THE KEYHOLDER ON THE GROUND, NEXT TO THE CHARIOT DRIVER'S CABIN. THAT'S WHY YOU FOUND ME UNCHAINING THE GUARDS.
THAT'S ENOUGH.

BLACK STAR TEMPLARS

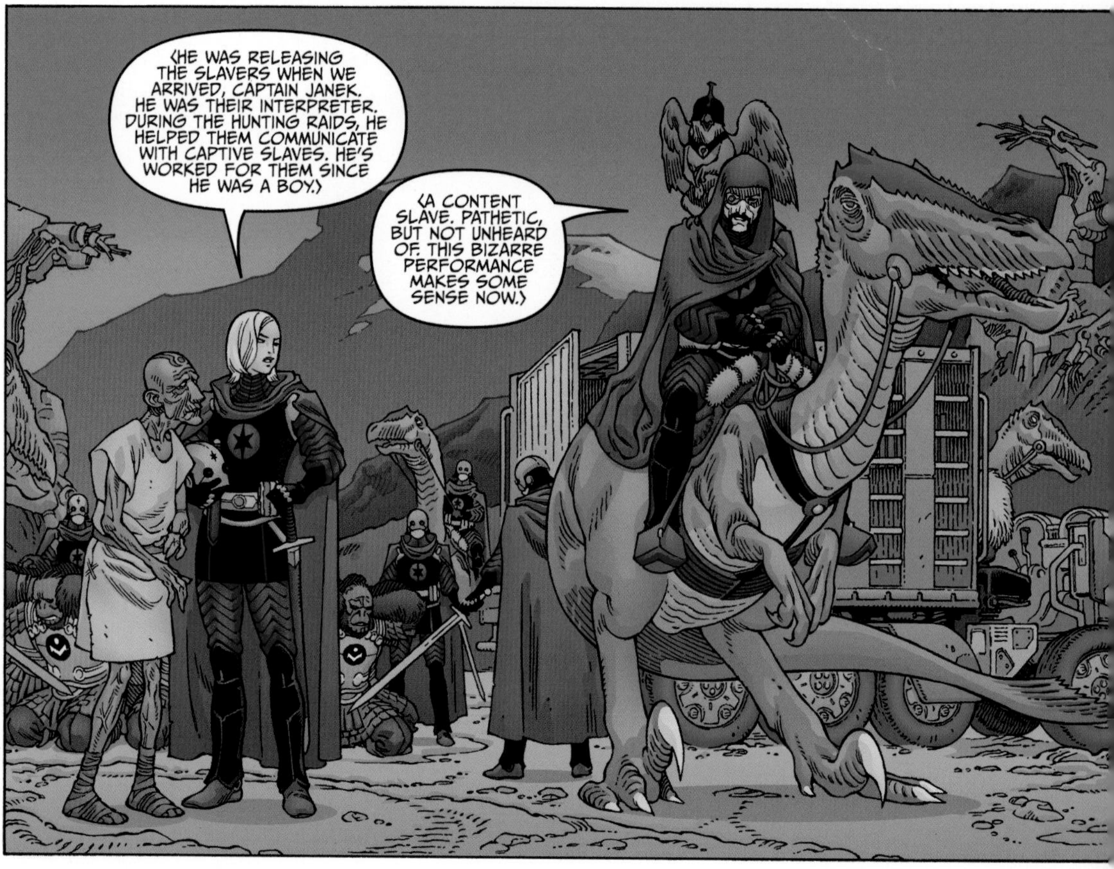
‹HE WAS RELEASING THE SLAVERS WHEN WE ARRIVED, CAPTAIN JANEK. HE WAS THEIR INTERPRETER. DURING THE HUNTING RAIDS, HE HELPED THEM COMMUNICATE WITH CAPTIVE SLAVES. HE'S WORKED FOR THEM SINCE HE WAS A BOY.›
‹A CONTENT SLAVE. PATHETIC, BUT NOT UNHEARD OF. THIS BIZARRE PERFORMANCE MAKES SOME SENSE NOW.›

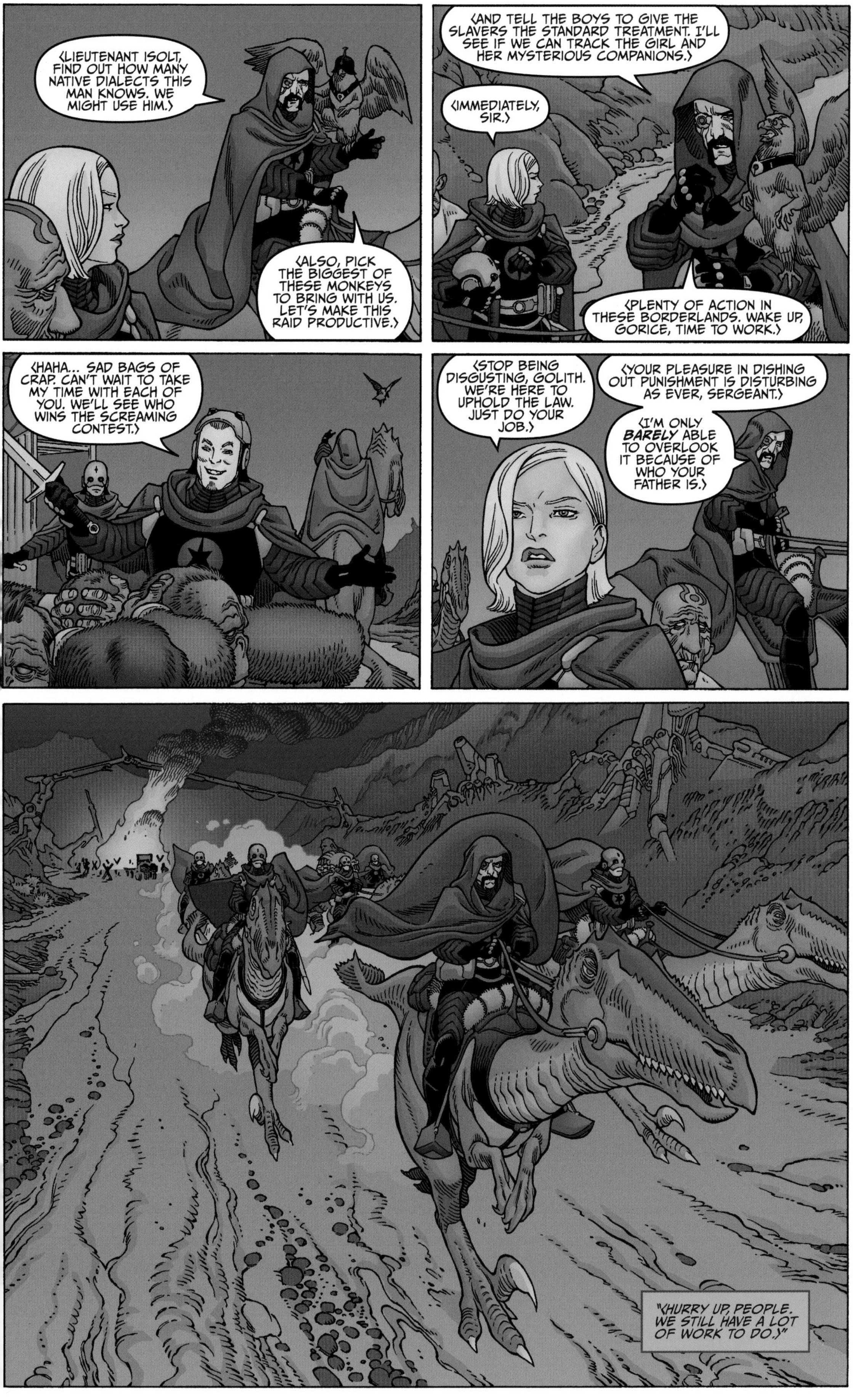
〈LIEUTENANT ISOLT, FIND OUT HOW MANY NATIVE DIALECTS THIS MAN KNOWS. WE MIGHT USE HIM.〉
〈ALSO, PICK THE BIGGEST OF THESE MONKEYS TO BRING WITH US. LET'S MAKE THIS RAID PRODUCTIVE.〉
〈AND TELL THE BOYS TO GIVE THE SLAVERS THE STANDARD TREATMENT. I'LL SEE IF WE CAN TRACK THE GIRL AND HER MYSTERIOUS COMPANIONS.〉
〈IMMEDIATELY, SIR.〉
〈PLENTY OF ACTION IN THESE BORDERLANDS. WAKE UP, GORICE, TIME TO WORK.〉
〈HAHA... SAD BAGS OF CRAP. CAN'T WAIT TO TAKE MY TIME WITH EACH OF YOU. WE'LL SEE WHO WINS THE SCREAMING CONTEST.〉
〈STOP BEING DISGUSTING, GOLITH. WE'RE HERE TO UPHOLD THE LAW. JUST DO YOUR JOB.〉
〈YOUR PLEASURE IN DISHING OUT PUNISHMENT IS DISTURBING AS EVER, SERGEANT.〉
〈I'M ONLY BARELY ABLE TO OVERLOOK IT BECAUSE OF WHO YOUR FATHER IS.〉
"〈HURRY UP, PEOPLE. WE STILL HAVE A LOT OF WORK TO DO.〉"

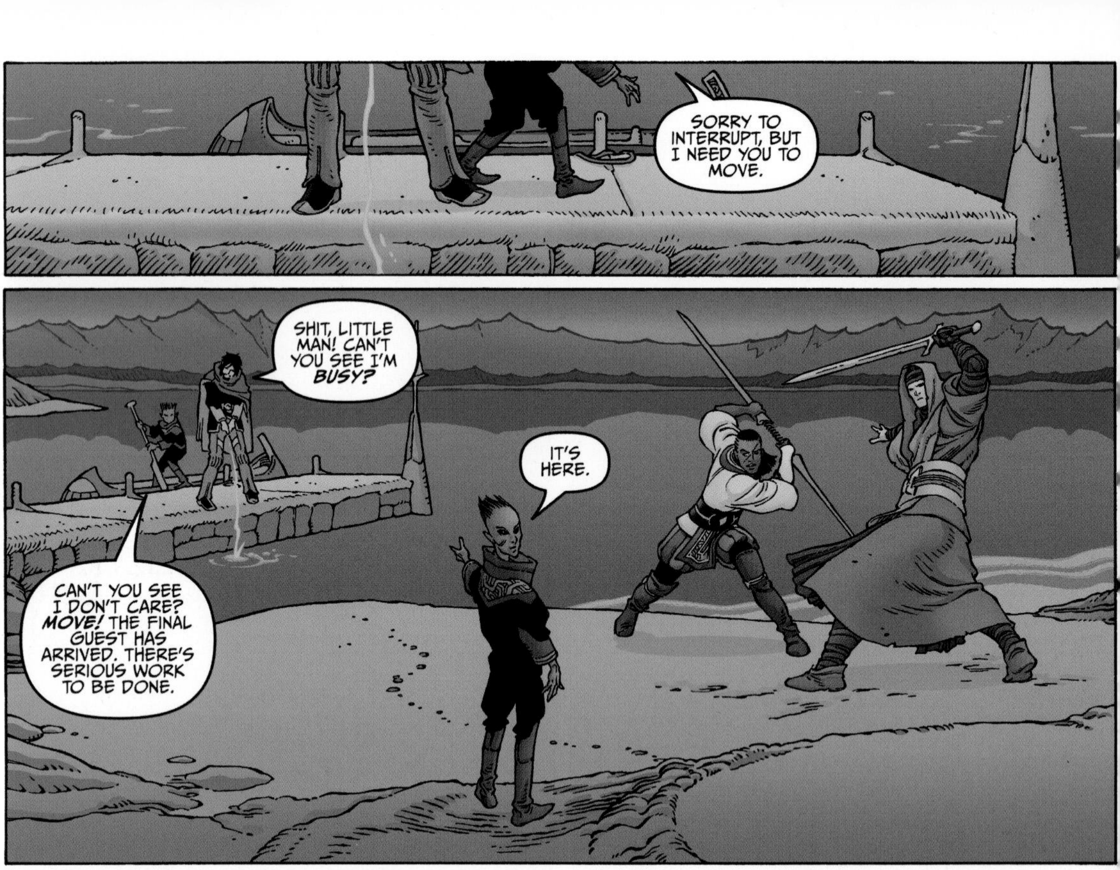
SORRY TO INTERRUPT, BUT I NEED YOU TO MOVE.
SHIT, LITTLE MAN! CAN'T YOU SEE I'M *BUSY?*
IT'S HERE.
CAN'T YOU SEE I DON'T CARE? ***MOVE!*** THE FINAL GUEST HAS ARRIVED. THERE'S SERIOUS WORK TO BE DONE.

THE GUARDIAN OF THE SACRED LAKE

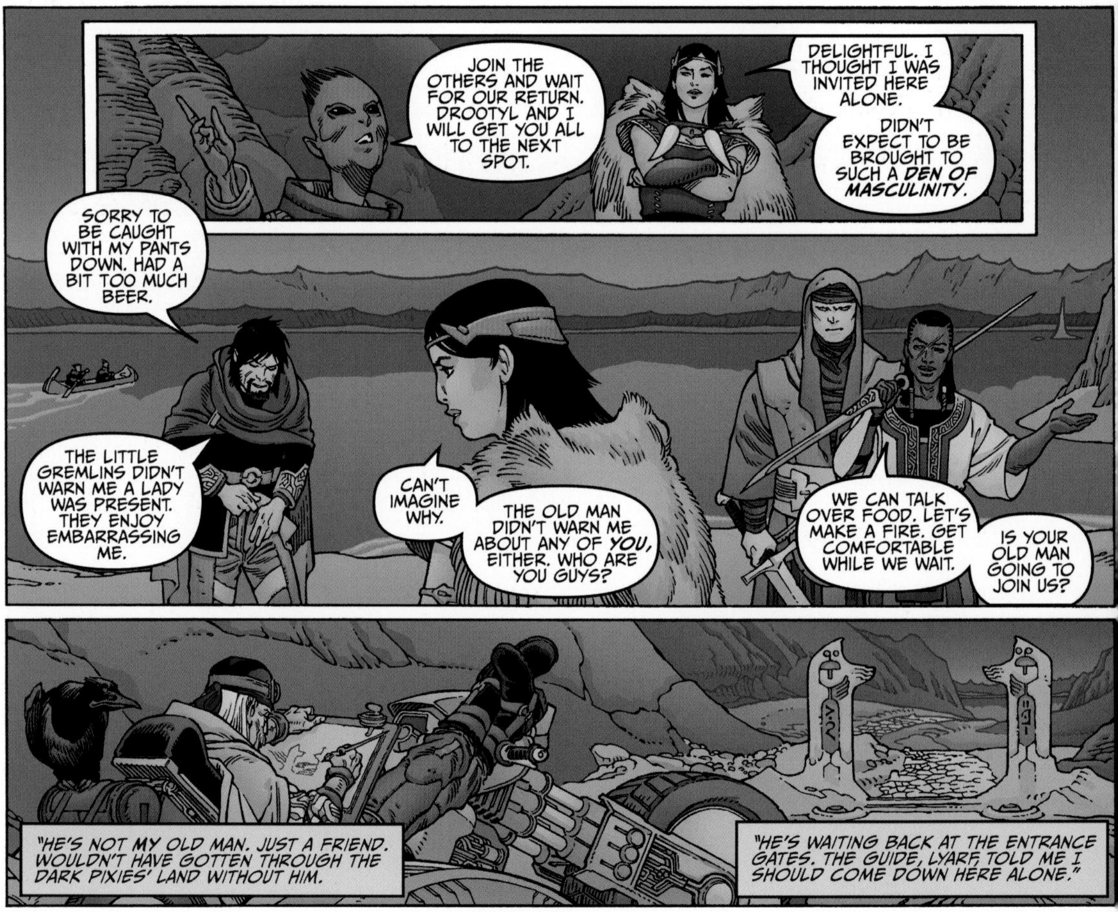
JOIN THE OTHERS AND WAIT FOR OUR RETURN. DROOTYL AND I WILL GET YOU ALL TO THE NEXT SPOT.
DELIGHTFUL. I THOUGHT I WAS INVITED HERE ALONE.
DIDN'T EXPECT TO BE BROUGHT TO SUCH A ***DEN OF MASCULINITY***.
SORRY TO BE CAUGHT WITH MY PANTS DOWN. HAD A BIT TOO MUCH BEER.
THE LITTLE GREMLINS DIDN'T WARN ME A LADY WAS PRESENT. THEY ENJOY EMBARRASSING ME.
CAN'T IMAGINE WHY.
THE OLD MAN DIDN'T WARN ME ABOUT ANY OF *YOU*, EITHER. WHO ARE YOU GUYS?
WE CAN TALK OVER FOOD. LET'S MAKE A FIRE. GET COMFORTABLE WHILE WE WAIT.
IS YOUR OLD MAN GOING TO JOIN US?
"HE'S NOT ***MY*** *OLD MAN. JUST A FRIEND. WOULDN'T HAVE GOTTEN THROUGH THE DARK PIXIES' LAND WITHOUT HIM.*
"HE'S WAITING BACK AT THE ENTRANCE GATES. THE GUIDE, LYARF, TOLD ME I SHOULD COME DOWN HERE ALONE."

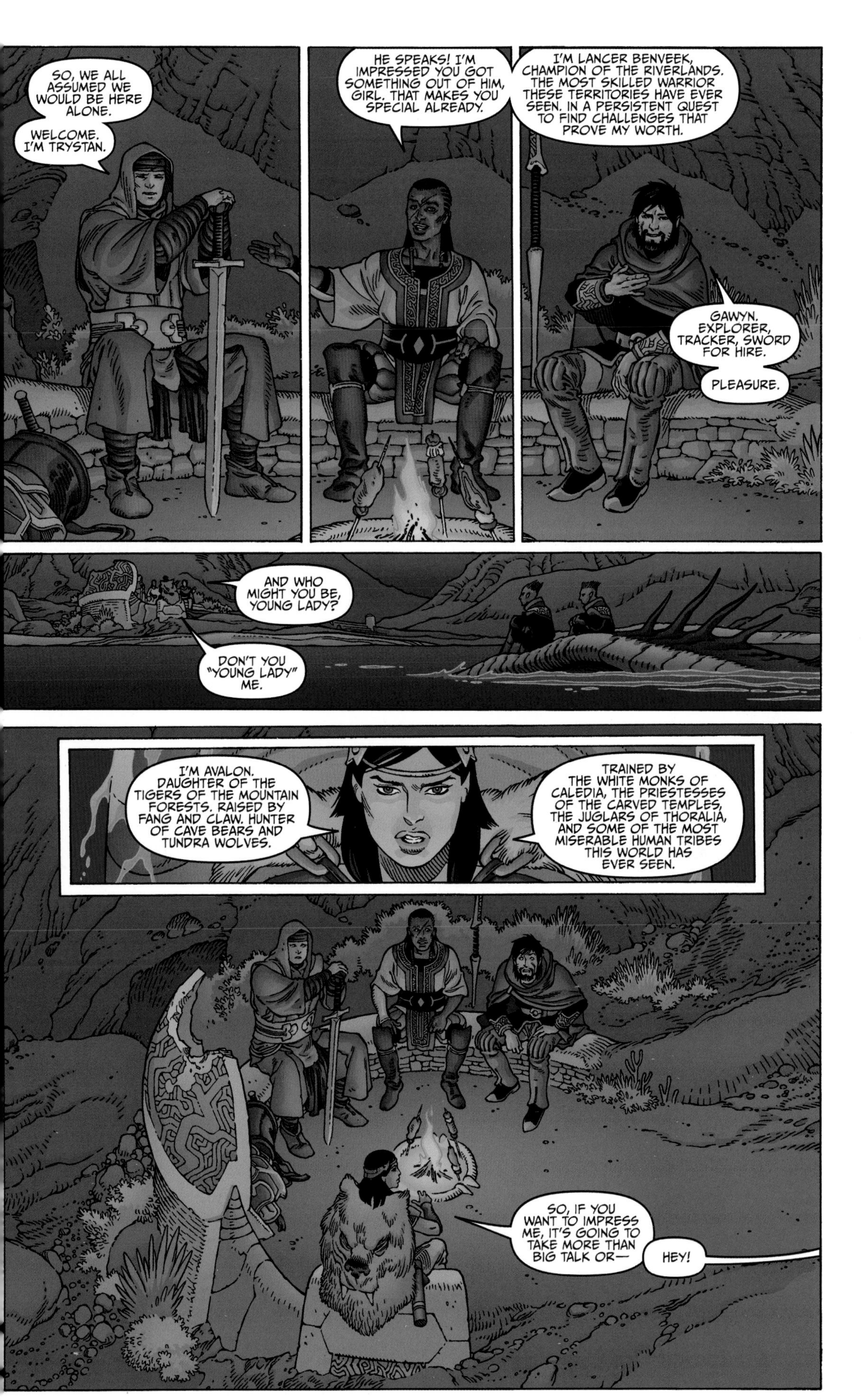

SO, WE ALL ASSUMED WE WOULD BE HERE ALONE.
WELCOME. I'M TRYSTAN.
HE SPEAKS! I'M IMPRESSED YOU GOT SOMETHING OUT OF HIM, GIRL. THAT MAKES YOU SPECIAL ALREADY.
I'M LANCER BENVEEK, CHAMPION OF THE RIVERLANDS. THE MOST SKILLED WARRIOR THESE TERRITORIES HAVE EVER SEEN. IN A PERSISTENT QUEST TO FIND CHALLENGES THAT PROVE MY WORTH.
GAWYN. EXPLORER, TRACKER, SWORD FOR HIRE.
PLEASURE.
AND WHO MIGHT YOU BE, YOUNG LADY?
DON'T YOU "YOUNG LADY" ME.
I'M AVALON. DAUGHTER OF THE TIGERS OF THE MOUNTAIN FORESTS. RAISED BY FANG AND CLAW. HUNTER OF CAVE BEARS AND TUNDRA WOLVES.
TRAINED BY THE WHITE MONKS OF CALEDIA, THE PRIESTESSES OF THE CARVED TEMPLES, THE JUGLARS OF THORALIA, AND SOME OF THE MOST MISERABLE HUMAN TRIBES THIS WORLD HAS EVER SEEN.
SO, IF YOU WANT TO IMPRESS ME, IT'S GOING TO TAKE MORE THAN BIG TALK OR—
HEY!

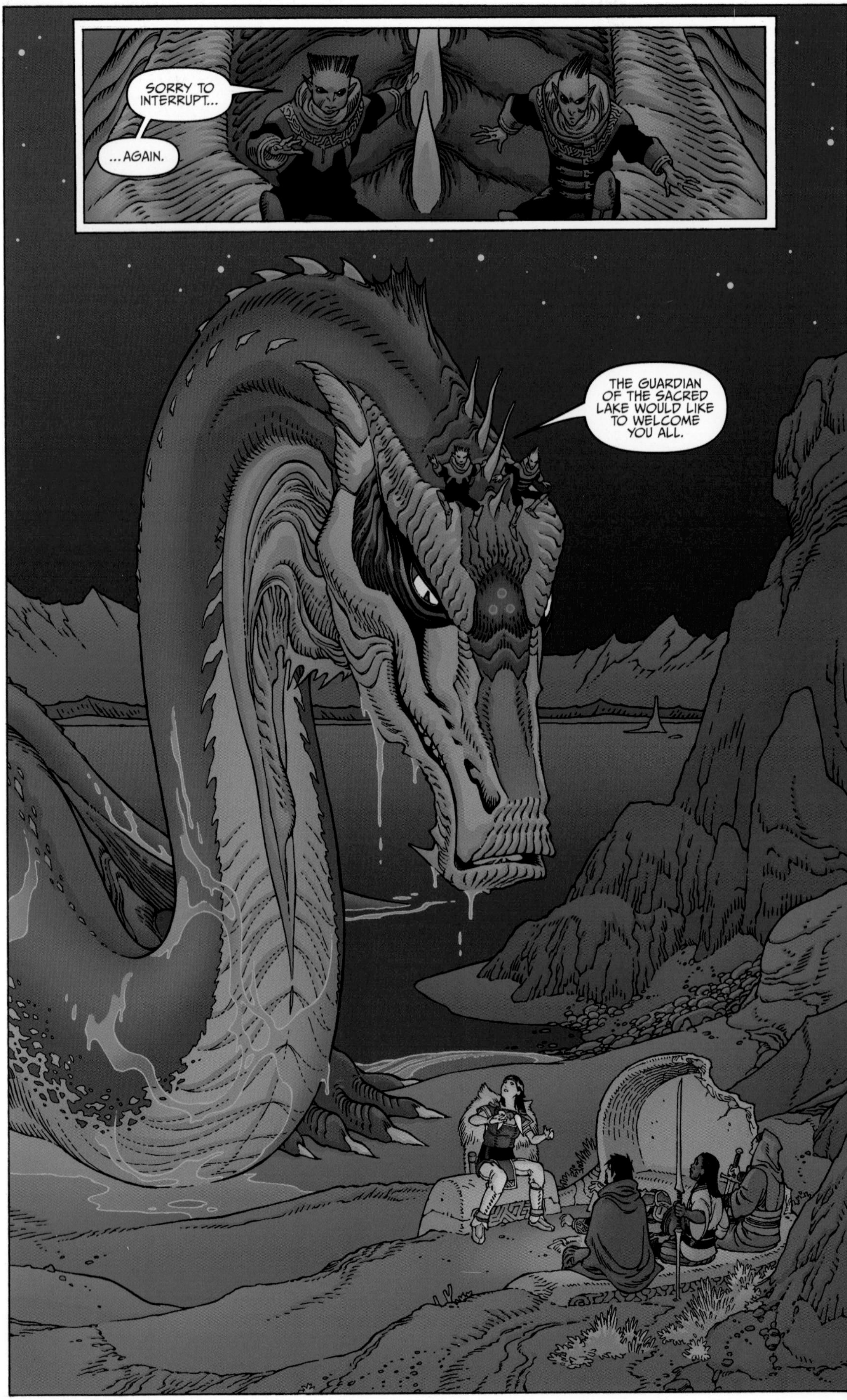
SORRY TO INTERRUPT...
...AGAIN.
THE GUARDIAN OF THE SACRED LAKE WOULD LIKE TO WELCOME YOU ALL.

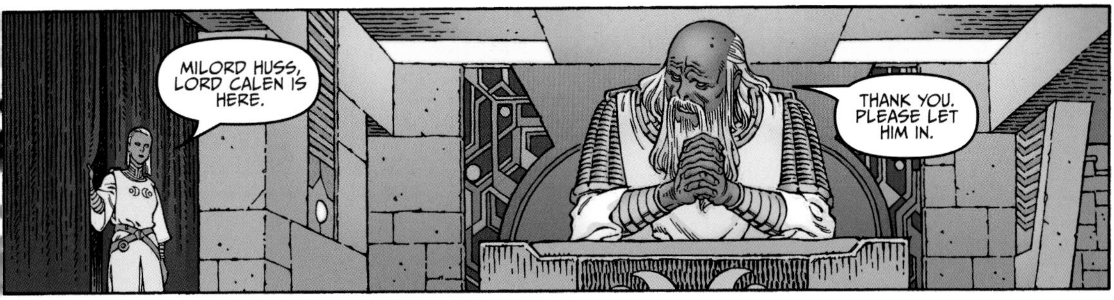
MILORD HUSS, LORD CALEN IS HERE.
THANK YOU. PLEASE LET HIM IN.

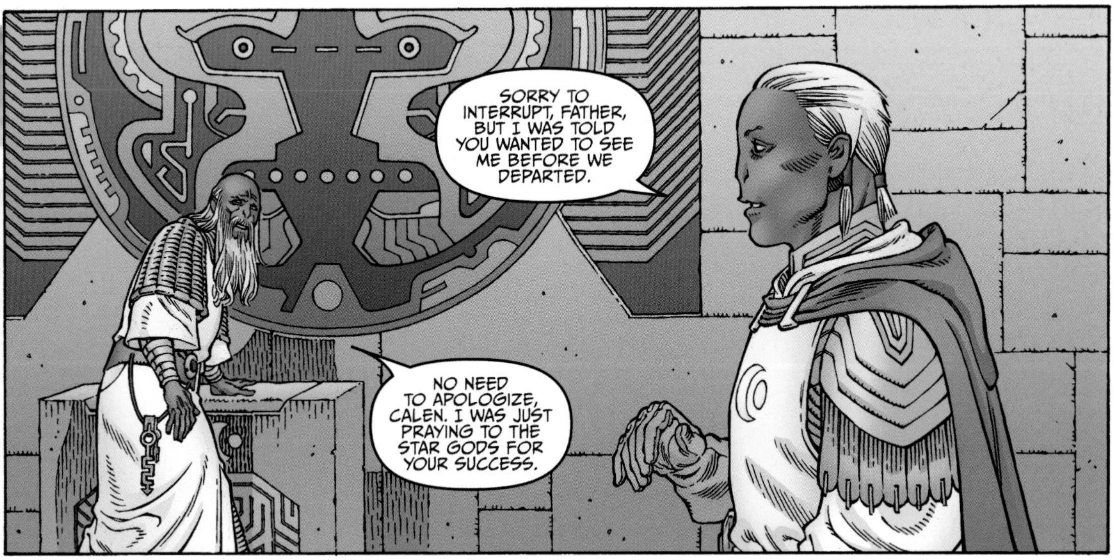
SORRY TO INTERRUPT, FATHER, BUT I WAS TOLD YOU WANTED TO SEE ME BEFORE WE DEPARTED.
NO NEED TO APOLOGIZE, CALEN. I WAS JUST PRAYING TO THE STAR GODS FOR YOUR SUCCESS.

THE WHITE MONKS OF CALEDIA

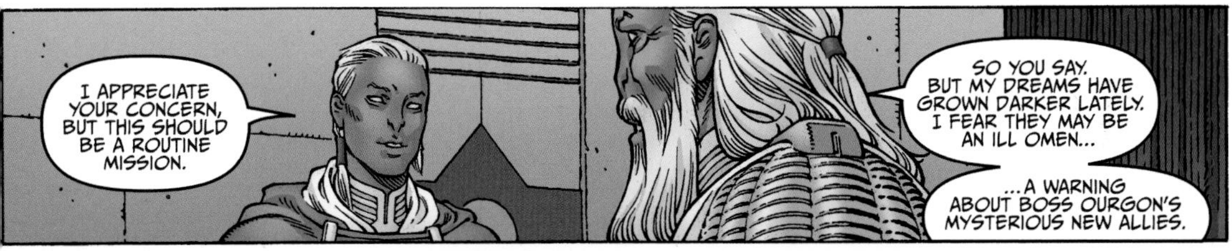
I APPRECIATE YOUR CONCERN, BUT THIS SHOULD BE A ROUTINE MISSION.
SO YOU SAY. BUT MY DREAMS HAVE GROWN DARKER LATELY. I FEAR THEY MAY BE AN ILL OMEN...
...A WARNING ABOUT BOSS OURGON'S MYSTERIOUS NEW ALLIES.

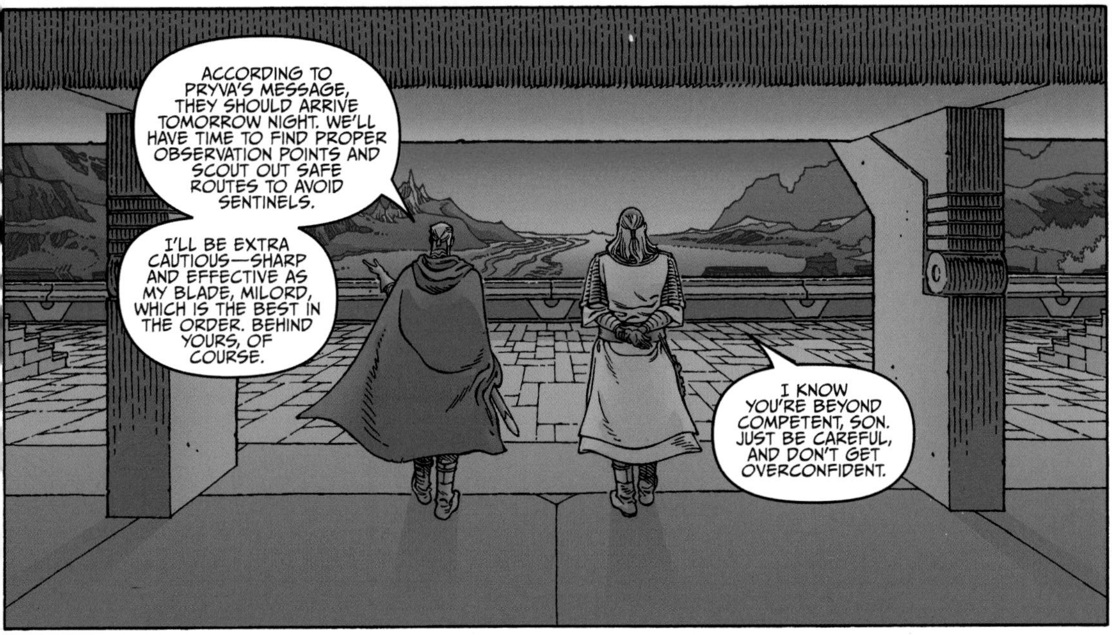
ACCORDING TO PRYVA'S MESSAGE, THEY SHOULD ARRIVE TOMORROW NIGHT. WE'LL HAVE TIME TO FIND PROPER OBSERVATION POINTS AND SCOUT OUT SAFE ROUTES TO AVOID SENTINELS.
I'LL BE EXTRA CAUTIOUS—SHARP AND EFFECTIVE AS MY BLADE, MILORD, WHICH IS THE BEST IN THE ORDER. BEHIND YOURS, OF COURSE.
I KNOW YOU'RE BEYOND COMPETENT, SON. JUST BE CAREFUL, AND DON'T GET OVERCONFIDENT.

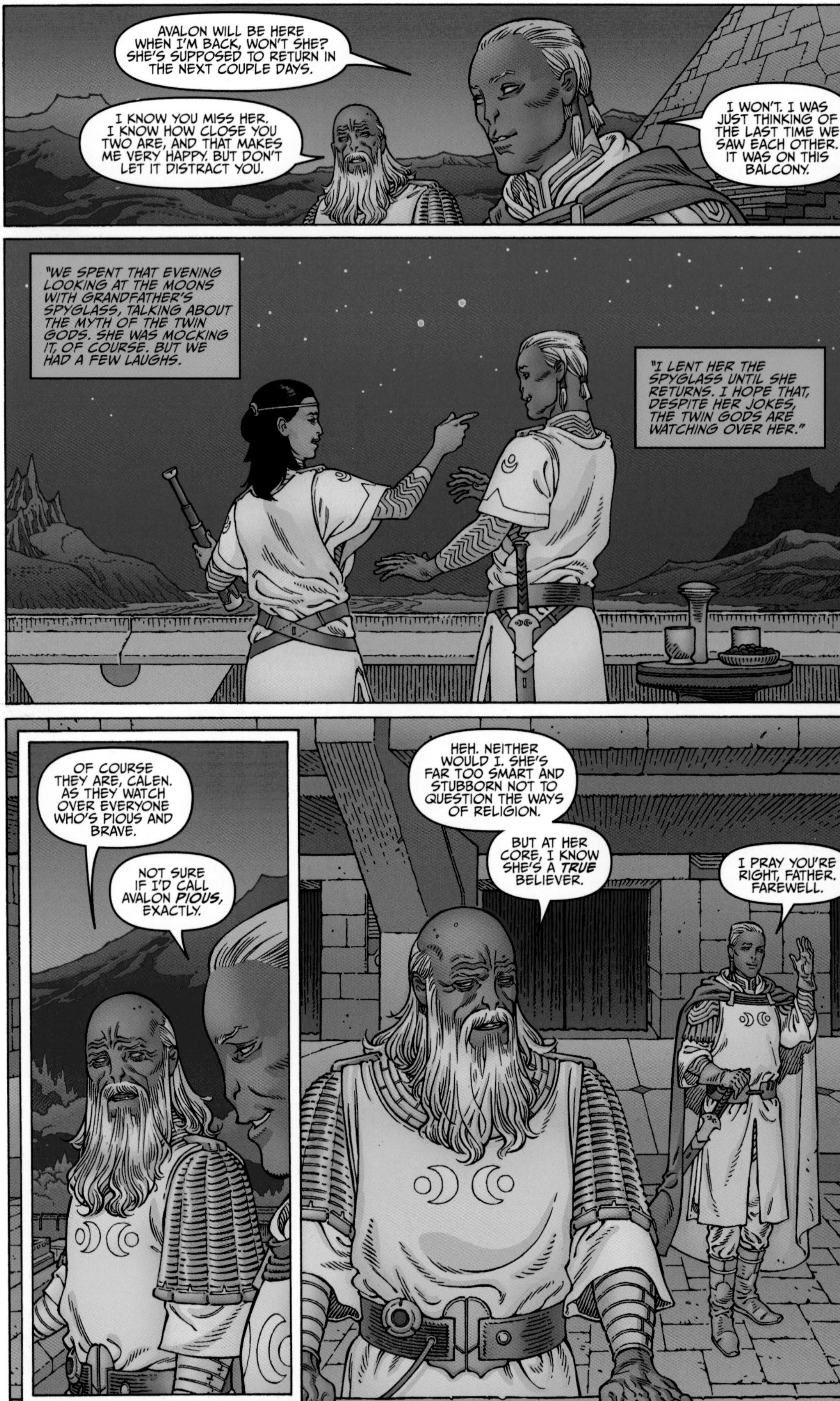
AVALON WILL BE HERE WHEN I'M BACK, WON'T SHE? SHE'S SUPPOSED TO RETURN IN THE NEXT COUPLE DAYS.
I KNOW YOU MISS HER. I KNOW HOW CLOSE YOU TWO ARE, AND THAT MAKES ME VERY HAPPY. BUT DON'T LET IT DISTRACT YOU.
I WON'T. I WAS JUST THINKING OF THE LAST TIME WE SAW EACH OTHER. IT WAS ON THIS BALCONY.
"WE SPENT THAT EVENING LOOKING AT THE MOONS WITH GRANDFATHER'S SPYGLASS, TALKING ABOUT THE MYTH OF THE TWIN GODS. SHE WAS MOCKING IT, OF COURSE. BUT WE HAD A FEW LAUGHS.
"I LENT HER THE SPYGLASS UNTIL SHE RETURNS. I HOPE THAT, DESPITE HER JOKES, THE TWIN GODS ARE WATCHING OVER HER."
OF COURSE THEY ARE, CALEN. AS THEY WATCH OVER EVERYONE WHO'S PIOUS AND BRAVE.
NOT SURE IF I'D CALL AVALON *PIOUS*, EXACTLY.
HEH. NEITHER WOULD I. SHE'S FAR TOO SMART AND STUBBORN NOT TO QUESTION THE WAYS OF RELIGION.
BUT AT HER CORE, I KNOW SHE'S A *TRUE* BELIEVER.
I PRAY YOU'RE RIGHT, FATHER. FAREWELL.

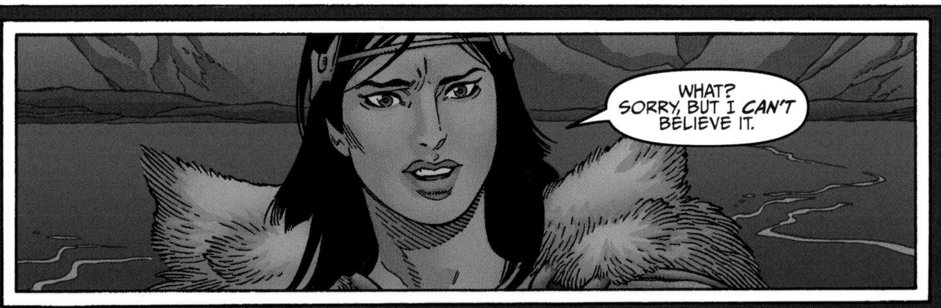
WHAT? SORRY, BUT I *CAN'T* BELIEVE IT.

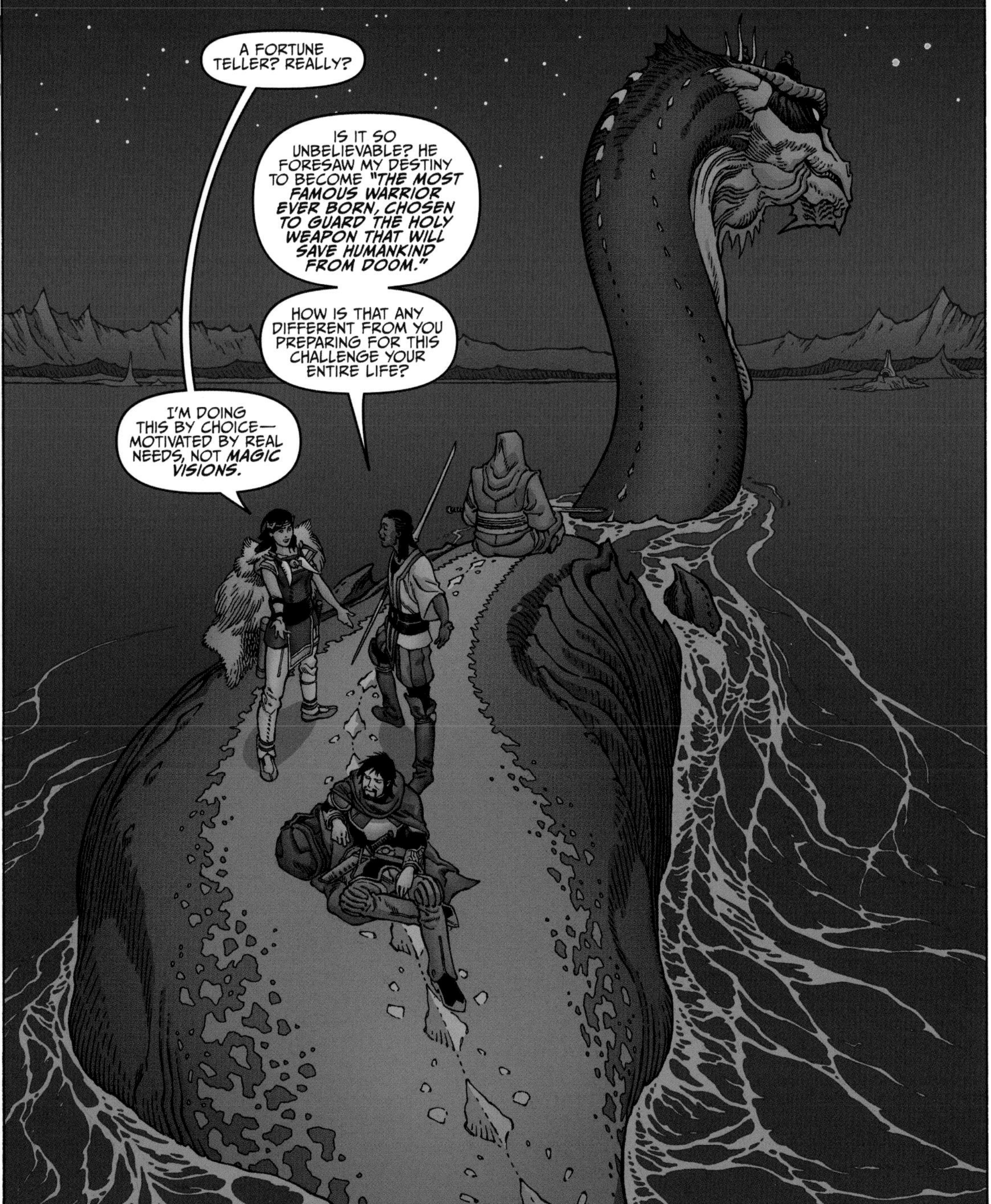
A FORTUNE TELLER? REALLY?
IS IT SO UNBELIEVABLE? HE FORESAW MY DESTINY TO BECOME ***"THE MOST FAMOUS WARRIOR EVER BORN, CHOSEN TO GUARD THE HOLY WEAPON THAT WILL SAVE HUMANKIND FROM DOOM."***
HOW IS THAT ANY DIFFERENT FROM YOU PREPARING FOR THIS CHALLENGE YOUR ENTIRE LIFE?
I'M DOING THIS BY CHOICE—MOTIVATED BY REAL NEEDS, NOT *MAGIC VISIONS.*

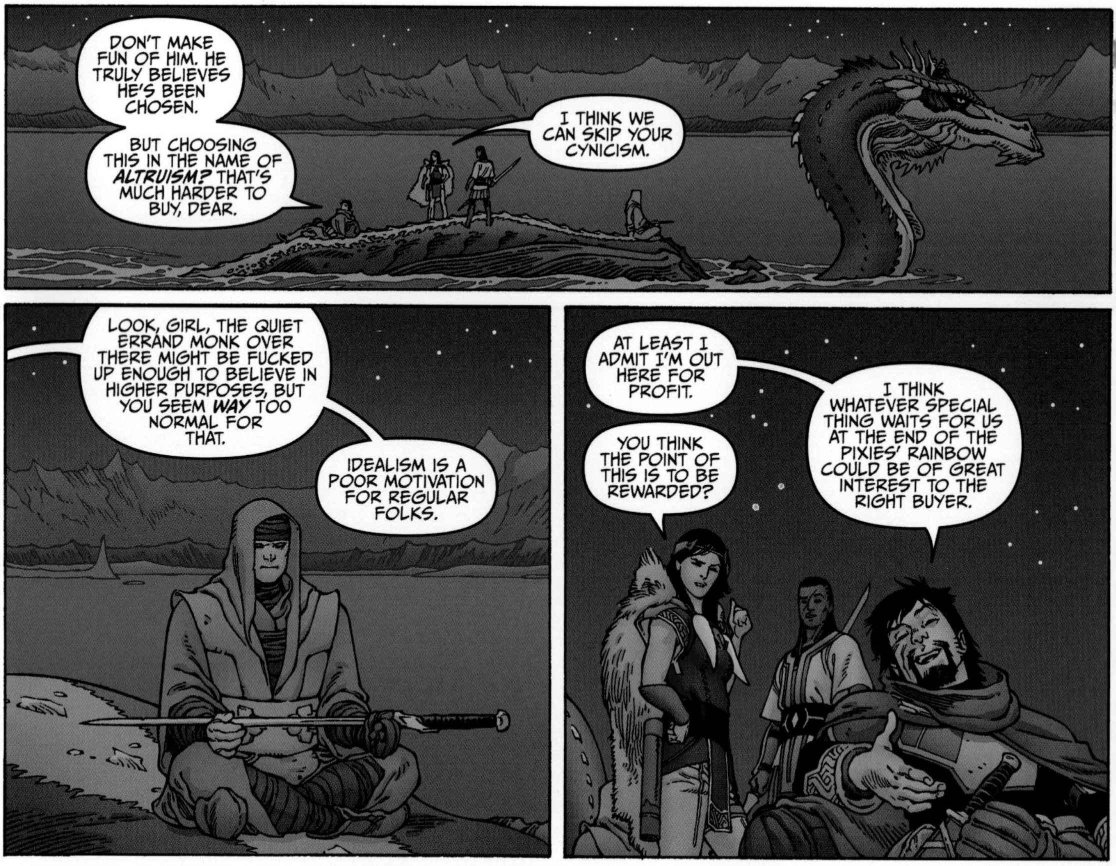
DON'T MAKE FUN OF HIM. HE TRULY BELIEVES HE'S BEEN CHOSEN.
BUT CHOOSING THIS IN THE NAME OF ALTRUISM? THAT'S MUCH HARDER TO BUY, DEAR.
I THINK WE CAN SKIP YOUR CYNICISM.
LOOK, GIRL, THE QUIET ERRAND MONK OVER THERE MIGHT BE FUCKED UP ENOUGH TO BELIEVE IN HIGHER PURPOSES, BUT YOU SEEM WAY TOO NORMAL FOR THAT.
IDEALISM IS A POOR MOTIVATION FOR REGULAR FOLKS.
AT LEAST I ADMIT I'M OUT HERE FOR PROFIT.
YOU THINK THE POINT OF THIS IS TO BE REWARDED?
I THINK WHATEVER SPECIAL THING WAITS FOR US AT THE END OF THE PIXIES' RAINBOW COULD BE OF GREAT INTEREST TO THE RIGHT BUYER.

THE SACRED CAVE

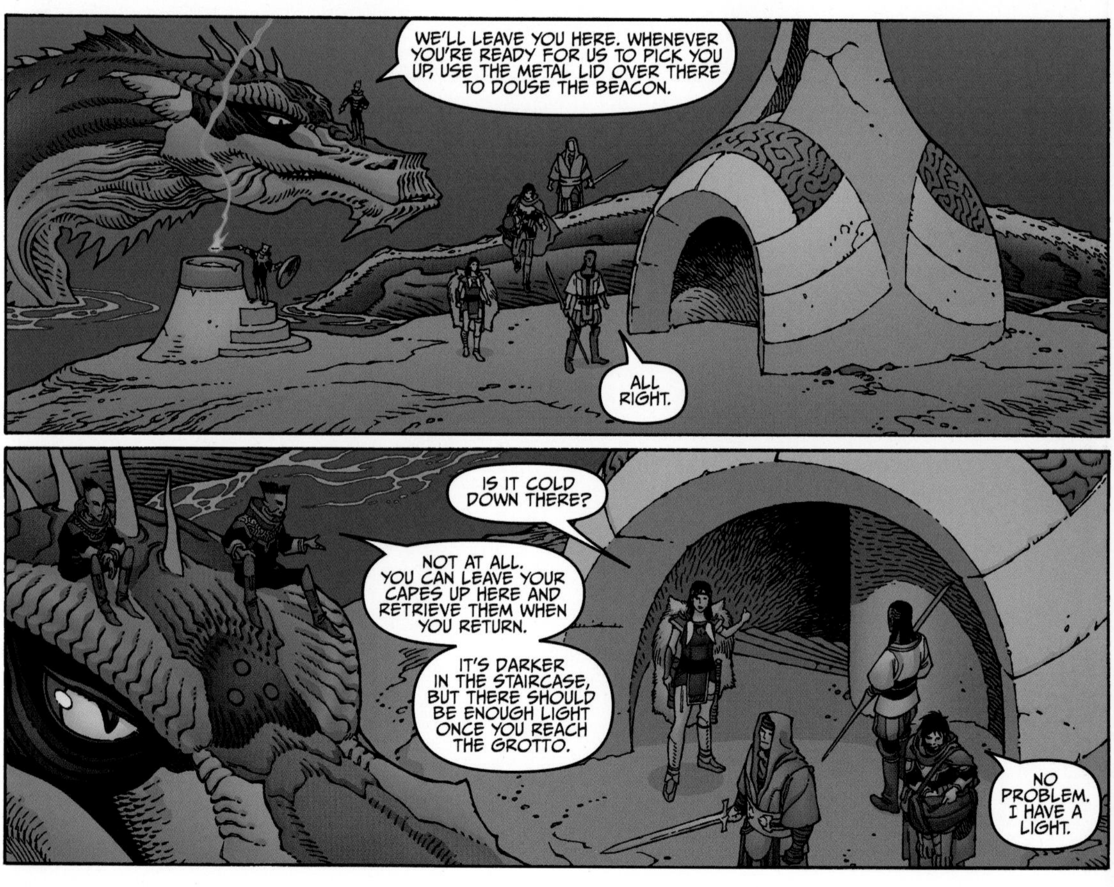
WE'LL LEAVE YOU HERE. WHENEVER YOU'RE READY FOR US TO PICK YOU UP, USE THE METAL LID OVER THERE TO DOUSE THE BEACON.
ALL RIGHT.
IS IT COLD DOWN THERE?
NOT AT ALL. YOU CAN LEAVE YOUR CAPES UP HERE AND RETRIEVE THEM WHEN YOU RETURN.
IT'S DARKER IN THE STAIRCASE, BUT THERE SHOULD BE ENOUGH LIGHT ONCE YOU REACH THE GROTTO.
NO PROBLEM. I HAVE A LIGHT.

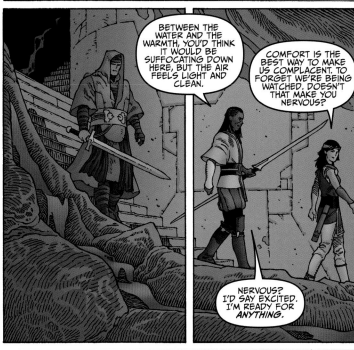

BETWEEN THE WATER AND THE WARMTH, YOU'D THINK IT WOULD BE SUFFOCATING DOWN HERE, BUT THE AIR FEELS LIGHT AND CLEAN.

COMFORT IS THE BEST WAY TO MAKE US COMPLACENT. TO FORGET WE'RE BEING WATCHED. DOESN'T THAT MAKE YOU NERVOUS?

NERVOUS? I'D SAY EXCITED. I'M READY FOR *ANYTHING.*

STAY CLOSE. LOOKS LIKE THE PATH AHEAD IS SURROUNDED BY LARGE POOLS. WE SHOULD PROBABLY BE QUIETER FROM HERE ON OUT.

WILL THAT MAKE A DIFFERENCE?

AS A SIGN OF RESPECT, IF NOTHING ELSE. IT'S ONE THING TO ASSUME WE'RE EXPECTED AND ANOTHER TO ANNOUNCE OURSELVES.

THE GLOW FROM THE WATER IS BRIGHTER DOWN HERE. SHOULD BE ENOUGH LIGHT FOR US TO...

WHAT?

37

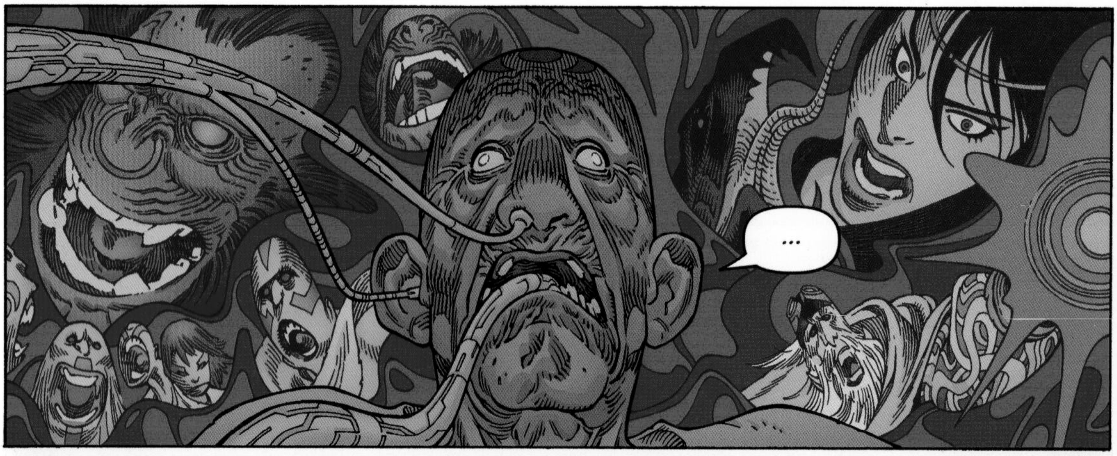
...

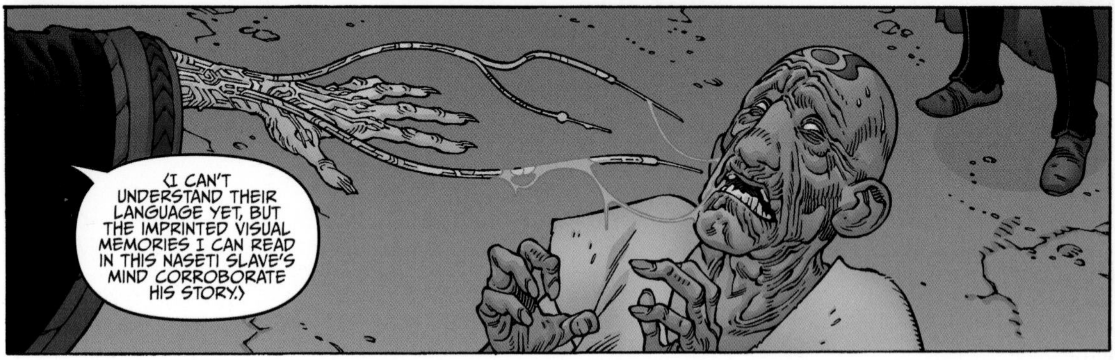
‹I CAN'T UNDERSTAND THEIR LANGUAGE YET, BUT THE IMPRINTED VISUAL MEMORIES I CAN READ IN THIS NASETI SLAVE'S MIND CORROBORATE HIS STORY.›

LORD MORGAN

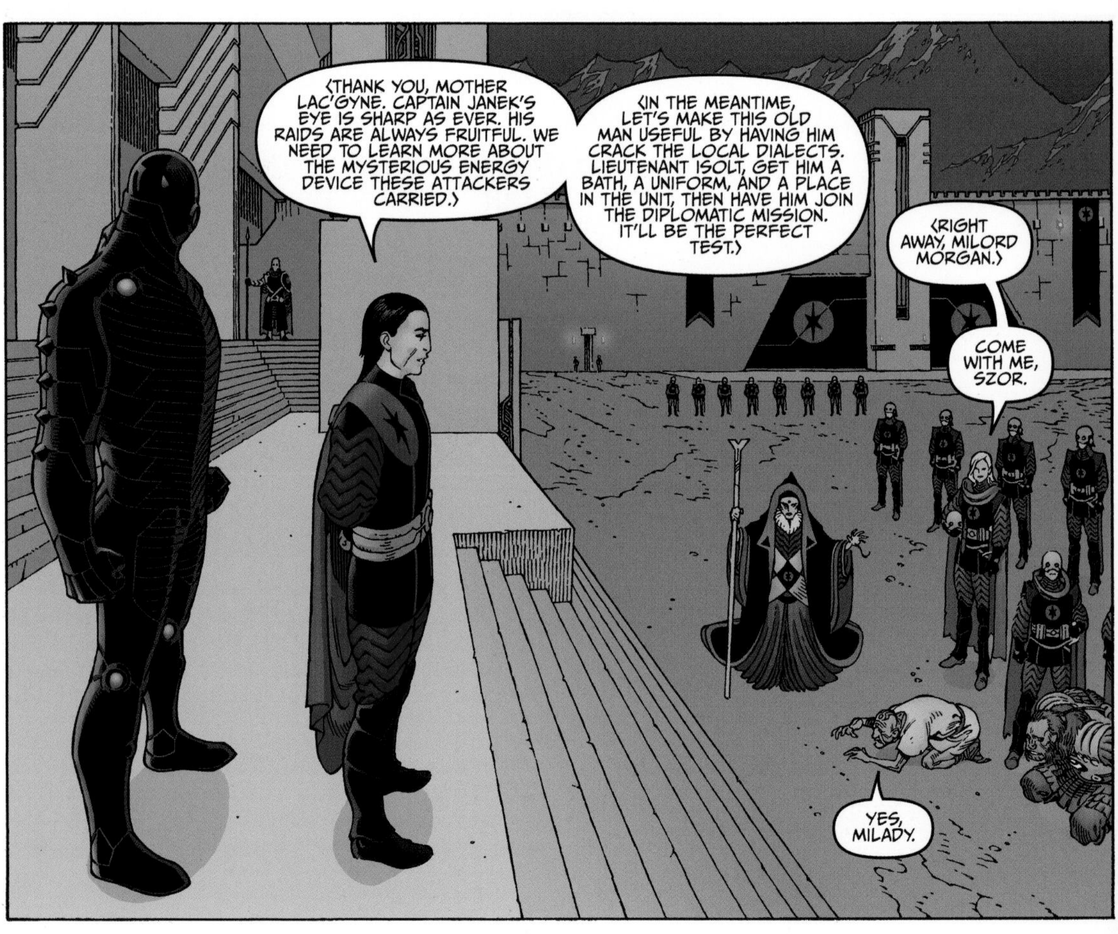
‹THANK YOU, MOTHER LAC'GYNE. CAPTAIN JANEK'S EYE IS SHARP AS EVER. HIS RAIDS ARE ALWAYS FRUITFUL. WE NEED TO LEARN MORE ABOUT THE MYSTERIOUS ENERGY DEVICE THESE ATTACKERS CARRIED.›
‹IN THE MEANTIME, LET'S MAKE THIS OLD MAN USEFUL BY HAVING HIM CRACK THE LOCAL DIALECTS. LIEUTENANT ISOLT, GET HIM A BATH, A UNIFORM, AND A PLACE IN THE UNIT, THEN HAVE HIM JOIN THE DIPLOMATIC MISSION. IT'LL BE THE PERFECT TEST.›
‹RIGHT AWAY, MILORD MORGAN.›
COME WITH ME, SZOR.
YES, MILADY.

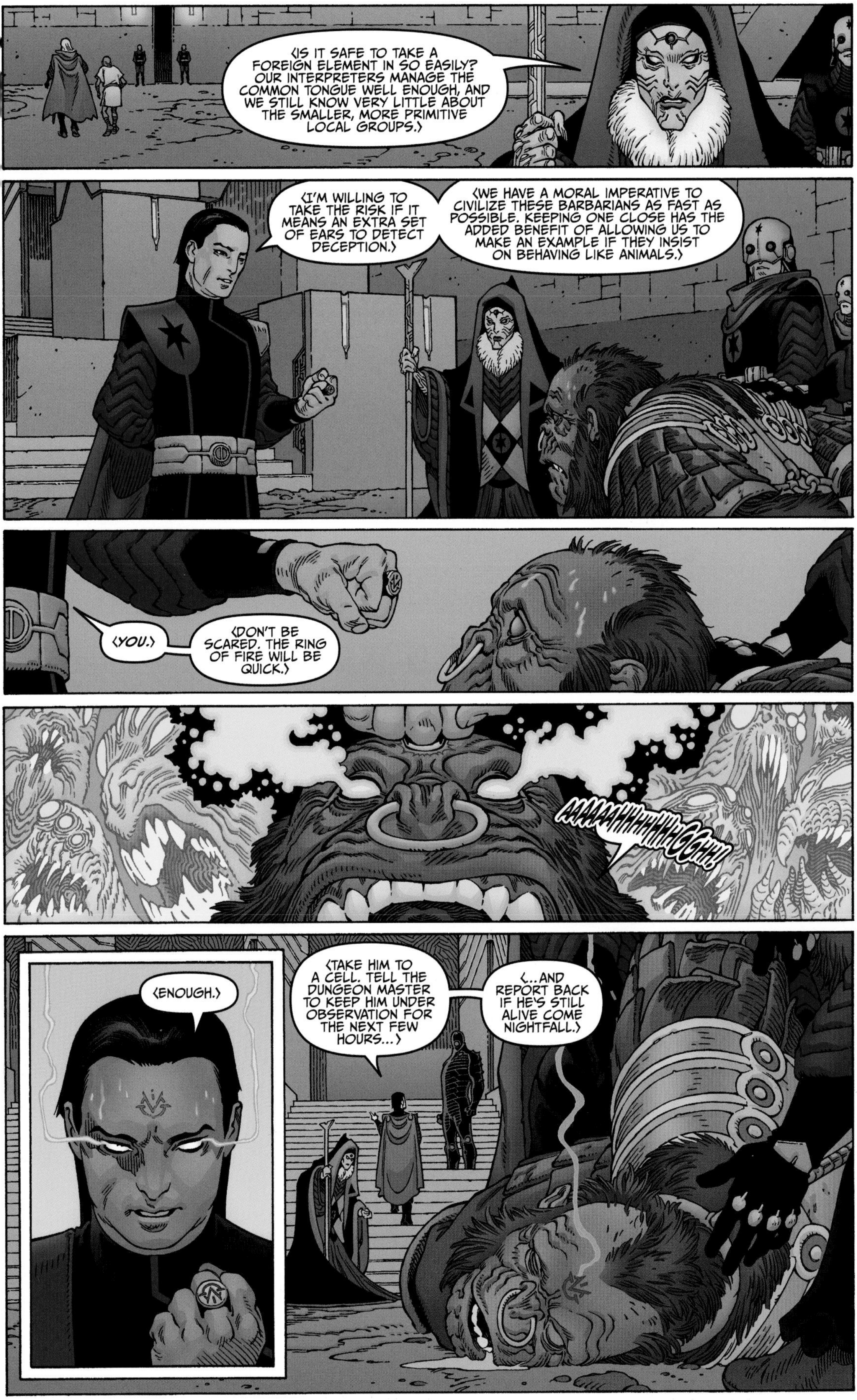
‹IS IT SAFE TO TAKE A FOREIGN ELEMENT IN SO EASILY? OUR INTERPRETERS MANAGE THE COMMON TONGUE WELL ENOUGH, AND WE STILL KNOW VERY LITTLE ABOUT THE SMALLER, MORE PRIMITIVE LOCAL GROUPS.›
‹I'M WILLING TO TAKE THE RISK IF IT MEANS AN EXTRA SET OF EARS TO DETECT DECEPTION.›
‹WE HAVE A MORAL IMPERATIVE TO CIVILIZE THESE BARBARIANS AS FAST AS POSSIBLE. KEEPING ONE CLOSE HAS THE ADDED BENEFIT OF ALLOWING US TO MAKE AN EXAMPLE IF THEY INSIST ON BEHAVING LIKE ANIMALS.›
‹YOU.›
‹DON'T BE SCARED. THE RING OF FIRE WILL BE QUICK.›
AAAAAAHHHHHHHGGHH!
‹ENOUGH.›
‹TAKE HIM TO A CELL. TELL THE DUNGEON MASTER TO KEEP HIM UNDER OBSERVATION FOR THE NEXT FEW HOURS...›
‹...AND REPORT BACK IF HE'S STILL ALIVE COME NIGHTFALL.›

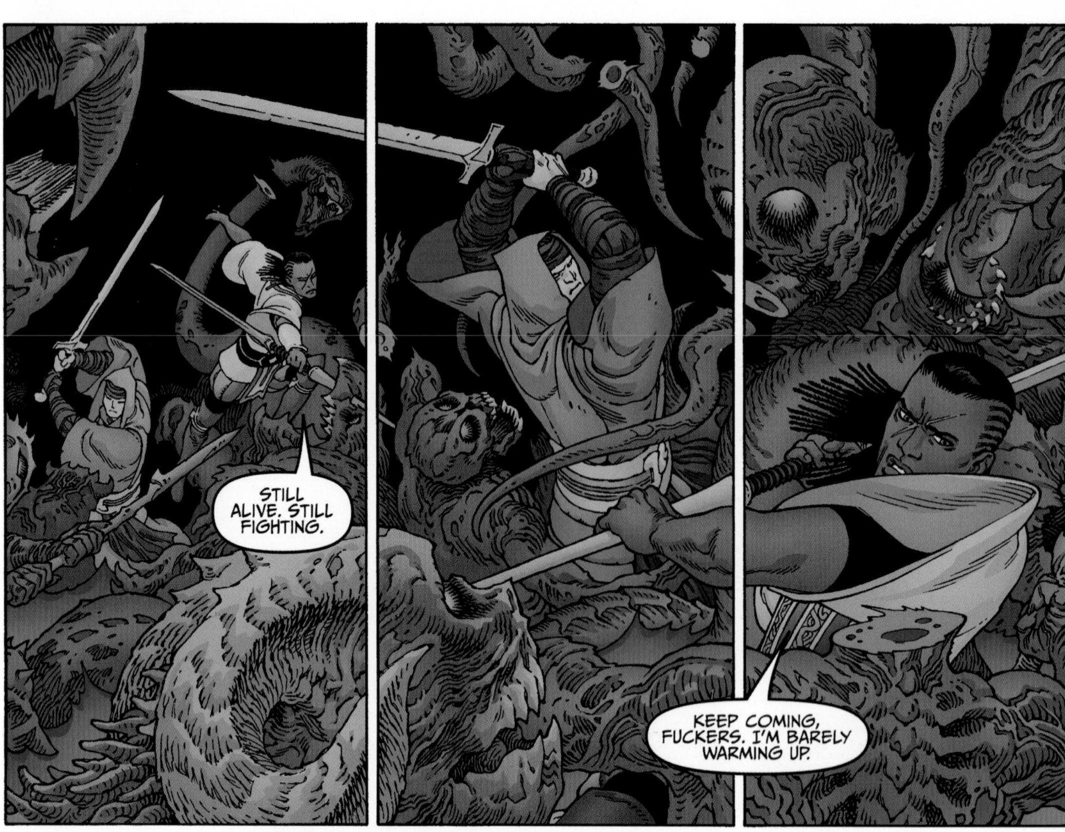
STILL ALIVE. STILL FIGHTING.
KEEP COMING, FUCKERS. I'M BARELY WARMING UP.

UNDERWORLD WARRIORS

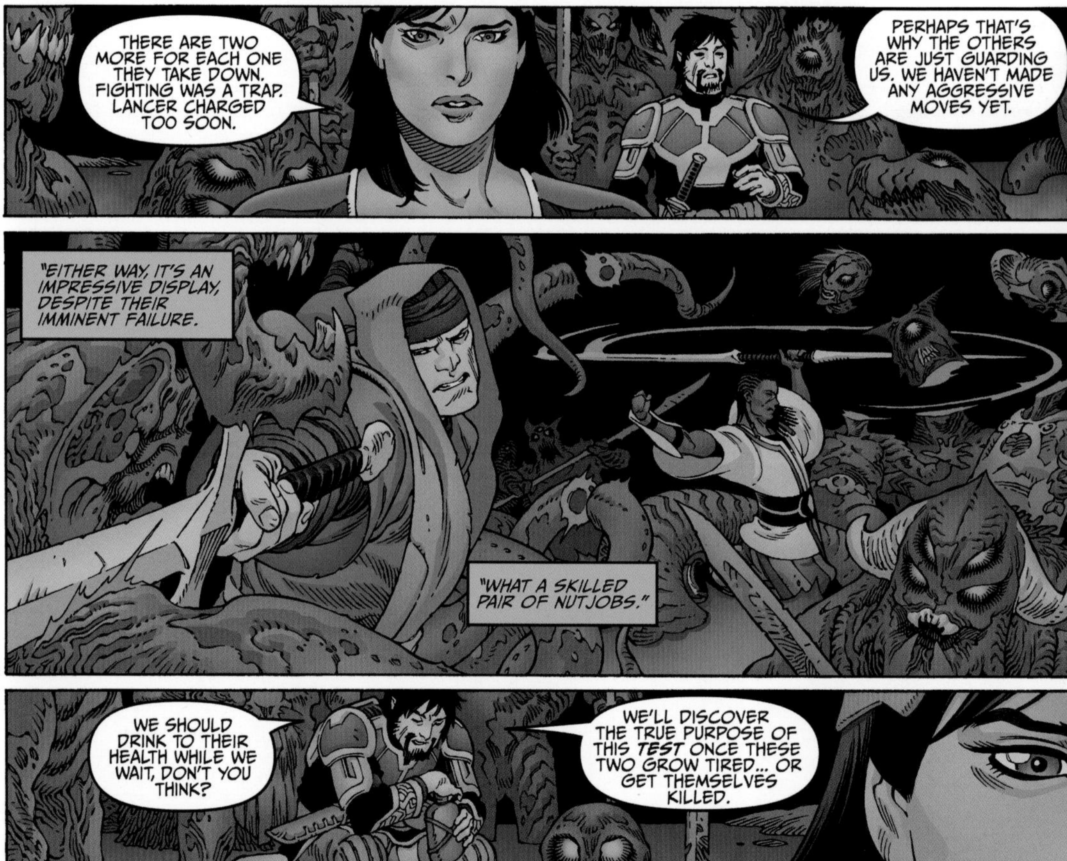
THERE ARE TWO MORE FOR EACH ONE THEY TAKE DOWN. FIGHTING WAS A TRAP. LANCER CHARGED TOO SOON.
PERHAPS THAT'S WHY THE OTHERS ARE JUST GUARDING US. WE HAVEN'T MADE ANY AGGRESSIVE MOVES YET.
"EITHER WAY, IT'S AN IMPRESSIVE DISPLAY, DESPITE THEIR IMMINENT FAILURE.
"WHAT A SKILLED PAIR OF NUTJOBS."
WE SHOULD DRINK TO THEIR HEALTH WHILE WE WAIT, DON'T YOU THINK?
WE'LL DISCOVER THE TRUE PURPOSE OF THIS TEST ONCE THESE TWO GROW TIRED... OR GET THEMSELVES KILLED.

KEEP MOVING. MAKE SPACE. YOU'RE FASTER... FASTER... FASTER...

...DAMN. DAMN!

HOW ABOUT WE DRINK TO YOUR "I'M FULL OF BULLSHIT" ATTITUDE. AND MY AWARENESS THAT IT'S JUST YOUR WAY OF GAINING ADVANTAGE OVER PEOPLE.

TO THAT, THEN. CHEERS!

YET, IN THE FACE OF HOPELESSNESS, WE SURRENDER ONLY TO THE HOLY LADY'S WILL.

YOU KNOW, I HAVE MY OWN WAY OF GAINING ADVANTAGE.

LIKE WHAT? BEGGING DOESN'T COUNT...

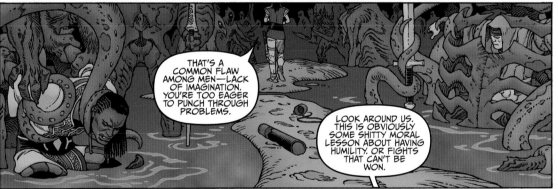

THAT'S A COMMON FLAW AMONG MEN—LACK OF IMAGINATION. YOU'RE TOO EAGER TO PUNCH THROUGH PROBLEMS.

LOOK AROUND US. THIS IS OBVIOUSLY SOME SHITTY MORAL LESSON ABOUT HAVING HUMILITY. OR FIGHTS THAT CAN'T BE WON.

OFTENTIMES, WINNING ISN'T ABOUT FIGHTING, BUT ABOUT CHOOSING THE PROPER WEAPON.

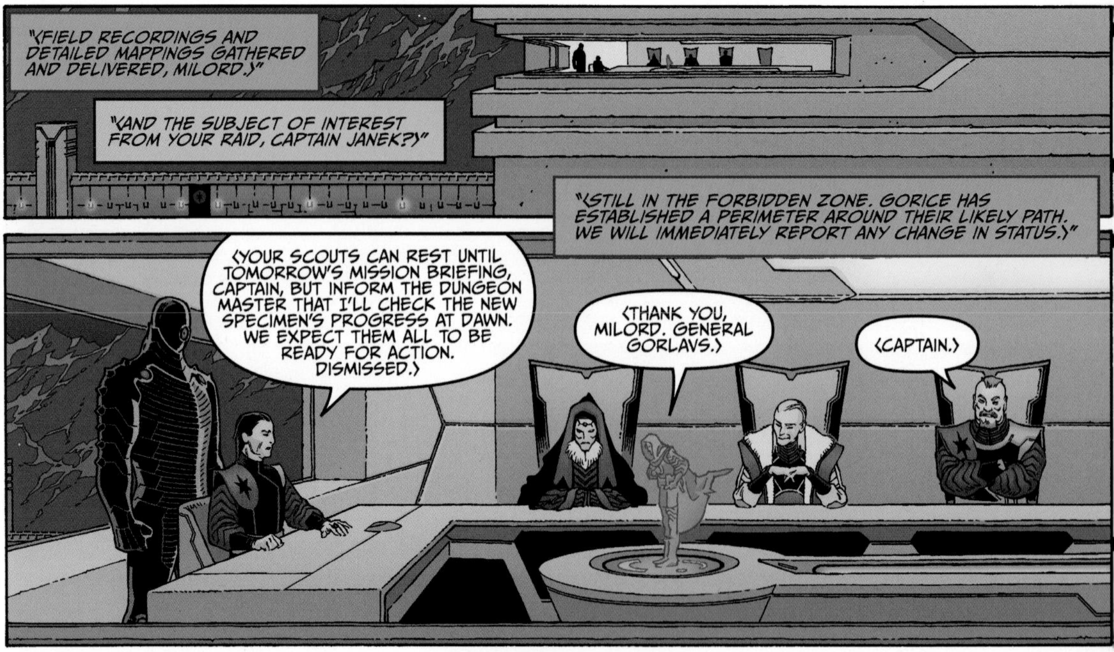

"<FIELD RECORDINGS AND DETAILED MAPPINGS GATHERED AND DELIVERED, MILORD.>"
"<AND THE SUBJECT OF INTEREST FROM YOUR RAID, CAPTAIN JANEK?>"
"<STILL IN THE FORBIDDEN ZONE. GORICE HAS ESTABLISHED A PERIMETER AROUND THEIR LIKELY PATH. WE WILL IMMEDIATELY REPORT ANY CHANGE IN STATUS.>"
<YOUR SCOUTS CAN REST UNTIL TOMORROW'S MISSION BRIEFING, CAPTAIN, BUT INFORM THE DUNGEON MASTER THAT I'LL CHECK THE NEW SPECIMEN'S PROGRESS AT DAWN. WE EXPECT THEM ALL TO BE READY FOR ACTION. DISMISSED.>
<THANK YOU, MILORD. GENERAL GORLAVS.>
<CAPTAIN.>

COUNCILS

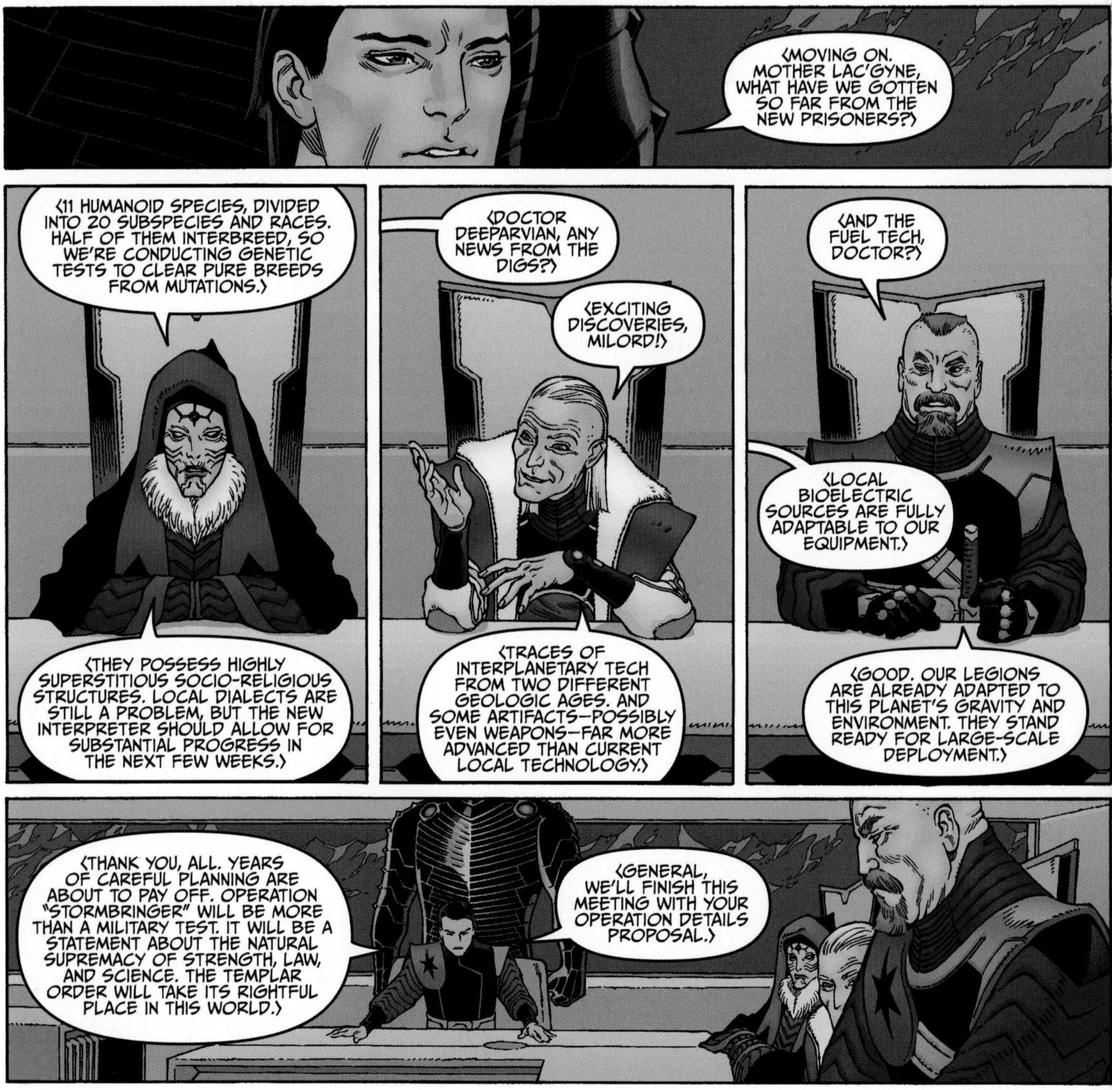

<MOVING ON. MOTHER LAC'GYNE, WHAT HAVE WE GOTTEN SO FAR FROM THE NEW PRISONERS?>
<11 HUMANOID SPECIES, DIVIDED INTO 20 SUBSPECIES AND RACES. HALF OF THEM INTERBREED, SO WE'RE CONDUCTING GENETIC TESTS TO CLEAR PURE BREEDS FROM MUTATIONS.>
<THEY POSSESS HIGHLY SUPERSTITIOUS SOCIO-RELIGIOUS STRUCTURES. LOCAL DIALECTS ARE STILL A PROBLEM, BUT THE NEW INTERPRETER SHOULD ALLOW FOR SUBSTANTIAL PROGRESS IN THE NEXT FEW WEEKS.>
<DOCTOR DEEPARVIAN, ANY NEWS FROM THE DIGS?>
<EXCITING DISCOVERIES, MILORD!>
<TRACES OF INTERPLANETARY TECH FROM TWO DIFFERENT GEOLOGIC AGES. AND SOME ARTIFACTS—POSSIBLY EVEN WEAPONS—FAR MORE ADVANCED THAN CURRENT LOCAL TECHNOLOGY.>
<AND THE FUEL TECH, DOCTOR?>
<LOCAL BIOELECTRIC SOURCES ARE FULLY ADAPTABLE TO OUR EQUIPMENT.>
<GOOD. OUR LEGIONS ARE ALREADY ADAPTED TO THIS PLANET'S GRAVITY AND ENVIRONMENT. THEY STAND READY FOR LARGE-SCALE DEPLOYMENT.>
<THANK YOU, ALL. YEARS OF CAREFUL PLANNING ARE ABOUT TO PAY OFF. OPERATION "STORMBRINGER" WILL BE MORE THAN A MILITARY TEST. IT WILL BE A STATEMENT ABOUT THE NATURAL SUPREMACY OF STRENGTH, LAW, AND SCIENCE. THE TEMPLAR ORDER WILL TAKE ITS RIGHTFUL PLACE IN THIS WORLD.>
<GENERAL, WE'LL FINISH THIS MEETING WITH YOUR OPERATION DETAILS PROPOSAL.>

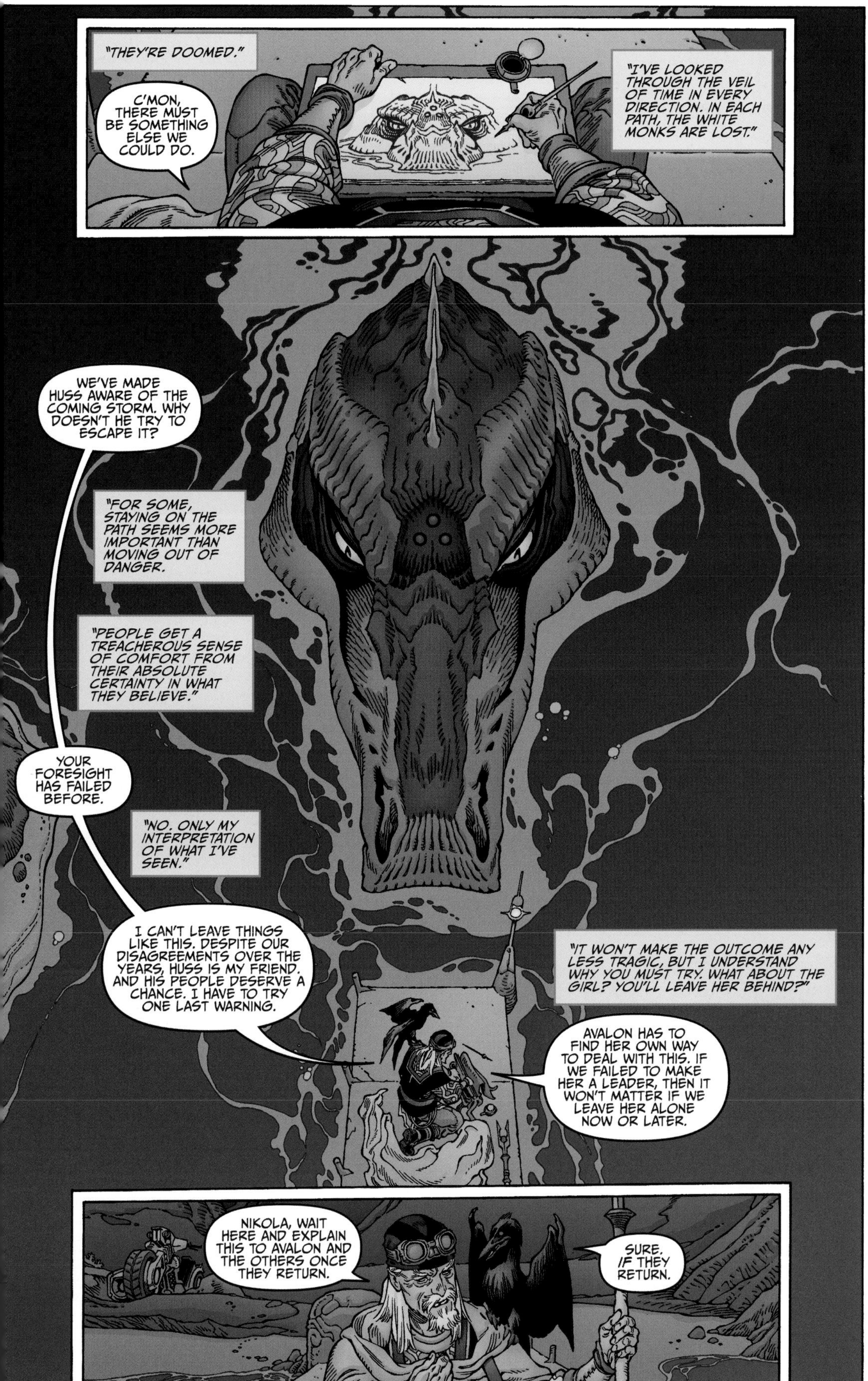
"THEY'RE DOOMED."
C'MON, THERE MUST BE SOMETHING ELSE WE COULD DO.
"I'VE LOOKED THROUGH THE VEIL OF TIME IN EVERY DIRECTION. IN EACH PATH, THE WHITE MONKS ARE LOST."
WE'VE MADE HUSS AWARE OF THE COMING STORM. WHY DOESN'T HE TRY TO ESCAPE IT?
"FOR SOME, STAYING ON THE PATH SEEMS MORE IMPORTANT THAN MOVING OUT OF DANGER.
"PEOPLE GET A TREACHEROUS SENSE OF COMFORT FROM THEIR ABSOLUTE CERTAINTY IN WHAT THEY BELIEVE."
YOUR FORESIGHT HAS FAILED BEFORE.
"NO. ONLY MY INTERPRETATION OF WHAT I'VE SEEN."
I CAN'T LEAVE THINGS LIKE THIS. DESPITE OUR DISAGREEMENTS OVER THE YEARS, HUSS IS MY FRIEND. AND HIS PEOPLE DESERVE A CHANCE. I HAVE TO TRY ONE LAST WARNING.
"IT WON'T MAKE THE OUTCOME ANY LESS TRAGIC, BUT I UNDERSTAND WHY YOU MUST TRY. WHAT ABOUT THE GIRL? YOU'LL LEAVE HER BEHIND?"
AVALON HAS TO FIND HER OWN WAY TO DEAL WITH THIS. IF WE FAILED TO MAKE HER A LEADER, THEN IT WON'T MATTER IF WE LEAVE HER ALONE NOW OR LATER.
NIKOLA, WAIT HERE AND EXPLAIN THIS TO AVALON AND THE OTHERS ONCE THEY RETURN.
SURE. IF THEY RETURN.

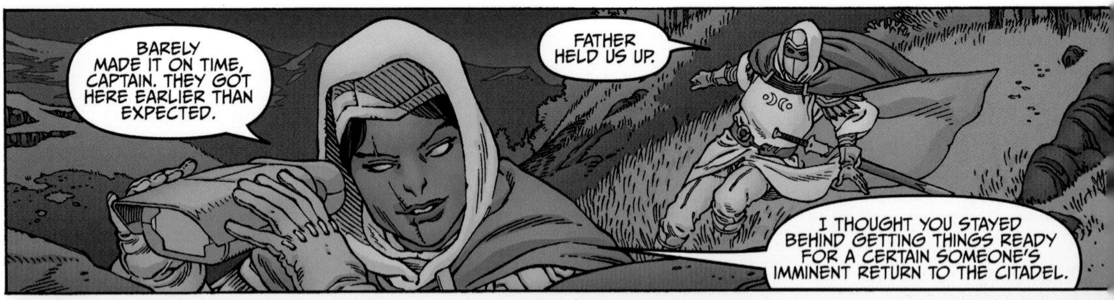
BARELY MADE IT ON TIME, CAPTAIN. THEY GOT HERE EARLIER THAN EXPECTED.
FATHER HELD US UP.
I THOUGHT YOU STAYED BEHIND GETTING THINGS READY FOR A CERTAIN SOMEONE'S IMMINENT RETURN TO THE CITADEL.

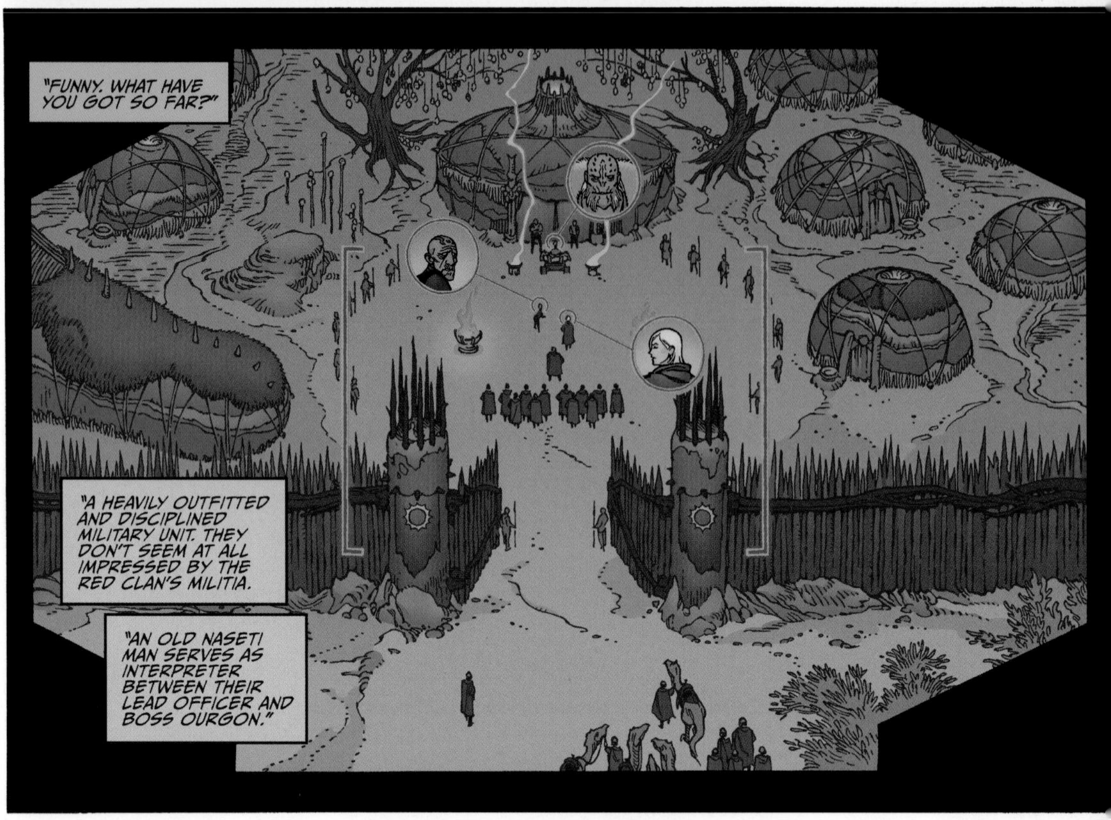
"FUNNY. WHAT HAVE YOU GOT SO FAR?"
"A HEAVILY OUTFITTED AND DISCIPLINED MILITARY UNIT. THEY DON'T SEEM AT ALL IMPRESSED BY THE RED CLAN'S MILITIA.
"AN OLD NASETI MAN SERVES AS INTERPRETER BETWEEN THEIR LEAD OFFICER AND BOSS OURGON."

THE COVENANT

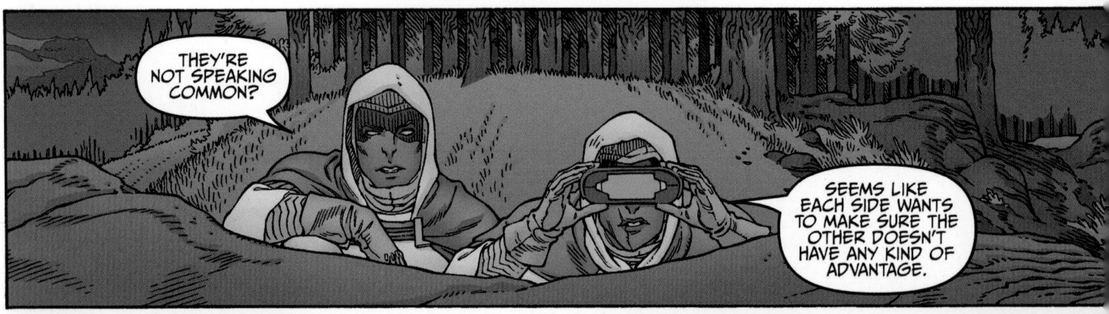
THEY'RE NOT SPEAKING COMMON?
SEEMS LIKE EACH SIDE WANTS TO MAKE SURE THE OTHER DOESN'T HAVE ANY KIND OF ADVANTAGE.

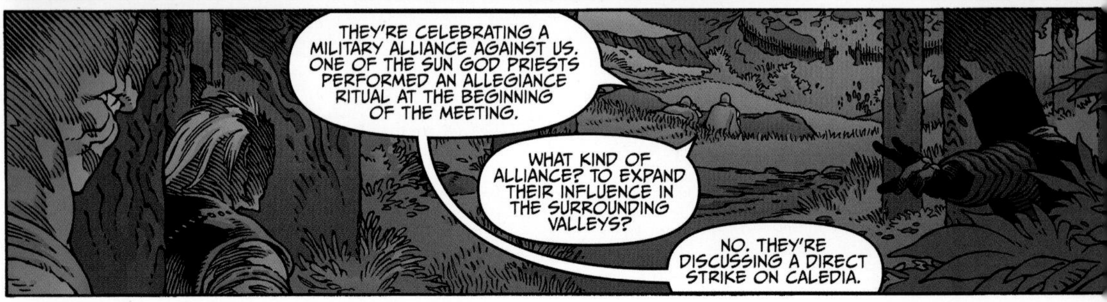
THEY'RE CELEBRATING A MILITARY ALLIANCE AGAINST US. ONE OF THE SUN GOD PRIESTS PERFORMED AN ALLEGIANCE RITUAL AT THE BEGINNING OF THE MEETING.
WHAT KIND OF ALLIANCE? TO EXPAND THEIR INFLUENCE IN THE SURROUNDING VALLEYS?
NO. THEY'RE DISCUSSING A DIRECT STRIKE ON CALEDIA.

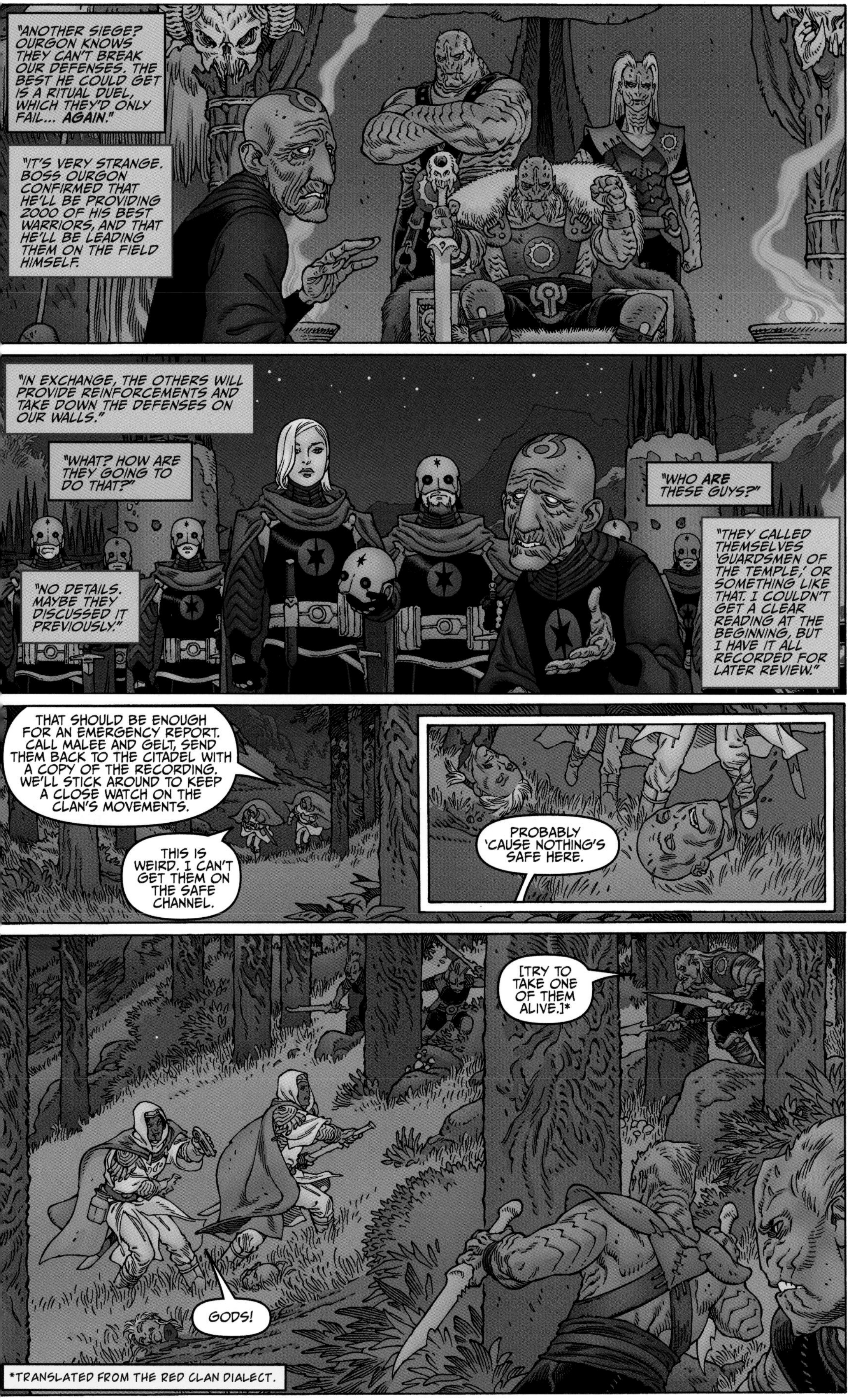

"ANOTHER SIEGE? OURGON KNOWS THEY CAN'T BREAK OUR DEFENSES. THE BEST HE COULD GET IS A RITUAL DUEL, WHICH THEY'D ONLY FAIL... AGAIN."
"IT'S VERY STRANGE. BOSS OURGON CONFIRMED THAT HE'LL BE PROVIDING 2000 OF HIS BEST WARRIORS, AND THAT HE'LL BE LEADING THEM ON THE FIELD HIMSELF.
"IN EXCHANGE, THE OTHERS WILL PROVIDE REINFORCEMENTS AND TAKE DOWN THE DEFENSES ON OUR WALLS."
"WHAT? HOW ARE THEY GOING TO DO THAT?"
"NO DETAILS. MAYBE THEY DISCUSSED IT PREVIOUSLY."
"WHO ARE THESE GUYS?"
"THEY CALLED THEMSELVES 'GUARDSMEN OF THE TEMPLE,' OR SOMETHING LIKE THAT. I COULDN'T GET A CLEAR READING AT THE BEGINNING, BUT I HAVE IT ALL RECORDED FOR LATER REVIEW."
THAT SHOULD BE ENOUGH FOR AN EMERGENCY REPORT. CALL MALEE AND GELT, SEND THEM BACK TO THE CITADEL WITH A COPY OF THE RECORDING. WE'LL STICK AROUND TO KEEP A CLOSE WATCH ON THE CLAN'S MOVEMENTS.
THIS IS WEIRD. I CAN'T GET THEM ON THE SAFE CHANNEL.
PROBABLY 'CAUSE NOTHING'S SAFE HERE.
[TRY TO TAKE ONE OF THEM ALIVE.]*
GODS!
*TRANSLATED FROM THE RED CLAN DIALECT.

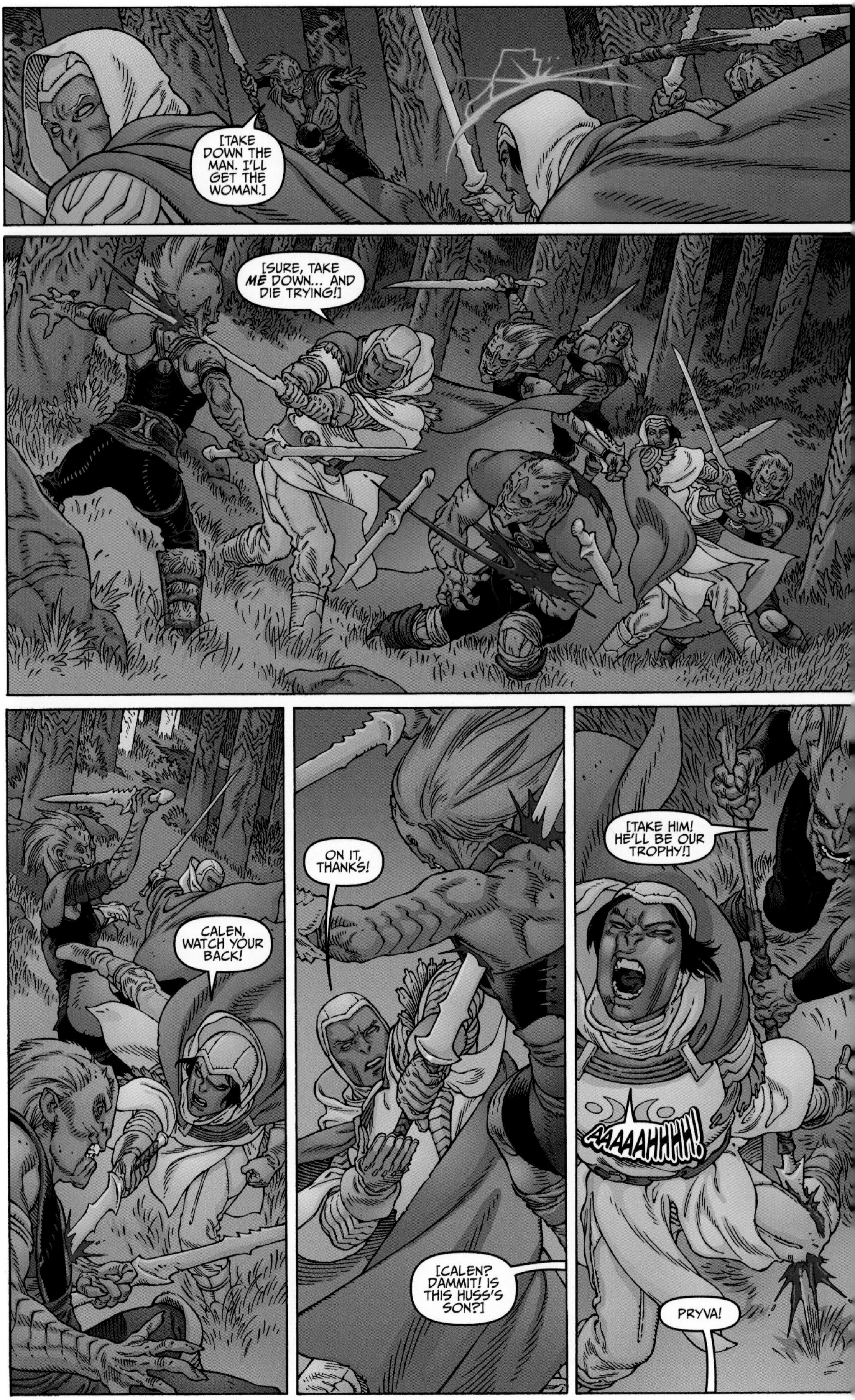

[TAKE DOWN THE MAN. I'LL GET THE WOMAN.]
[SURE, TAKE *ME* DOWN... AND DIE TRYING!]
CALEN, WATCH YOUR BACK!
ON IT, THANKS!
[CALEN? DAMMIT! IS THIS HUSS'S SON?]
[TAKE HIM! HE'LL BE OUR TROPHY!]
AAAAAHHHH!
PRYVA!

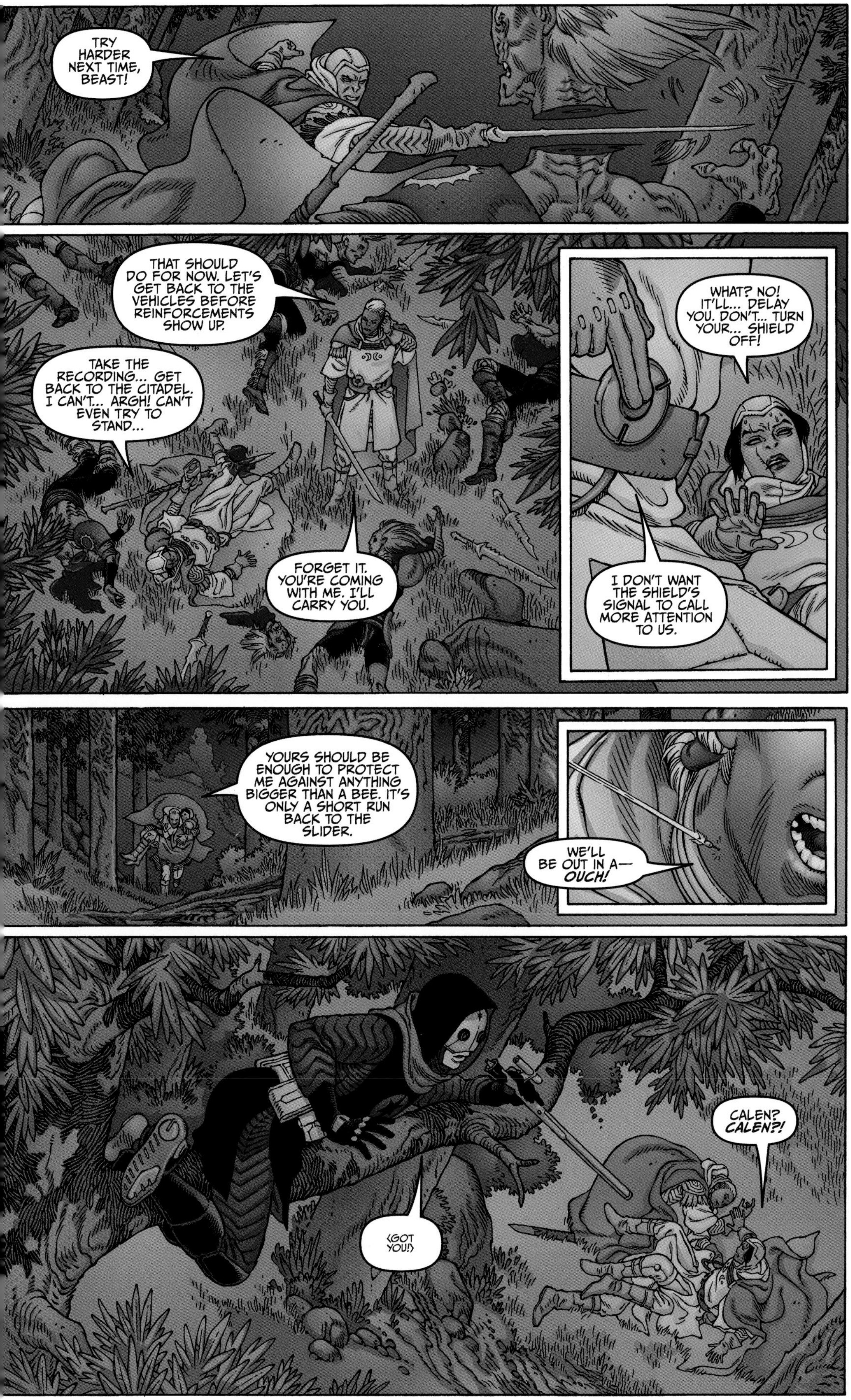
TRY HARDER NEXT TIME, BEAST!
THAT SHOULD DO FOR NOW. LET'S GET BACK TO THE VEHICLES BEFORE REINFORCEMENTS SHOW UP.
TAKE THE RECORDING... GET BACK TO THE CITADEL. I CAN'T... ARGH! CAN'T EVEN TRY TO STAND...
FORGET IT. YOU'RE COMING WITH ME. I'LL CARRY YOU.
WHAT? NO! IT'LL... DELAY YOU. DON'T... TURN YOUR... SHIELD OFF!
I DON'T WANT THE SHIELD'S SIGNAL TO CALL MORE ATTENTION TO US.
YOURS SHOULD BE ENOUGH TO PROTECT ME AGAINST ANYTHING BIGGER THAN A BEE. IT'S ONLY A SHORT RUN BACK TO THE SLIDER.
WE'LL BE OUT IN A— OUCH!
CALEN? CALEN?!
‹GOT YOU!›

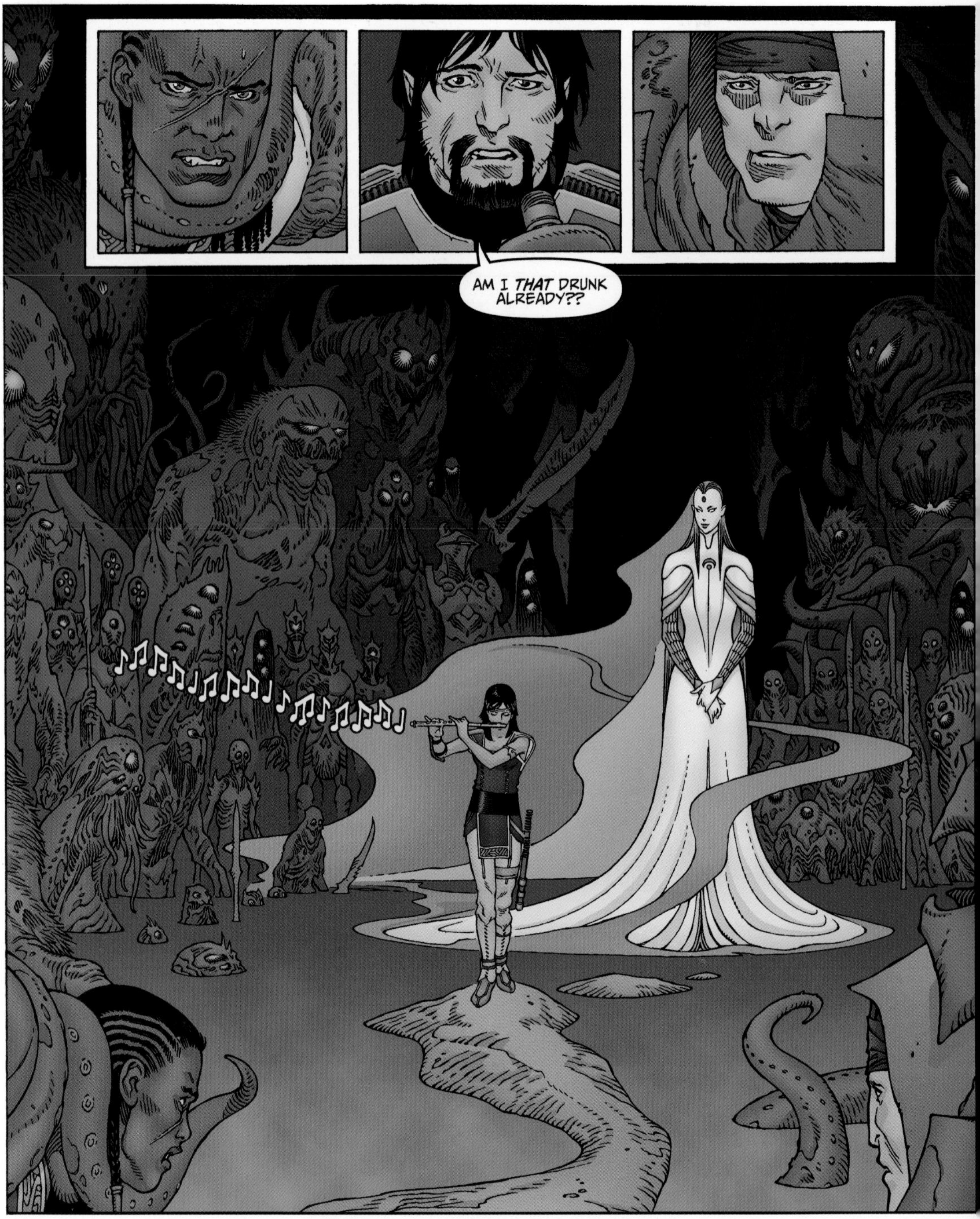
AM I *THAT* DRUNK ALREADY??

THE LADY'S GIFT

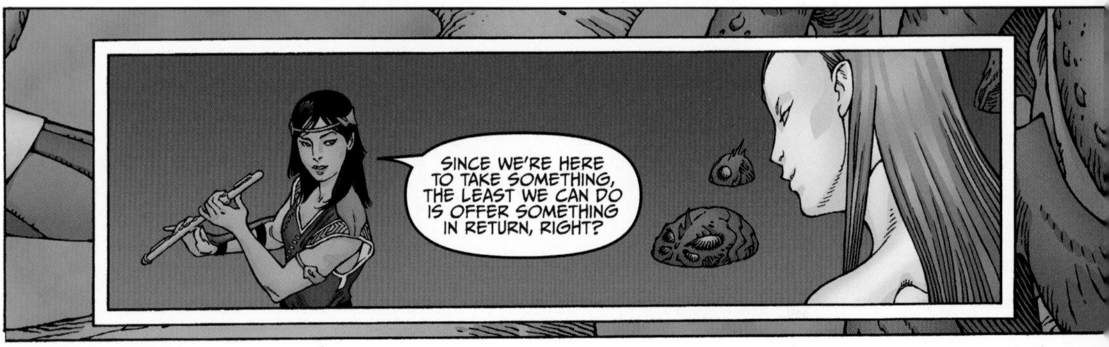
SINCE WE'RE HERE TO TAKE SOMETHING, THE LEAST WE CAN DO IS OFFER SOMETHING IN RETURN, RIGHT?

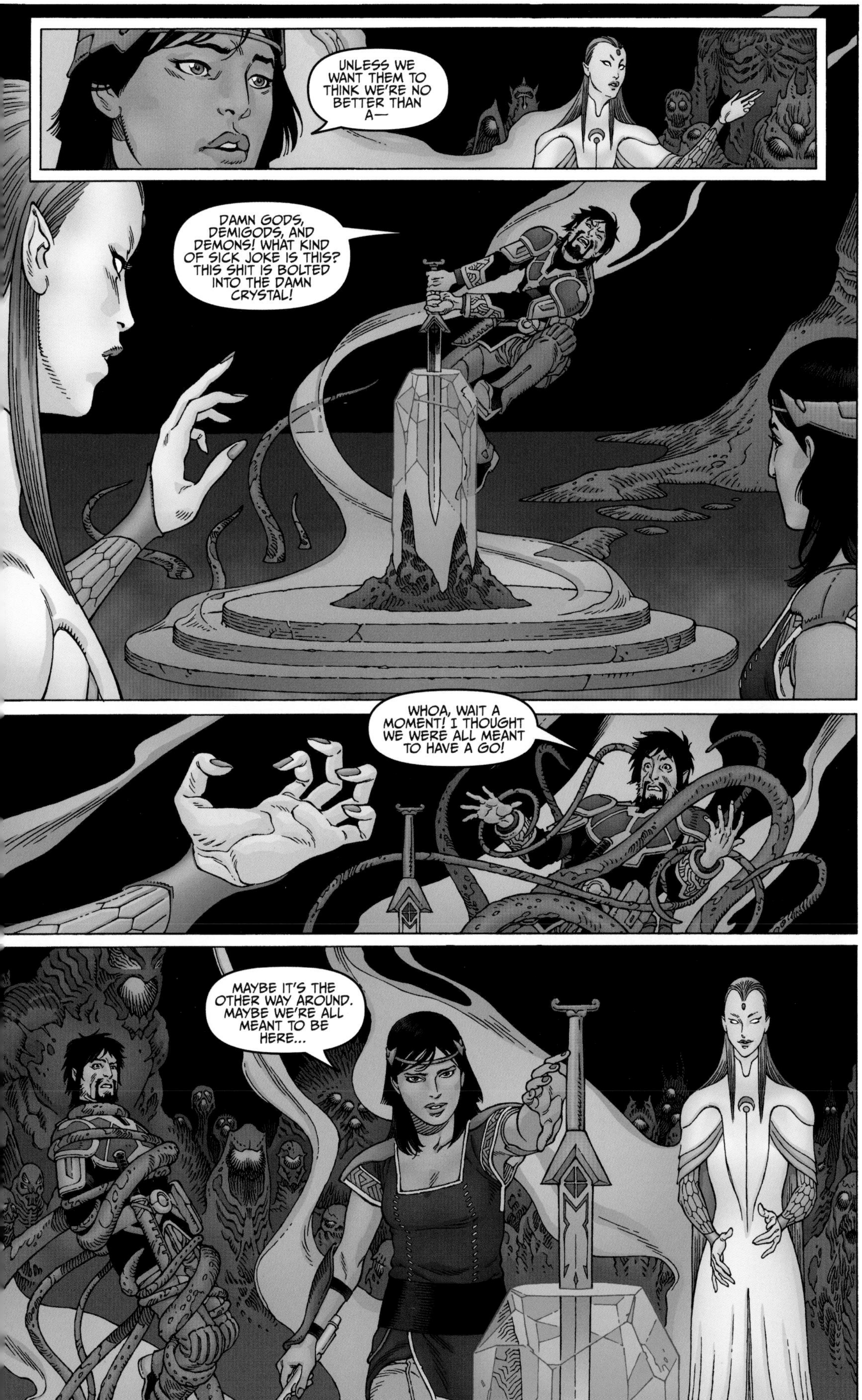
UNLESS WE WANT THEM TO THINK WE'RE NO BETTER THAN A—
DAMN GODS, DEMIGODS, AND DEMONS! WHAT KIND OF SICK JOKE IS THIS? THIS SHIT IS BOLTED INTO THE DAMN CRYSTAL!
WHOA, WAIT A MOMENT! I THOUGHT WE WERE ALL MEANT TO HAVE A GO!
MAYBE IT'S THE OTHER WAY AROUND. MAYBE WE'RE ALL MEANT TO BE HERE...

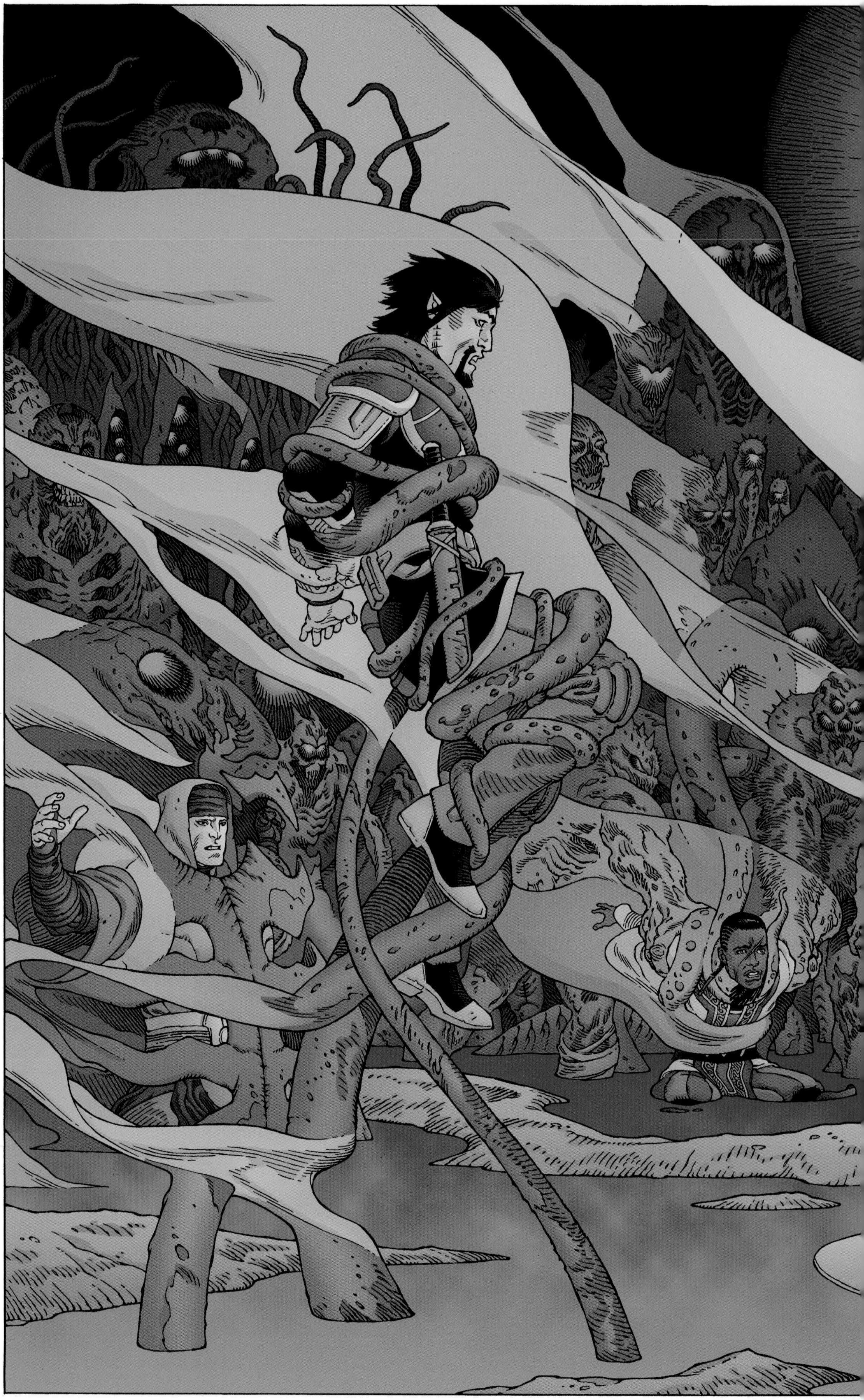

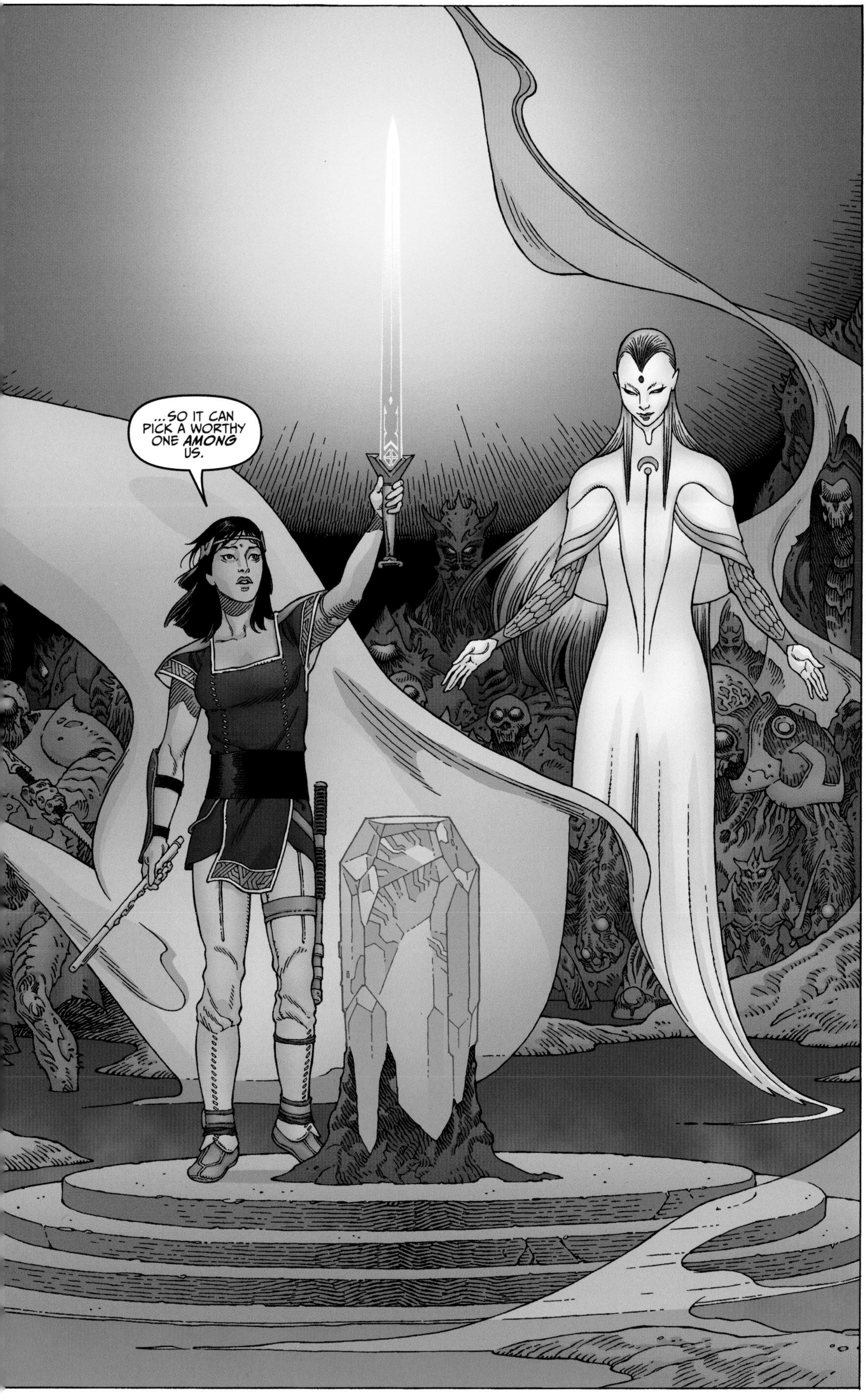
...SO IT CAN PICK A WORTHY ONE *AMONG* US.

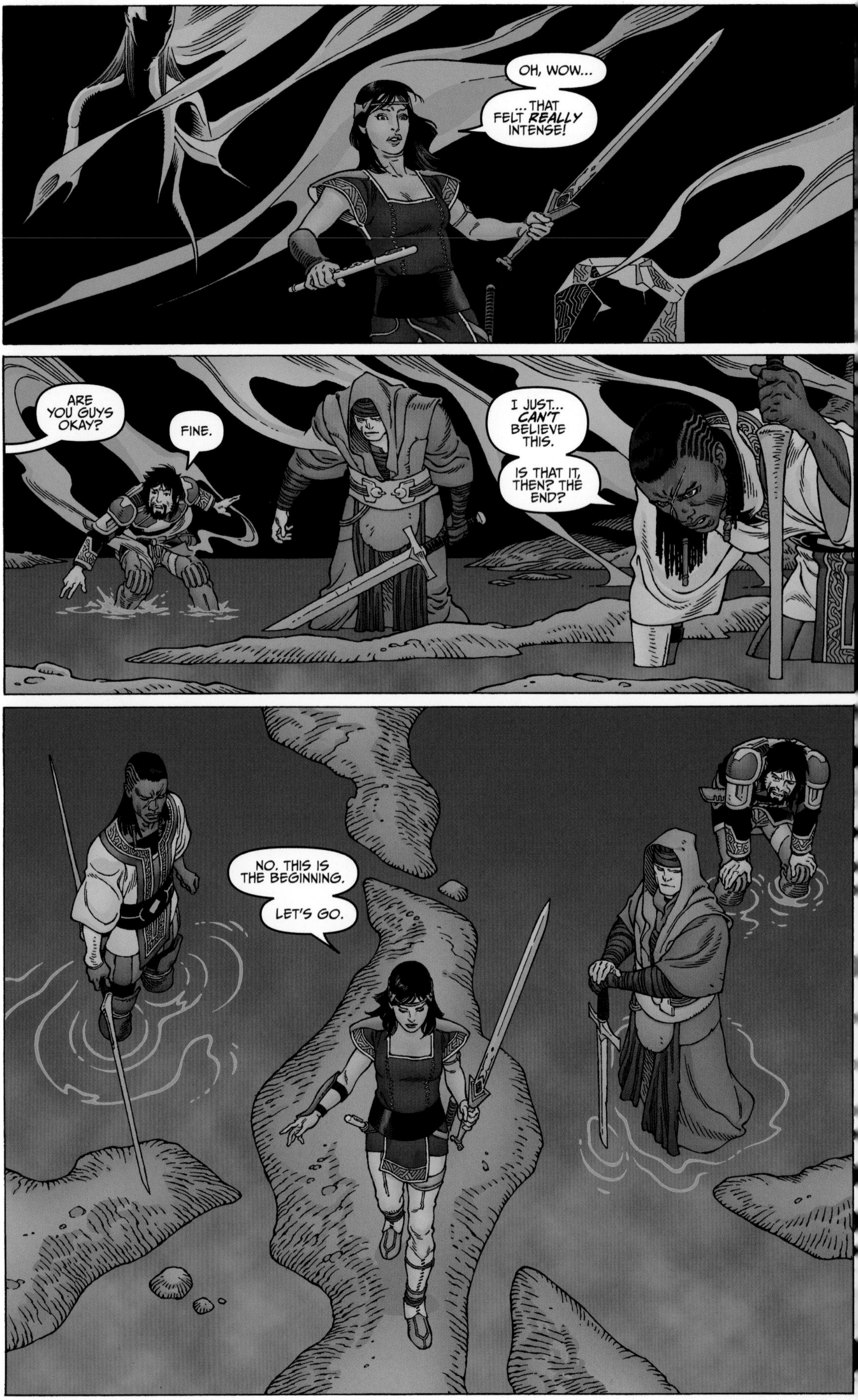
OH, WOW...
...THAT FELT REALLY INTENSE!
ARE YOU GUYS OKAY?
FINE.
I JUST... CAN'T BELIEVE THIS.
IS THAT IT, THEN? THE END?
NO. THIS IS THE BEGINNING.
LET'S GO.

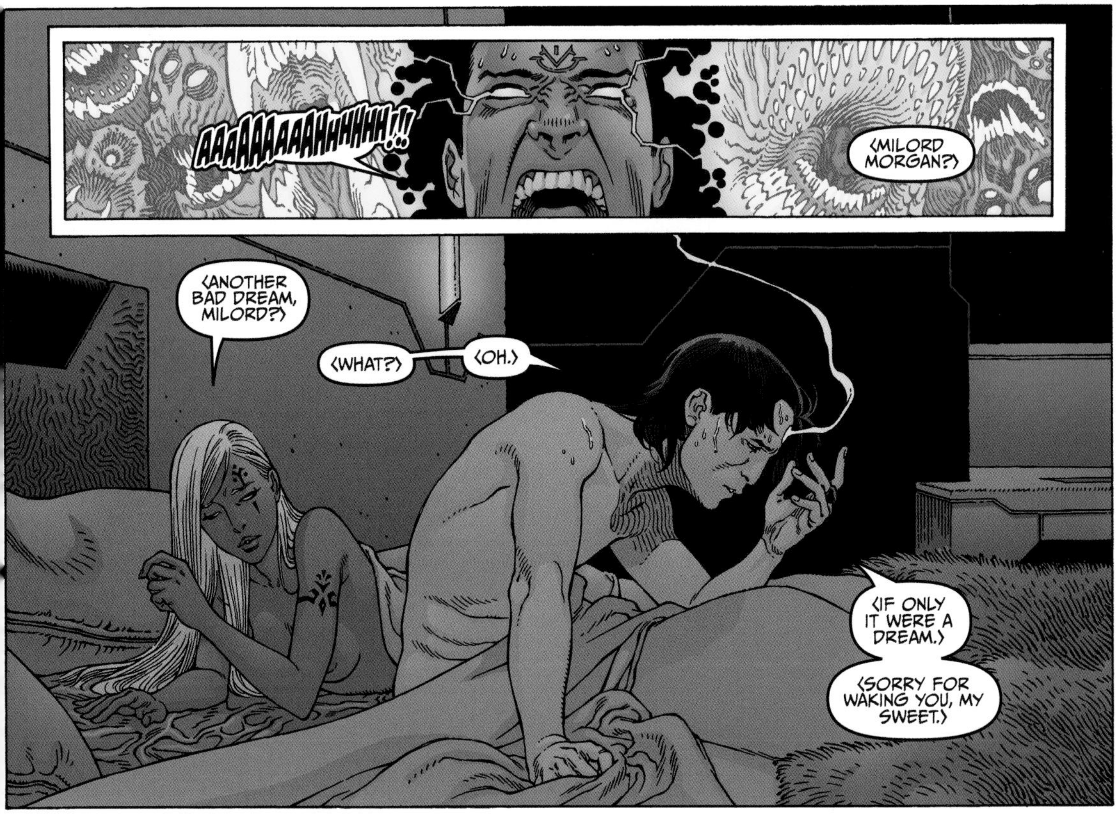
AAAAAAAAAHHHHHH!!!
‹MILORD MORGAN?›
‹ANOTHER BAD DREAM, MILORD?›
‹WHAT?›
‹OH.›
‹IF ONLY IT WERE A DREAM.›
‹SORRY FOR WAKING YOU, MY SWEET.›

NIGHTMARES

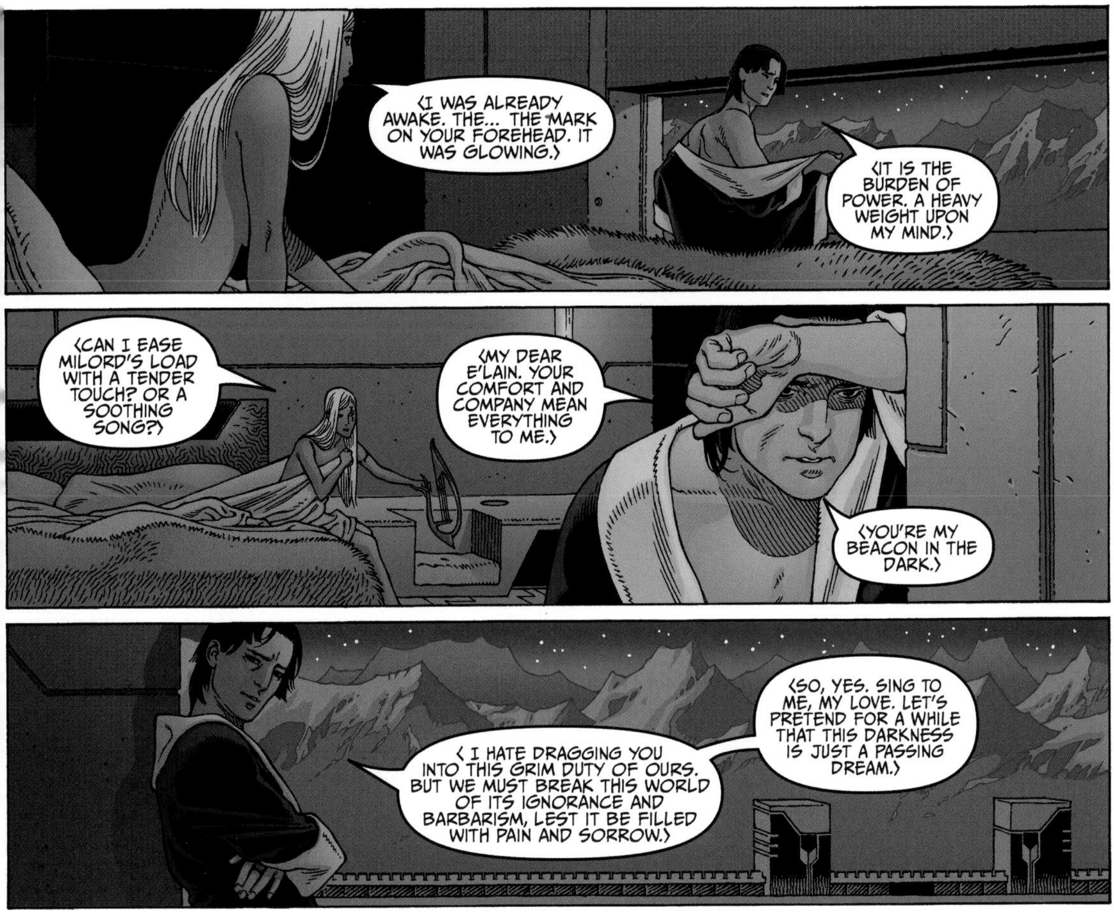
‹I WAS ALREADY AWAKE. THE... THE MARK ON YOUR FOREHEAD. IT WAS GLOWING.›
‹IT IS THE BURDEN OF POWER. A HEAVY WEIGHT UPON MY MIND.›
‹CAN I EASE MILORD'S LOAD WITH A TENDER TOUCH? OR A SOOTHING SONG?›
‹MY DEAR E'LAIN. YOUR COMFORT AND COMPANY MEAN EVERYTHING TO ME.›
‹YOU'RE MY BEACON IN THE DARK.›
‹ I HATE DRAGGING YOU INTO THIS GRIM DUTY OF OURS. BUT WE MUST BREAK THIS WORLD OF ITS IGNORANCE AND BARBARISM, LEST IT BE FILLED WITH PAIN AND SORROW.›
‹SO, YES. SING TO ME, MY LOVE. LET'S PRETEND FOR A WHILE THAT THIS DARKNESS IS JUST A PASSING DREAM.›

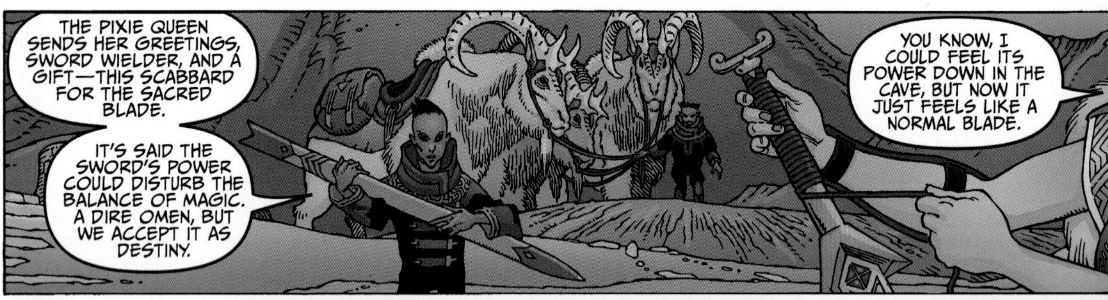
THE PIXIE QUEEN SENDS HER GREETINGS, SWORD WIELDER, AND A GIFT—THIS SCABBARD FOR THE SACRED BLADE.
IT'S SAID THE SWORD'S POWER COULD DISTURB THE BALANCE OF MAGIC. A DIRE OMEN, BUT WE ACCEPT IT AS DESTINY.
YOU KNOW, I COULD FEEL ITS POWER DOWN IN THE CAVE, BUT NOW IT JUST FEELS LIKE A NORMAL BLADE.

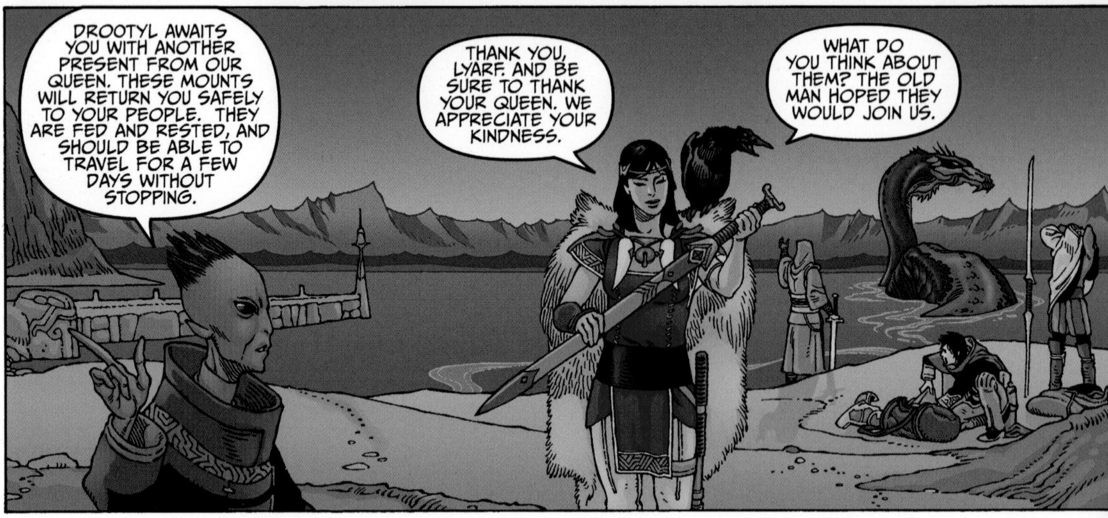
DROOTYL AWAITS YOU WITH ANOTHER PRESENT FROM OUR QUEEN. THESE MOUNTS WILL RETURN YOU SAFELY TO YOUR PEOPLE. THEY ARE FED AND RESTED, AND SHOULD BE ABLE TO TRAVEL FOR A FEW DAYS WITHOUT STOPPING.
THANK YOU, LYARF. AND BE SURE TO THANK YOUR QUEEN. WE APPRECIATE YOUR KINDNESS.
WHAT DO YOU THINK ABOUT THEM? THE OLD MAN HOPED THEY WOULD JOIN US.

CROSSROADS AND CHOICES

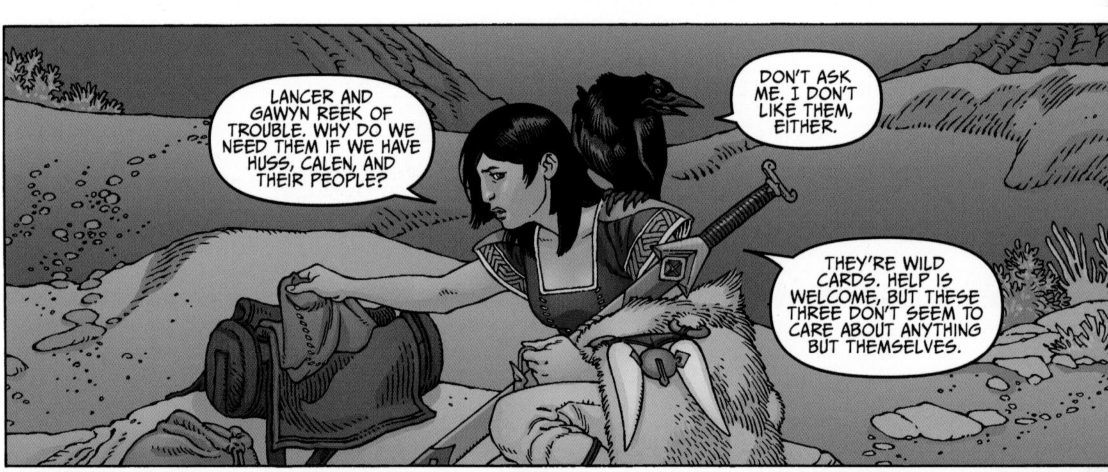
LANCER AND GAWYN REEK OF TROUBLE. WHY DO WE NEED THEM IF WE HAVE HUSS, CALEN, AND THEIR PEOPLE?
DON'T ASK ME. I DON'T LIKE THEM, EITHER.
THEY'RE WILD CARDS. HELP IS WELCOME, BUT THESE THREE DON'T SEEM TO CARE ABOUT ANYTHING BUT THEMSELVES.

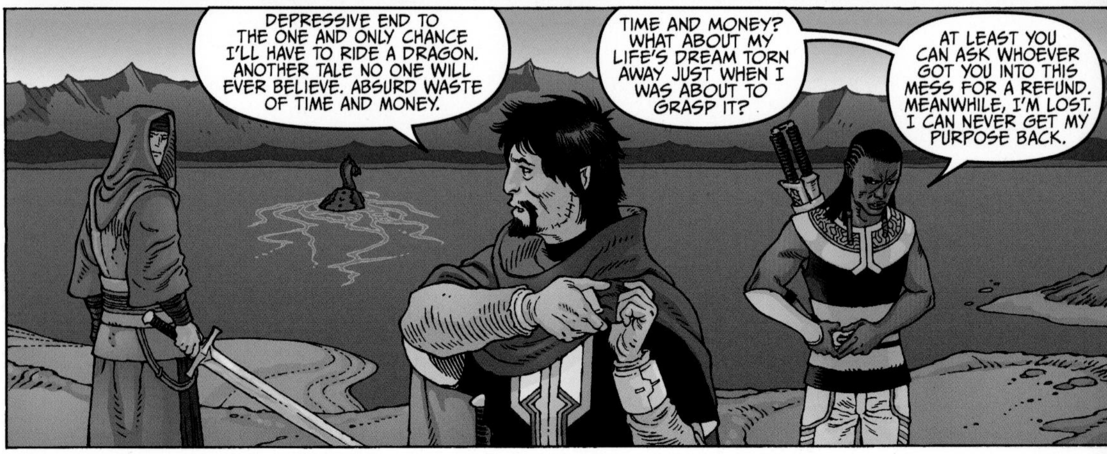
DEPRESSIVE END TO THE ONE AND ONLY CHANCE I'LL HAVE TO RIDE A DRAGON. ANOTHER TALE NO ONE WILL EVER BELIEVE. ABSURD WASTE OF TIME AND MONEY.
TIME AND MONEY? WHAT ABOUT MY LIFE'S DREAM TORN AWAY JUST WHEN I WAS ABOUT TO GRASP IT?
AT LEAST YOU CAN ASK WHOEVER GOT YOU INTO THIS MESS FOR A REFUND. MEANWHILE, I'M LOST. I CAN NEVER GET MY PURPOSE BACK.

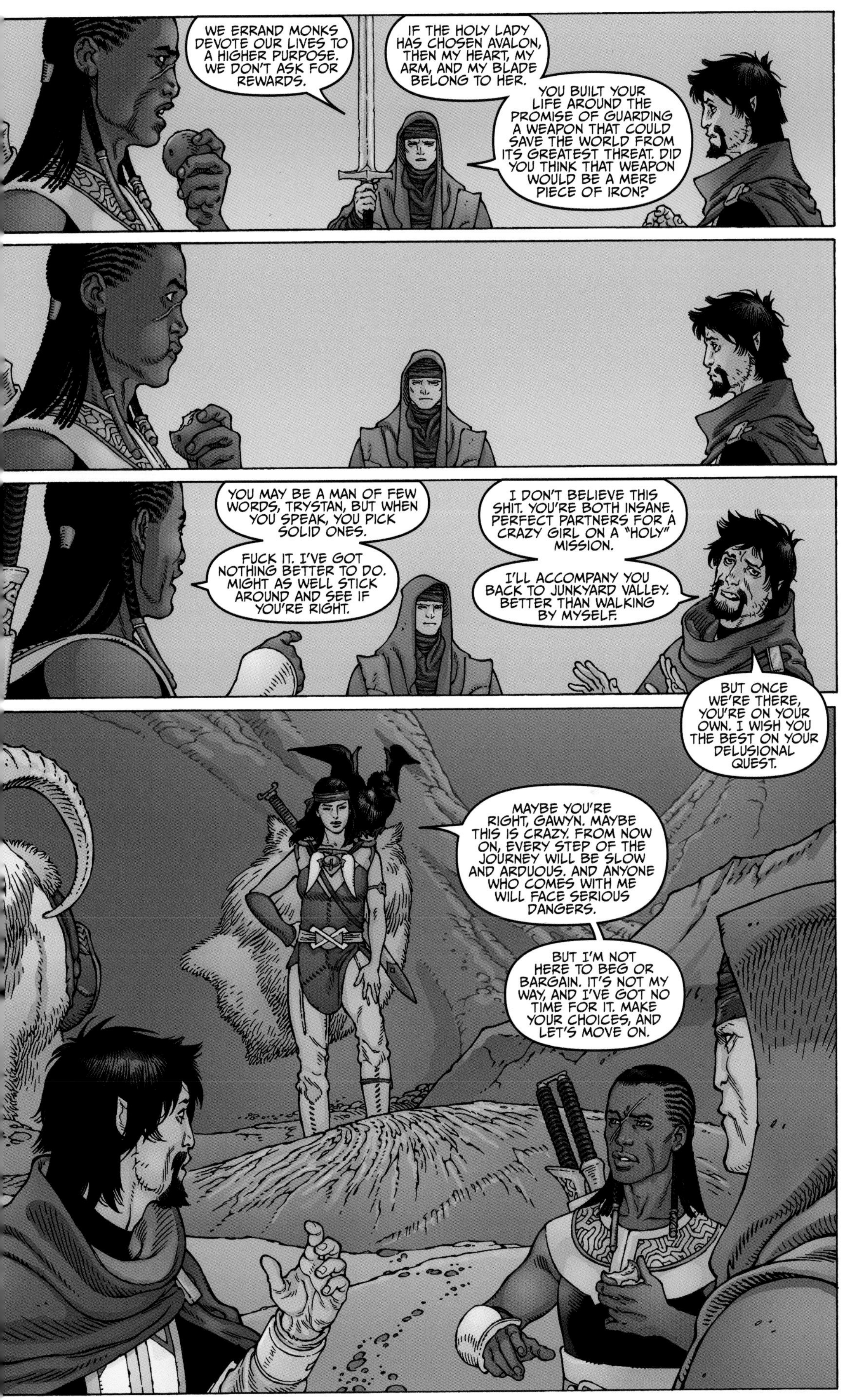
WE ERRAND MONKS DEVOTE OUR LIVES TO A HIGHER PURPOSE. WE DON'T ASK FOR REWARDS.
IF THE HOLY LADY HAS CHOSEN AVALON, THEN MY HEART, MY ARM, AND MY BLADE BELONG TO HER.
YOU BUILT YOUR LIFE AROUND THE PROMISE OF GUARDING A WEAPON THAT COULD SAVE THE WORLD FROM ITS GREATEST THREAT. DID YOU THINK THAT WEAPON WOULD BE A MERE PIECE OF IRON?
YOU MAY BE A MAN OF FEW WORDS, TRYSTAN, BUT WHEN YOU SPEAK, YOU PICK SOLID ONES.
FUCK IT. I'VE GOT NOTHING BETTER TO DO. MIGHT AS WELL STICK AROUND AND SEE IF YOU'RE RIGHT.
I DON'T BELIEVE THIS SHIT. YOU'RE BOTH INSANE. PERFECT PARTNERS FOR A CRAZY GIRL ON A "HOLY" MISSION.
I'LL ACCOMPANY YOU BACK TO JUNKYARD VALLEY. BETTER THAN WALKING BY MYSELF.
BUT ONCE WE'RE THERE, YOU'RE ON YOUR OWN. I WISH YOU THE BEST ON YOUR DELUSIONAL QUEST.
MAYBE YOU'RE RIGHT, GAWYN. MAYBE THIS IS CRAZY. FROM NOW ON, EVERY STEP OF THE JOURNEY WILL BE SLOW AND ARDUOUS. AND ANYONE WHO COMES WITH ME WILL FACE SERIOUS DANGERS.
BUT I'M NOT HERE TO BEG OR BARGAIN. IT'S NOT MY WAY, AND I'VE GOT NO TIME FOR IT. MAKE YOUR CHOICES, AND LET'S MOVE ON.

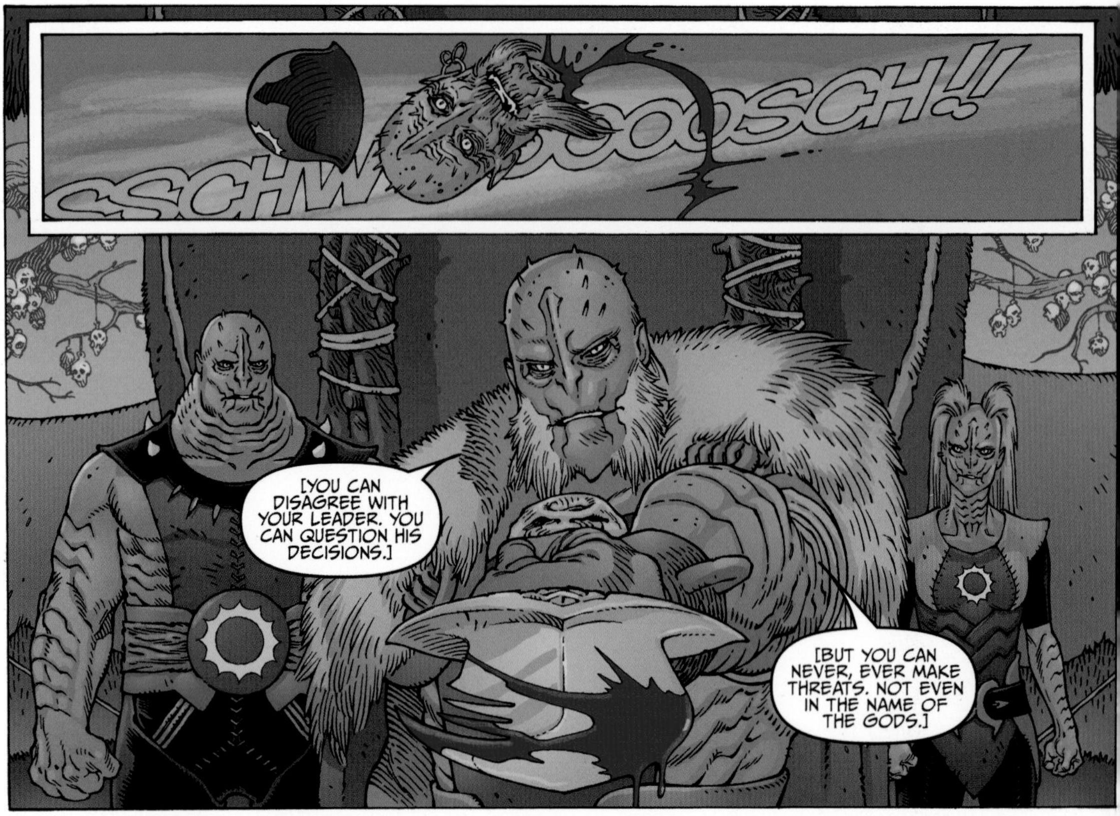
SSCHWOOOSCH!!
[YOU CAN DISAGREE WITH YOUR LEADER. YOU CAN QUESTION HIS DECISIONS.]
[BUT YOU CAN NEVER, EVER MAKE THREATS. NOT EVEN IN THE NAME OF THE GODS.]

THE BOLDEST AND THE STRONGEST

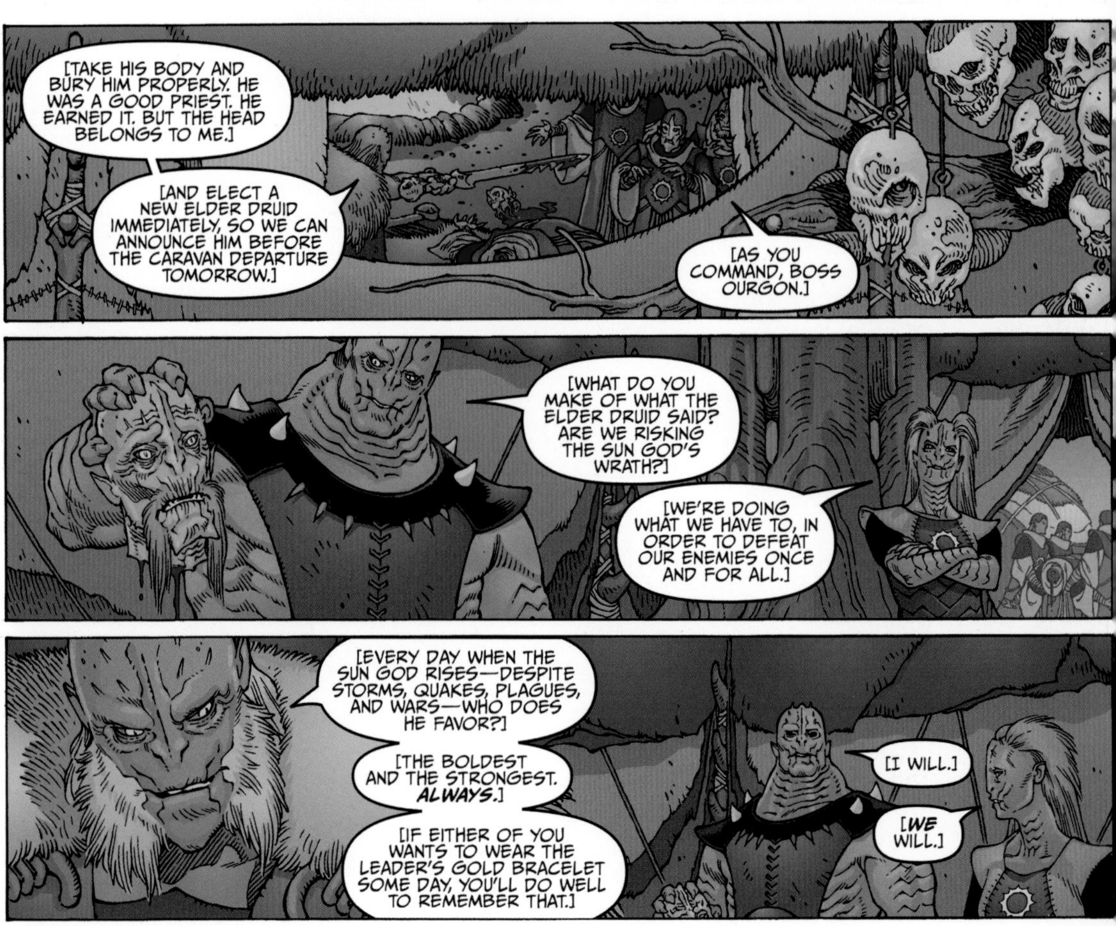
[TAKE HIS BODY AND BURY HIM PROPERLY. HE WAS A GOOD PRIEST. HE EARNED IT. BUT THE HEAD BELONGS TO ME.]
[AND ELECT A NEW ELDER DRUID IMMEDIATELY, SO WE CAN ANNOUNCE HIM BEFORE THE CARAVAN DEPARTURE TOMORROW.]
[AS YOU COMMAND, BOSS OURGON.]
[WHAT DO YOU MAKE OF WHAT THE ELDER DRUID SAID? ARE WE RISKING THE SUN GOD'S WRATH?]
[WE'RE DOING WHAT WE HAVE TO, IN ORDER TO DEFEAT OUR ENEMIES ONCE AND FOR ALL.]
[EVERY DAY WHEN THE SUN GOD RISES—DESPITE STORMS, QUAKES, PLAGUES, AND WARS—WHO DOES HE FAVOR?]
[THE BOLDEST AND THE STRONGEST. ***ALWAYS.***]
[IF EITHER OF YOU WANTS TO WEAR THE LEADER'S GOLD BRACELET SOME DAY, YOU'LL DO WELL TO REMEMBER THAT.]
[I WILL.]
[***WE*** WILL.]

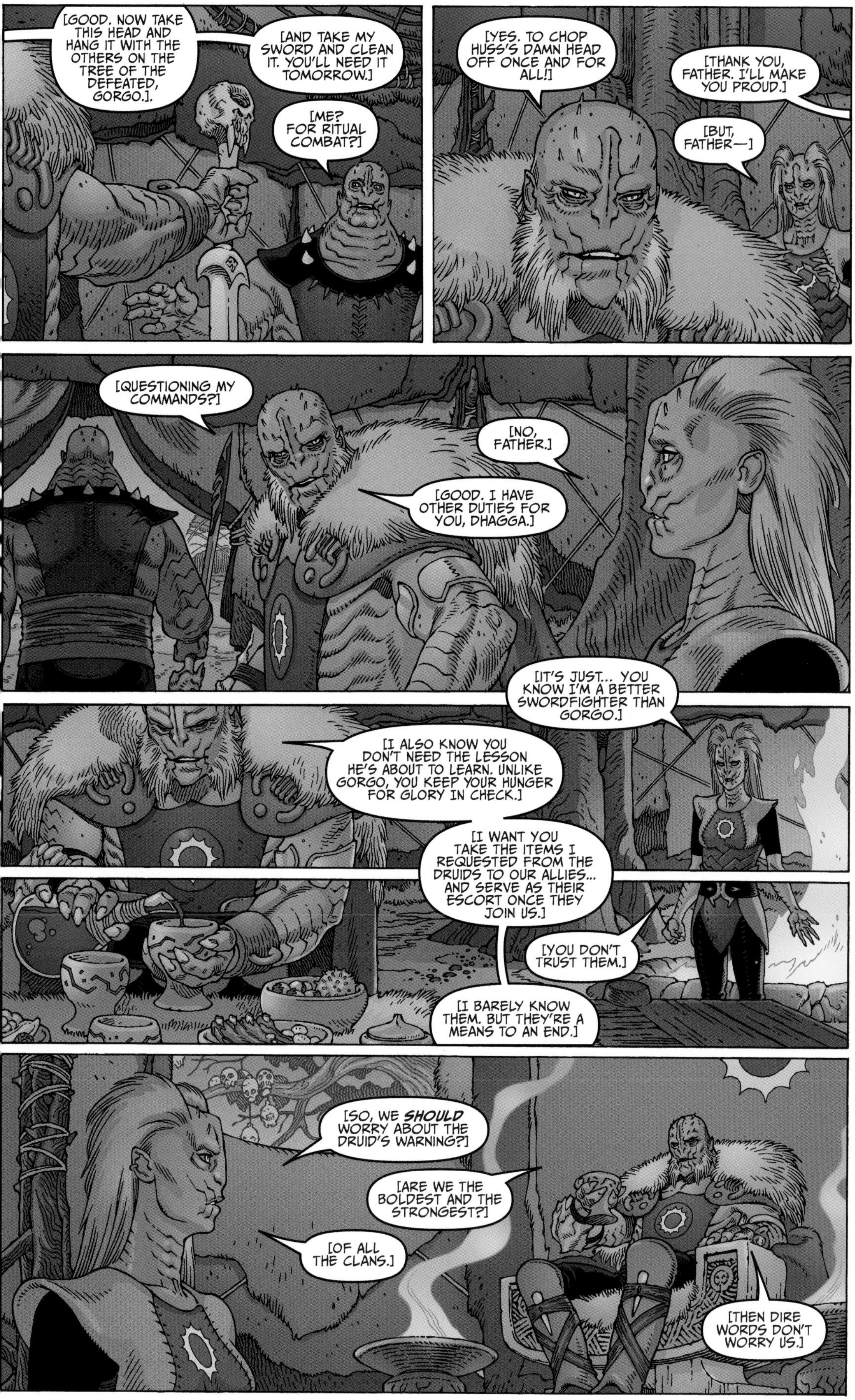
[GOOD. NOW TAKE THIS HEAD AND HANG IT WITH THE OTHERS ON THE TREE OF THE DEFEATED, GORGO.].
[AND TAKE MY SWORD AND CLEAN IT. YOU'LL NEED IT TOMORROW.]
[ME? FOR RITUAL COMBAT?]
[YES. TO CHOP HUSS'S DAMN HEAD OFF ONCE AND FOR ALL!]
[THANK YOU, FATHER. I'LL MAKE YOU PROUD.]
[BUT, FATHER—]
[QUESTIONING MY COMMANDS?]
[NO, FATHER.]
[GOOD. I HAVE OTHER DUTIES FOR YOU, DHAGGA.]
[IT'S JUST... YOU KNOW I'M A BETTER SWORDFIGHTER THAN GORGO.]
[I ALSO KNOW YOU DON'T NEED THE LESSON HE'S ABOUT TO LEARN. UNLIKE GORGO, YOU KEEP YOUR HUNGER FOR GLORY IN CHECK.]
[I WANT YOU TAKE THE ITEMS I REQUESTED FROM THE DRUIDS TO OUR ALLIES... AND SERVE AS THEIR ESCORT ONCE THEY JOIN US.]
[YOU DON'T TRUST THEM.]
[I BARELY KNOW THEM. BUT THEY'RE A MEANS TO AN END.]
[SO, WE ***SHOULD*** WORRY ABOUT THE DRUID'S WARNING?]
[ARE WE THE BOLDEST AND THE STRONGEST?]
[OF ALL THE CLANS.]
[THEN DIRE WORDS DON'T WORRY US.]

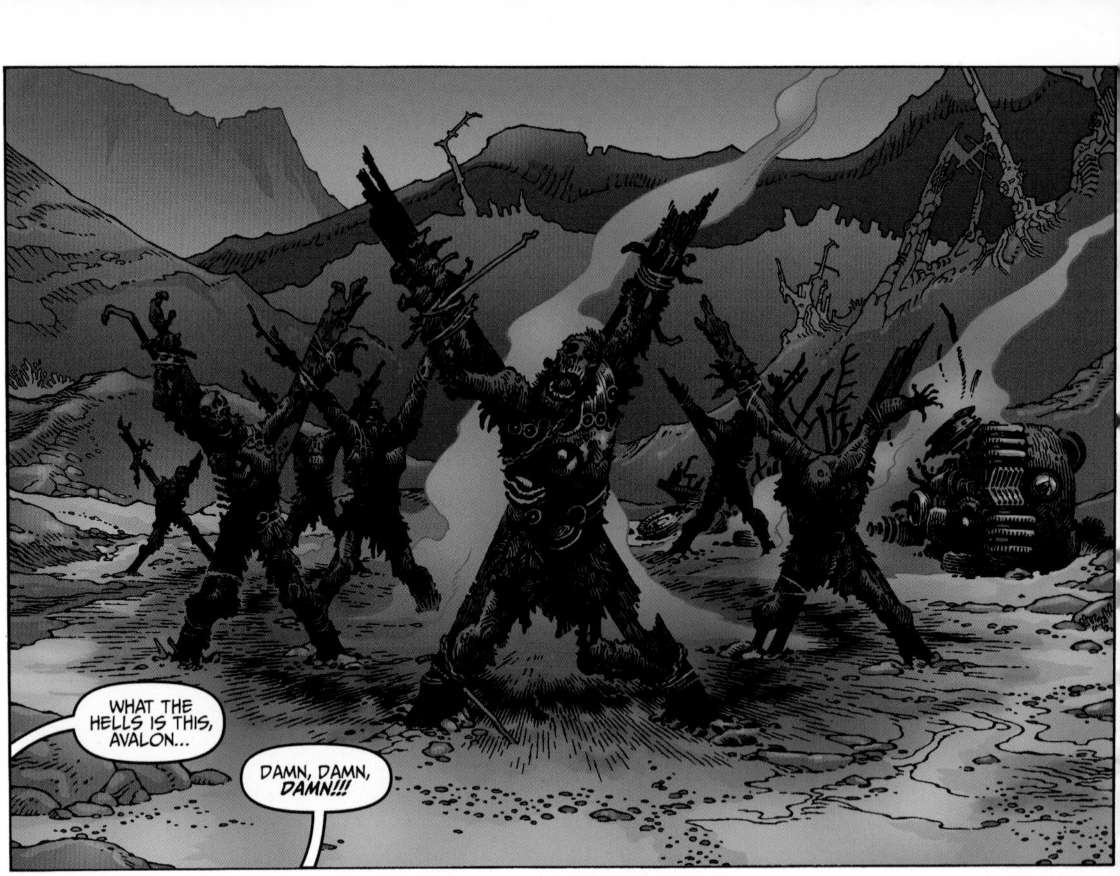
WHAT THE HELLS IS THIS, AVALON...
DAMN, DAMN, *DAMN!!!*

VIA CRUCIS

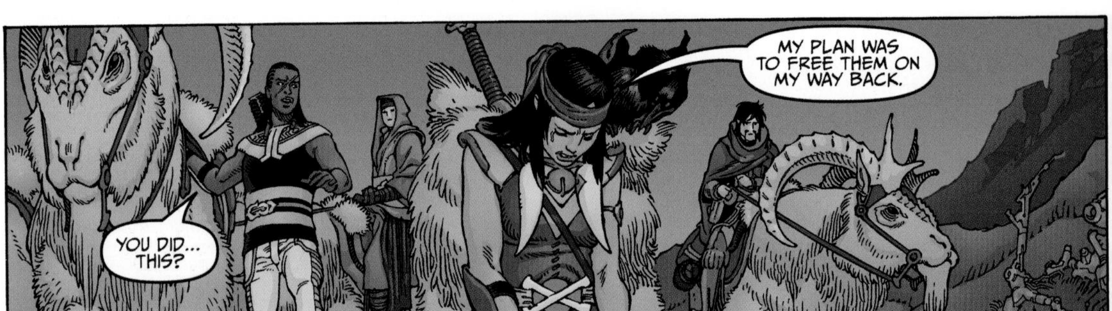
MY PLAN WAS TO FREE THEM ON MY WAY BACK.
YOU DID... THIS?
I WANTED TO TEACH THEM A LESSON ABOUT SLAVERY, BUT NOT LIKE THIS...

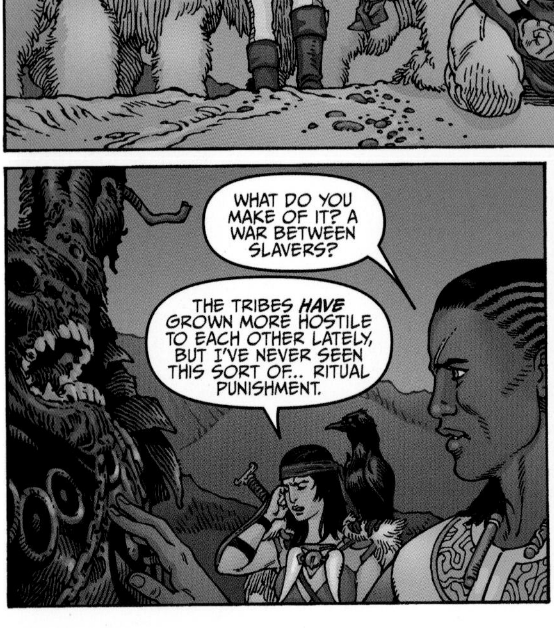
WHAT DO YOU MAKE OF IT? A WAR BETWEEN SLAVERS?
THE TRIBES *HAVE* GROWN MORE HOSTILE TO EACH OTHER LATELY, BUT I'VE NEVER SEEN THIS SORT OF... RITUAL PUNISHMENT.

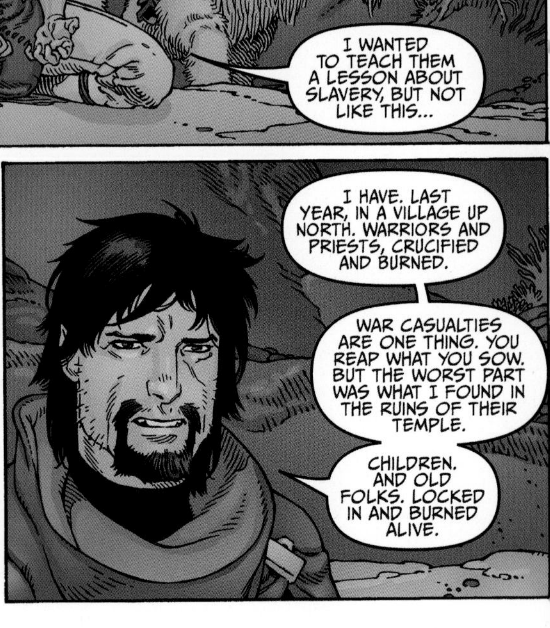
I HAVE. LAST YEAR, IN A VILLAGE UP NORTH. WARRIORS AND PRIESTS, CRUCIFIED AND BURNED.
WAR CASUALTIES ARE ONE THING. YOU REAP WHAT YOU SOW. BUT THE WORST PART WAS WHAT I FOUND IN THE RUINS OF THEIR TEMPLE.
CHILDREN. AND OLD FOLKS. LOCKED IN AND BURNED ALIVE.

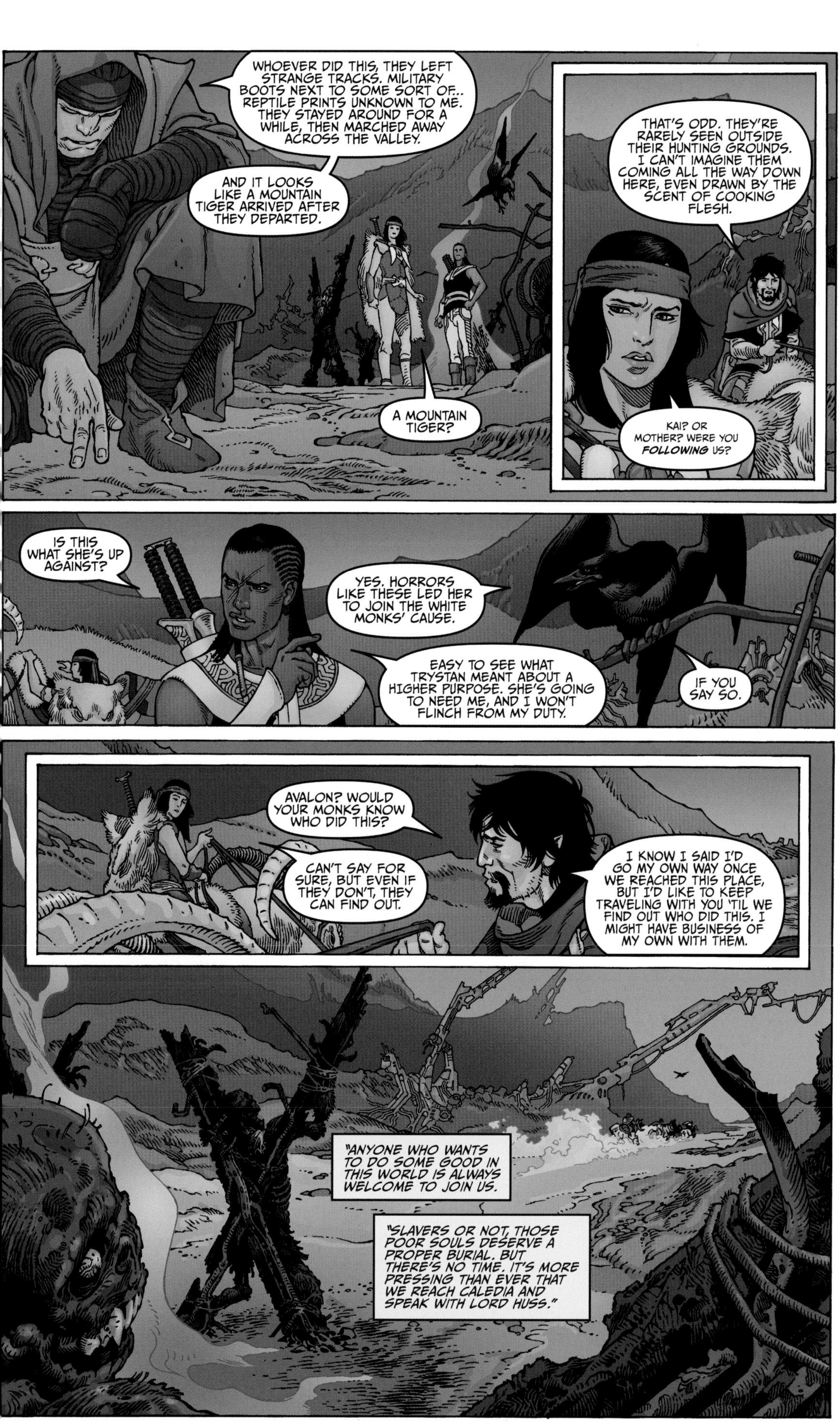
WHOEVER DID THIS, THEY LEFT STRANGE TRACKS. MILITARY BOOTS NEXT TO SOME SORT OF... REPTILE PRINTS UNKNOWN TO ME. THEY STAYED AROUND FOR A WHILE, THEN MARCHED AWAY ACROSS THE VALLEY.
AND IT LOOKS LIKE A MOUNTAIN TIGER ARRIVED AFTER THEY DEPARTED.
A MOUNTAIN TIGER?
THAT'S ODD. THEY'RE RARELY SEEN OUTSIDE THEIR HUNTING GROUNDS. I CAN'T IMAGINE THEM COMING ALL THE WAY DOWN HERE, EVEN DRAWN BY THE SCENT OF COOKING FLESH.
KAI? OR MOTHER? WERE YOU FOLLOWING US?
IS THIS WHAT SHE'S UP AGAINST?
YES. HORRORS LIKE THESE LED HER TO JOIN THE WHITE MONKS' CAUSE.
EASY TO SEE WHAT TRYSTAN MEANT ABOUT A HIGHER PURPOSE. SHE'S GOING TO NEED ME, AND I WON'T FLINCH FROM MY DUTY.
IF YOU SAY SO.
AVALON? WOULD YOUR MONKS KNOW WHO DID THIS?
CAN'T SAY FOR SURE, BUT EVEN IF THEY DON'T, THEY CAN FIND OUT.
I KNOW I SAID I'D GO MY OWN WAY ONCE WE REACHED THIS PLACE, BUT I'D LIKE TO KEEP TRAVELING WITH YOU 'TIL WE FIND OUT WHO DID THIS. I MIGHT HAVE BUSINESS OF MY OWN WITH THEM.
"ANYONE WHO WANTS TO DO SOME GOOD IN THIS WORLD IS ALWAYS WELCOME TO JOIN US.
"SLAVERS OR NOT, THOSE POOR SOULS DESERVE A PROPER BURIAL. BUT THERE'S NO TIME. IT'S MORE PRESSING THAN EVER THAT WE REACH CALEDIA AND SPEAK WITH LORD HUSS."

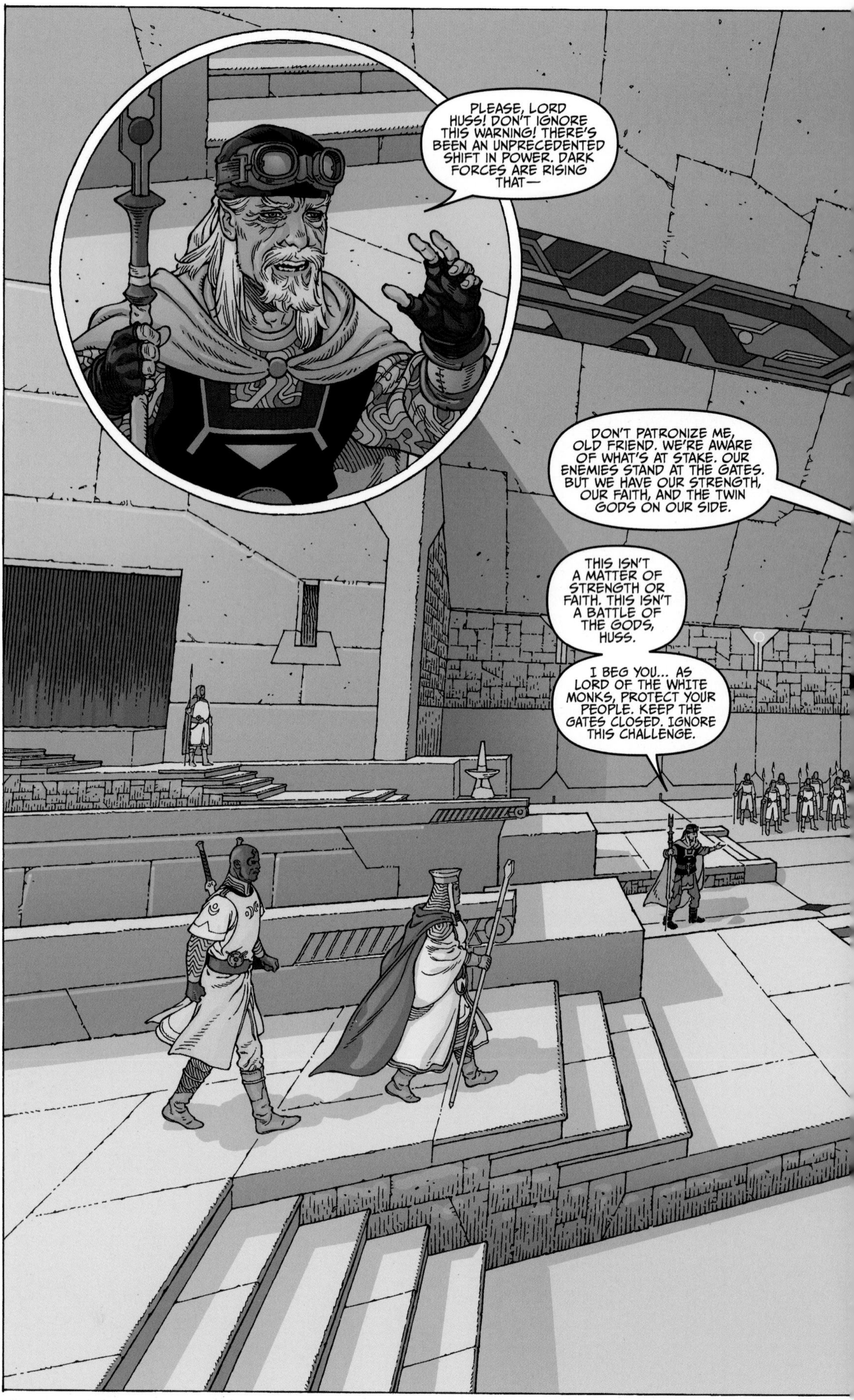
PLEASE, LORD HUSS! DON'T IGNORE THIS WARNING! THERE'S BEEN AN UNPRECEDENTED SHIFT IN POWER. DARK FORCES ARE RISING THAT—
DON'T PATRONIZE ME, OLD FRIEND. WE'RE AWARE OF WHAT'S AT STAKE. OUR ENEMIES STAND AT THE GATES. BUT WE HAVE OUR STRENGTH, OUR FAITH, AND THE TWIN GODS ON OUR SIDE.
THIS ISN'T A MATTER OF STRENGTH OR FAITH. THIS ISN'T A BATTLE OF THE GODS, HUSS.
I BEG YOU... AS LORD OF THE WHITE MONKS, PROTECT YOUR PEOPLE. KEEP THE GATES CLOSED. IGNORE THIS CHALLENGE.

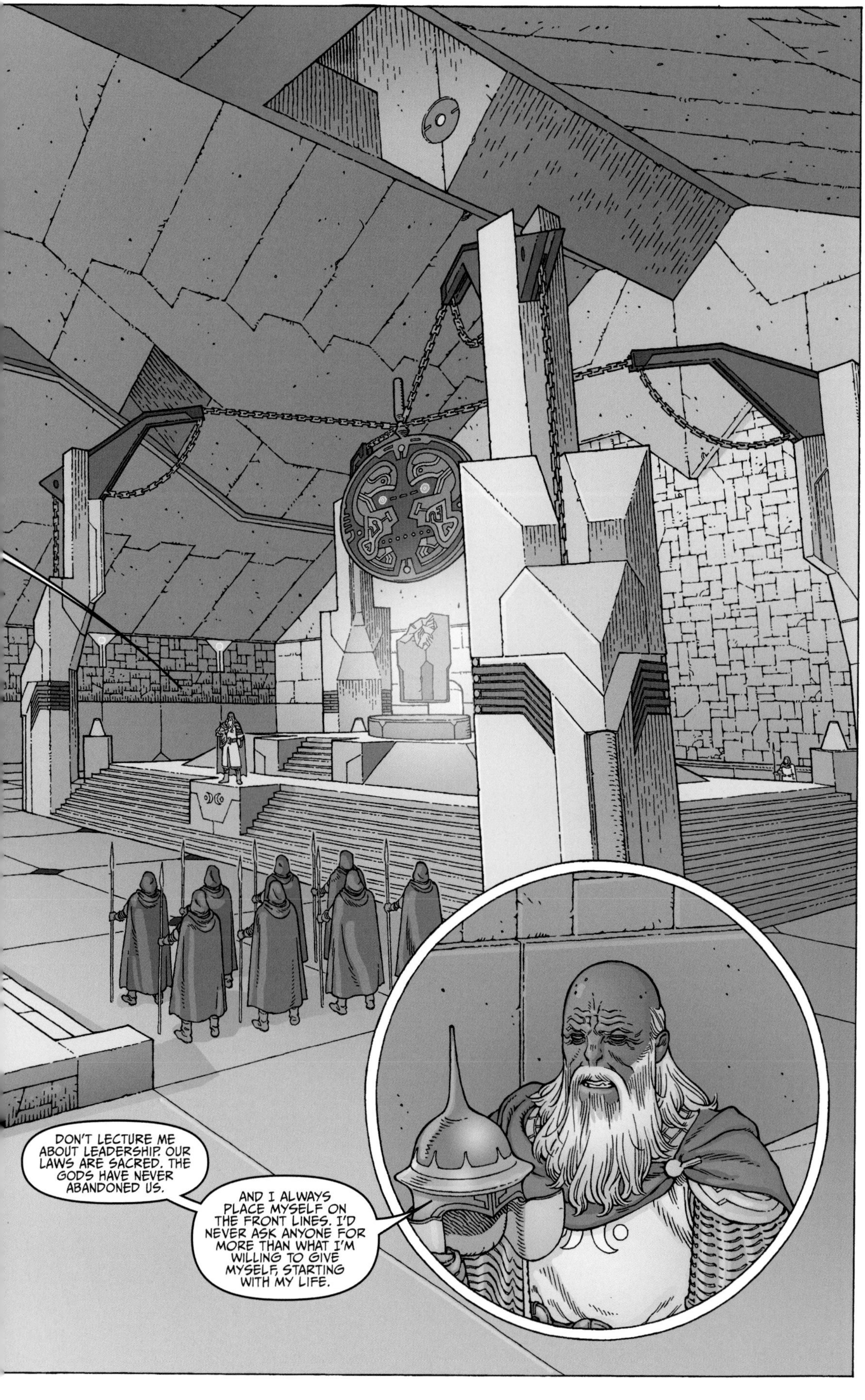
DON'T LECTURE ME ABOUT LEADERSHIP. OUR LAWS ARE SACRED. THE GODS HAVE NEVER ABANDONED US.
AND I ALWAYS PLACE MYSELF ON THE FRONT LINES. I'D NEVER ASK ANYONE FOR MORE THAN WHAT I'M WILLING TO GIVE MYSELF, STARTING WITH MY LIFE.

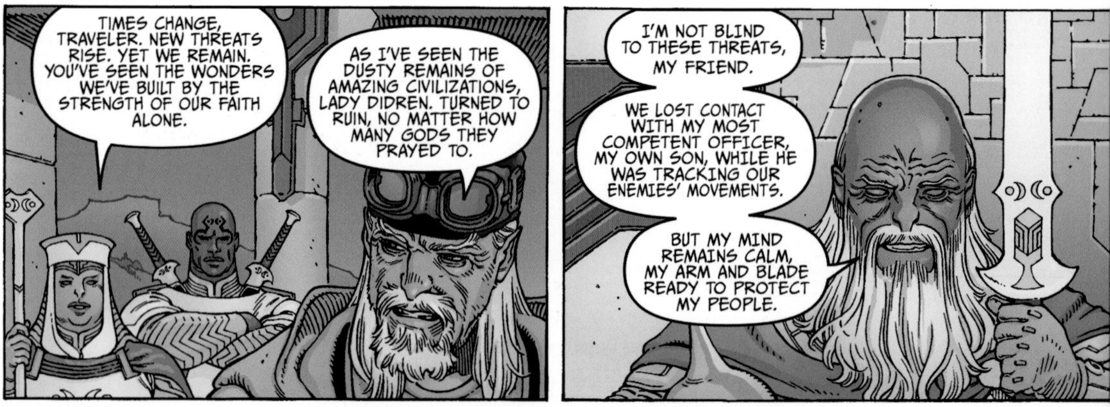

TIMES CHANGE, TRAVELER. NEW THREATS RISE. YET WE REMAIN. YOU'VE SEEN THE WONDERS WE'VE BUILT BY THE STRENGTH OF OUR FAITH ALONE.
AS I'VE SEEN THE DUSTY REMAINS OF AMAZING CIVILIZATIONS, LADY DIDREN. TURNED TO RUIN, NO MATTER HOW MANY GODS THEY PRAYED TO.
I'M NOT BLIND TO THESE THREATS, MY FRIEND.
WE LOST CONTACT WITH MY MOST COMPETENT OFFICER, MY OWN SON, WHILE HE WAS TRACKING OUR ENEMIES' MOVEMENTS.
BUT MY MIND REMAINS CALM, MY ARM AND BLADE READY TO PROTECT MY PEOPLE.

THE CITADEL SIEGE

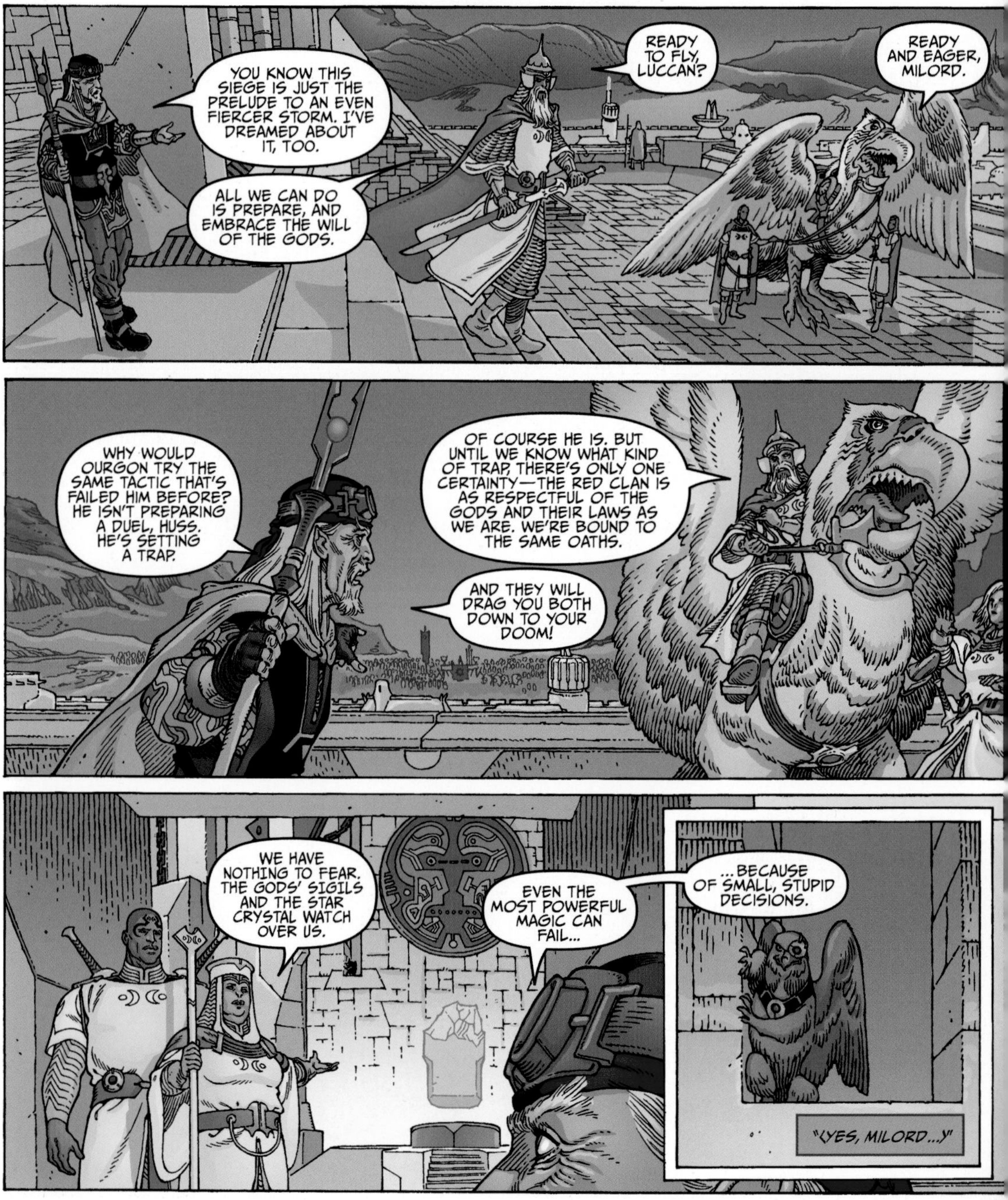

YOU KNOW THIS SIEGE IS JUST THE PRELUDE TO AN EVEN FIERCER STORM. I'VE DREAMED ABOUT IT, TOO.
ALL WE CAN DO IS PREPARE, AND EMBRACE THE WILL OF THE GODS.
READY TO FLY, LUCCAN?
READY AND EAGER, MILORD.
WHY WOULD OURGON TRY THE SAME TACTIC THAT'S FAILED HIM BEFORE? HE ISN'T PREPARING A DUEL, HUSS. HE'S SETTING A TRAP.
OF COURSE HE IS. BUT UNTIL WE KNOW WHAT KIND OF TRAP, THERE'S ONLY ONE CERTAINTY—THE RED CLAN IS AS RESPECTFUL OF THE GODS AND THEIR LAWS AS WE ARE. WE'RE BOUND TO THE SAME OATHS.
AND THEY WILL DRAG YOU BOTH DOWN TO YOUR DOOM!
WE HAVE NOTHING TO FEAR. THE GODS' SIGILS AND THE STAR CRYSTAL WATCH OVER US.
EVEN THE MOST POWERFUL MAGIC CAN FAIL...
...BECAUSE OF SMALL, STUPID DECISIONS.
‹YES, MILORD...›

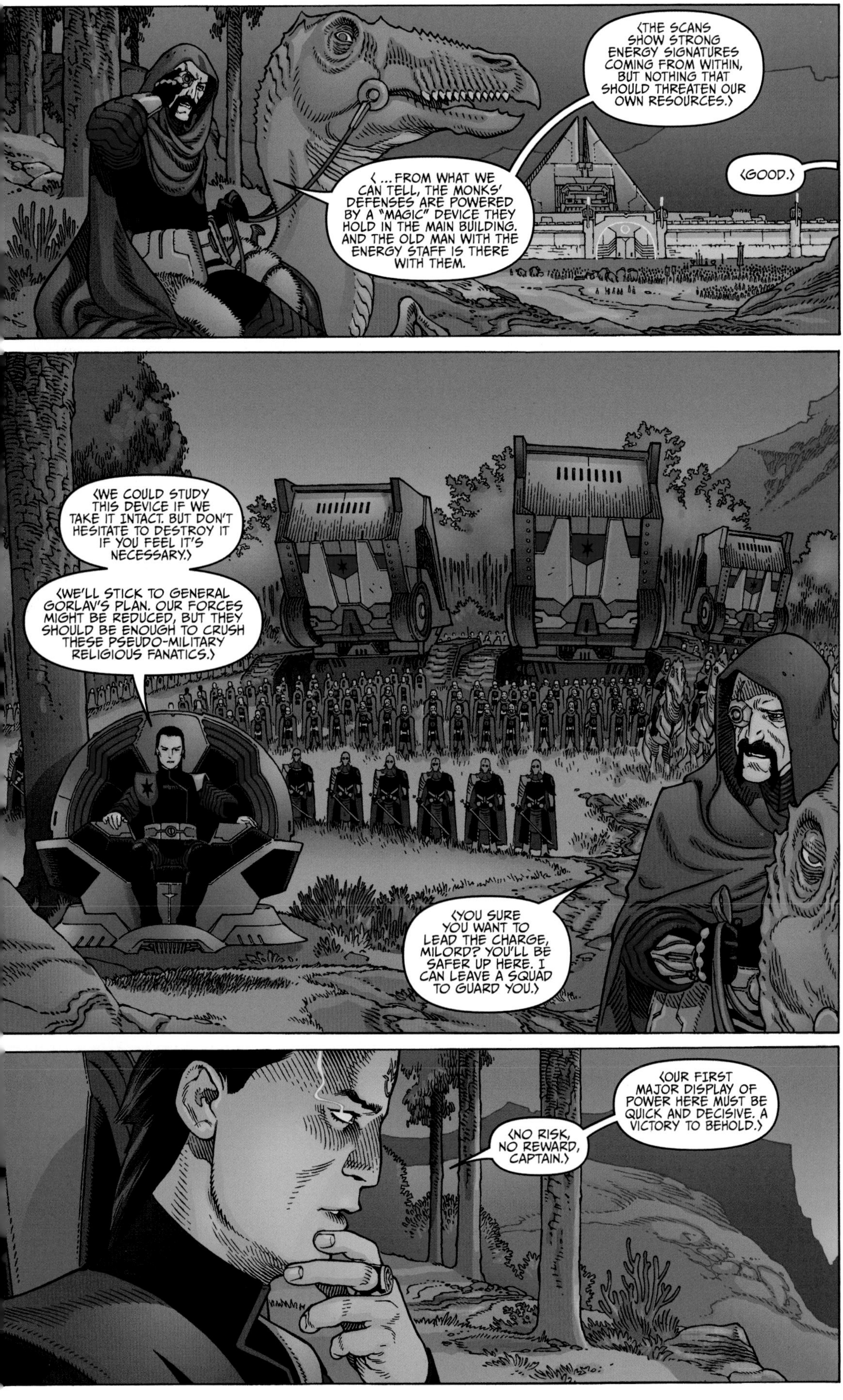
‹ ...FROM WHAT WE CAN TELL, THE MONKS' DEFENSES ARE POWERED BY A "MAGIC" DEVICE THEY HOLD IN THE MAIN BUILDING. AND THE OLD MAN WITH THE ENERGY STAFF IS THERE WITH THEM.
‹THE SCANS SHOW STRONG ENERGY SIGNATURES COMING FROM WITHIN, BUT NOTHING THAT SHOULD THREATEN OUR OWN RESOURCES.›
‹GOOD.›
‹WE COULD STUDY THIS DEVICE IF WE TAKE IT INTACT. BUT DON'T HESITATE TO DESTROY IT IF YOU FEEL IT'S NECESSARY.›
‹WE'LL STICK TO GENERAL GORLAV'S PLAN. OUR FORCES MIGHT BE REDUCED, BUT THEY SHOULD BE ENOUGH TO CRUSH THESE PSEUDO-MILITARY RELIGIOUS FANATICS.›
‹YOU SURE YOU WANT TO LEAD THE CHARGE, MILORD? YOU'LL BE SAFER UP HERE. I CAN LEAVE A SQUAD TO GUARD YOU.›
‹OUR FIRST MAJOR DISPLAY OF POWER HERE MUST BE QUICK AND DECISIVE. A VICTORY TO BEHOLD.›
‹NO RISK, NO REWARD, CAPTAIN.›

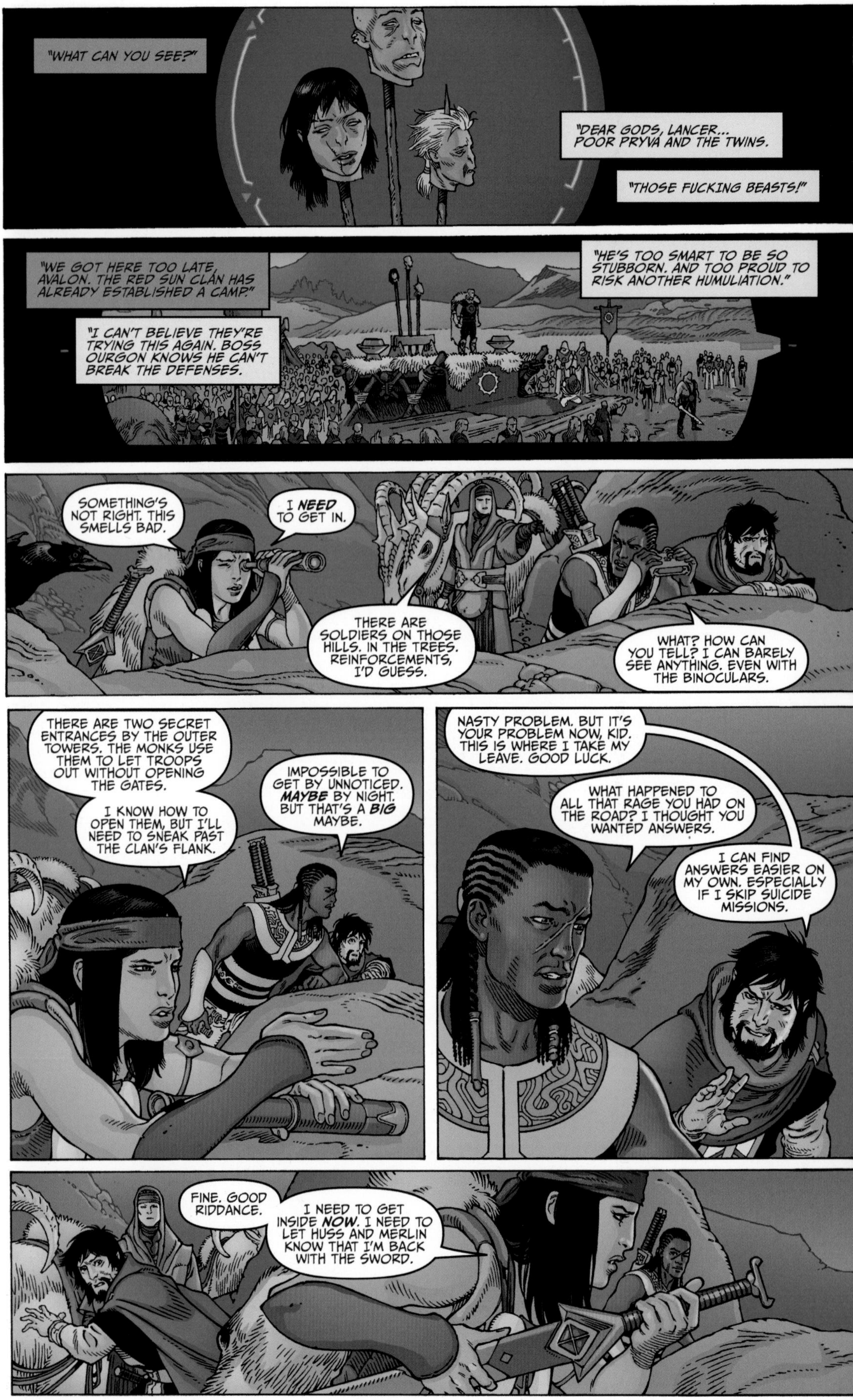
"WHAT CAN YOU SEE?"
"DEAR GODS, LANCER... POOR PRYVA AND THE TWINS.
"THOSE FUCKING BEASTS!"
"WE GOT HERE TOO LATE, AVALON. THE RED SUN CLAN HAS ALREADY ESTABLISHED A CAMP."
"I CAN'T BELIEVE THEY'RE TRYING THIS AGAIN. BOSS OURGON KNOWS HE CAN'T BREAK THE DEFENSES.
"HE'S TOO SMART TO BE SO STUBBORN. AND TOO PROUD TO RISK ANOTHER HUMULIATION."
SOMETHING'S NOT RIGHT. THIS SMELLS BAD.
I NEED TO GET IN.
THERE ARE SOLDIERS ON THOSE HILLS. IN THE TREES. REINFORCEMENTS, I'D GUESS.
WHAT? HOW CAN YOU TELL? I CAN BARELY SEE ANYTHING. EVEN WITH THE BINOCULARS.
THERE ARE TWO SECRET ENTRANCES BY THE OUTER TOWERS. THE MONKS USE THEM TO LET TROOPS OUT WITHOUT OPENING THE GATES.
I KNOW HOW TO OPEN THEM, BUT I'LL NEED TO SNEAK PAST THE CLAN'S FLANK.
IMPOSSIBLE TO GET BY UNNOTICED. MAYBE BY NIGHT. BUT THAT'S A BIG MAYBE.
NASTY PROBLEM. BUT IT'S YOUR PROBLEM NOW, KID. THIS IS WHERE I TAKE MY LEAVE. GOOD LUCK.
WHAT HAPPENED TO ALL THAT RAGE YOU HAD ON THE ROAD? I THOUGHT YOU WANTED ANSWERS.
I CAN FIND ANSWERS EASIER ON MY OWN. ESPECIALLY IF I SKIP SUICIDE MISSIONS.
FINE. GOOD RIDDANCE.
I NEED TO GET INSIDE NOW. I NEED TO LET HUSS AND MERLIN KNOW THAT I'M BACK WITH THE SWORD.

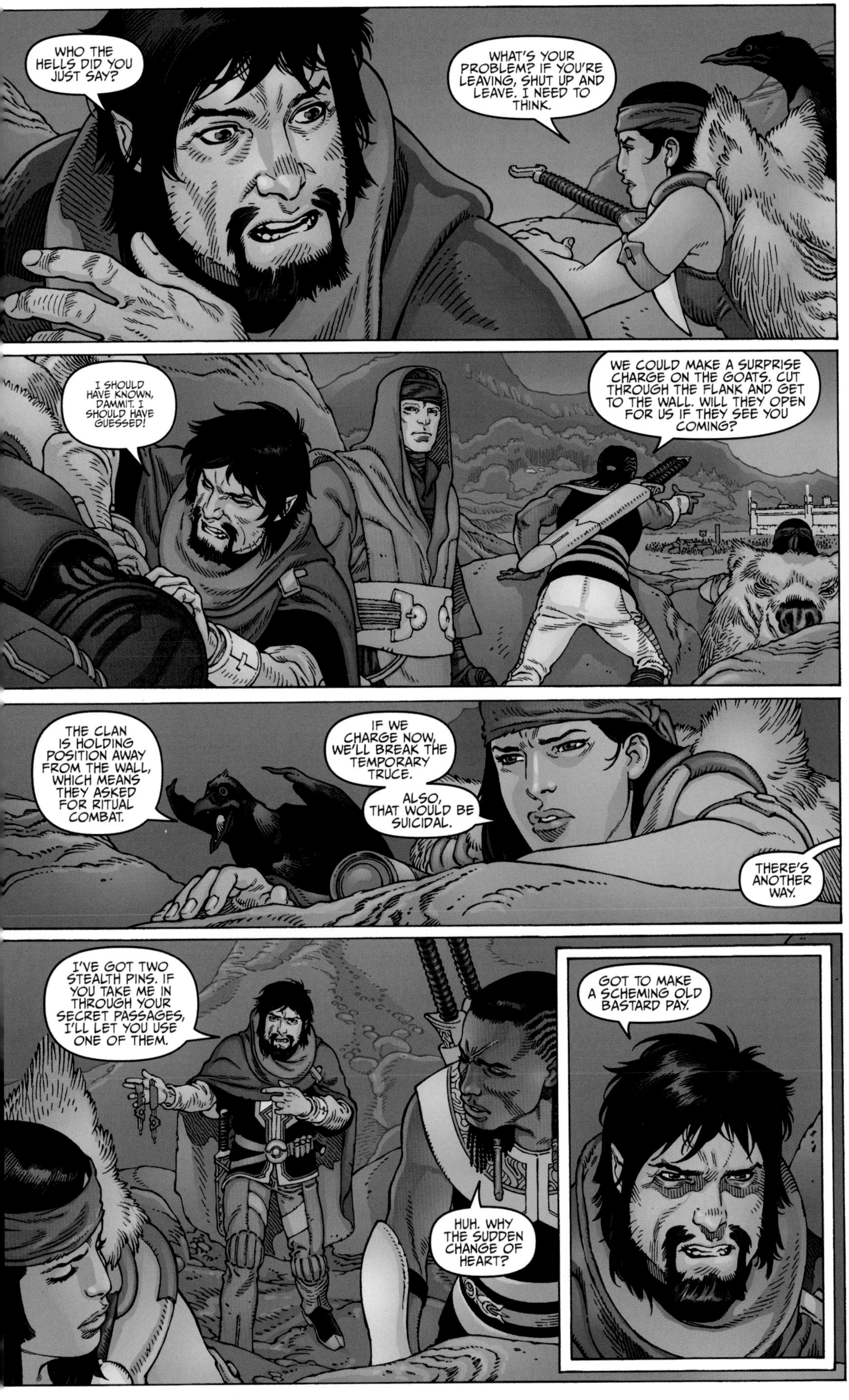
WHO THE HELLS DID YOU JUST SAY?
WHAT'S YOUR PROBLEM? IF YOU'RE LEAVING, SHUT UP AND LEAVE. I NEED TO THINK.
I SHOULD HAVE KNOWN, DAMMIT. I SHOULD HAVE GUESSED!
WE COULD MAKE A SURPRISE CHARGE ON THE GOATS. CUT THROUGH THE FLANK AND GET TO THE WALL. WILL THEY OPEN FOR US IF THEY SEE YOU COMING?
THE CLAN IS HOLDING POSITION AWAY FROM THE WALL, WHICH MEANS THEY ASKED FOR RITUAL COMBAT.
IF WE CHARGE NOW, WE'LL BREAK THE TEMPORARY TRUCE.
ALSO, THAT WOULD BE SUICIDAL.
THERE'S ANOTHER WAY.
I'VE GOT TWO STEALTH PINS. IF YOU TAKE ME IN THROUGH YOUR SECRET PASSAGES, I'LL LET YOU USE ONE OF THEM.
HUH. WHY THE SUDDEN CHANGE OF HEART?
GOT TO MAKE A SCHEMING OLD BASTARD PAY.

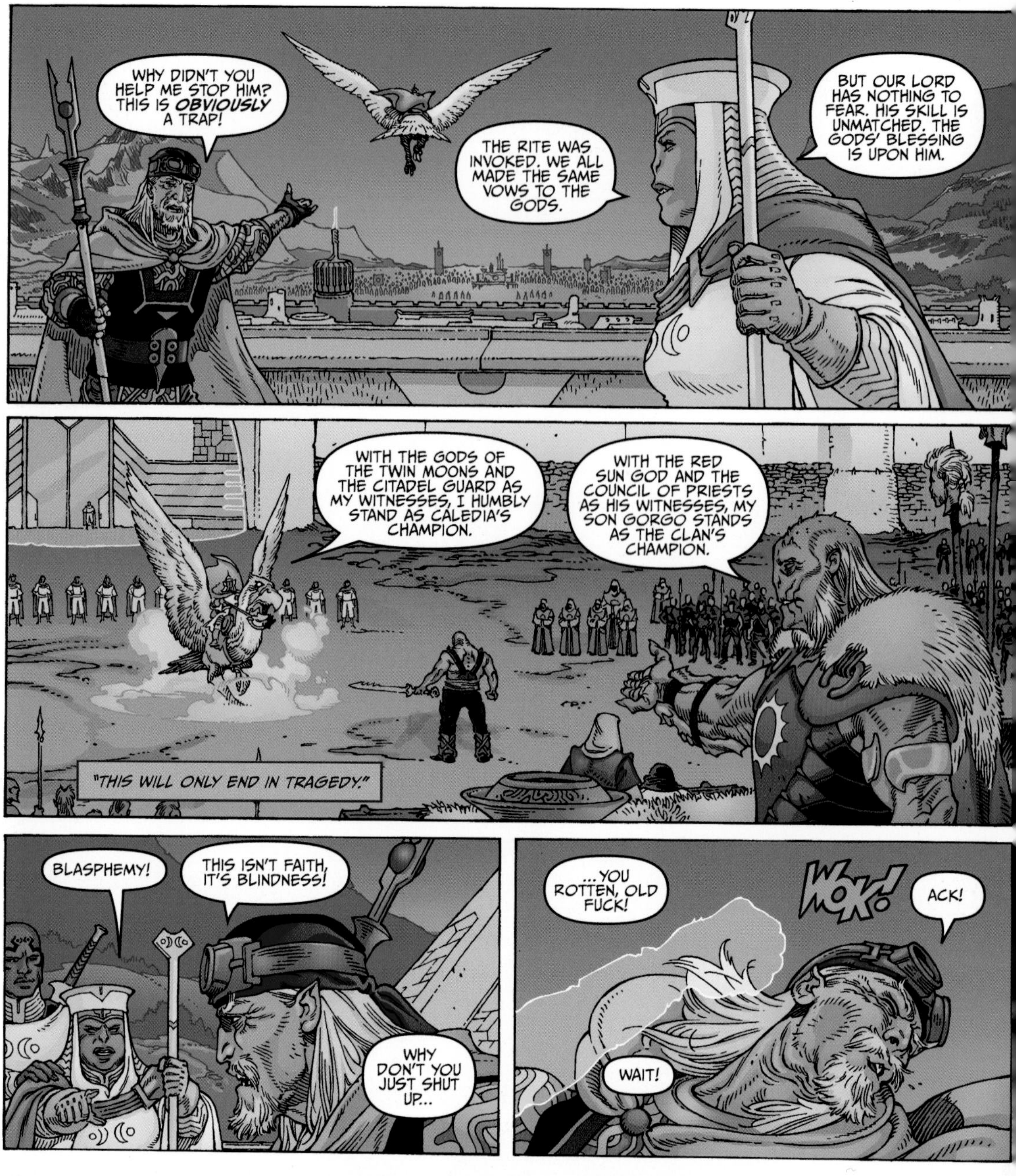
WHY DIDN'T YOU HELP ME STOP HIM? THIS IS *OBVIOUSLY* A TRAP!
THE RITE WAS INVOKED. WE ALL MADE THE SAME VOWS TO THE GODS.
BUT OUR LORD HAS NOTHING TO FEAR. HIS SKILL IS UNMATCHED. THE GODS' BLESSING IS UPON HIM.
WITH THE GODS OF THE TWIN MOONS AND THE CITADEL GUARD AS MY WITNESSES, I HUMBLY STAND AS CALEDIA'S CHAMPION.
WITH THE RED SUN GOD AND THE COUNCIL OF PRIESTS AS HIS WITNESSES, MY SON GORGO STANDS AS THE CLAN'S CHAMPION.
"THIS WILL ONLY END IN TRAGEDY."
BLASPHEMY!
THIS ISN'T FAITH, IT'S BLINDNESS!
WHY DON'T YOU JUST SHUT UP...
...YOU ROTTEN, OLD FUCK!
WOK!
ACK!
WAIT!

THE GODS' TRIAL

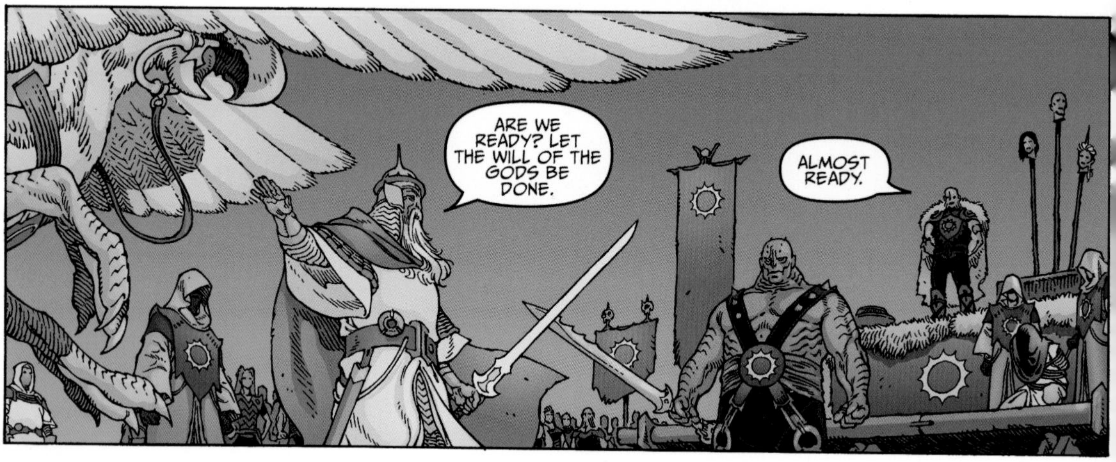
ARE WE READY? LET THE WILL OF THE GODS BE DONE.
ALMOST READY.

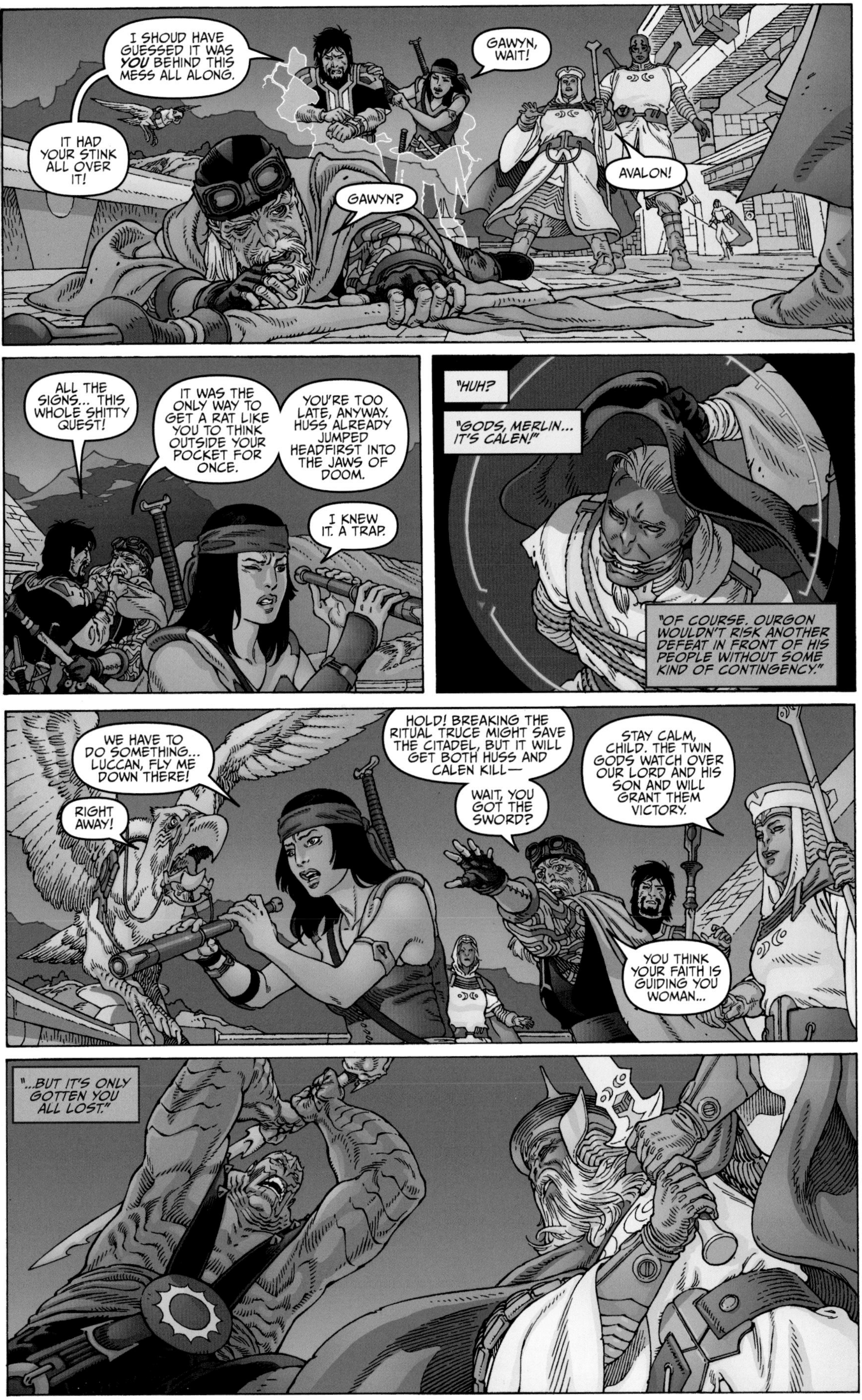
I SHOUD HAVE GUESSED IT WAS YOU BEHIND THIS MESS ALL ALONG.
IT HAD YOUR STINK ALL OVER IT!
GAWYN, WAIT!
GAWYN?
AVALON!
ALL THE SIGNS... THIS WHOLE SHITTY QUEST!
IT WAS THE ONLY WAY TO GET A RAT LIKE YOU TO THINK OUTSIDE YOUR POCKET FOR ONCE.
YOU'RE TOO LATE, ANYWAY. HUSS ALREADY JUMPED HEADFIRST INTO THE JAWS OF DOOM.
I KNEW IT. A TRAP.
"HUH?
"GODS, MERLIN... IT'S CALEN!"
"OF COURSE. OURGON WOULDN'T RISK ANOTHER DEFEAT IN FRONT OF HIS PEOPLE WITHOUT SOME KIND OF CONTINGENCY."
WE HAVE TO DO SOMETHING... LUCCAN, FLY ME DOWN THERE!
RIGHT AWAY!
HOLD! BREAKING THE RITUAL TRUCE MIGHT SAVE THE CITADEL, BUT IT WILL GET BOTH HUSS AND CALEN KILL—
WAIT, YOU GOT THE SWORD?
STAY CALM, CHILD. THE TWIN GODS WATCH OVER OUR LORD AND HIS SON AND WILL GRANT THEM VICTORY.
YOU THINK YOUR FAITH IS GUIDING YOU WOMAN...
"...BUT IT'S ONLY GOTTEN YOU ALL LOST."

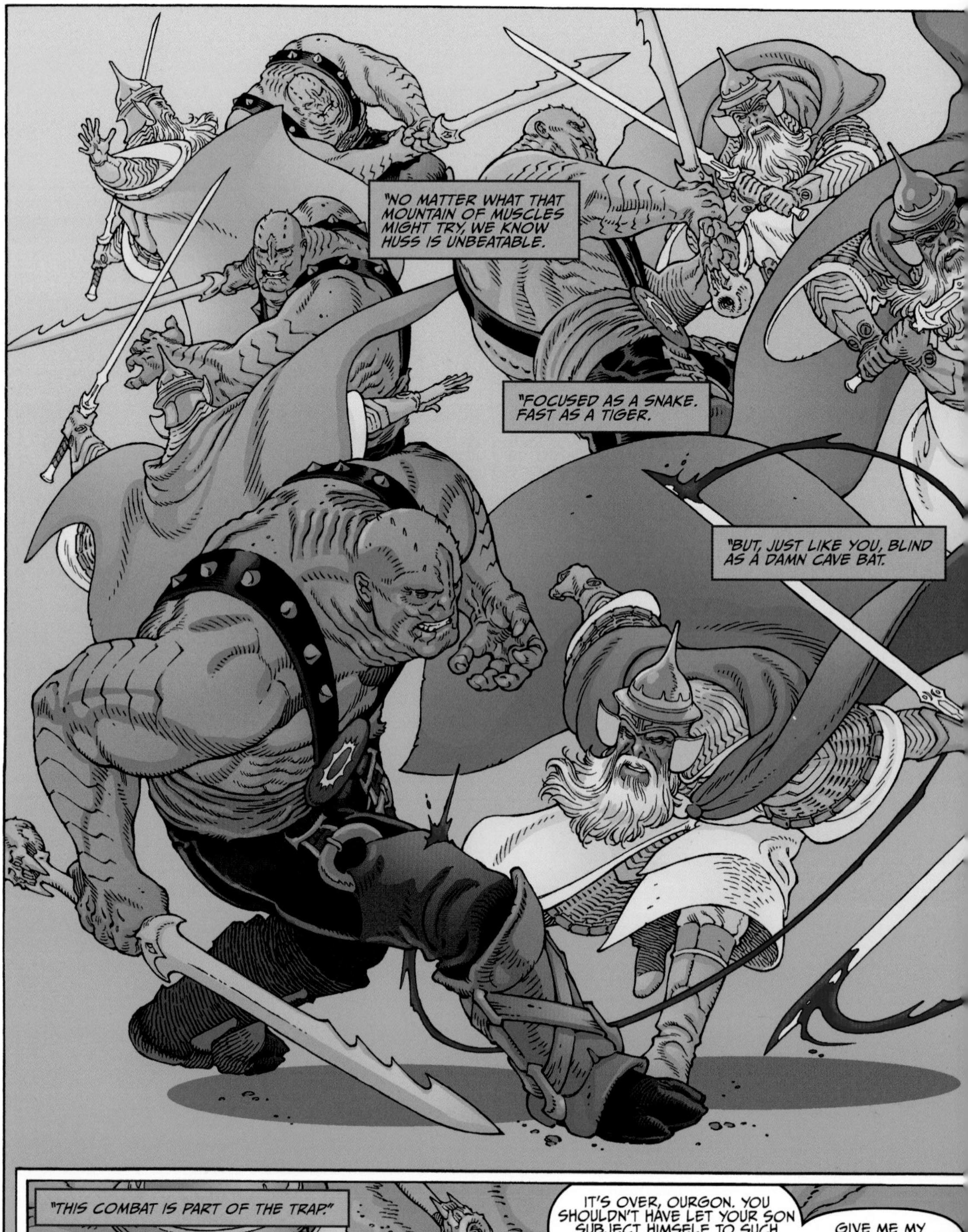
"NO MATTER WHAT THAT MOUNTAIN OF MUSCLES MIGHT TRY, WE KNOW HUSS IS UNBEATABLE.
"FOCUSED AS A SNAKE. FAST AS A TIGER.
"BUT, JUST LIKE YOU, BLIND AS A DAMN CAVE BAT.

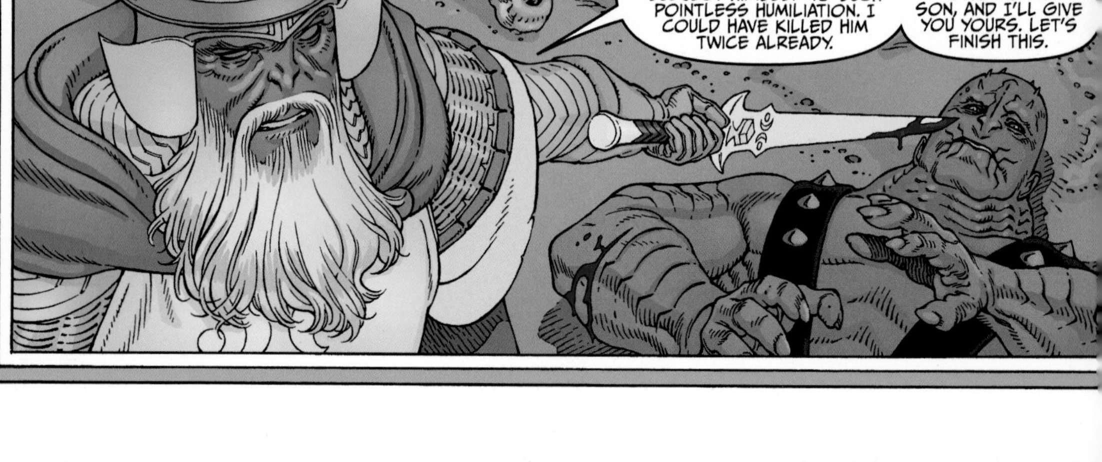
"THIS COMBAT IS PART OF THE TRAP."
IT'S OVER, OURGON. YOU SHOULDN'T HAVE LET YOUR SON SUBJECT HIMSELF TO SUCH POINTLESS HUMILIATION. I COULD HAVE KILLED HIM TWICE ALREADY.
GIVE ME MY SON, AND I'LL GIVE YOU YOURS. LET'S FINISH THIS.

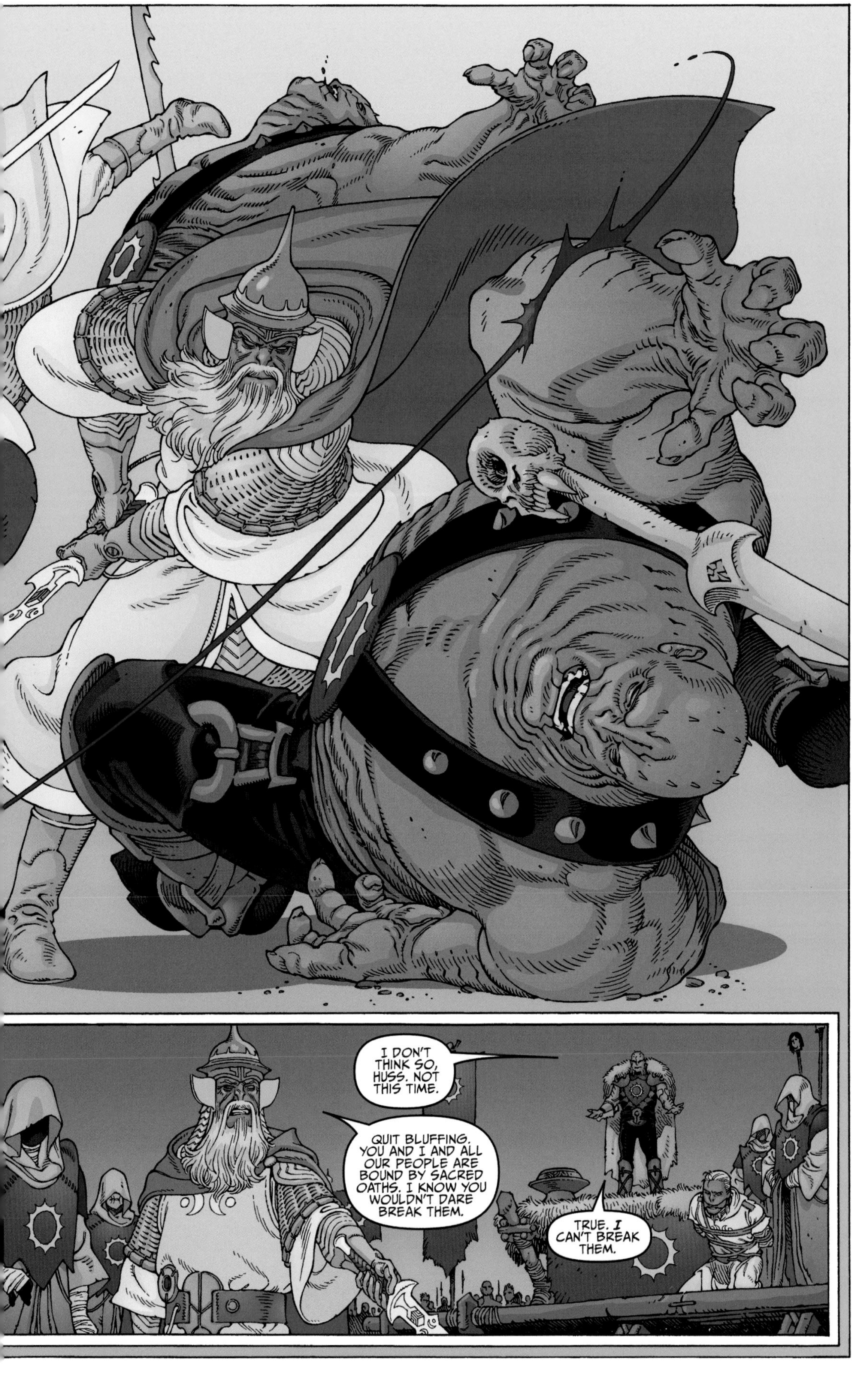
I DON'T THINK SO, HUSS. NOT THIS TIME.
QUIT BLUFFING. YOU AND I AND ALL OUR PEOPLE ARE BOUND BY SACRED OATHS. I KNOW YOU WOULDN'T DARE BREAK THEM.
TRUE. *I* CAN'T BREAK THEM.

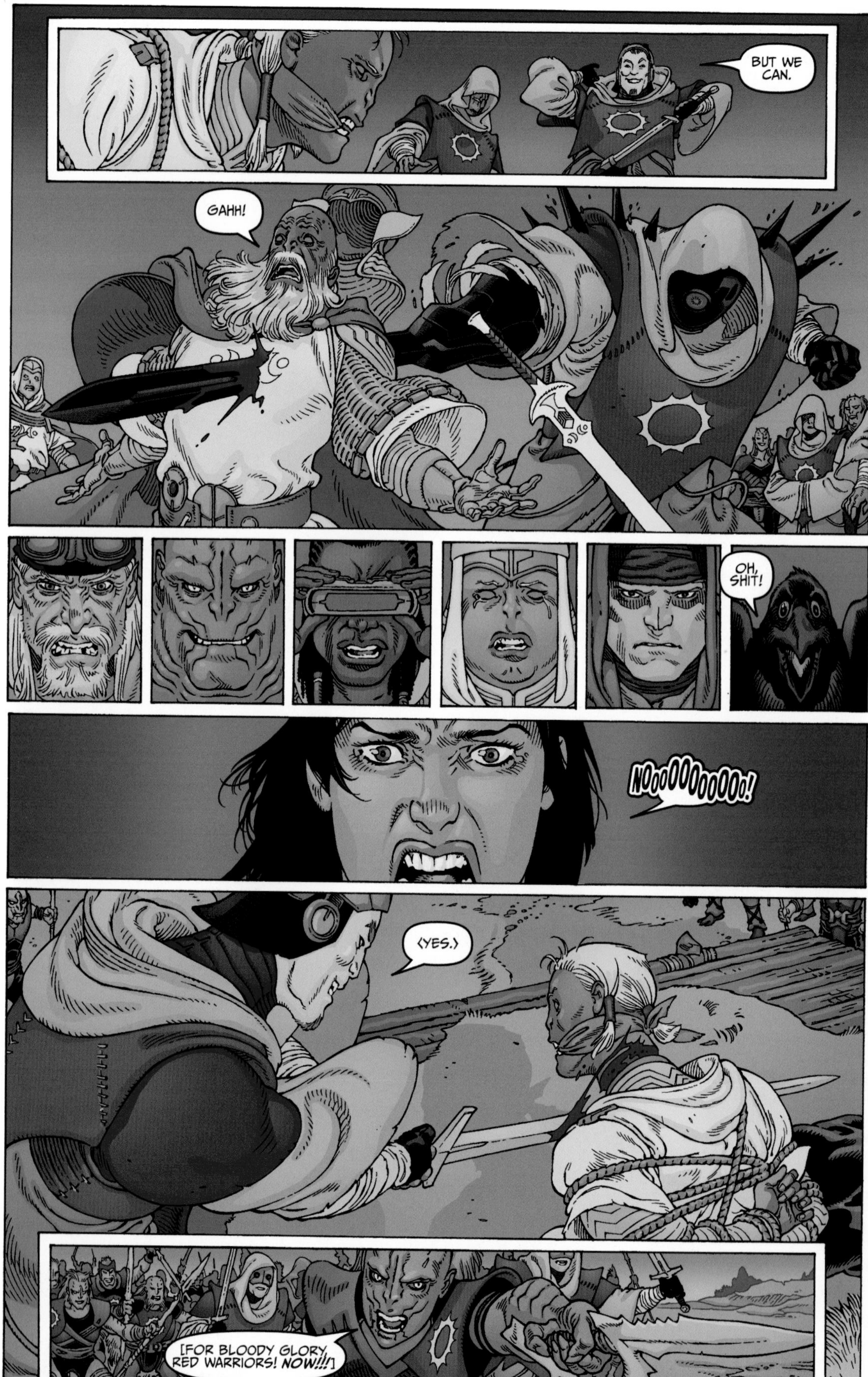

BUT WE CAN.
GAHH!
OH, SHIT!
NOOOOOOOOOO!
‹YES.›
[FOR BLOODY GLORY, RED WARRIORS! NOW!!!]

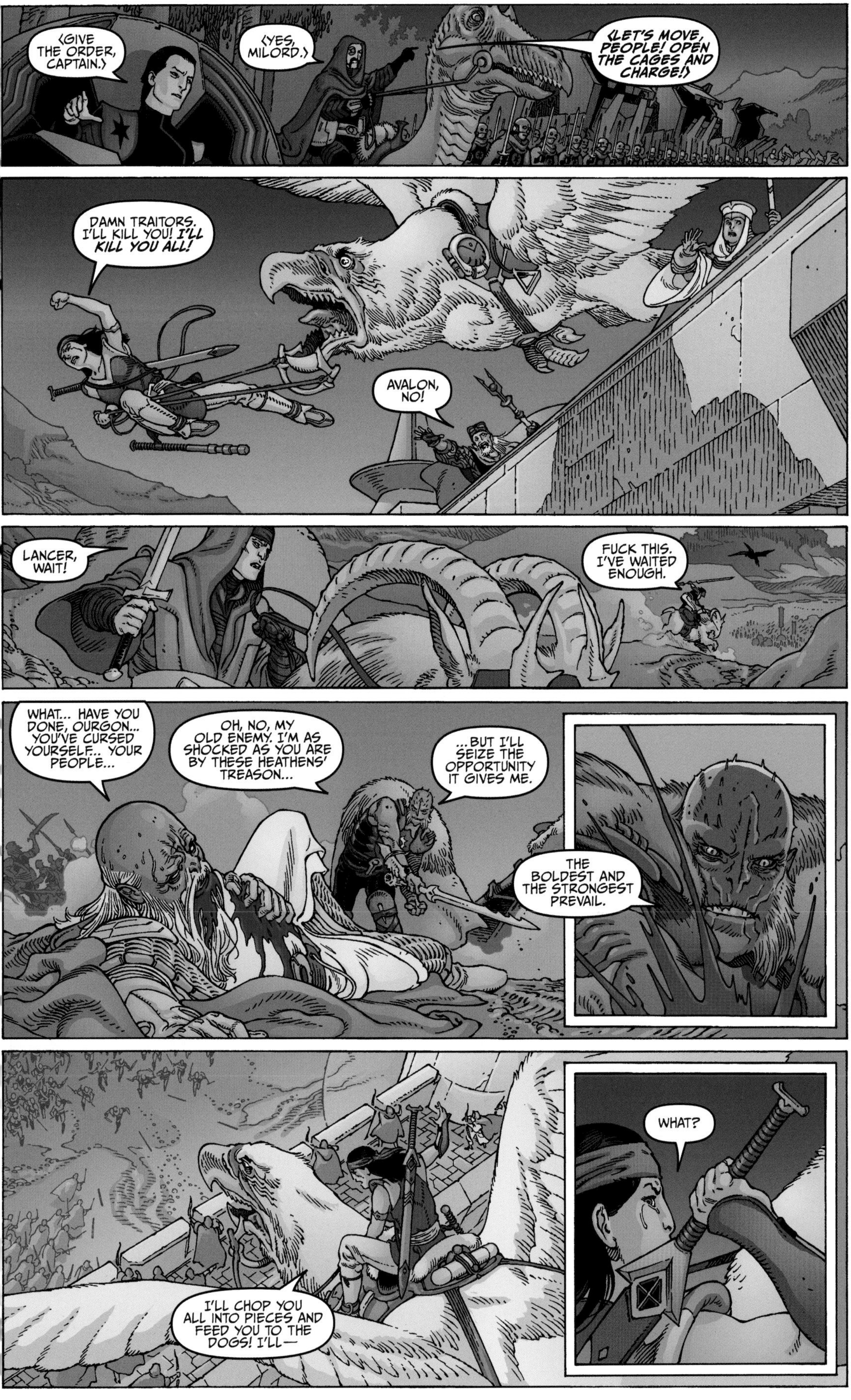

‹GIVE THE ORDER, CAPTAIN.›
‹YES, MILORD.›
‹LET'S MOVE, PEOPLE! OPEN THE CAGES AND CHARGE!›
DAMN TRAITORS. I'LL KILL YOU! *I'LL KILL YOU ALL!*
AVALON, NO!
LANCER, WAIT!
FUCK THIS. I'VE WAITED ENOUGH.
WHAT... HAVE YOU DONE, OURGON... YOU'VE CURSED YOURSELF... YOUR PEOPLE...
OH, NO, MY OLD ENEMY. I'M AS SHOCKED AS YOU ARE BY THESE HEATHENS' TREASON...
...BUT I'LL SEIZE THE OPPORTUNITY IT GIVES ME.
THE BOLDEST AND THE STRONGEST PREVAIL.
I'LL CHOP YOU ALL INTO PIECES AND FEED YOU TO THE DOGS! I'LL—
WHAT?

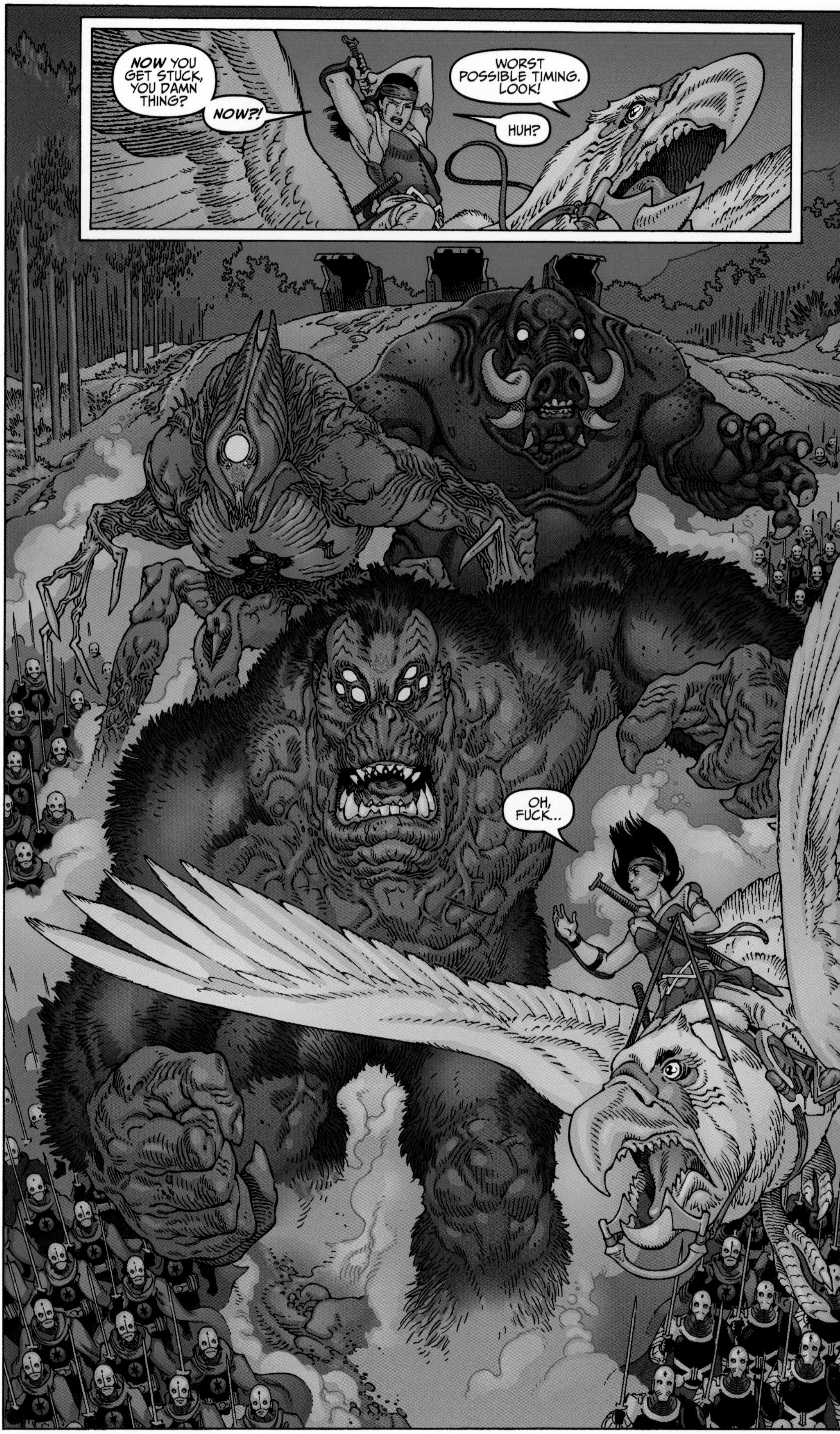

NOW YOU GET STUCK, YOU DAMN THING?
NOW?!
WORST POSSIBLE TIMING. LOOK!
HUH?
OH, FUCK...

LANCER AND TRYSTAN FIGHT LIKE DEMIGODS OF LEGEND.

THEY STRUCK THE ENEMY LINES LIKE LIGHTNING AND REGROUPED WITH THE MONKS NEAR THE WALLS' DEFENSES.

BUT THEY WON'T HOLD FOR LONG AGAINST THE RED CLAN AND THEIR ALLIES, EVEN WITH THE REINFORCEMENTS SENT FROM THE CITADEL.

THAT BLACK DEMON IS A LIVING, KILLING STORM.

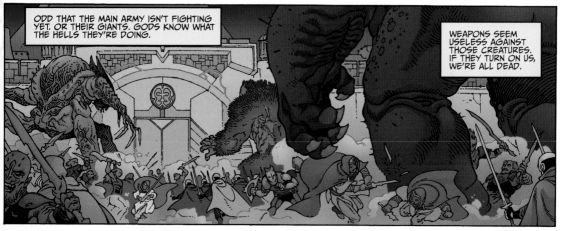

ODD THAT THE MAIN ARMY ISN'T FIGHTING YET. OR THEIR GIANTS. GODS KNOW WHAT THE HELLS THEY'RE DOING.

WEAPONS SEEM USELESS AGAINST THOSE CREATURES. IF THEY TURN ON US, WE'RE ALL DEAD.

JUST LIKE LORD HUSS AND CALEN.

GATES OF CHAOS

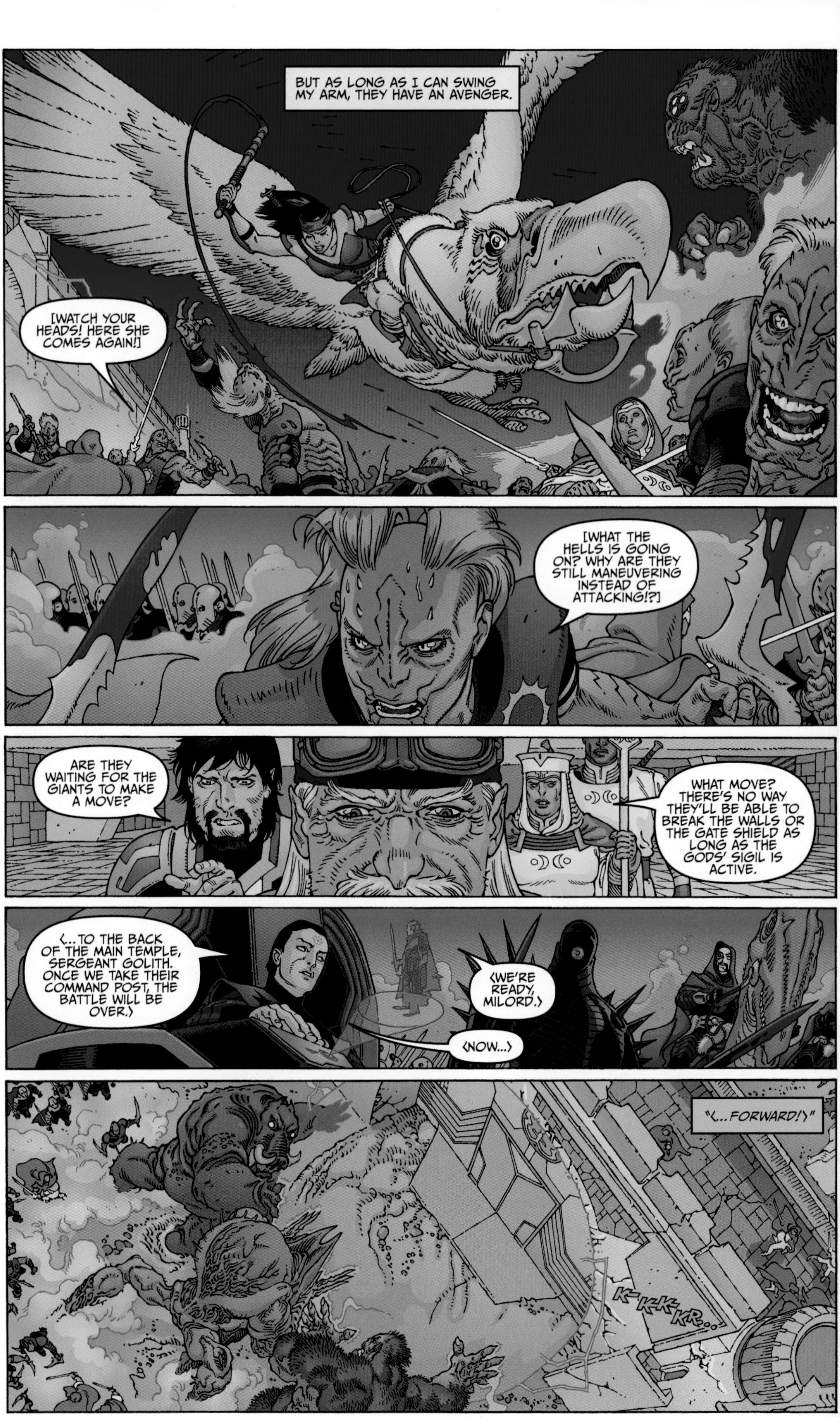
BUT AS LONG AS I CAN SWING MY ARM, THEY HAVE AN AVENGER.
[WATCH YOUR HEADS! HERE SHE COMES AGAIN!]
[WHAT THE HELLS IS GOING ON? WHY ARE THEY STILL MANEUVERING INSTEAD OF ATTACKING!?]
ARE THEY WAITING FOR THE GIANTS TO MAKE A MOVE?
WHAT MOVE? THERE'S NO WAY THEY'LL BE ABLE TO BREAK THE WALLS OR THE GATE SHIELD AS LONG AS THE GODS' SIGIL IS ACTIVE.
‹...TO THE BACK OF THE MAIN TEMPLE, SERGEANT GOLITH. ONCE WE TAKE THEIR COMMAND POST, THE BATTLE WILL BE OVER.›
‹WE'RE READY, MILORD.›
‹NOW...›
"‹...FORWARD!›"
K-K-K-KR...

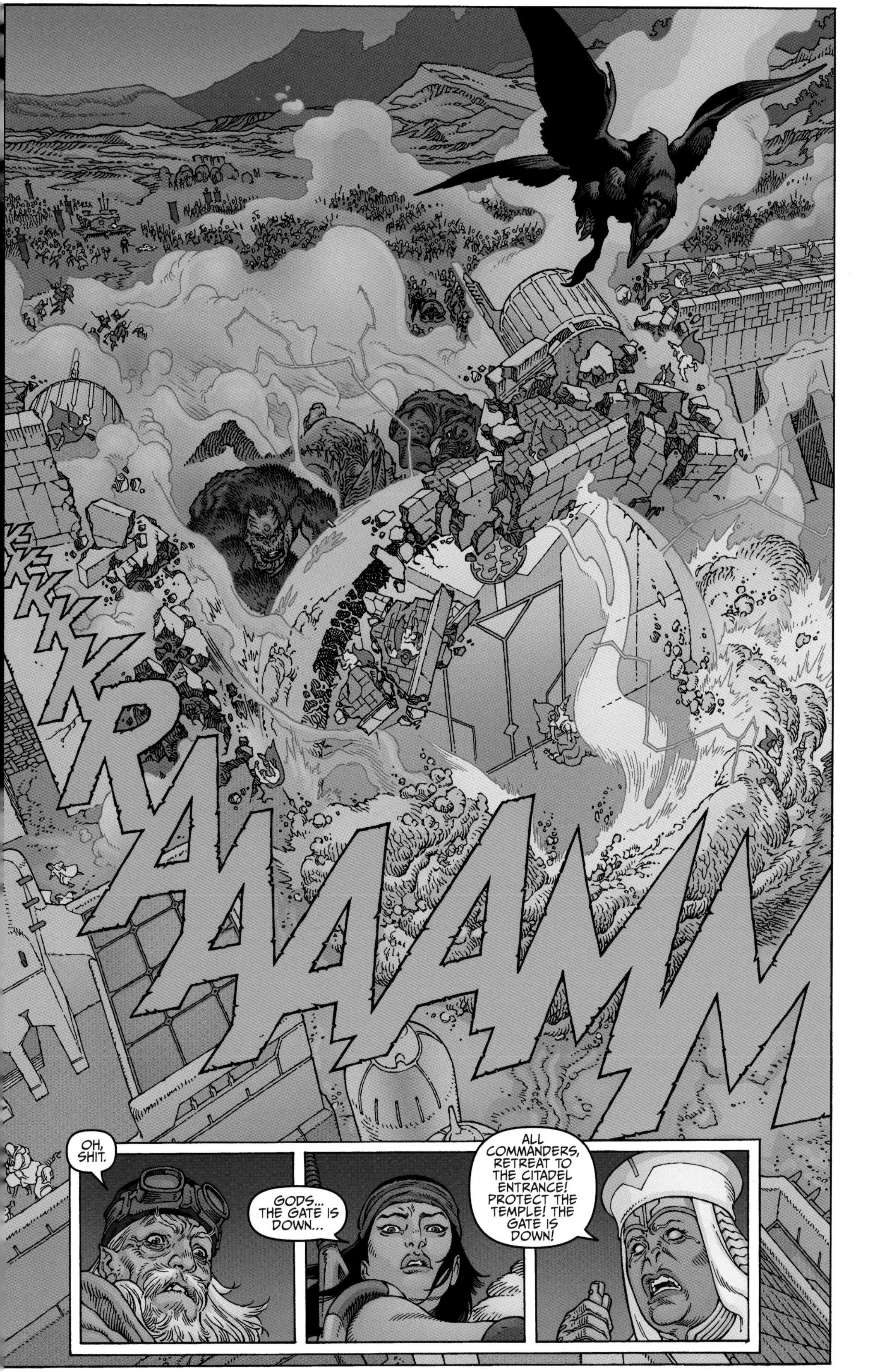
KKKKRAAAMM
OH, SHIT.
GODS... THE GATE IS DOWN...
ALL COMMANDERS, RETREAT TO THE CITADEL ENTRANCE! PROTECT THE TEMPLE! THE GATE IS DOWN!

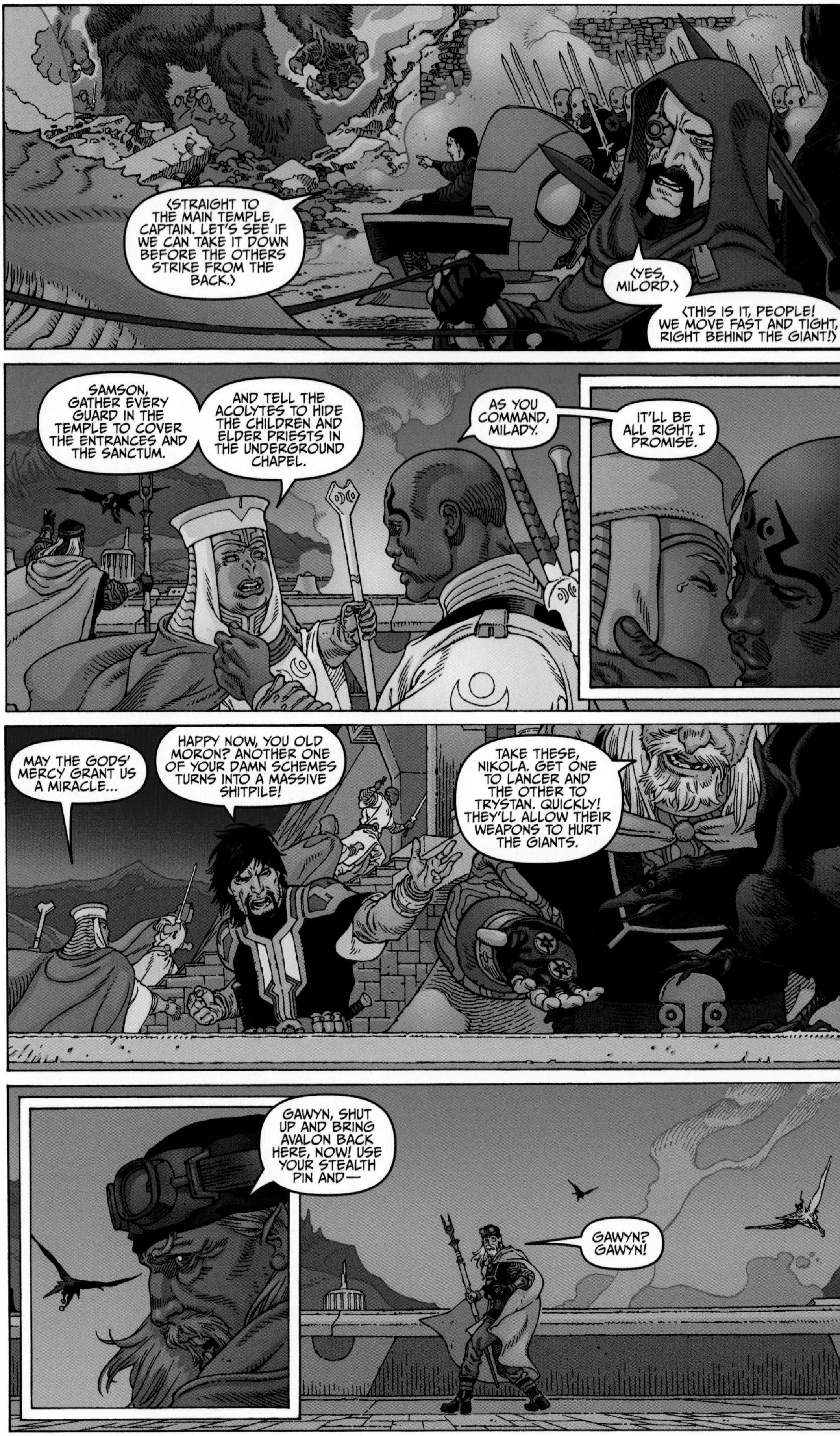

‹STRAIGHT TO THE MAIN TEMPLE, CAPTAIN. LET'S SEE IF WE CAN TAKE IT DOWN BEFORE THE OTHERS STRIKE FROM THE BACK.›
‹YES, MILORD.›
‹THIS IS IT, PEOPLE! WE MOVE FAST AND TIGHT, RIGHT BEHIND THE GIANT!›
SAMSON, GATHER EVERY GUARD IN THE TEMPLE TO COVER THE ENTRANCES AND THE SANCTUM.
AND TELL THE ACOLYTES TO HIDE THE CHILDREN AND ELDER PRIESTS IN THE UNDERGROUND CHAPEL.
AS YOU COMMAND, MILADY.
IT'LL BE ALL RIGHT, I PROMISE.
MAY THE GODS' MERCY GRANT US A MIRACLE...
HAPPY NOW, YOU OLD MORON? ANOTHER ONE OF YOUR DAMN SCHEMES TURNS INTO A MASSIVE SHITPILE!
TAKE THESE, NIKOLA. GET ONE TO LANCER AND THE OTHER TO TRYSTAN. QUICKLY! THEY'LL ALLOW THEIR WEAPONS TO HURT THE GIANTS.
GAWYN, SHUT UP AND BRING AVALON BACK HERE, NOW! USE YOUR STEALTH PIN AND—
GAWYN? GAWYN!

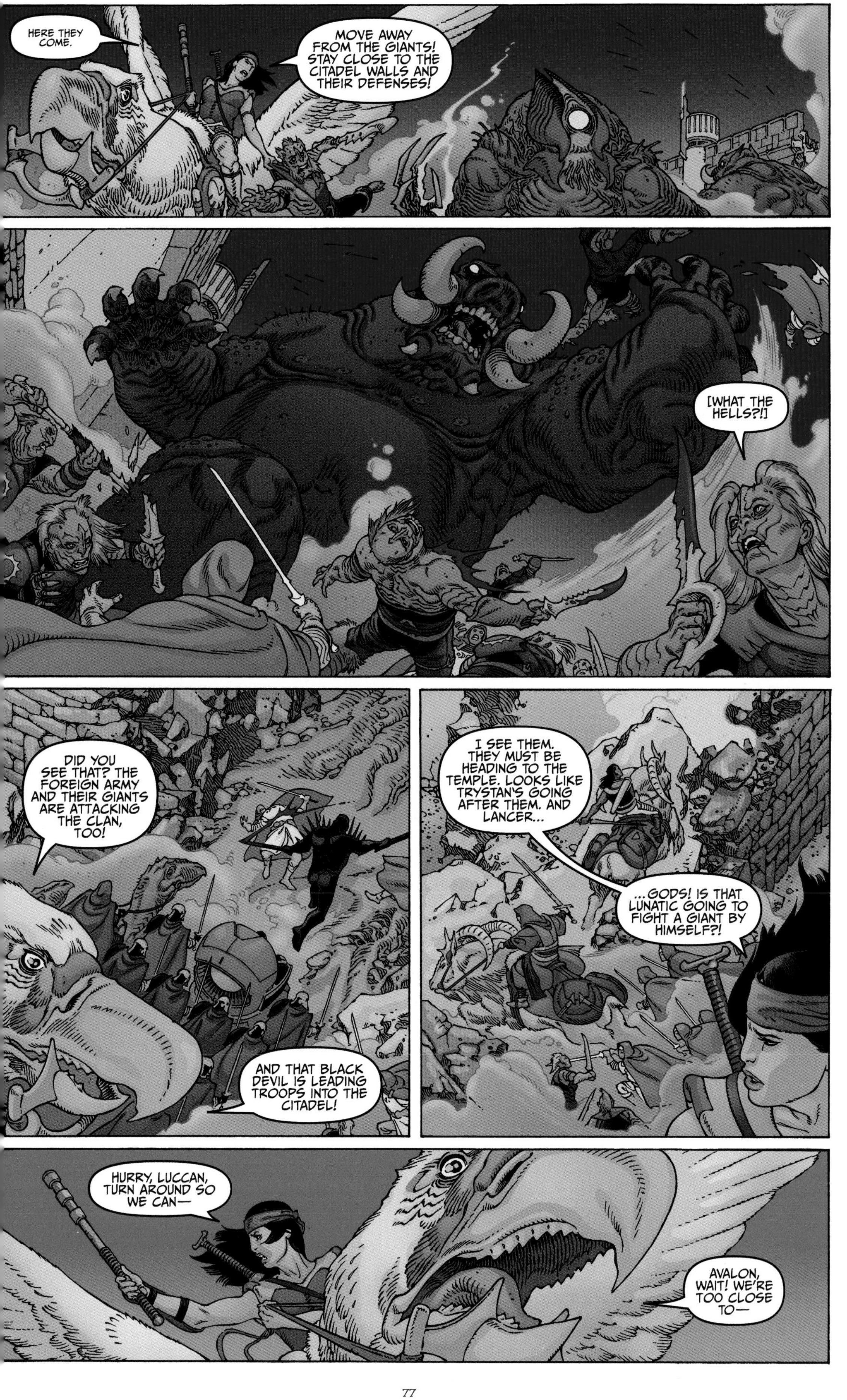
HERE THEY COME.
MOVE AWAY FROM THE GIANTS! STAY CLOSE TO THE CITADEL WALLS AND THEIR DEFENSES!
[WHAT THE HELLS?!]
DID YOU SEE THAT? THE FOREIGN ARMY AND THEIR GIANTS ARE ATTACKING THE CLAN, TOO!
AND THAT BLACK DEVIL IS LEADING TROOPS INTO THE CITADEL!
I SEE THEM. THEY MUST BE HEADING TO THE TEMPLE. LOOKS LIKE TRYSTAN'S GOING AFTER THEM. AND LANCER...
...GODS! IS THAT LUNATIC GOING TO FIGHT A GIANT BY HIMSELF?!
HURRY, LUCCAN, TURN AROUND SO WE CAN—
AVALON, WAIT! WE'RE TOO CLOSE TO—

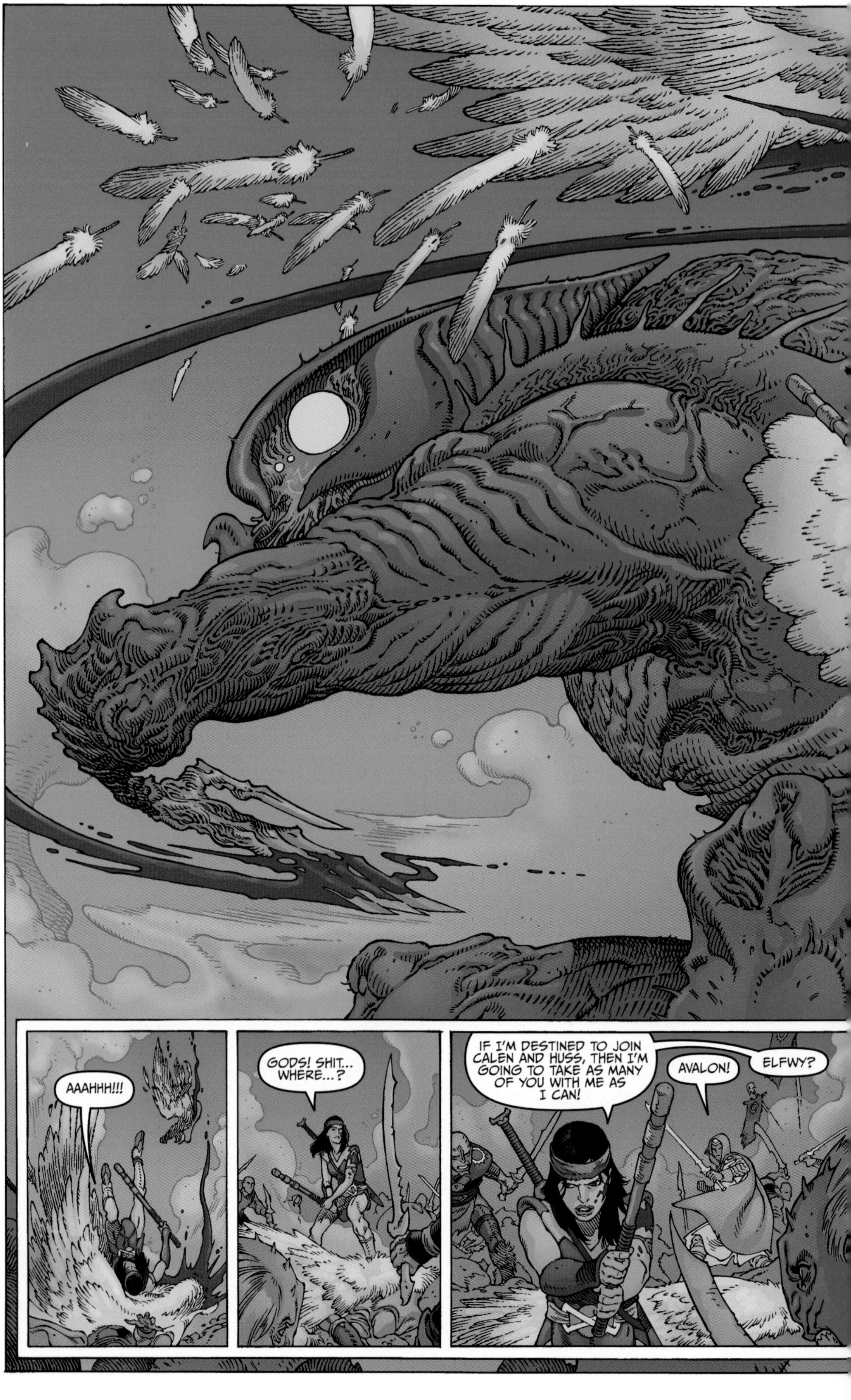
AAAHHH!!!
GODS! SHIT... WHERE...?
IF I'M DESTINED TO JOIN CALEN AND HUSS, THEN I'M GOING TO TAKE AS MANY OF YOU WITH ME AS I CAN!
AVALON!
ELFWY?

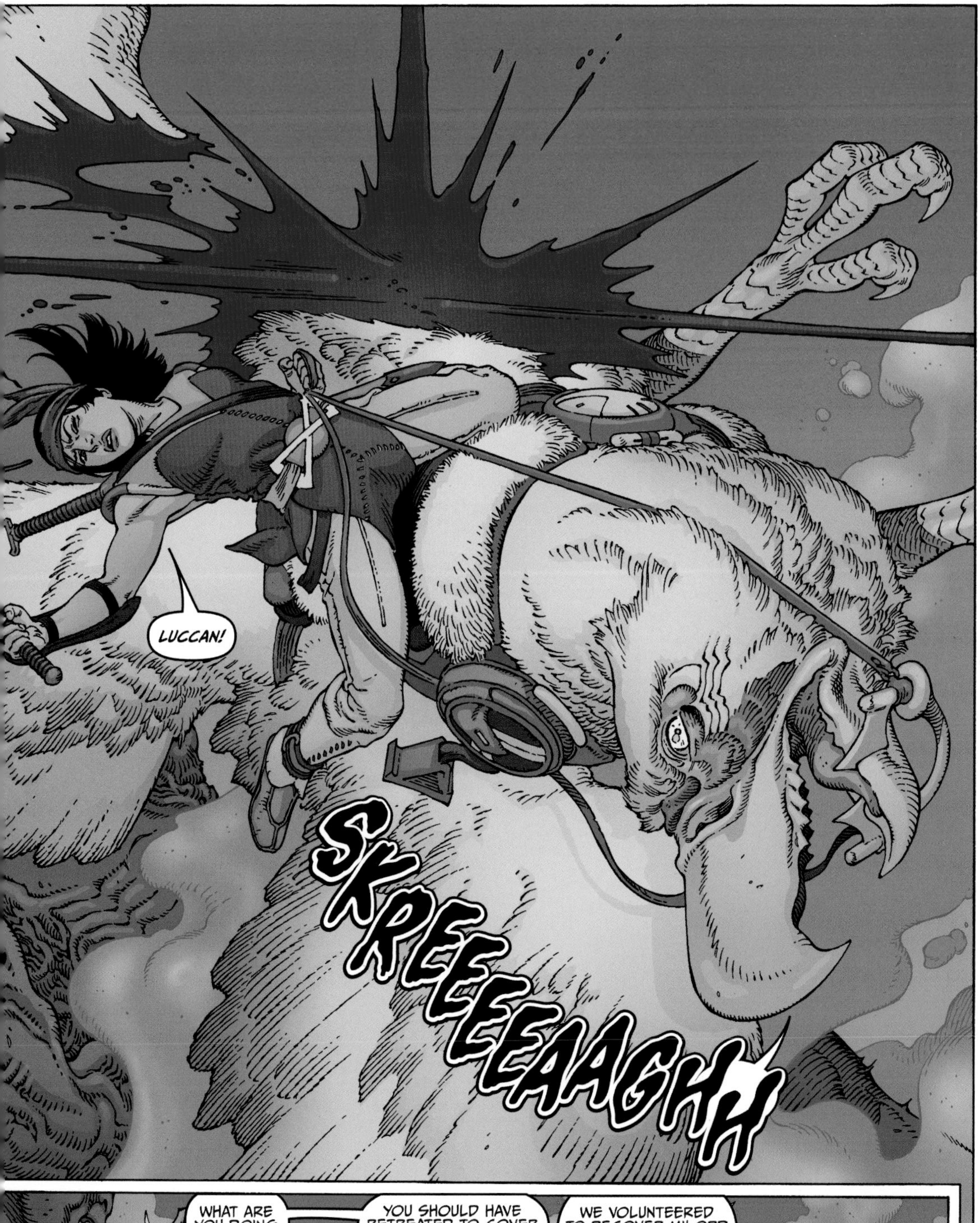
LUCCAN!
SKREEEEAAGHH

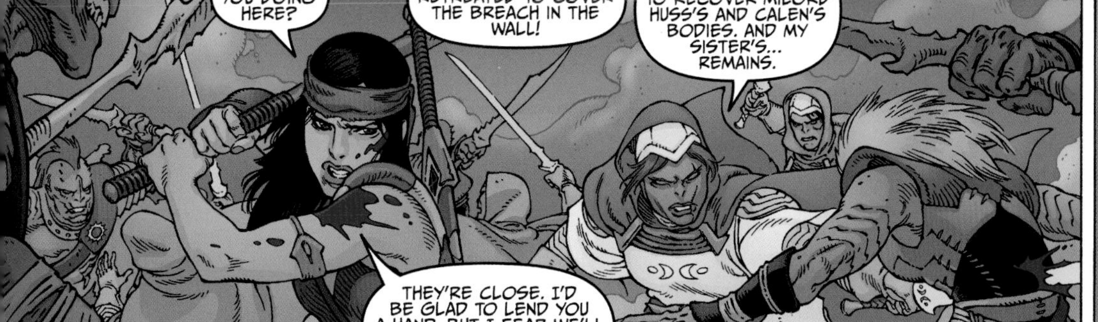
WHAT ARE YOU DOING HERE?
YOU SHOULD HAVE RETREATED TO COVER THE BREACH IN THE WALL!
WE VOLUNTEERED TO RECOVER MILORD HUSS'S AND CALEN'S BODIES. AND MY SISTER'S... REMAINS.
THEY'RE CLOSE. I'D BE GLAD TO LEND YOU A HAND. BUT I FEAR WE'LL BE JOINING OUR FALLEN FRIENDS ALL TOO SOON.

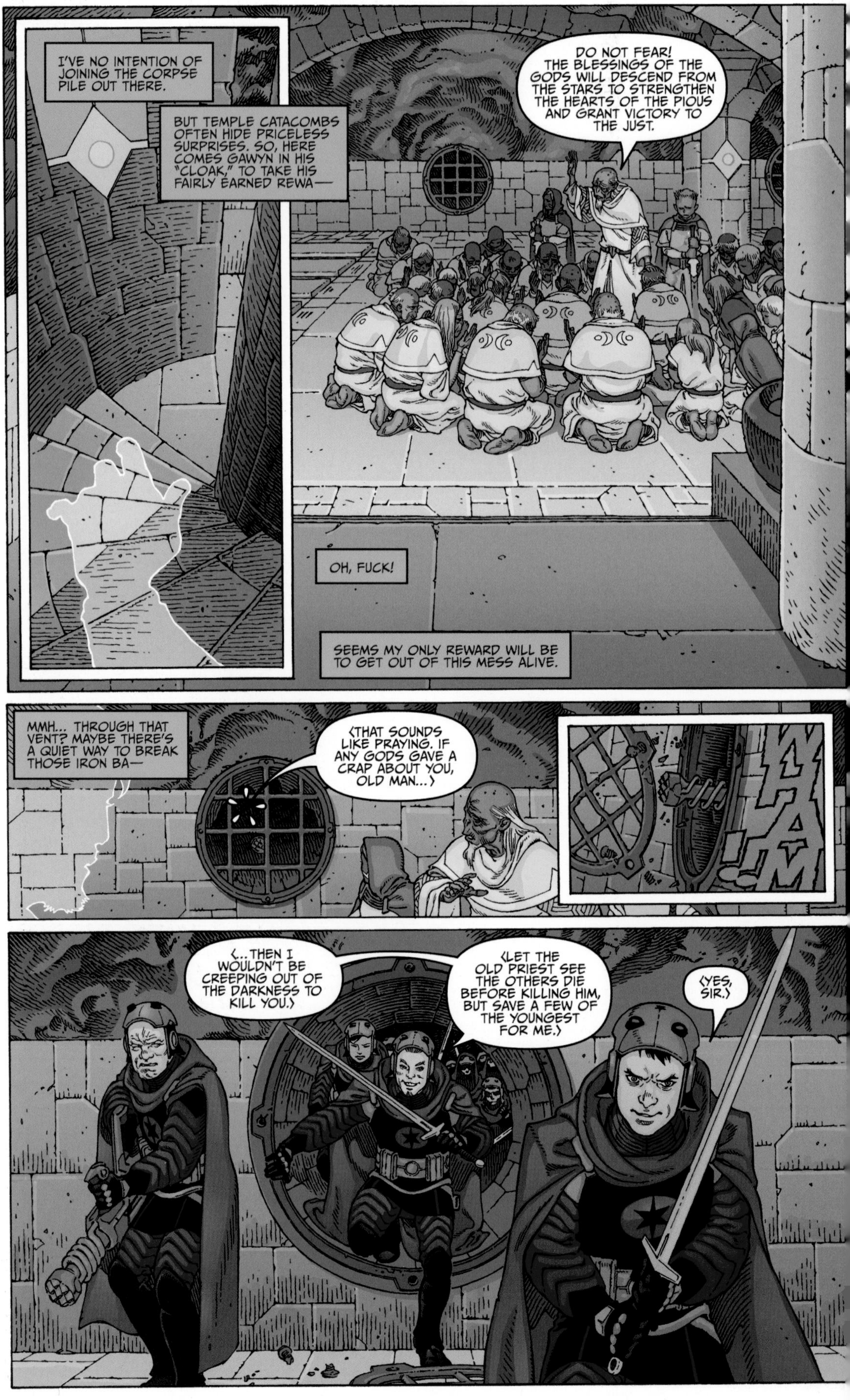
I'VE NO INTENTION OF JOINING THE CORPSE PILE OUT THERE.
BUT TEMPLE CATACOMBS OFTEN HIDE PRICELESS SURPRISES. SO, HERE COMES GAWYN IN HIS "CLOAK," TO TAKE HIS FAIRLY EARNED REWA—
DO NOT FEAR! THE BLESSINGS OF THE GODS WILL DESCEND FROM THE STARS TO STRENGTHEN THE HEARTS OF THE PIOUS AND GRANT VICTORY TO THE JUST.
OH, FUCK!
SEEMS MY ONLY REWARD WILL BE TO GET OUT OF THIS MESS ALIVE.
MMH... THROUGH THAT VENT? MAYBE THERE'S A QUIET WAY TO BREAK THOSE IRON BA—
⟨THAT SOUNDS LIKE PRAYING. IF ANY GODS GAVE A CRAP ABOUT YOU, OLD MAN...⟩
WHAM
⟨...THEN I WOULDN'T BE CREEPING OUT OF THE DARKNESS TO KILL YOU.⟩
⟨LET THE OLD PRIEST SEE THE OTHERS DIE BEFORE KILLING HIM, BUT SAVE A FEW OF THE YOUNGEST FOR ME.⟩
⟨YES, SIR.⟩

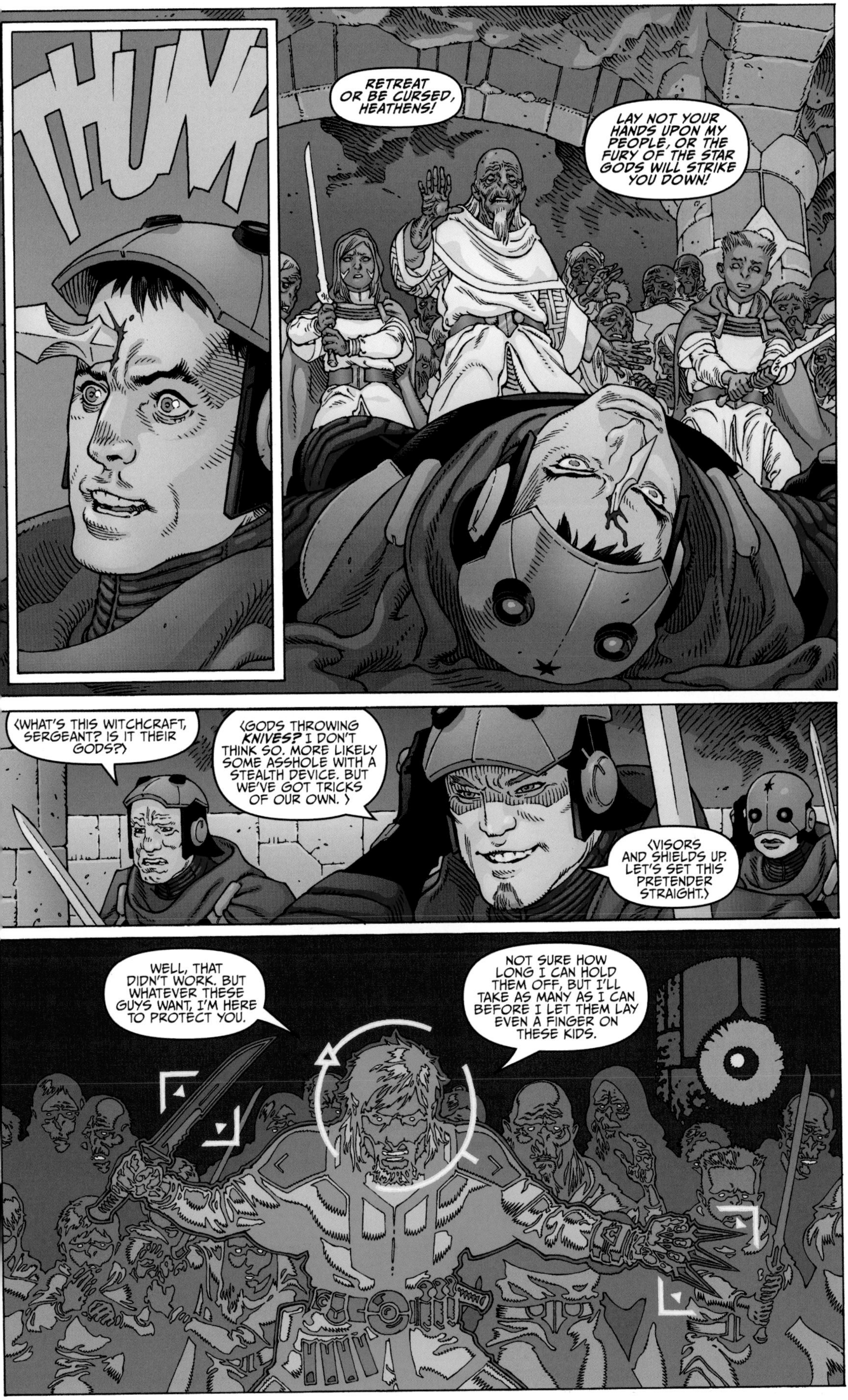
THUNK
RETREAT OR BE CURSED, HEATHENS!
LAY NOT YOUR HANDS UPON MY PEOPLE, OR THE FURY OF THE STAR GODS WILL STRIKE YOU DOWN!
‹WHAT'S THIS WITCHCRAFT, SERGEANT? IS IT THEIR GODS?›
‹GODS THROWING *KNIVES?* I DON'T THINK SO. MORE LIKELY SOME ASSHOLE WITH A STEALTH DEVICE. BUT WE'VE GOT TRICKS OF OUR OWN.›
‹VISORS AND SHIELDS UP. LET'S SET THIS PRETENDER STRAIGHT.›
WELL, THAT DIDN'T WORK. BUT WHATEVER THESE GUYS WANT, I'M HERE TO PROTECT YOU.
NOT SURE HOW LONG I CAN HOLD THEM OFF, BUT I'LL TAKE AS MANY AS I CAN BEFORE I LET THEM LAY EVEN A FINGER ON THESE KIDS.

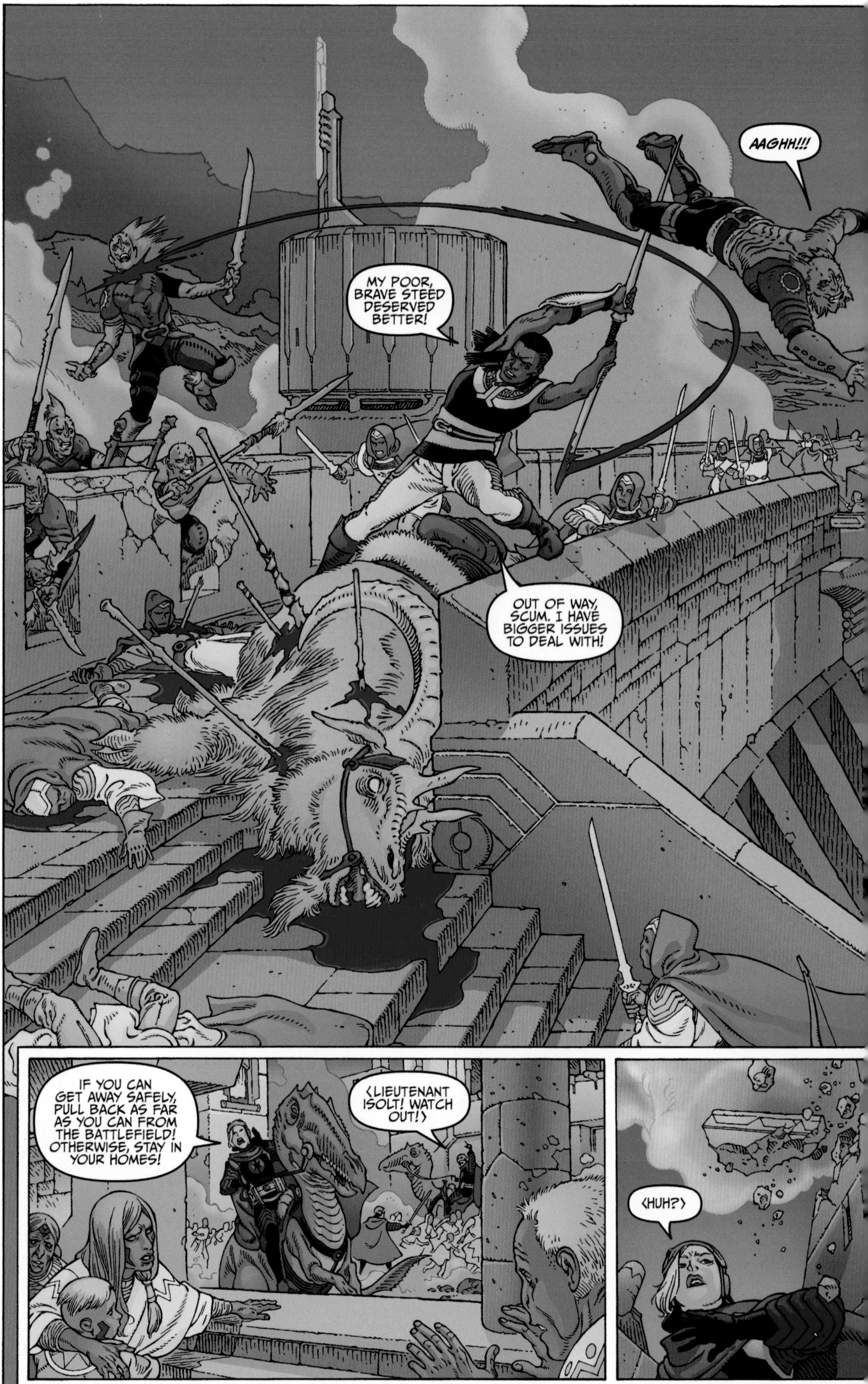
AAGHH!!!
MY POOR, BRAVE STEED DESERVED BETTER!
OUT OF WAY, SCUM. I HAVE BIGGER ISSUES TO DEAL WITH!
IF YOU CAN GET AWAY SAFELY, PULL BACK AS FAR AS YOU CAN FROM THE BATTLEFIELD! OTHERWISE, STAY IN YOUR HOMES!
<LIEUTENANT ISOLT! WATCH OUT!>
<HUH?>

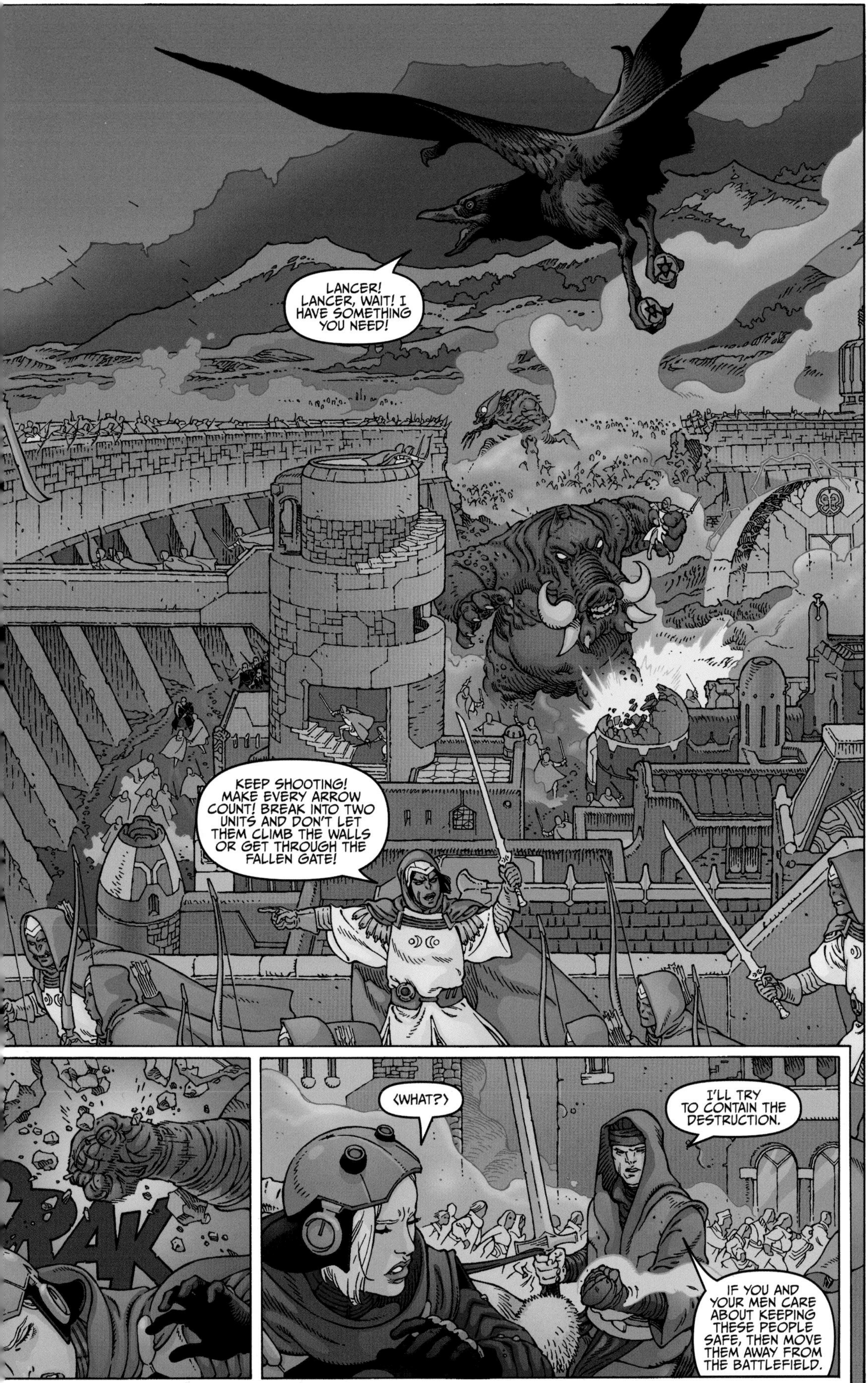
LANCER! LANCER, WAIT! I HAVE SOMETHING YOU NEED!
KEEP SHOOTING! MAKE EVERY ARROW COUNT! BREAK INTO TWO UNITS AND DON'T LET THEM CLIMB THE WALLS OR GET THROUGH THE FALLEN GATE!
RAK
‹WHAT?›
I'LL TRY TO CONTAIN THE DESTRUCTION.
IF YOU AND YOUR MEN CARE ABOUT KEEPING THESE PEOPLE SAFE, THEN MOVE THEM AWAY FROM THE BATTLEFIELD.

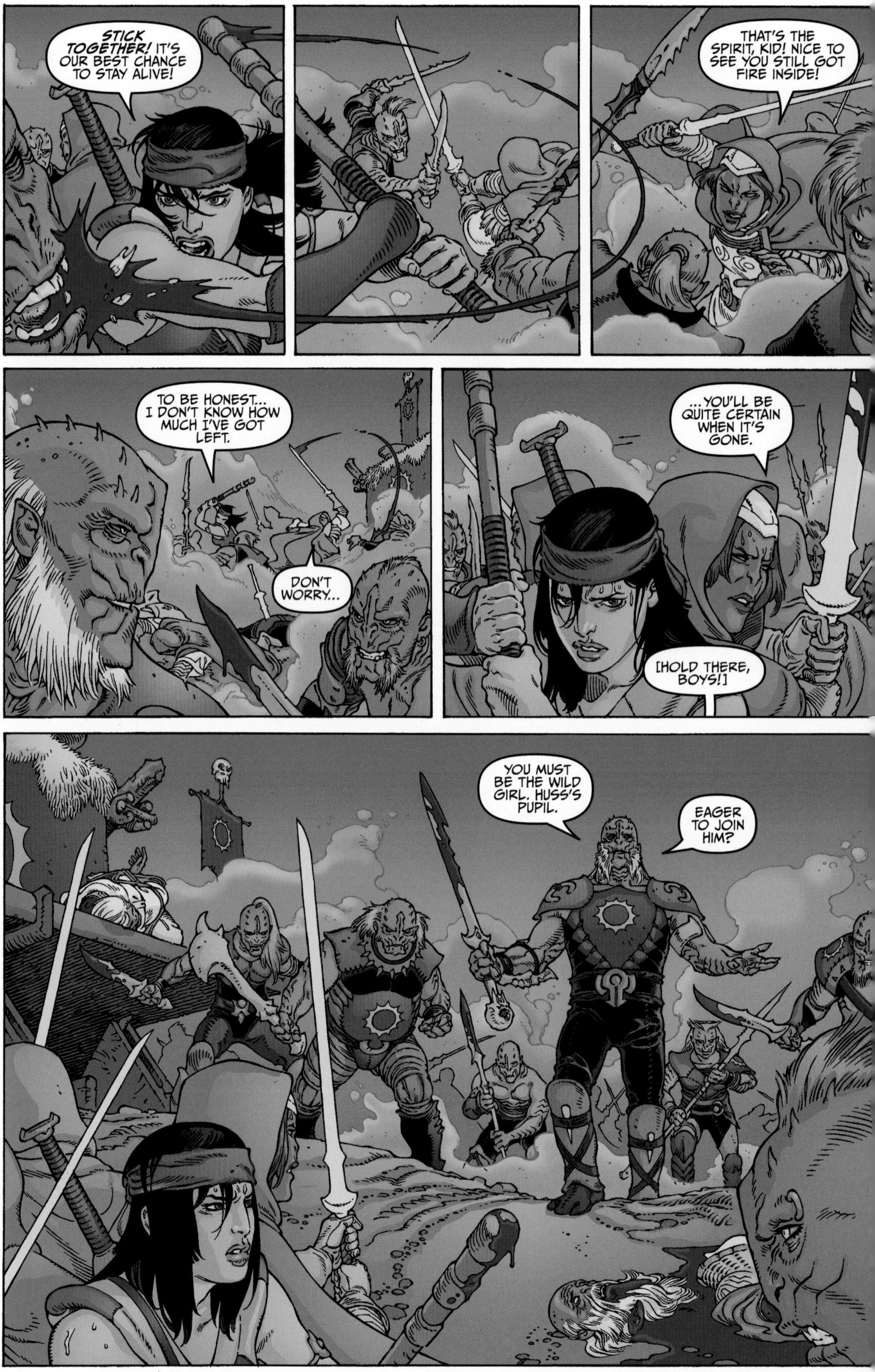
STICK TOGETHER! IT'S OUR BEST CHANCE TO STAY ALIVE!
THAT'S THE SPIRIT, KID! NICE TO SEE YOU STILL GOT FIRE INSIDE!
TO BE HONEST... I DON'T KNOW HOW MUCH I'VE GOT LEFT.
DON'T WORRY...
...YOU'LL BE QUITE CERTAIN WHEN IT'S GONE.
[HOLD THERE, BOYS!]
YOU MUST BE THE WILD GIRL. HUSS'S PUPIL.
EAGER TO JOIN HIM?

BROKEN OATHS, BROKEN WARRIORS

ALMOST THERE...

...THAT'S YOUR LAST BLOW. I'VE GOT YOU NOW!

INCOMING!

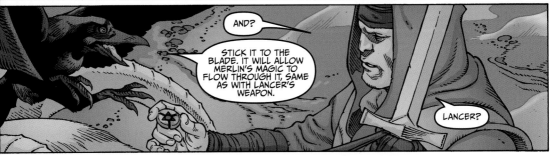

AND?

STICK IT TO THE BLADE. IT WILL ALLOW MERLIN'S MAGIC TO FLOW THROUGH IT, SAME AS WITH LANCER'S WEAPON.

LANCER?

YEEEEHAAAAA!

AAGGGGHH!

⟨MILORD!⟩

⟨ONE PUPPET'S DEAD. SOMEONE— *SOMETHING*—STRONG ENOUGH TO MATCH THE POWER OF THE RING.⟩

⟨MUST BE THAT OLD BASTARD'S STAFF. WE HAVE TO STOP HIM!⟩

⟨DON'T WORRY, MILORD.⟩

⟨GORICE IS ON HIM...⟩

"⟨...AND SHARING HIS LOCATION DATA.⟩"

YES, LANCER, YES! ONE DOWN, TWO MORE TO GO!

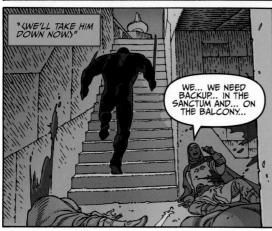

"⟨WE'LL TAKE HIM DOWN NOW.⟩"

WE... WE NEED BACKUP... IN THE SANCTUM AND... ON THE BALCONY...

HEY, WAIT! AT LEAST ONE OF YOU SHOULD HEAD OUT TO HELP AVAL—

86

AAAARRGHH!

THEY'RE HEADING TO THE SANCTUM...

...WE COULDN'T STOP THEM... THE GIANT...

DON'T WORRY, WE'RE ON IT!

THERE! STOP HIM!

TAKE HIM BACK TO THE SANCTUM.

YOU'RE NO... MATCH FOR THIS ONE... TOO DAMN LATE...

"WE'LL JOIN SAMSON AND MAKE OUR LAST STAND THERE.

"WE MUST PROTECT THE STAR CRYSTAL AT ALL COSTS."

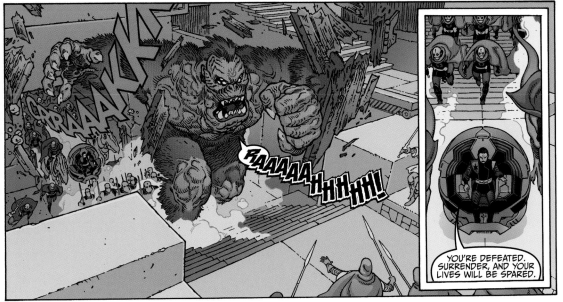

GRAAAKK!

GRAAAA

RAAAAAHHHHH!

YOU'RE DEFEATED. SURRENDER, AND YOUR LIVES WILL BE SPARED.

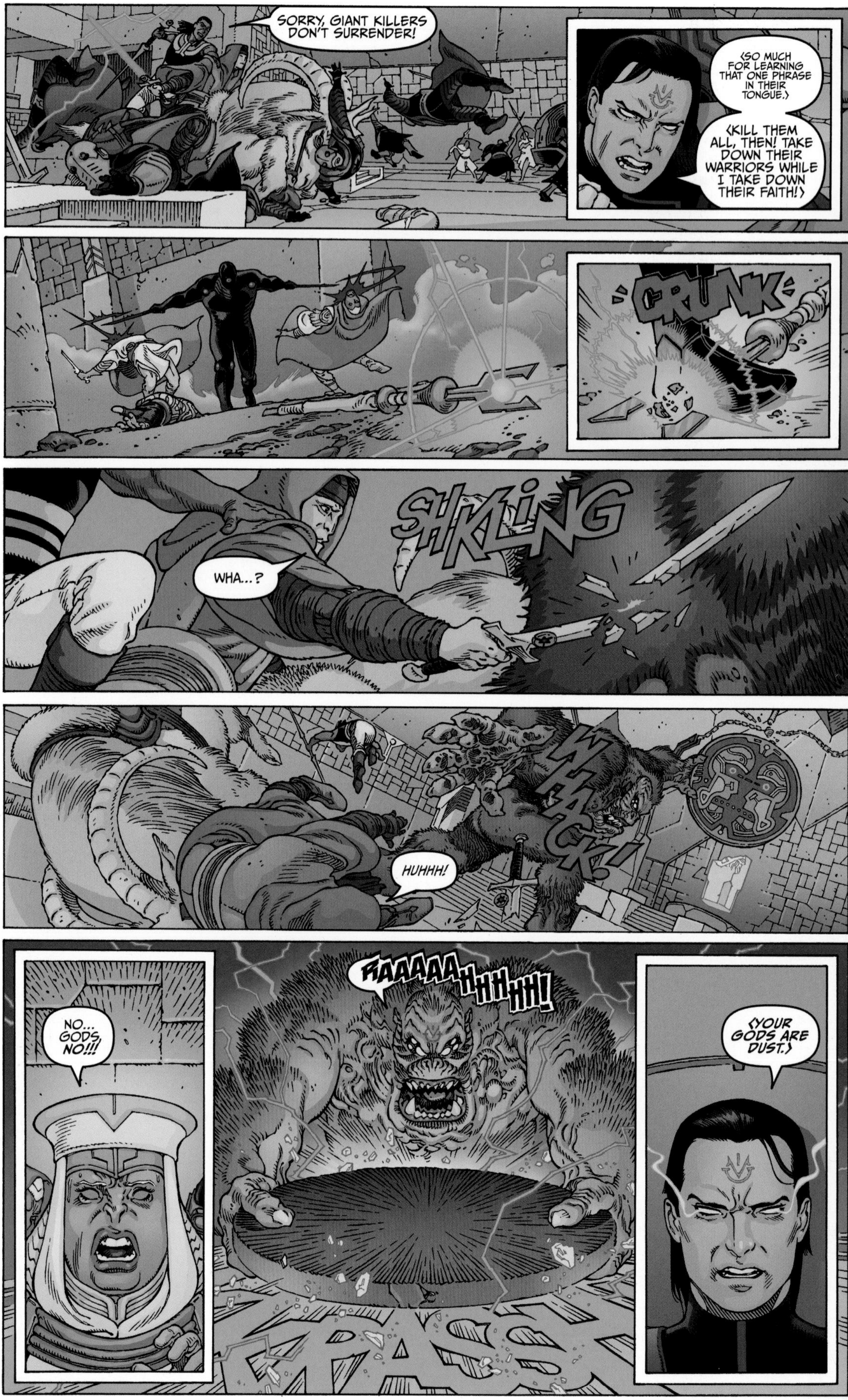

SORRY, GIANT KILLERS DON'T SURRENDER!
‹SO MUCH FOR LEARNING THAT ONE PHRASE IN THEIR TONGUE.›
‹KILL THEM ALL, THEN! TAKE DOWN THEIR WARRIORS WHILE I TAKE DOWN THEIR FAITH!›
CRUNK
SHKLING
WHA...?
WHACK!
HUHHH!
NO... GODS, NO!!!
RAAAAAHHHHH!
‹YOUR GODS ARE DUST.›

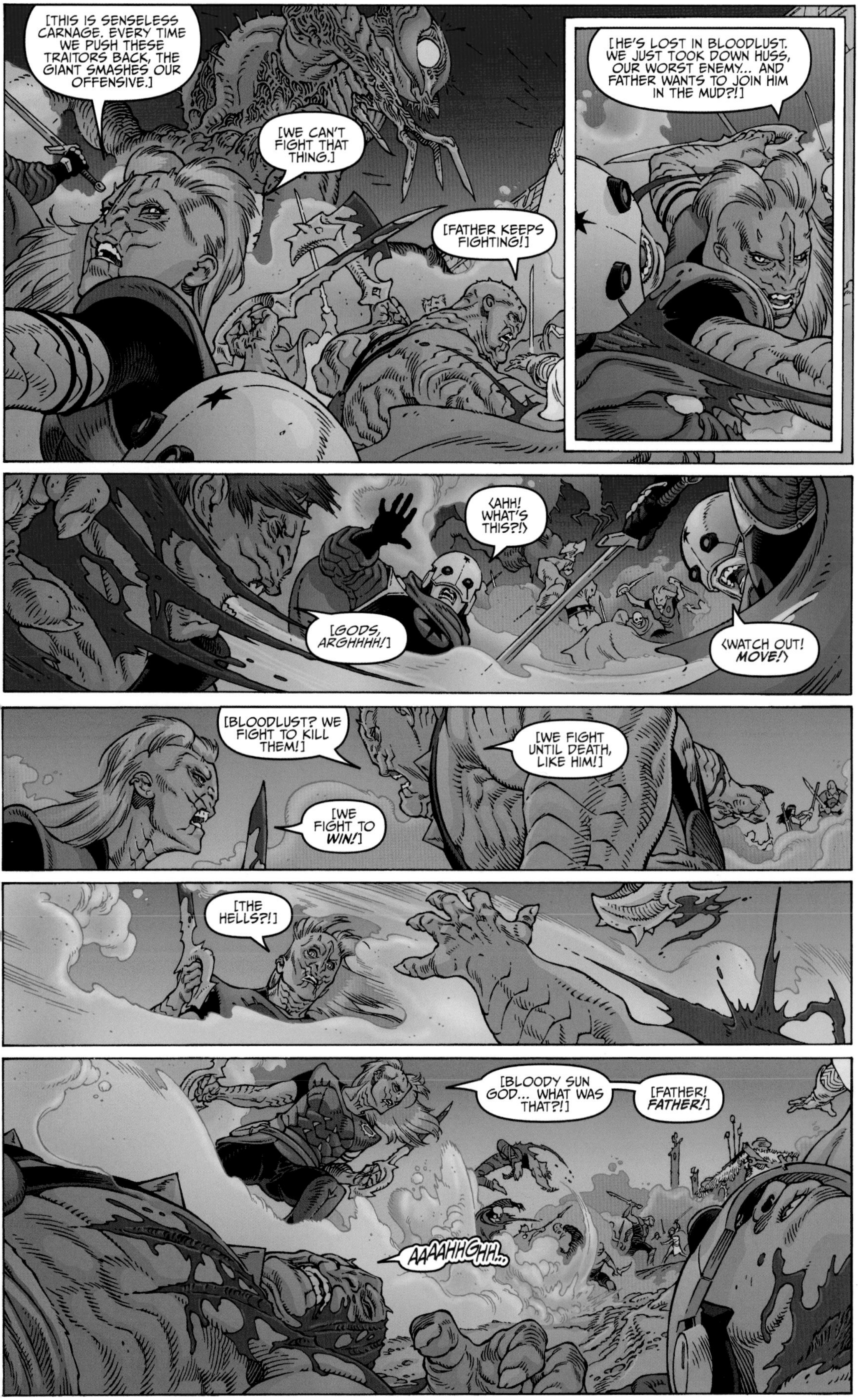

[THIS IS SENSELESS CARNAGE. EVERY TIME WE PUSH THESE TRAITORS BACK, THE GIANT SMASHES OUR OFFENSIVE.]
[WE CAN'T FIGHT THAT THING.]
[FATHER KEEPS FIGHTING!]
[HE'S LOST IN BLOODLUST. WE JUST TOOK DOWN HUSS, OUR WORST ENEMY... AND FATHER WANTS TO JOIN HIM IN THE MUD?!]
<AHH! WHAT'S THIS?!>
[GODS, ARGHHHH!]
<WATCH OUT! *MOVE!*>
[BLOODLUST? WE FIGHT TO KILL THEM!]
[WE FIGHT UNTIL DEATH, LIKE HIM!]
[WE FIGHT TO *WIN!*]
[THE HELLS?!]
[BLOODY SUN GOD... WHAT WAS THAT?!]
[FATHER! *FATHER!*]
AAAAHHGHH...

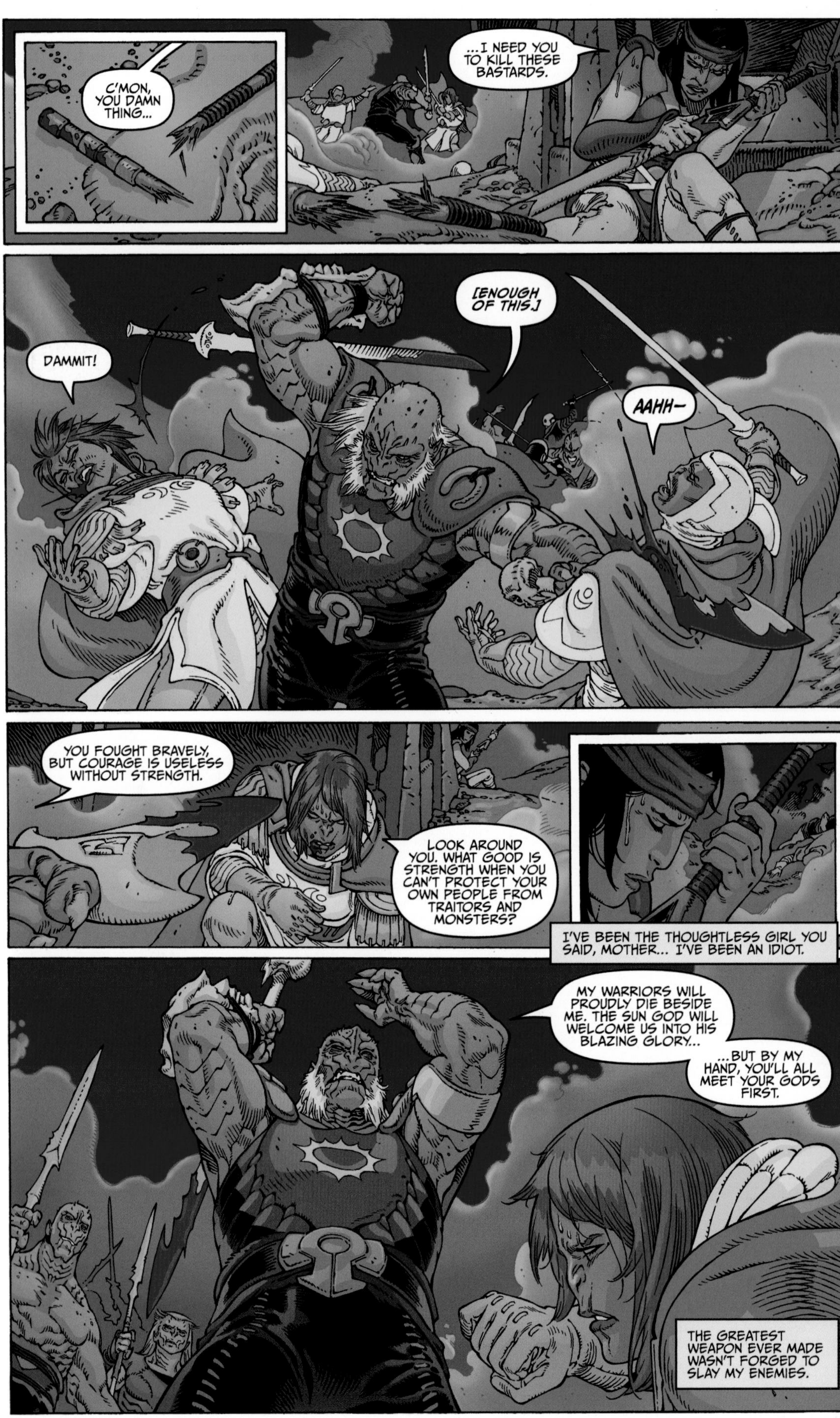
C'MON, YOU DAMN THING...
...I NEED YOU TO KILL THESE BASTARDS.
DAMMIT!
[ENOUGH OF THIS.]
AAHH-
YOU FOUGHT BRAVELY, BUT COURAGE IS USELESS WITHOUT STRENGTH.
LOOK AROUND YOU. WHAT GOOD IS STRENGTH WHEN YOU CAN'T PROTECT YOUR OWN PEOPLE FROM TRAITORS AND MONSTERS?
I'VE BEEN THE THOUGHTLESS GIRL YOU SAID, MOTHER... I'VE BEEN AN IDIOT.
MY WARRIORS WILL PROUDLY DIE BESIDE ME. THE SUN GOD WILL WELCOME US INTO HIS BLAZING GLORY...
...BUT BY MY HAND, YOU'LL ALL MEET YOUR GODS FIRST.
THE GREATEST WEAPON EVER MADE WASN'T FORGED TO SLAY MY ENEMIES.

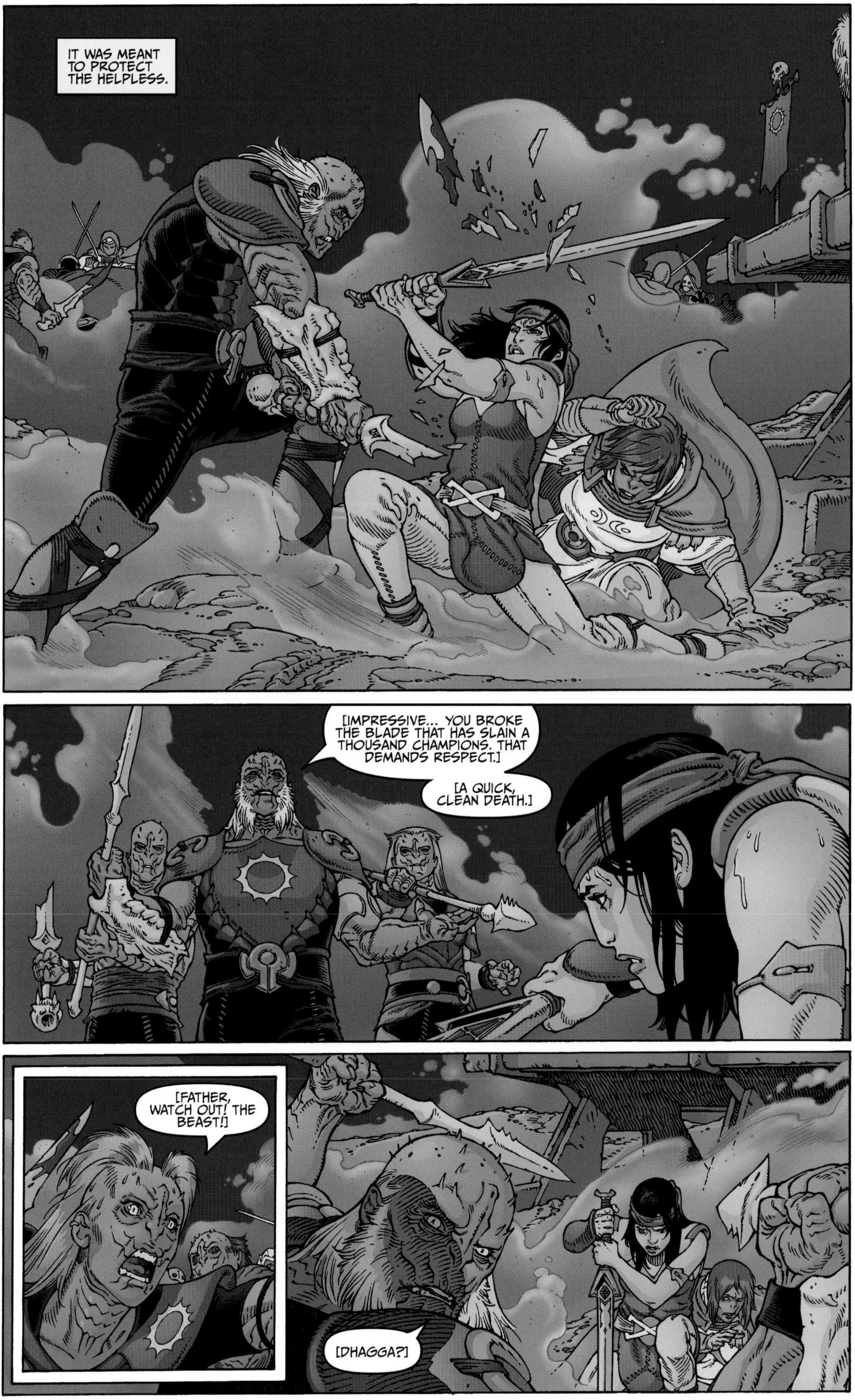
IT WAS MEANT TO PROTECT THE HELPLESS.
[IMPRESSIVE... YOU BROKE THE BLADE THAT HAS SLAIN A THOUSAND CHAMPIONS. THAT DEMANDS RESPECT.]
[A QUICK, CLEAN DEATH.]
[FATHER, WATCH OUT! THE BEAST!]
[DHAGGA?]

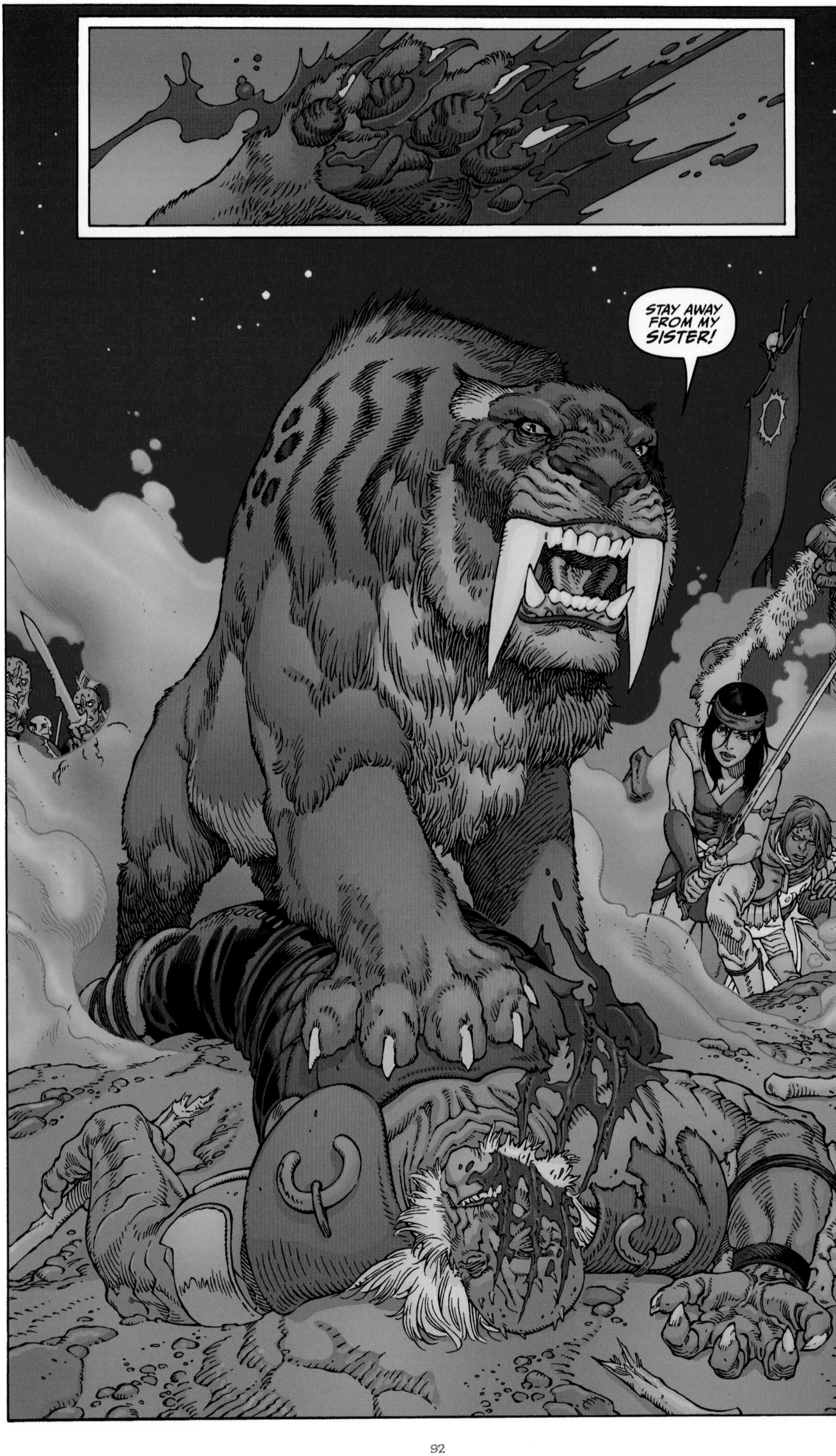
STAY AWAY FROM MY SISTER!

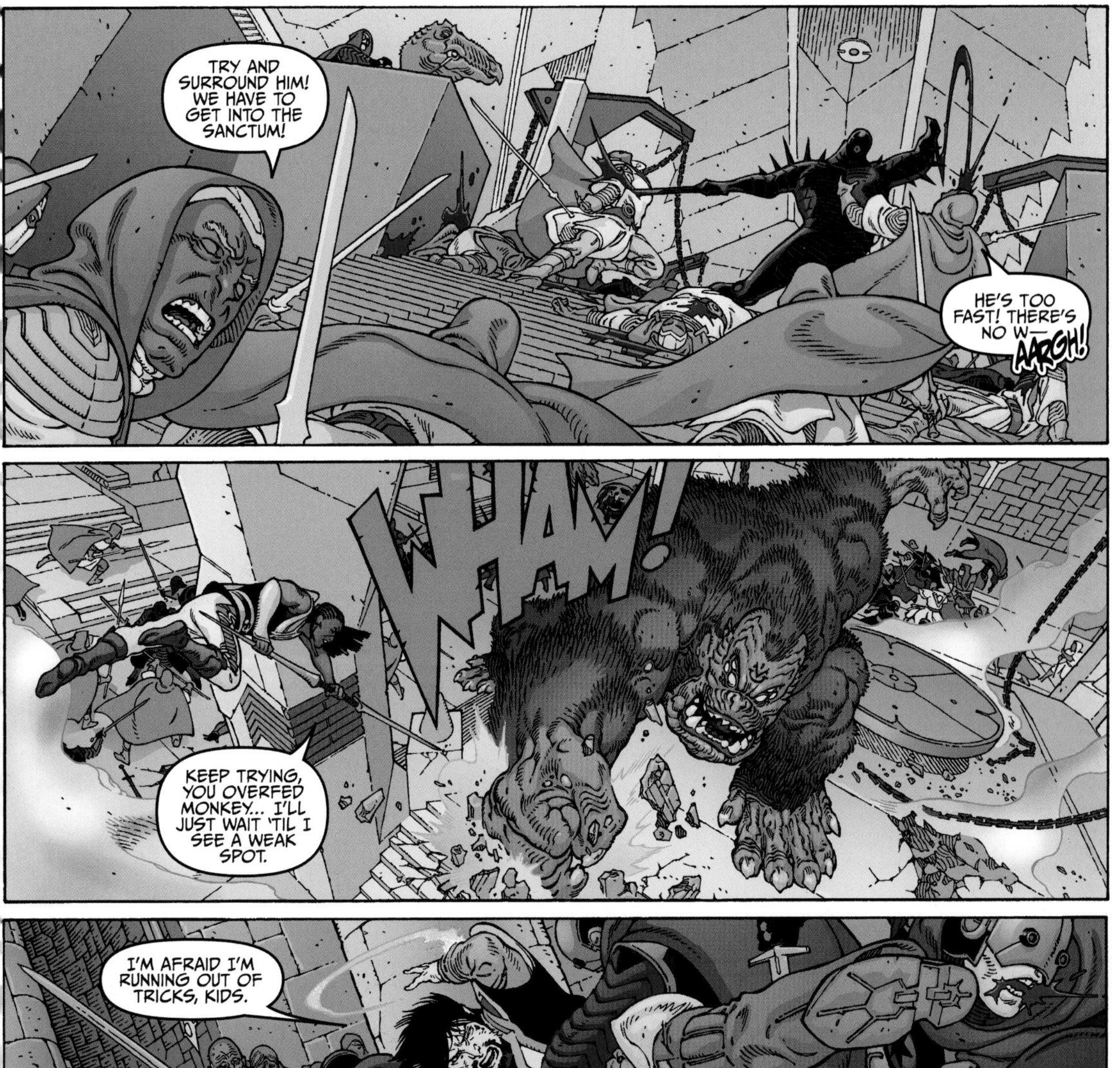
TRY AND SURROUND HIM! WE HAVE TO GET INTO THE SANCTUM!
HE'S TOO FAST! THERE'S NO W—
AARGH!
WHAM!
KEEP TRYING, YOU OVERFED MONKEY... I'LL JUST WAIT 'TIL I SEE A WEAK SPOT.
I'M AFRAID I'M RUNNING OUT OF TRICKS, KIDS.
BE READY TO RUN BACK UPSTAIRS. AND PRAY THAT IT'S SAFER UP THERE THAN IT IS DOWN HERE.

LAST STAND

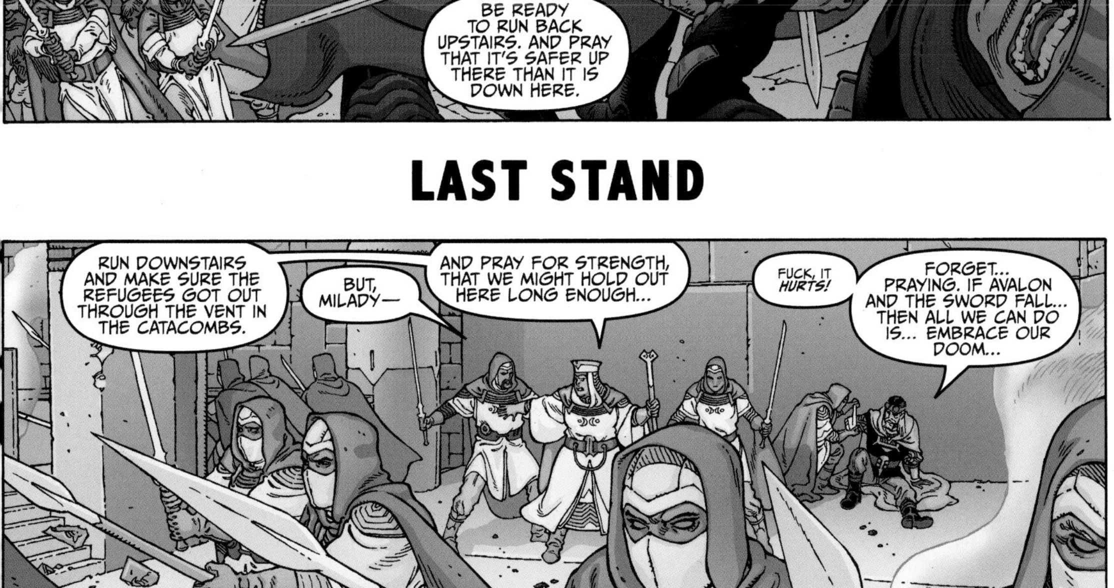
RUN DOWNSTAIRS AND MAKE SURE THE REFUGEES GOT OUT THROUGH THE VENT IN THE CATACOMBS.
BUT, MILADY—
AND PRAY FOR STRENGTH, THAT WE MIGHT HOLD OUT HERE LONG ENOUGH...
FUCK, IT *HURTS!*
FORGET... PRAYING. IF AVALON AND THE SWORD FALL... THEN ALL WE CAN DO IS... EMBRACE OUR DOOM...

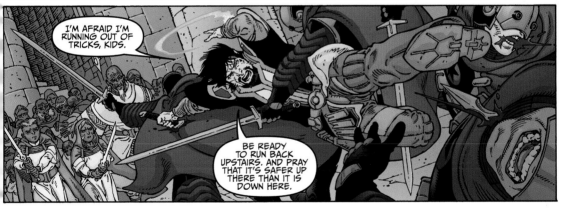

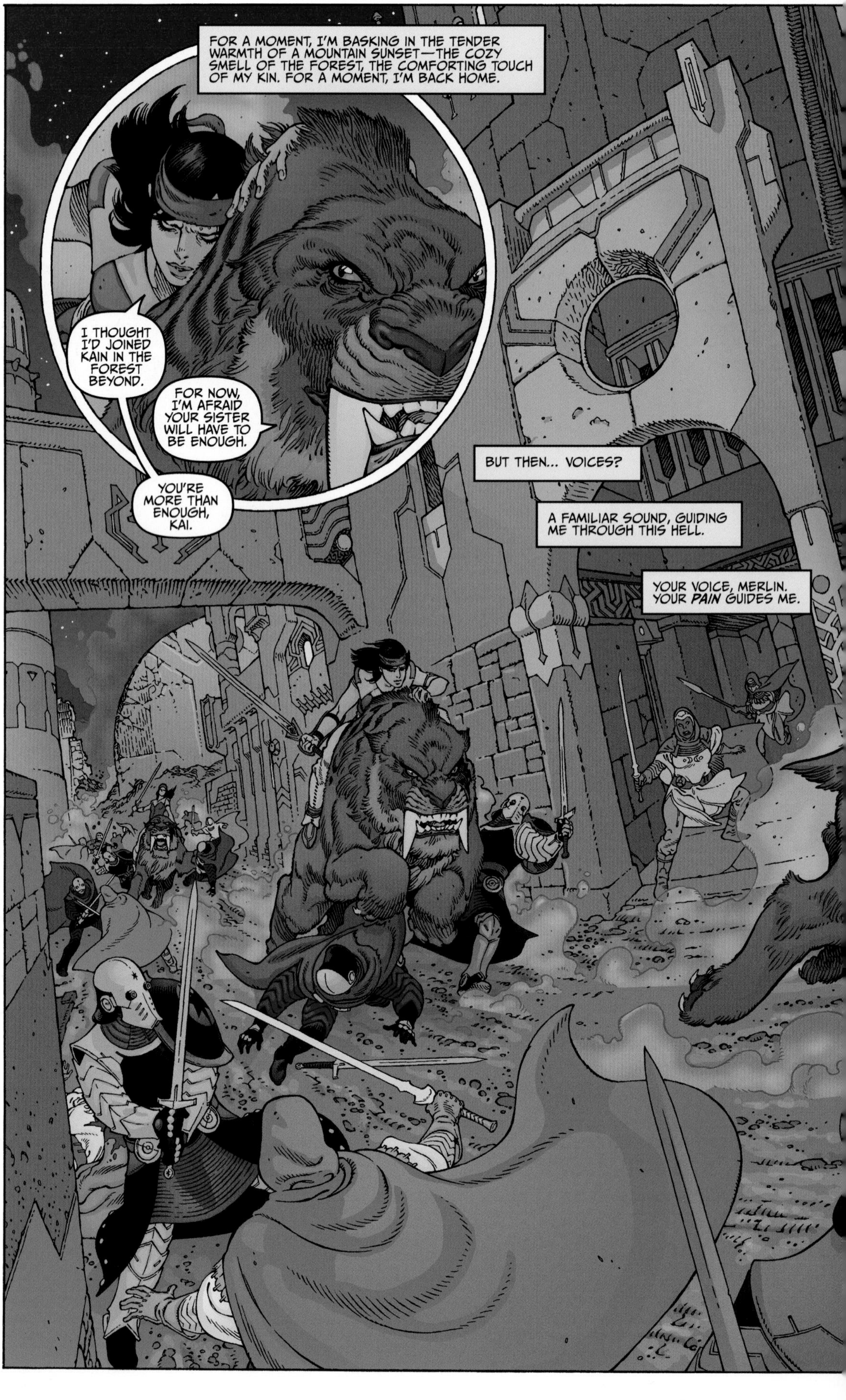
FOR A MOMENT, I'M BASKING IN THE TENDER WARMTH OF A MOUNTAIN SUNSET—THE COZY SMELL OF THE FOREST, THE COMFORTING TOUCH OF MY KIN. FOR A MOMENT, I'M BACK HOME.
I THOUGHT I'D JOINED KAIN IN THE FOREST BEYOND.
FOR NOW, I'M AFRAID YOUR SISTER WILL HAVE TO BE ENOUGH.
YOU'RE MORE THAN ENOUGH, KAI.
BUT THEN... VOICES?
A FAMILIAR SOUND, GUIDING ME THROUGH THIS HELL.
YOUR VOICE, MERLIN. YOUR *PAIN* GUIDES ME.

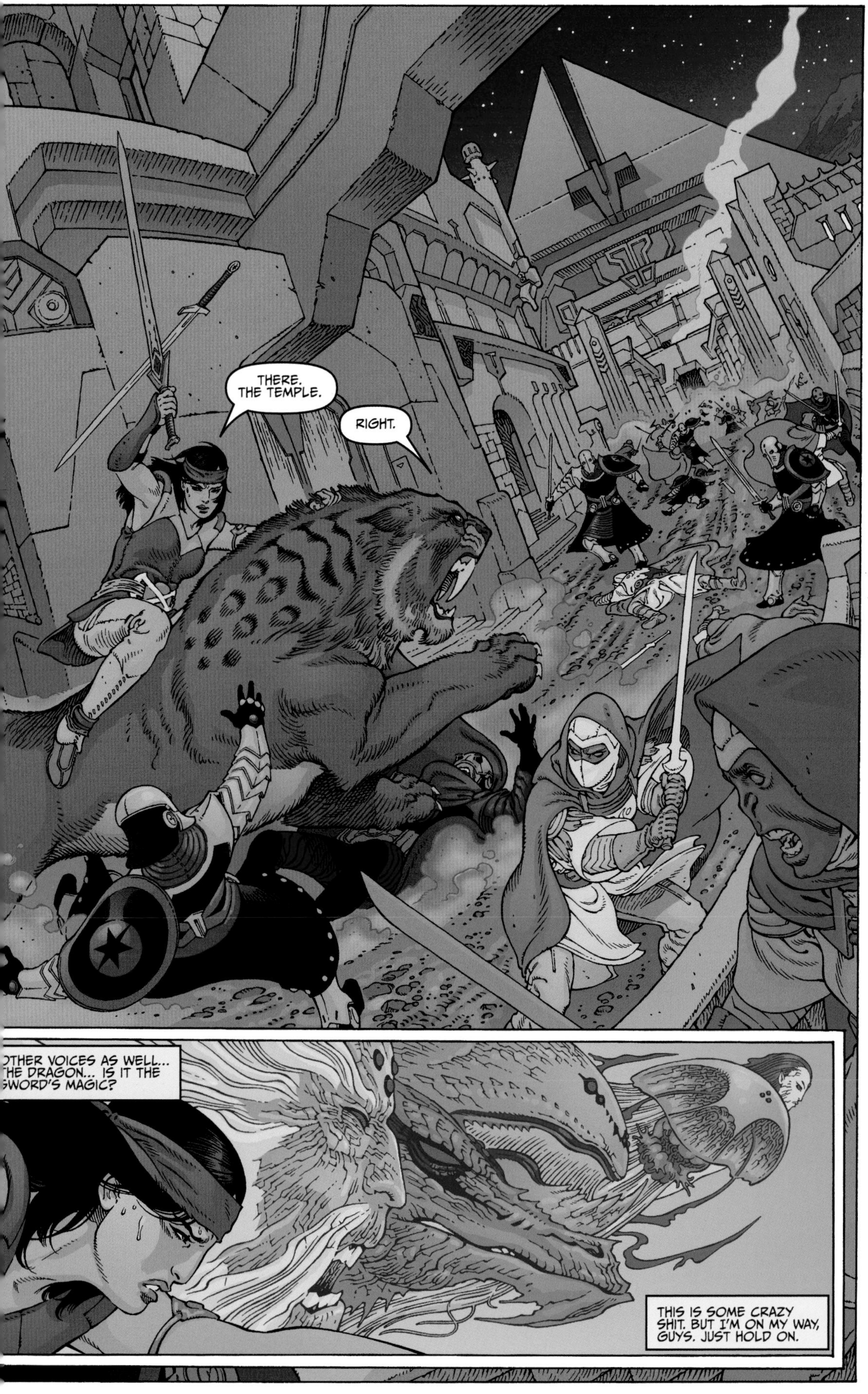
THERE. THE TEMPLE.
RIGHT.
OTHER VOICES AS WELL... THE DRAGON... IS IT THE SWORD'S MAGIC?
THIS IS SOME CRAZY SHIT. BUT I'M ON MY WAY, GUYS. JUST HOLD ON.

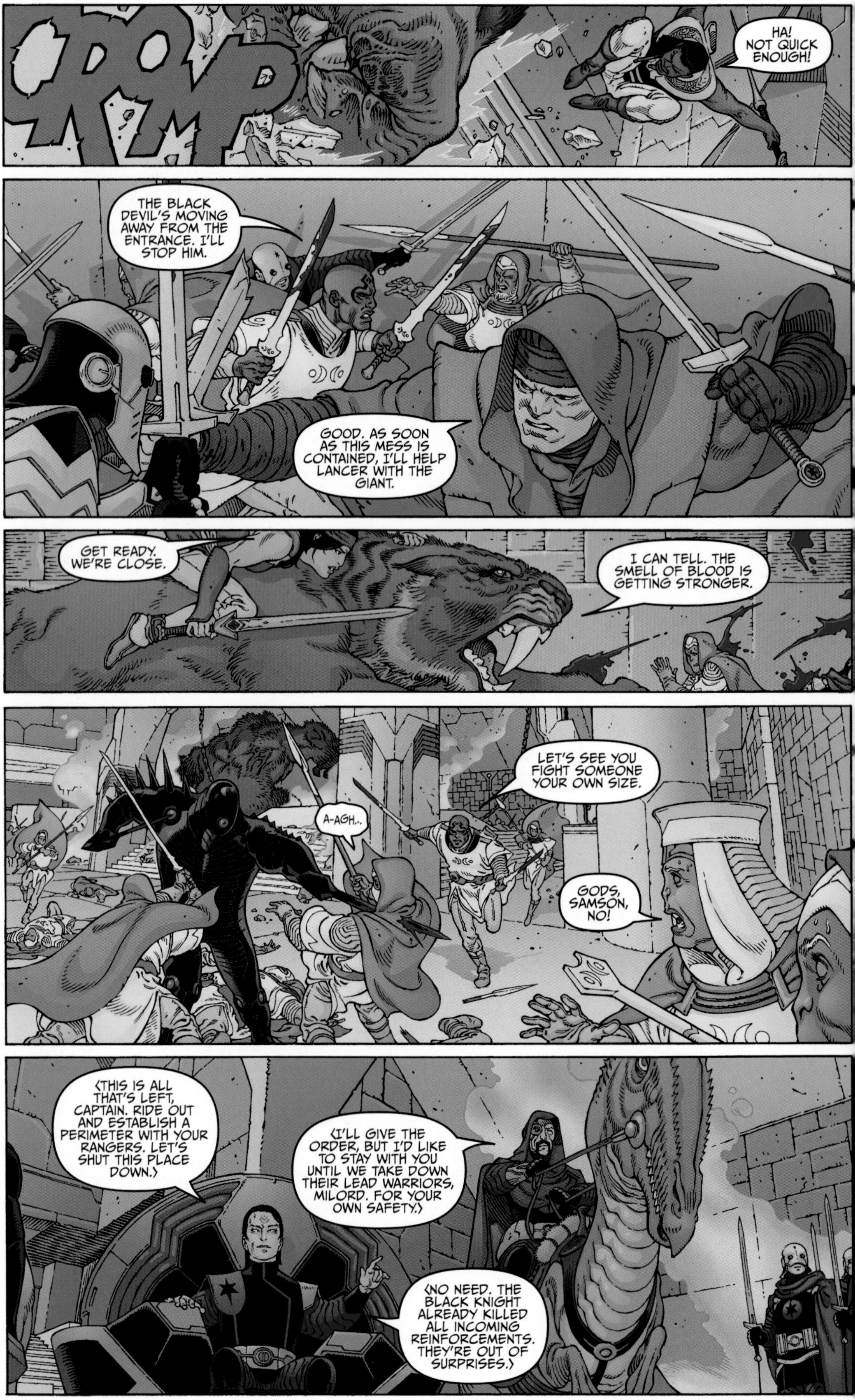
THROOMP
HA! NOT QUICK ENOUGH!
THE BLACK DEVIL'S MOVING AWAY FROM THE ENTRANCE. I'LL STOP HIM.
GOOD. AS SOON AS THIS MESS IS CONTAINED, I'LL HELP LANCER WITH THE GIANT.
GET READY. WE'RE CLOSE.
I CAN TELL. THE SMELL OF BLOOD IS GETTING STRONGER.
LET'S SEE YOU FIGHT SOMEONE YOUR OWN SIZE.
A-AGH...
GODS, SAMSON, NO!
‹THIS IS ALL THAT'S LEFT, CAPTAIN. RIDE OUT AND ESTABLISH A PERIMETER WITH YOUR RANGERS. LET'S SHUT THIS PLACE DOWN.›
‹I'LL GIVE THE ORDER, BUT I'D LIKE TO STAY WITH YOU UNTIL WE TAKE DOWN THEIR LEAD WARRIORS, MILORD. FOR YOUR OWN SAFETY.›
‹NO NEED. THE BLACK KNIGHT ALREADY KILLED ALL INCOMING REINFORCEMENTS. THEY'RE OUT OF SURPRISES.›

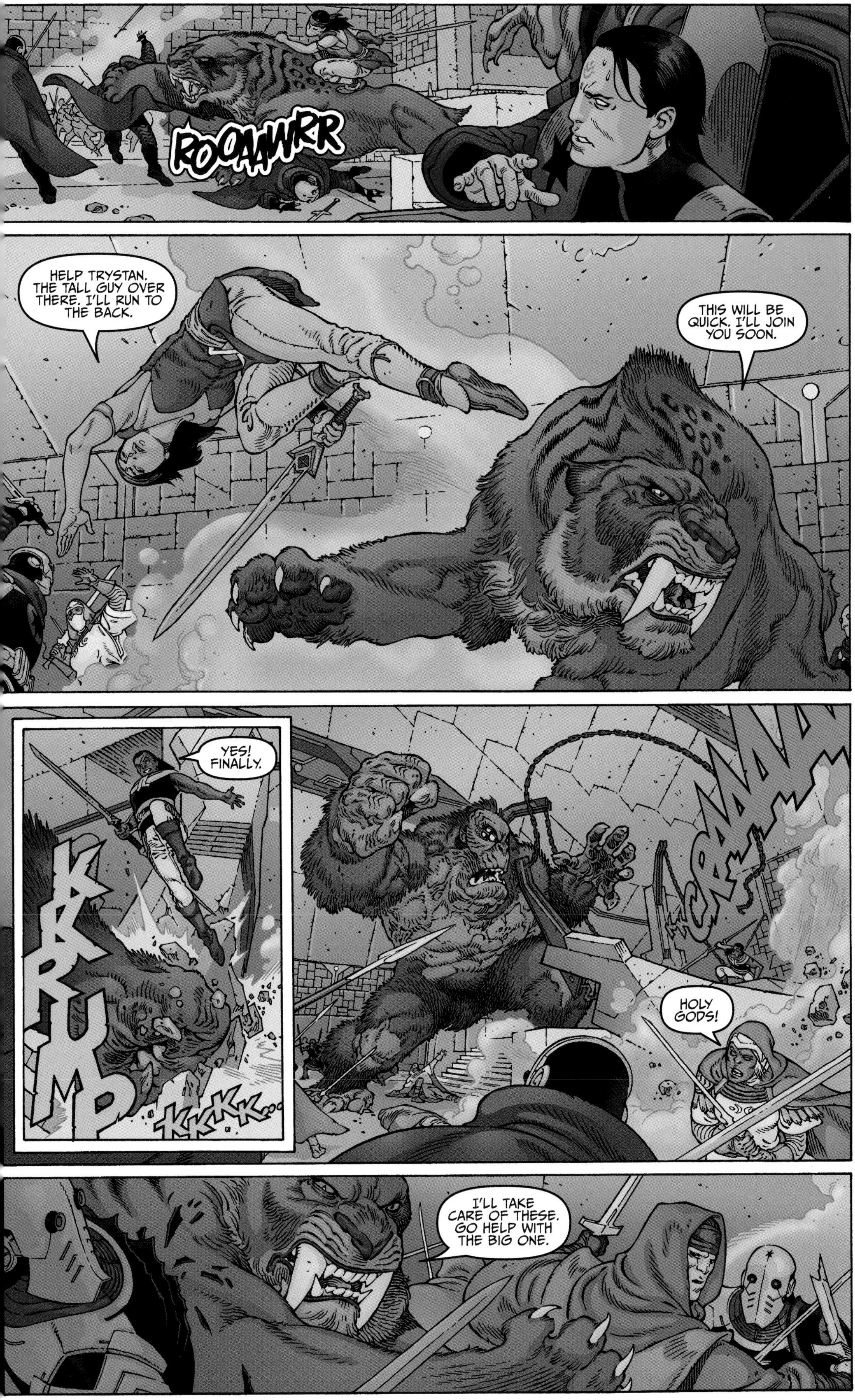
ROOAAWRR
HELP TRYSTAN. THE TALL GUY OVER THERE. I'LL RUN TO THE BACK.
THIS WILL BE QUICK. I'LL JOIN YOU SOON.
YES! FINALLY.
KRUMP
KKKK...
HOLY GODS!
I'LL TAKE CARE OF THESE. GO HELP WITH THE BIG ONE.

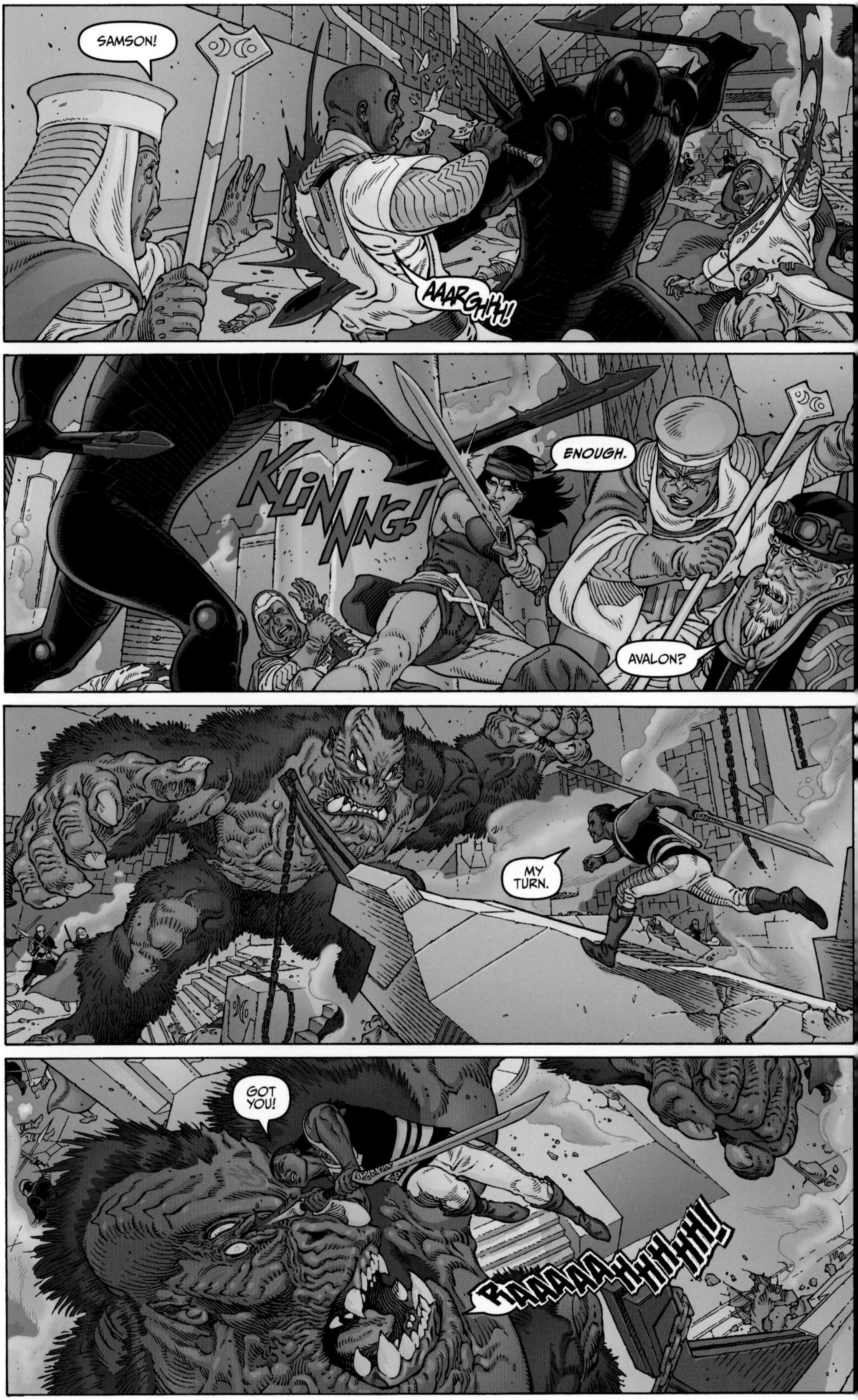
SAMSON!
AAARGHHH!
KLINNNG!
ENOUGH.
AVALON?
MY TURN.
GOT YOU!
RAAAAAHHHHH!

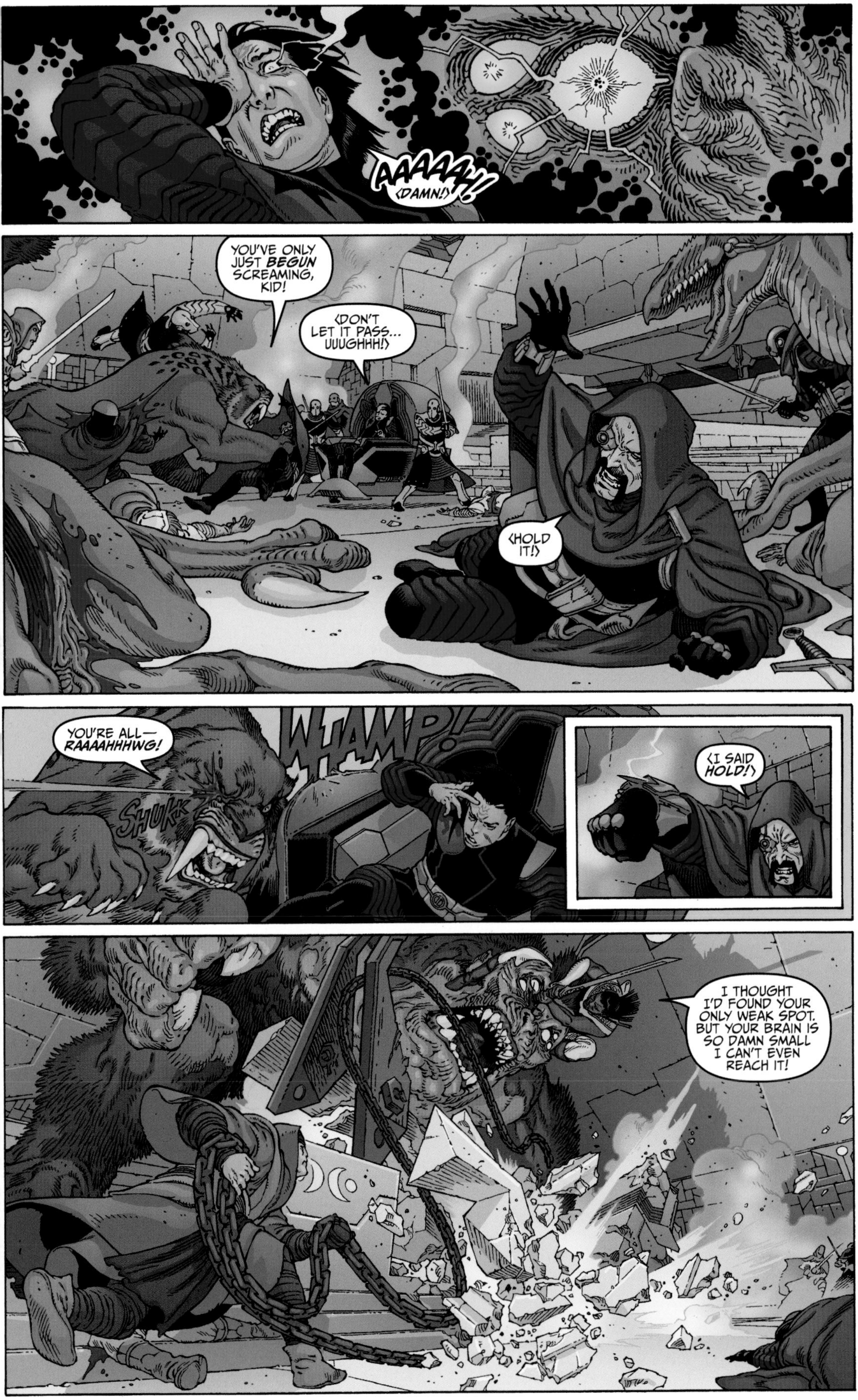
AAAAAH!!
‹DAMN!›
YOU'VE ONLY JUST BEGUN SCREAMING, KID!
‹DON'T LET IT PASS... UUUGHHH!›
‹HOLD IT!›
YOU'RE ALL— RAAAAHHHWG!
WHAMP!
SHUKK
‹I SAID HOLD!›
I THOUGHT I'D FOUND YOUR ONLY WEAK SPOT. BUT YOUR BRAIN IS SO DAMN SMALL I CAN'T EVEN REACH IT!

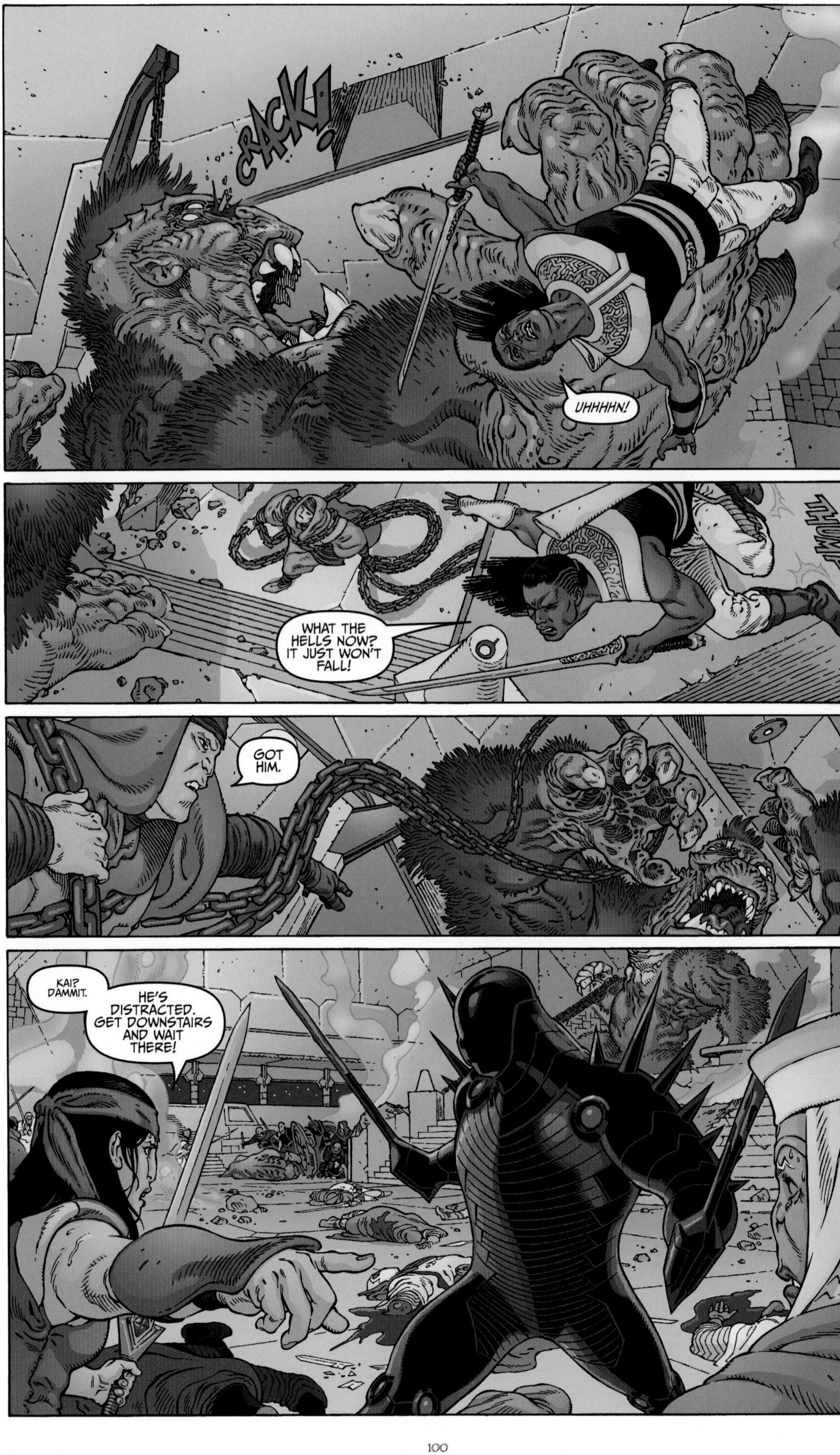
CRACK!
UHHHHN!
THUMP
WHAT THE HELLS NOW? IT JUST WON'T FALL!
GOT HIM.
KAI? DAMMIT.
HE'S DISTRACTED. GET DOWNSTAIRS AND WAIT THERE!

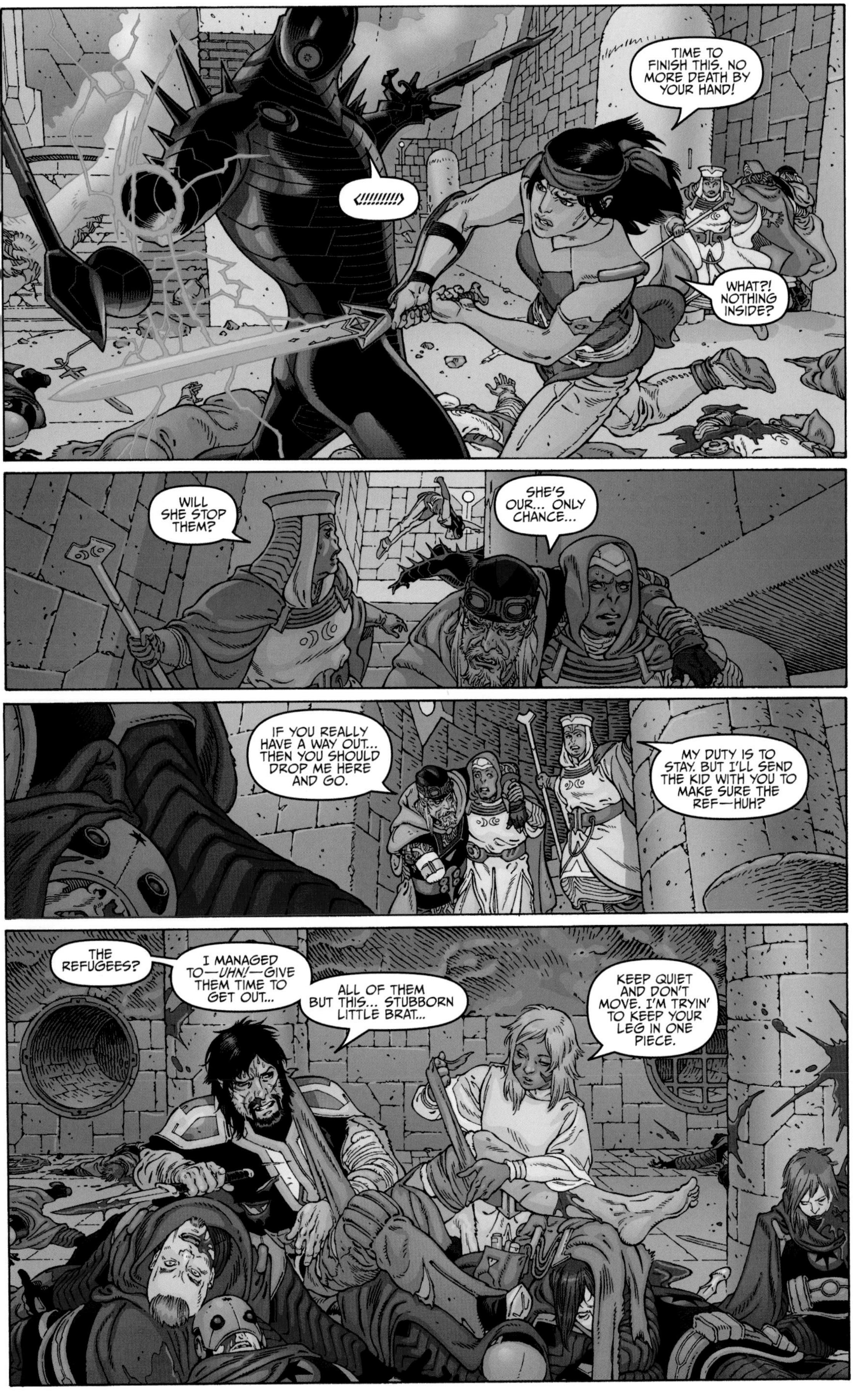

TIME TO FINISH THIS. NO MORE DEATH BY YOUR HAND!
<!!!!!!!!>
WHAT?! NOTHING INSIDE?
WILL SHE STOP THEM?
SHE'S OUR... ONLY CHANCE...
IF YOU REALLY HAVE A WAY OUT... THEN YOU SHOULD DROP ME HERE AND GO.
MY DUTY IS TO STAY. BUT I'LL SEND THE KID WITH YOU TO MAKE SURE THE REF—HUH?
THE REFUGEES?
I MANAGED TO—*UHN!*—GIVE THEM TIME TO GET OUT...
ALL OF THEM BUT THIS... STUBBORN LITTLE BRAT...
KEEP QUIET AND DON'T MOVE. I'M TRYIN' TO KEEP YOUR LEG IN ONE PIECE.

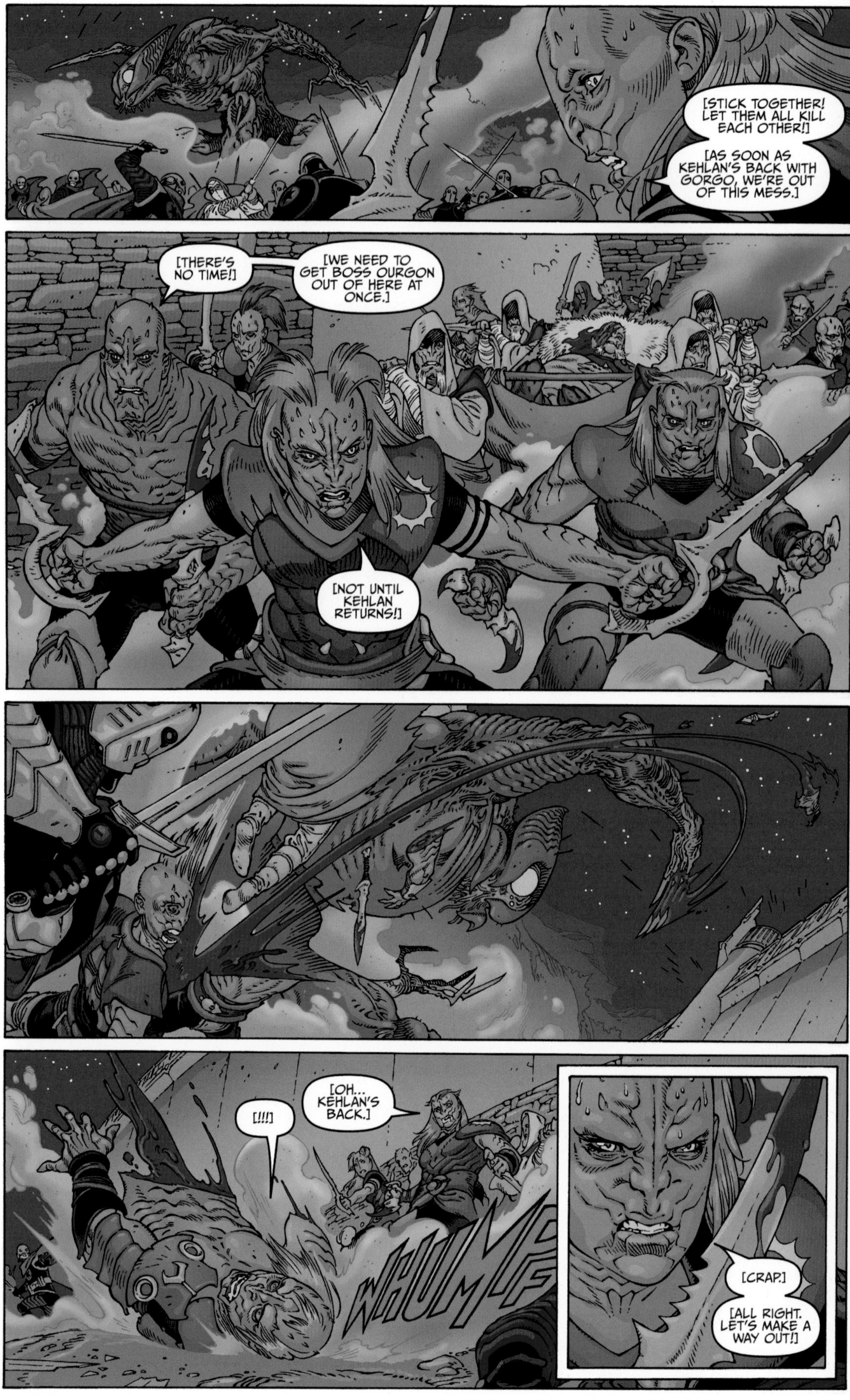
[STICK TOGETHER! LET THEM ALL KILL EACH OTHER!]
[AS SOON AS KEHLAN'S BACK WITH GORGO, WE'RE OUT OF THIS MESS.]
[THERE'S NO TIME!]
[WE NEED TO GET BOSS OURGON OUT OF HERE AT ONCE.]
[NOT UNTIL KEHLAN RETURNS!]
[!!!]
[OH... KEHLAN'S BACK.]
WHUMF
[CRAP.]
[ALL RIGHT. LET'S MAKE A WAY OUT!]

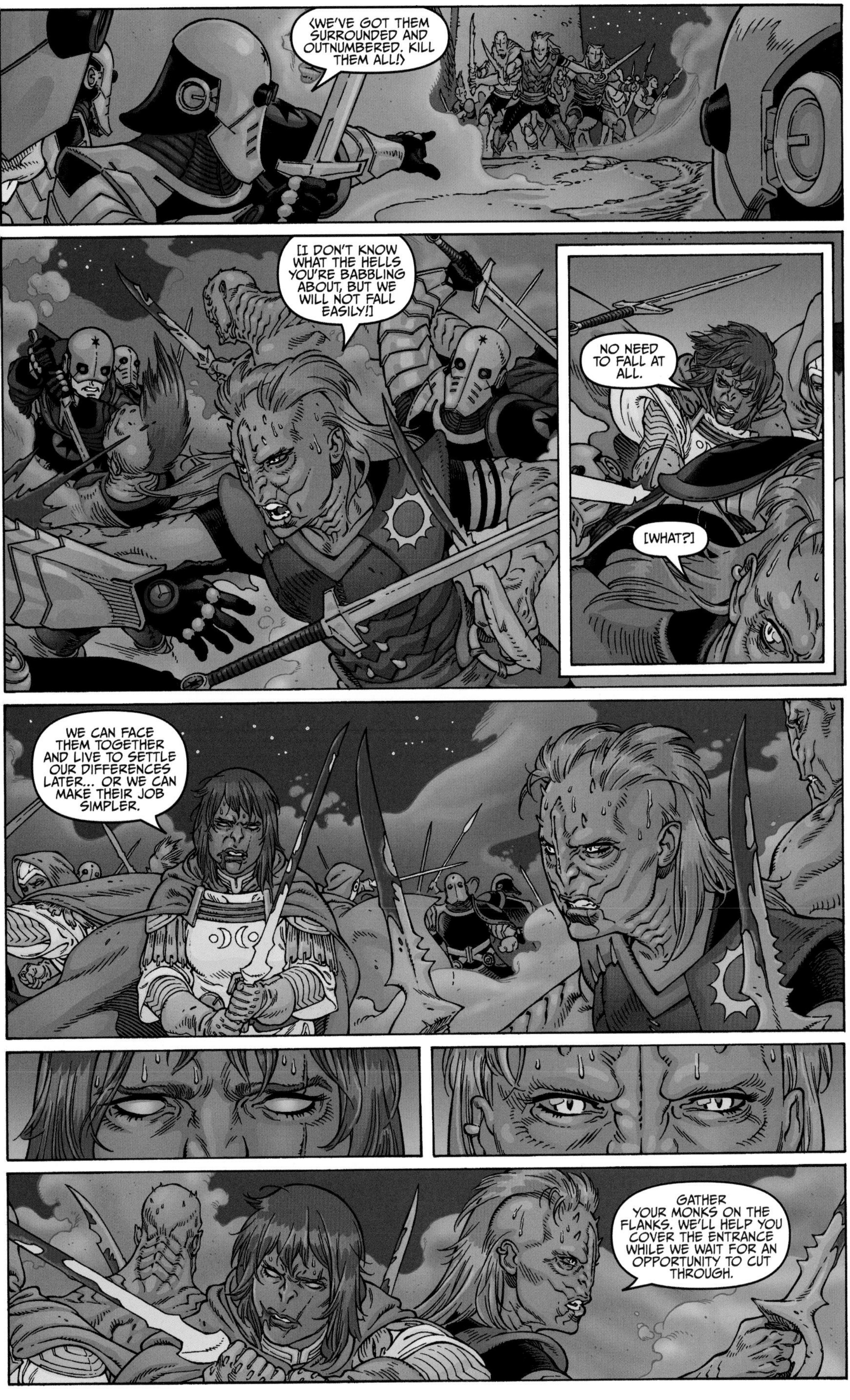

‹WE'VE GOT THEM SURROUNDED AND OUTNUMBERED. KILL THEM ALL!›
[I DON'T KNOW WHAT THE HELLS YOU'RE BABBLING ABOUT, BUT WE WILL NOT FALL EASILY!]
NO NEED TO FALL AT ALL.
[WHAT?]
WE CAN FACE THEM TOGETHER AND LIVE TO SETTLE OUR DIFFERENCES LATER... OR WE CAN MAKE THEIR JOB SIMPLER.
GATHER YOUR MONKS ON THE FLANKS. WE'LL HELP YOU COVER THE ENTRANCE WHILE WE WAIT FOR AN OPPORTUNITY TO CUT THROUGH.

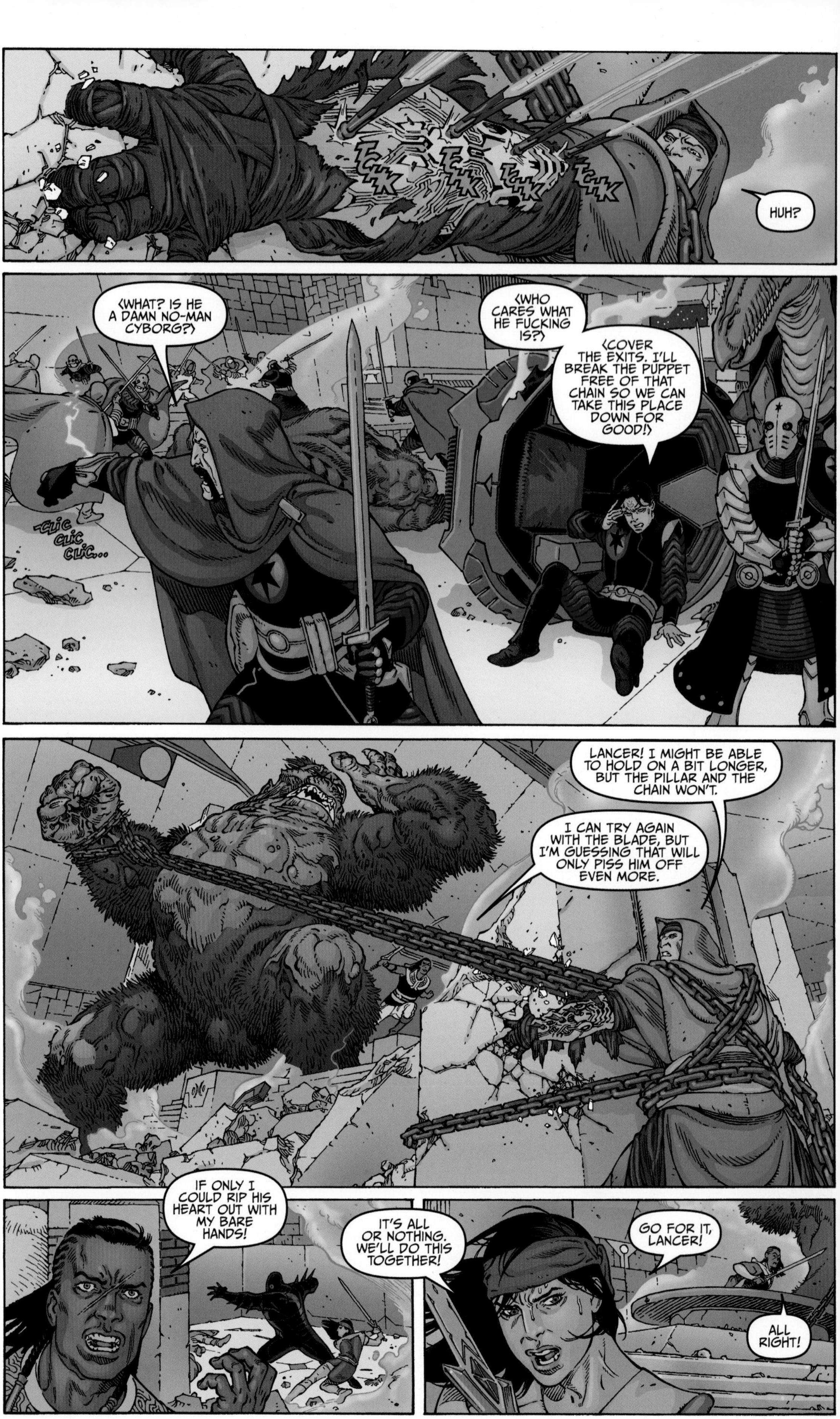
TCHK TCHK TCHK TCHK
HUH?
‹WHAT? IS HE A DAMN NO-MAN CYBORG?›
‹WHO CARES WHAT HE FUCKING IS?›
‹COVER THE EXITS. I'LL BREAK THE PUPPET FREE OF THAT CHAIN SO WE CAN TAKE THIS PLACE DOWN FOR GOOD!›
-CLIC CLIC CLIC...
LANCER! I MIGHT BE ABLE TO HOLD ON A BIT LONGER, BUT THE PILLAR AND THE CHAIN WON'T.
I CAN TRY AGAIN WITH THE BLADE, BUT I'M GUESSING THAT WILL ONLY PISS HIM OFF EVEN MORE.
IF ONLY I COULD RIP HIS HEART OUT WITH MY BARE HANDS!
IT'S ALL OR NOTHING. WE'LL DO THIS TOGETHER!
GO FOR IT, LANCER!
ALL RIGHT!

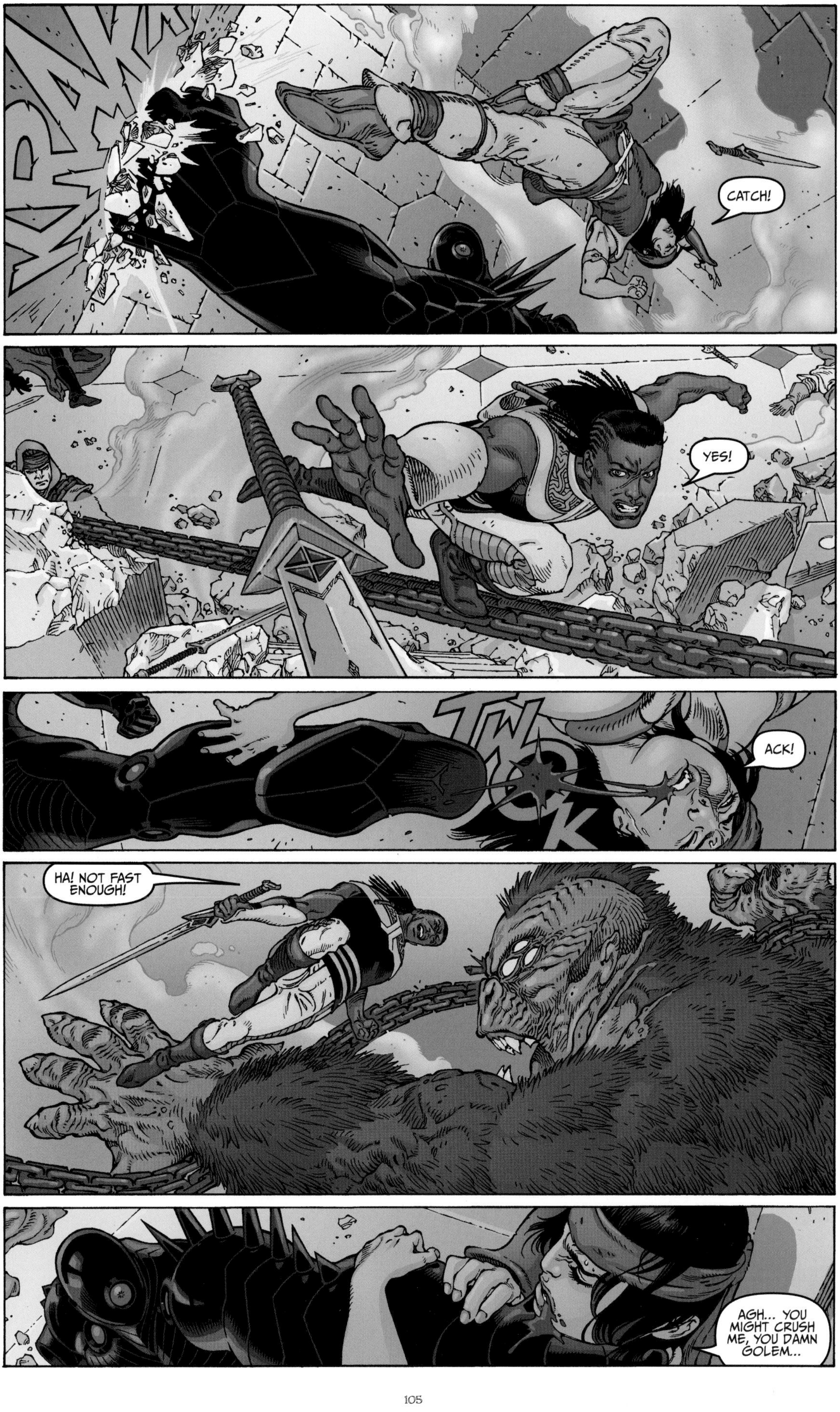
CATCH!
YES!
ACK!
HA! NOT FAST ENOUGH!
AGH... YOU MIGHT CRUSH ME, YOU DAMN GOLEM...

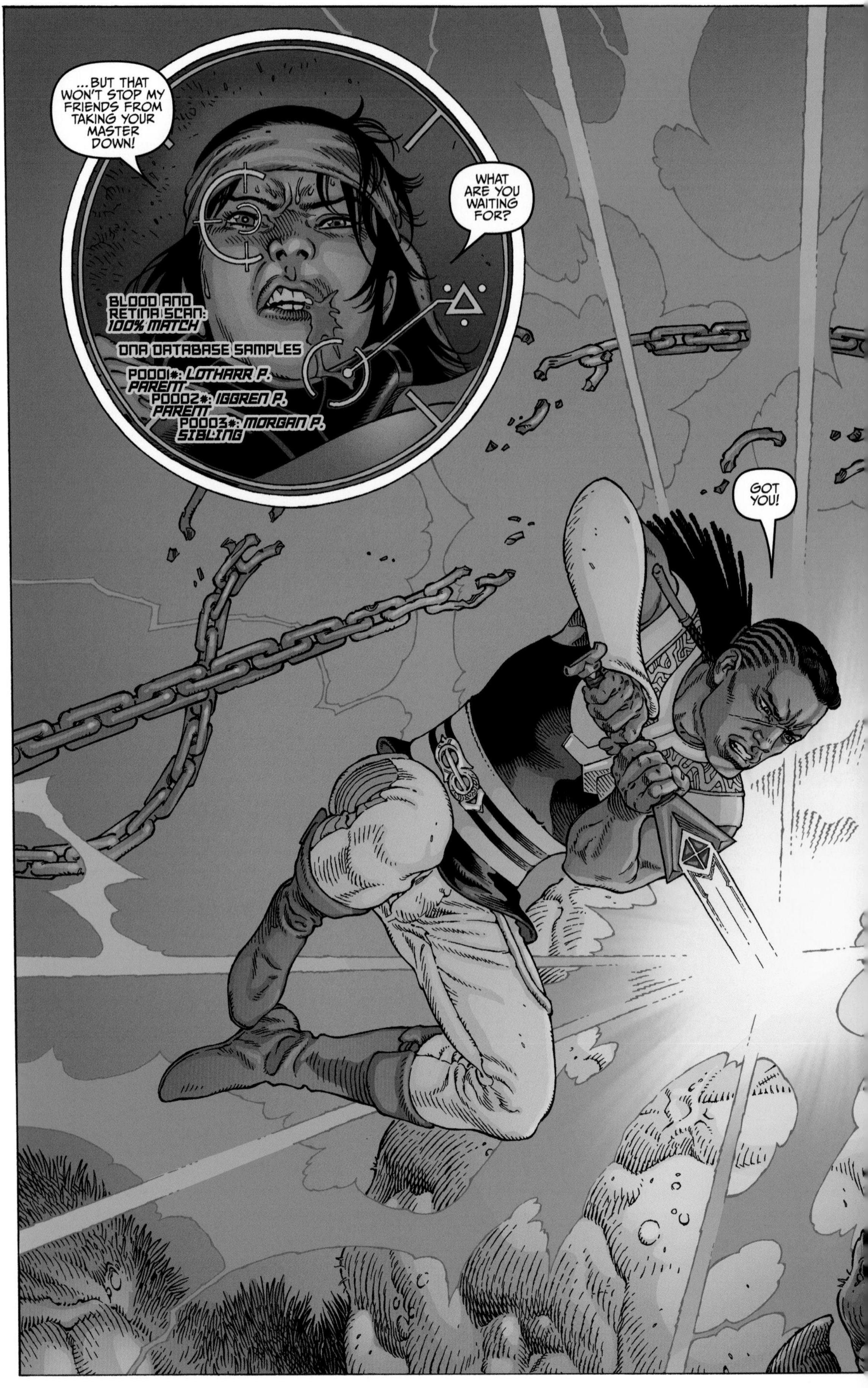

...BUT THAT WON'T STOP MY FRIENDS FROM TAKING YOUR MASTER DOWN!
WHAT ARE YOU WAITING FOR?
BLOOD AND RETINA SCAN: 100% MATCH
DNA DATABASE SAMPLES
P0001#: LOTHARR P. PARENT
P0002#: IBBREN P. PARENT
P0003#: MORGAN P. SIBLING
GOT YOU!

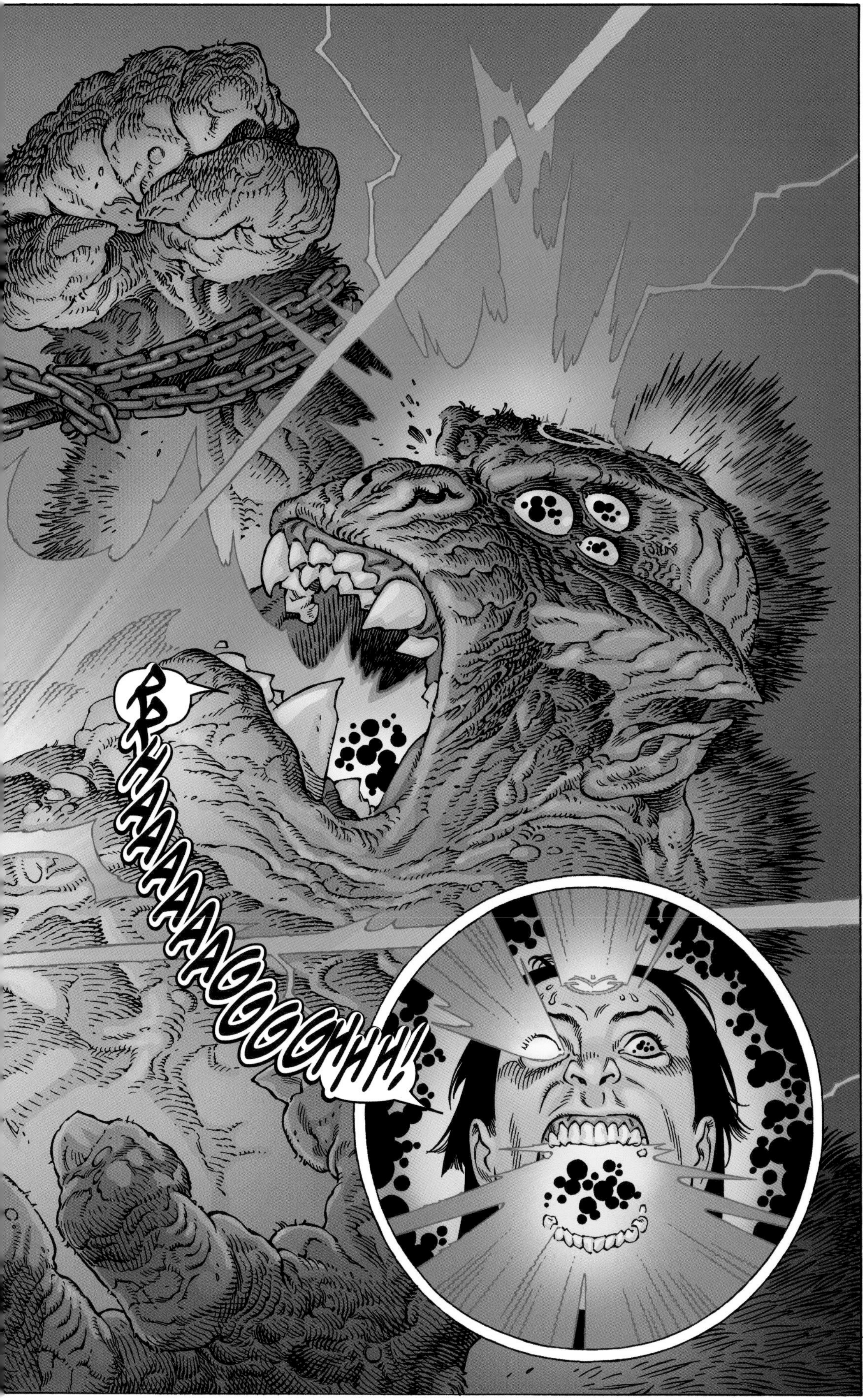
RRHAAAAAGGGGHHH!

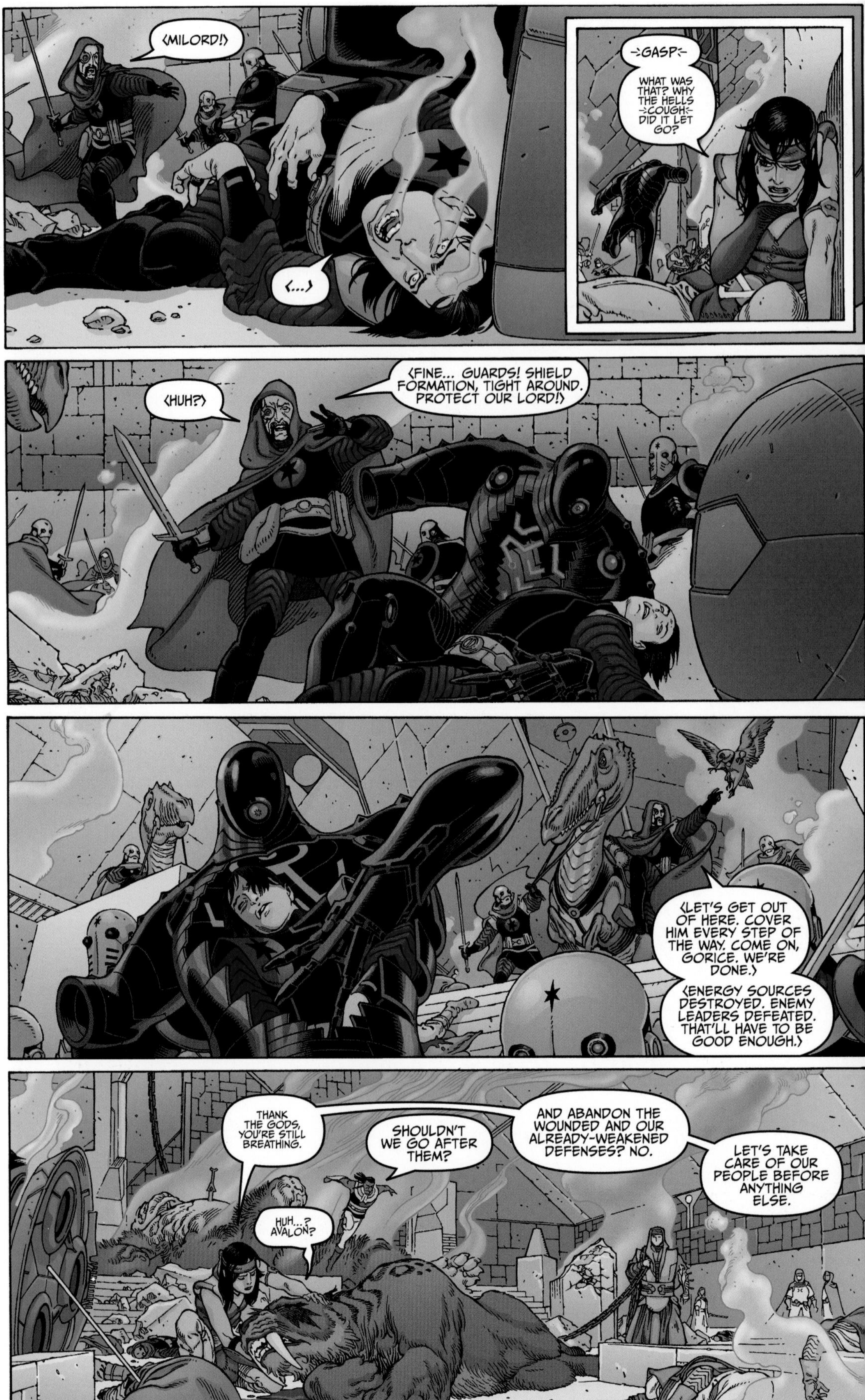

⟨MILORD!⟩
⟨...⟩
-:-GASP-:-
WHAT WAS THAT? WHY THE HELLS -:-COUGH-:- DID IT LET GO?
⟨HUH?⟩
⟨FINE... GUARDS! SHIELD FORMATION, TIGHT AROUND. PROTECT OUR LORD!⟩
⟨LET'S GET OUT OF HERE. COVER HIM EVERY STEP OF THE WAY. COME ON, GORICE. WE'RE DONE.⟩
⟨ENERGY SOURCES DESTROYED. ENEMY LEADERS DEFEATED. THAT'LL HAVE TO BE GOOD ENOUGH.⟩
THANK THE GODS, YOU'RE STILL BREATHING.
HUH...? AVALON?
SHOULDN'T WE GO AFTER THEM?
AND ABANDON THE WOUNDED AND OUR ALREADY-WEAKENED DEFENSES? NO.
LET'S TAKE CARE OF OUR PEOPLE BEFORE ANYTHING ELSE.

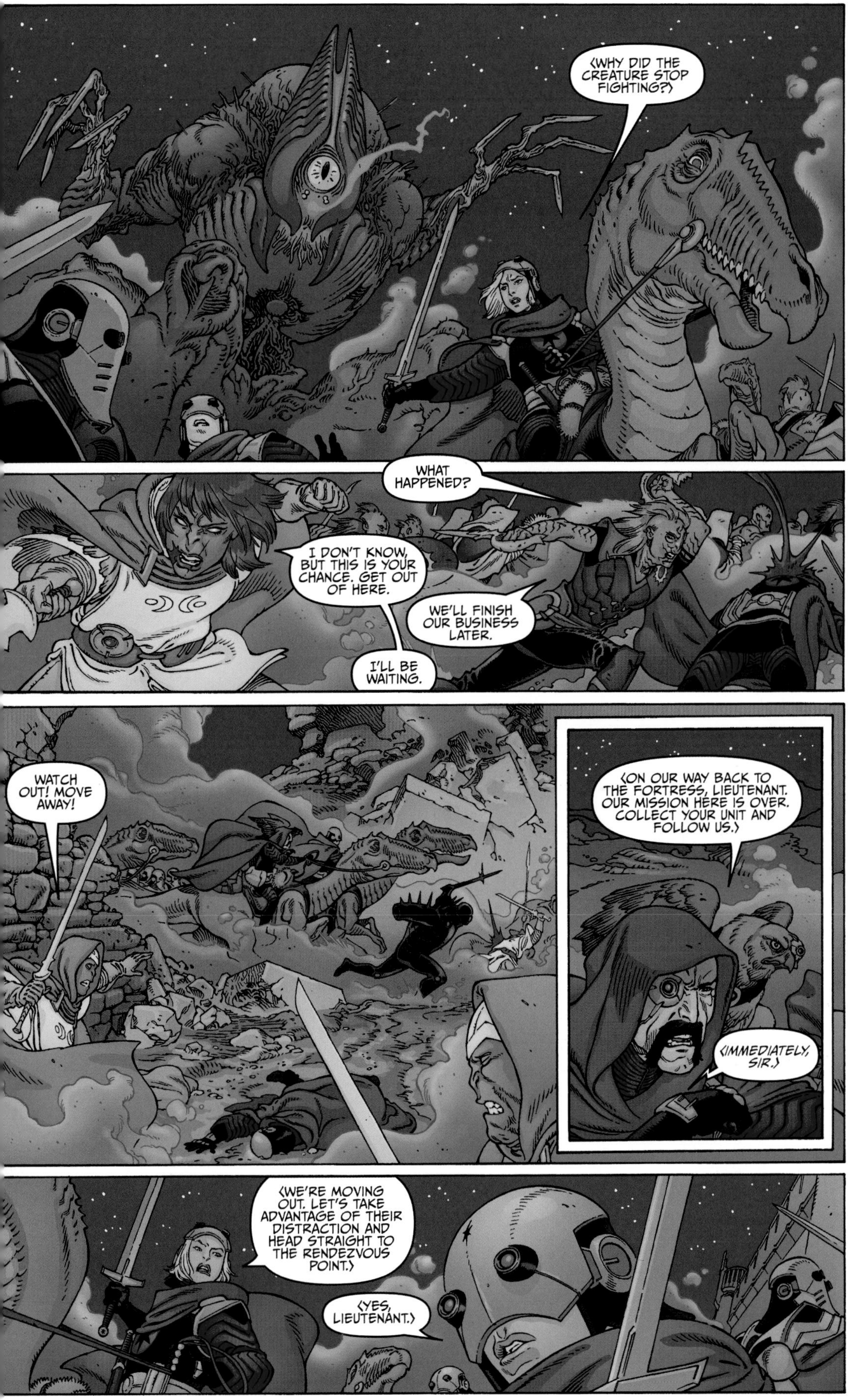

‹WHY DID THE CREATURE STOP FIGHTING?›
WHAT HAPPENED?
I DON'T KNOW, BUT THIS IS YOUR CHANCE. GET OUT OF HERE.
WE'LL FINISH OUR BUSINESS LATER.
I'LL BE WAITING.
WATCH OUT! MOVE AWAY!
‹ON OUR WAY BACK TO THE FORTRESS, LIEUTENANT. OUR MISSION HERE IS OVER. COLLECT YOUR UNIT AND FOLLOW US.›
‹IMMEDIATELY, SIR.›
‹WE'RE MOVING OUT. LET'S TAKE ADVANTAGE OF THEIR DISTRACTION AND HEAD STRAIGHT TO THE RENDEZVOUS POINT.›
‹YES, LIEUTENANT.›

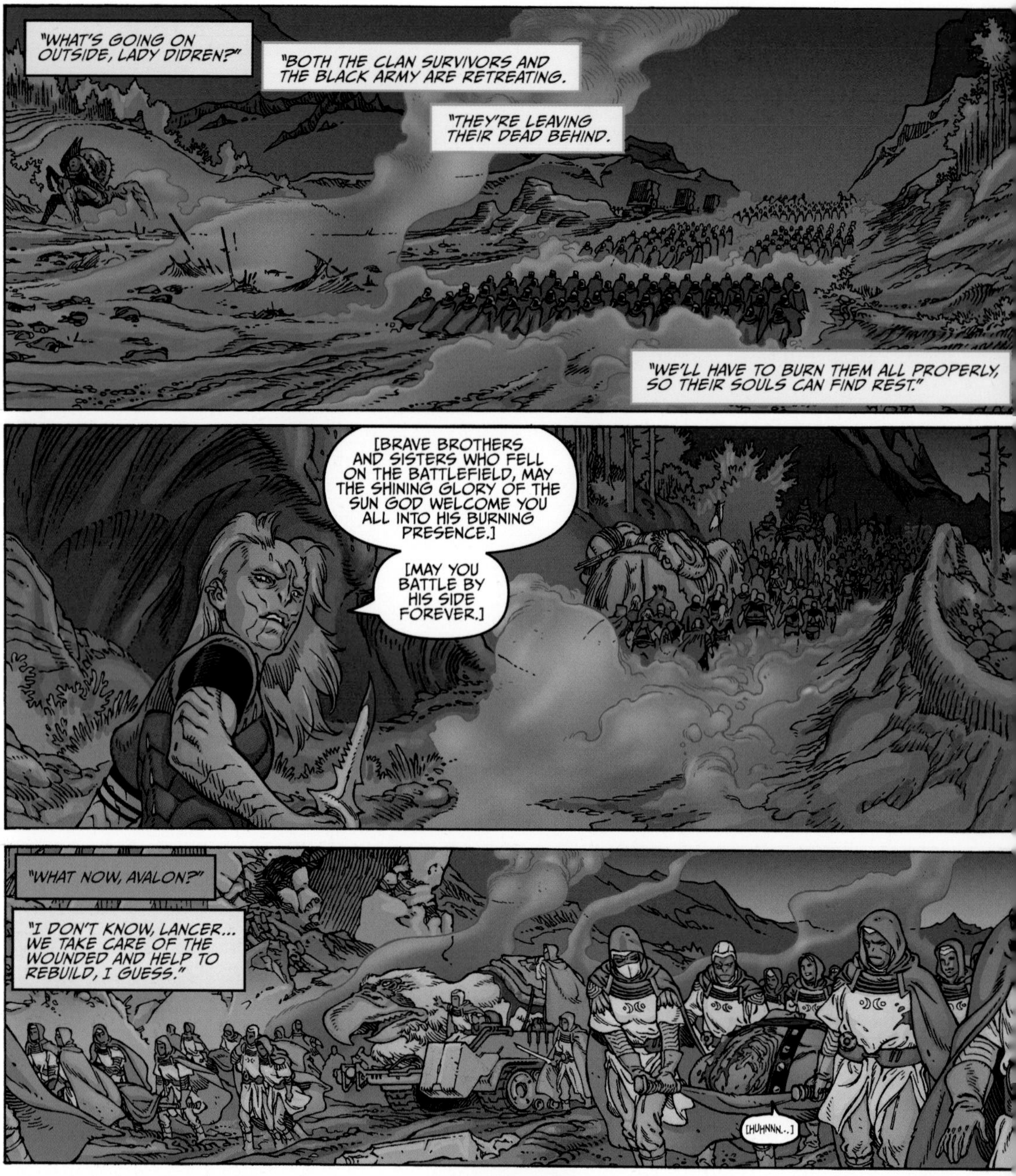
"WHAT'S GOING ON OUTSIDE, LADY DIDREN?"
"BOTH THE CLAN SURVIVORS AND THE BLACK ARMY ARE RETREATING.
"THEY'RE LEAVING THEIR DEAD BEHIND.
"WE'LL HAVE TO BURN THEM ALL PROPERLY, SO THEIR SOULS CAN FIND REST."
[BRAVE BROTHERS AND SISTERS WHO FELL ON THE BATTLEFIELD, MAY THE SHINING GLORY OF THE SUN GOD WELCOME YOU ALL INTO HIS BURNING PRESENCE.]
[MAY YOU BATTLE BY HIS SIDE FOREVER.]
"WHAT NOW, AVALON?"
"I DON'T KNOW, LANCER... WE TAKE CARE OF THE WOUNDED AND HELP TO REBUILD, I GUESS."
[HUHNNN...]

DAWN

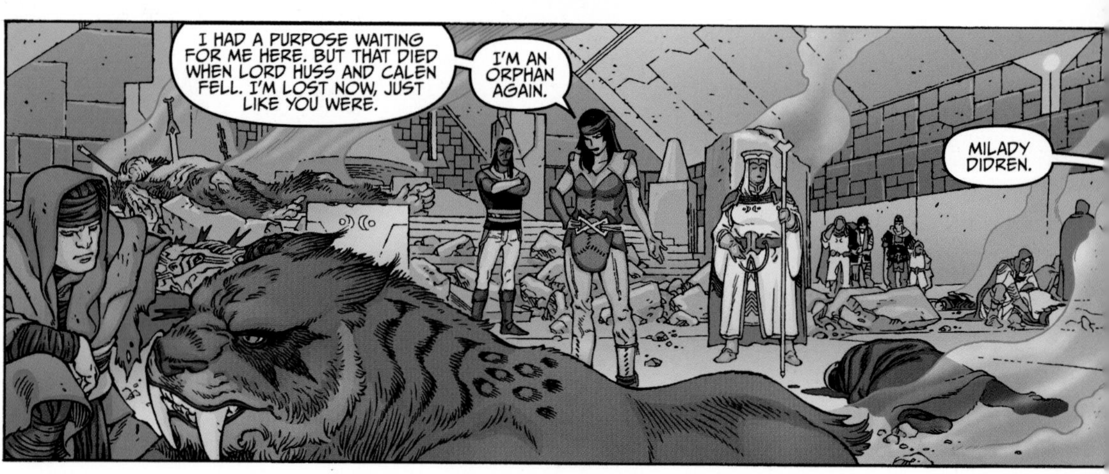
I HAD A PURPOSE WAITING FOR ME HERE. BUT THAT DIED WHEN LORD HUSS AND CALEN FELL. I'M LOST NOW, JUST LIKE YOU WERE.
I'M AN ORPHAN AGAIN.
MILADY DIDREN.

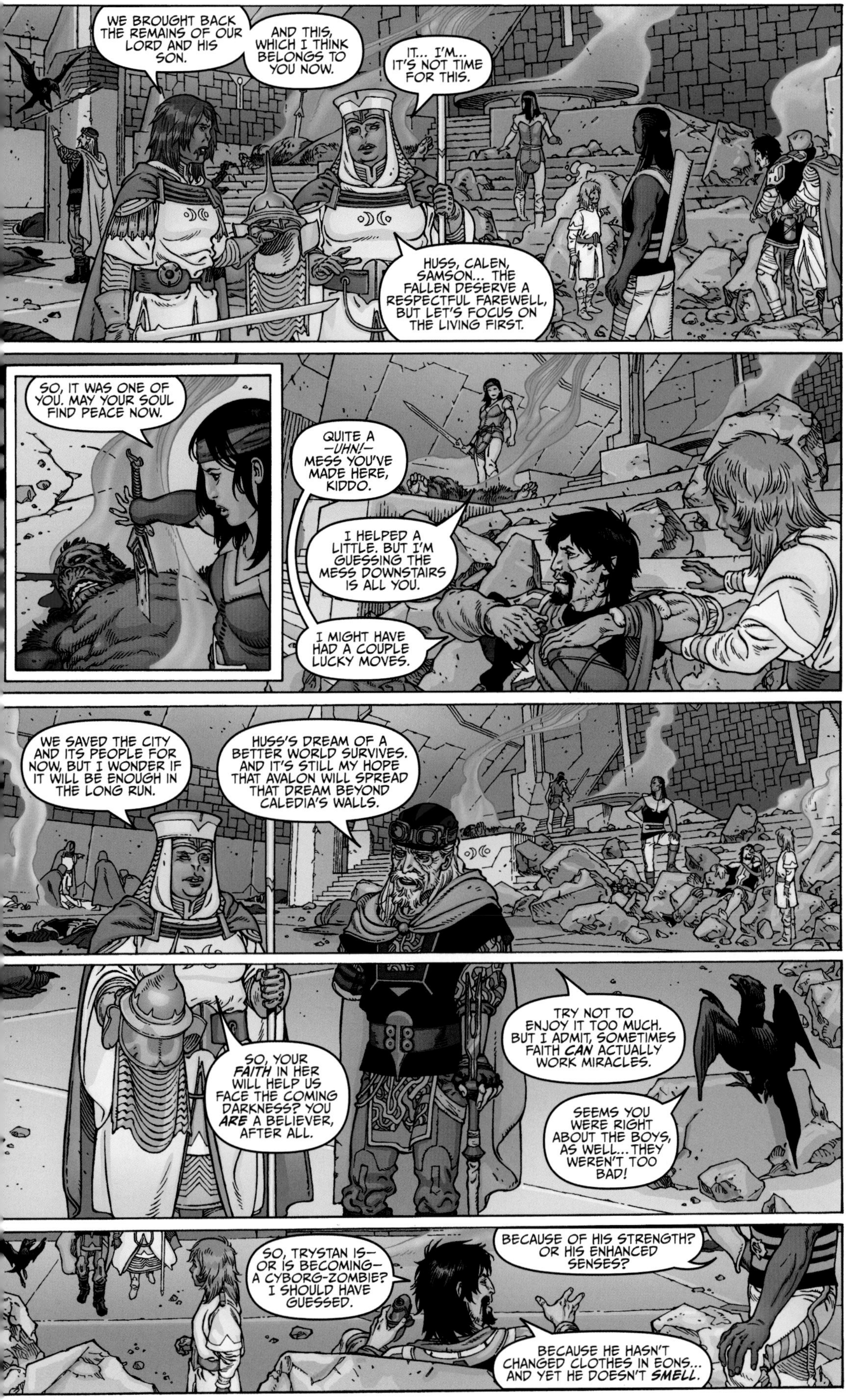
WE BROUGHT BACK THE REMAINS OF OUR LORD AND HIS SON.
AND THIS, WHICH I THINK BELONGS TO YOU NOW.
IT... I'M... IT'S NOT TIME FOR THIS.
HUSS, CALEN, SAMSON... THE FALLEN DESERVE A RESPECTFUL FAREWELL, BUT LET'S FOCUS ON THE LIVING FIRST.
SO, IT WAS ONE OF YOU. MAY YOUR SOUL FIND PEACE NOW.
QUITE A —UHN!— MESS YOU'VE MADE HERE, KIDDO.
I HELPED A LITTLE. BUT I'M GUESSING THE MESS DOWNSTAIRS IS ALL YOU.
I MIGHT HAVE HAD A COUPLE LUCKY MOVES.
WE SAVED THE CITY AND ITS PEOPLE FOR NOW, BUT I WONDER IF IT WILL BE ENOUGH IN THE LONG RUN.
HUSS'S DREAM OF A BETTER WORLD SURVIVES. AND IT'S STILL MY HOPE THAT AVALON WILL SPREAD THAT DREAM BEYOND CALEDIA'S WALLS.
SO, YOUR FAITH IN HER WILL HELP US FACE THE COMING DARKNESS? YOU ARE A BELIEVER, AFTER ALL.
TRY NOT TO ENJOY IT TOO MUCH. BUT I ADMIT, SOMETIMES FAITH CAN ACTUALLY WORK MIRACLES.
SEEMS YOU WERE RIGHT ABOUT THE BOYS, AS WELL... THEY WEREN'T TOO BAD!
SO, TRYSTAN IS— OR IS BECOMING— A CYBORG-ZOMBIE? I SHOULD HAVE GUESSED.
BECAUSE OF HIS STRENGTH? OR HIS ENHANCED SENSES?
BECAUSE HE HASN'T CHANGED CLOTHES IN EONS... AND YET HE DOESN'T SMELL.

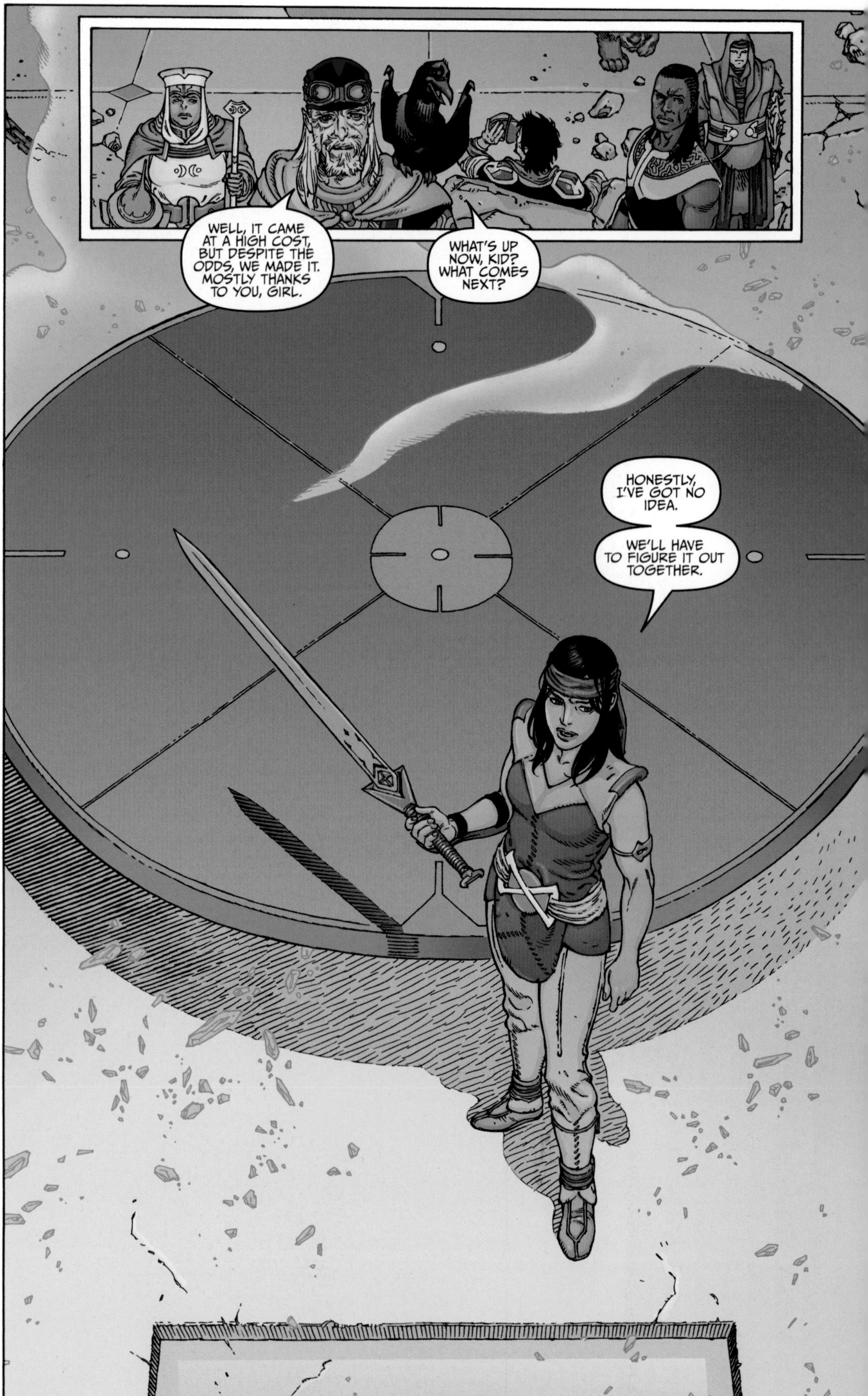
WELL, IT CAME AT A HIGH COST, BUT DESPITE THE ODDS, WE MADE IT. MOSTLY THANKS TO YOU, GIRL.
WHAT'S UP NOW, KID? WHAT COMES NEXT?
HONESTLY, I'VE GOT NO IDEA.
WE'LL HAVE TO FIGURE IT OUT TOGETHER.

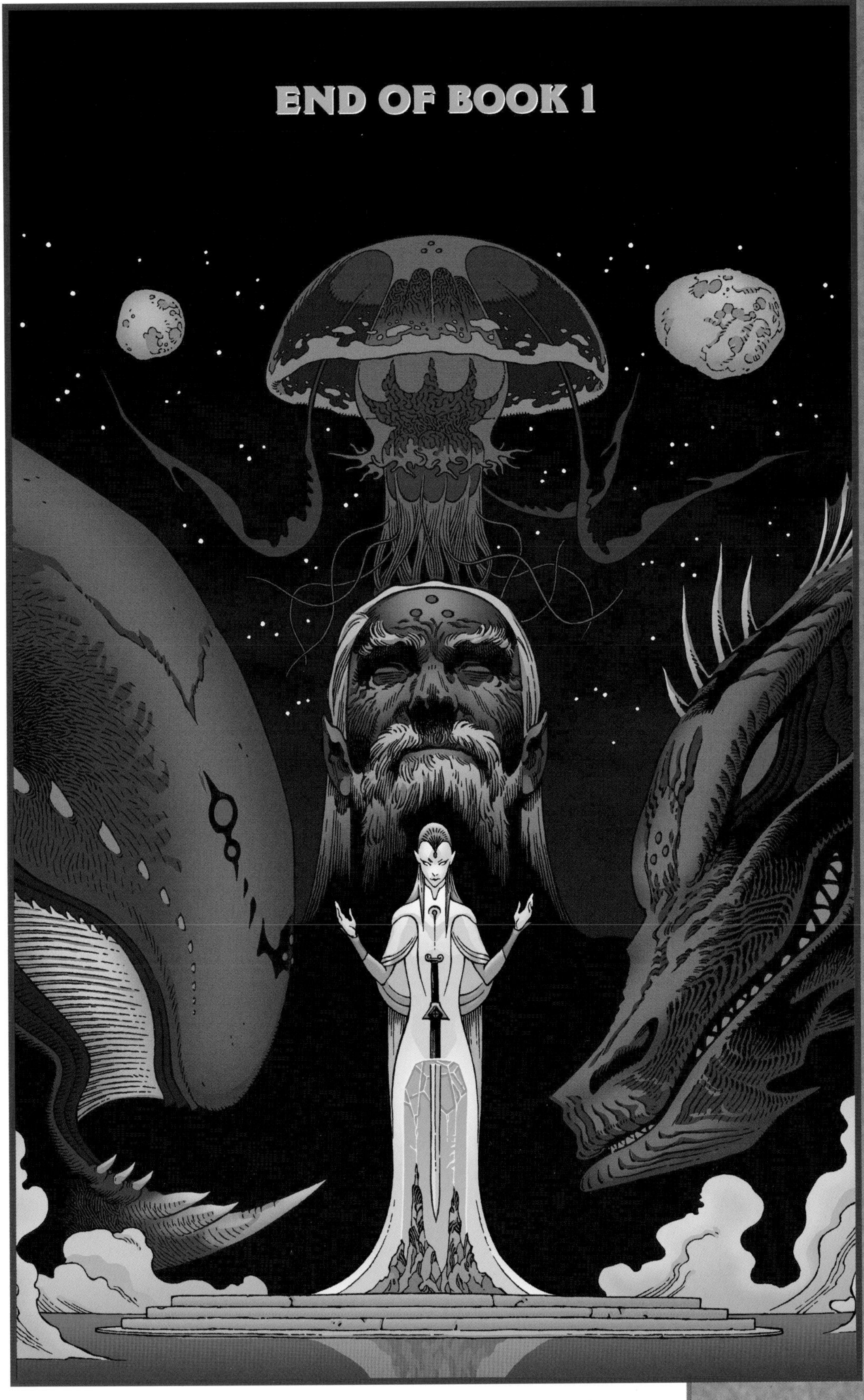
END OF BOOK 1

GABRIEL RODRÍGUEZ
Art Gallery

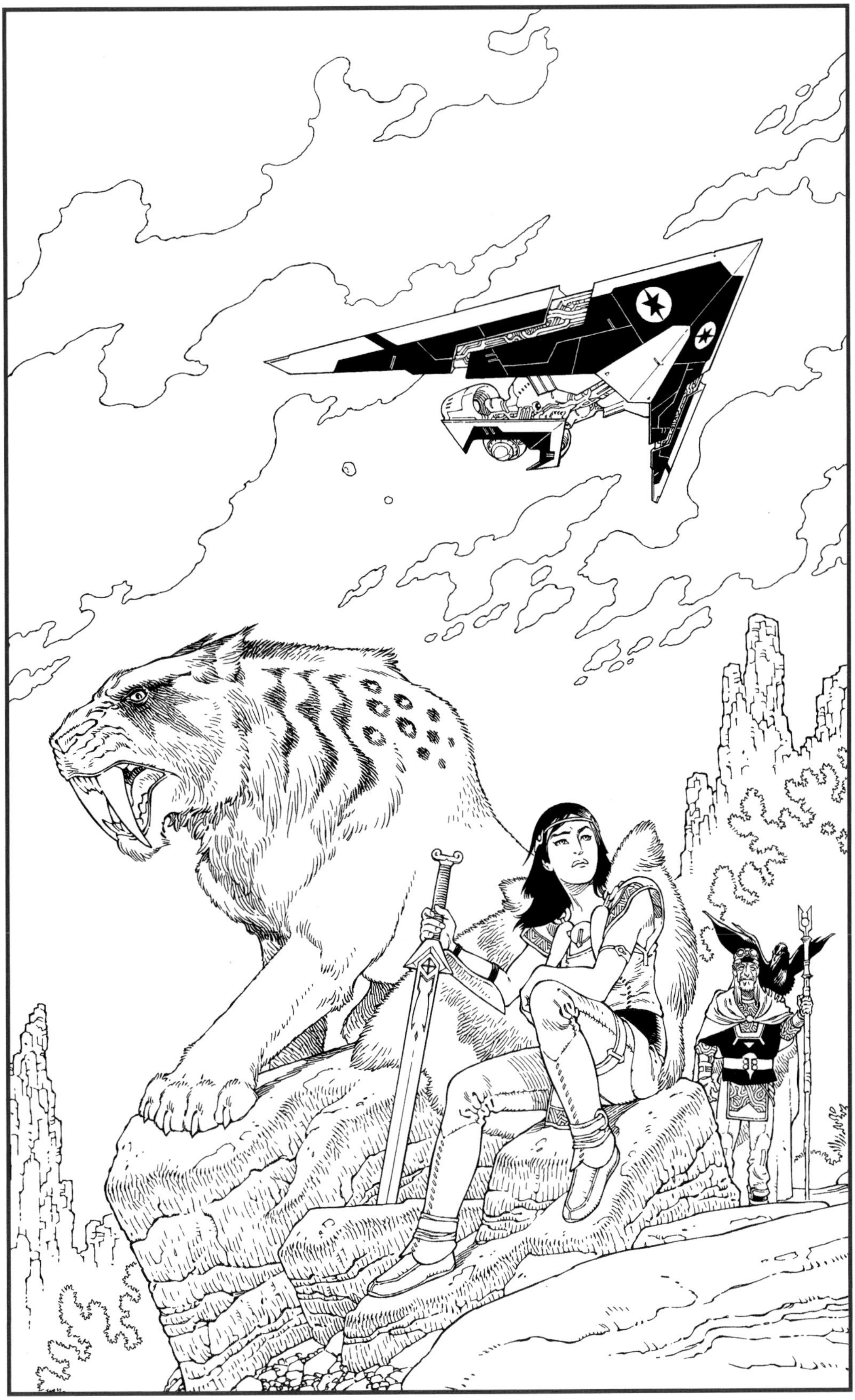

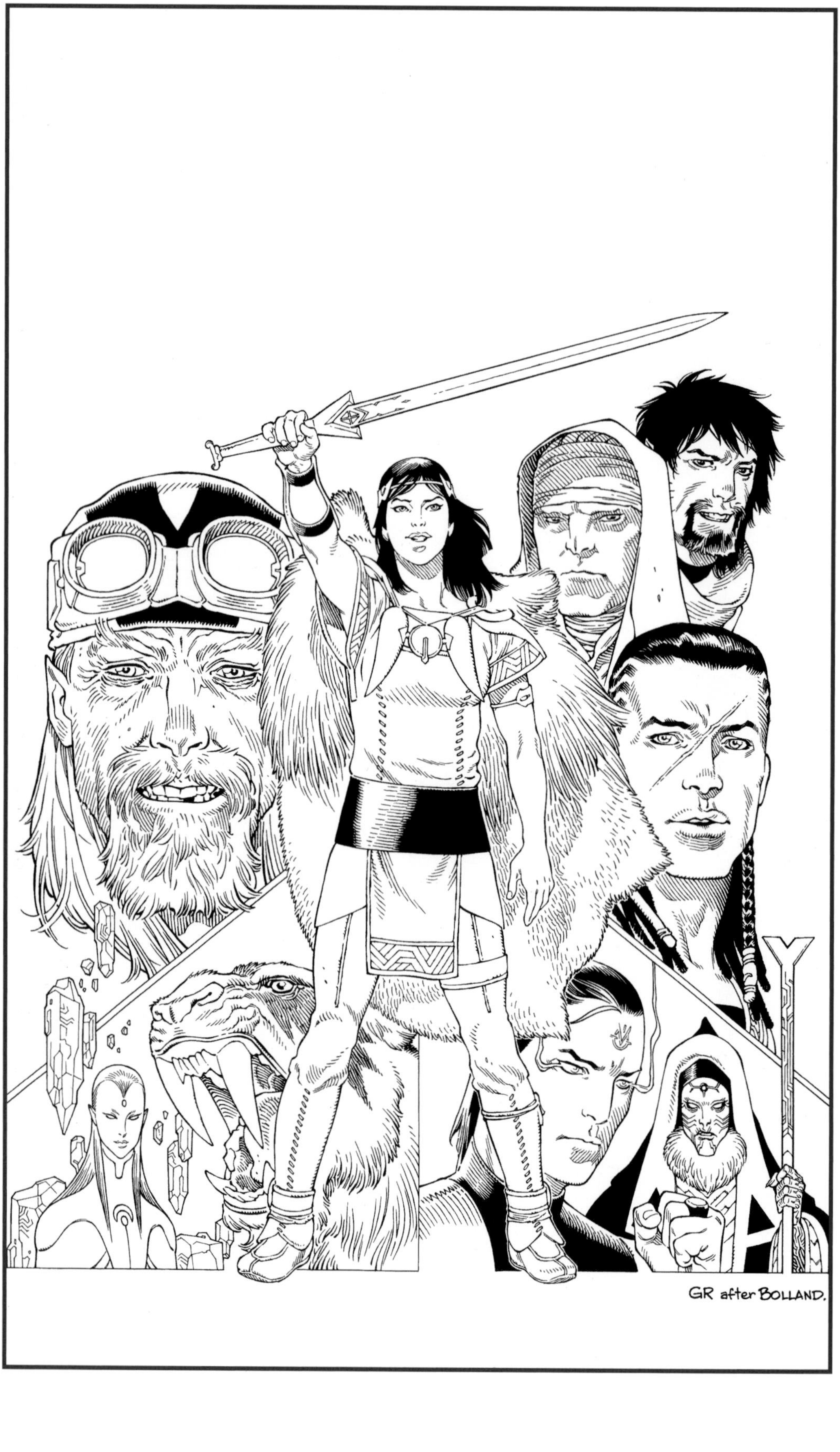
GR after BOLLAND.

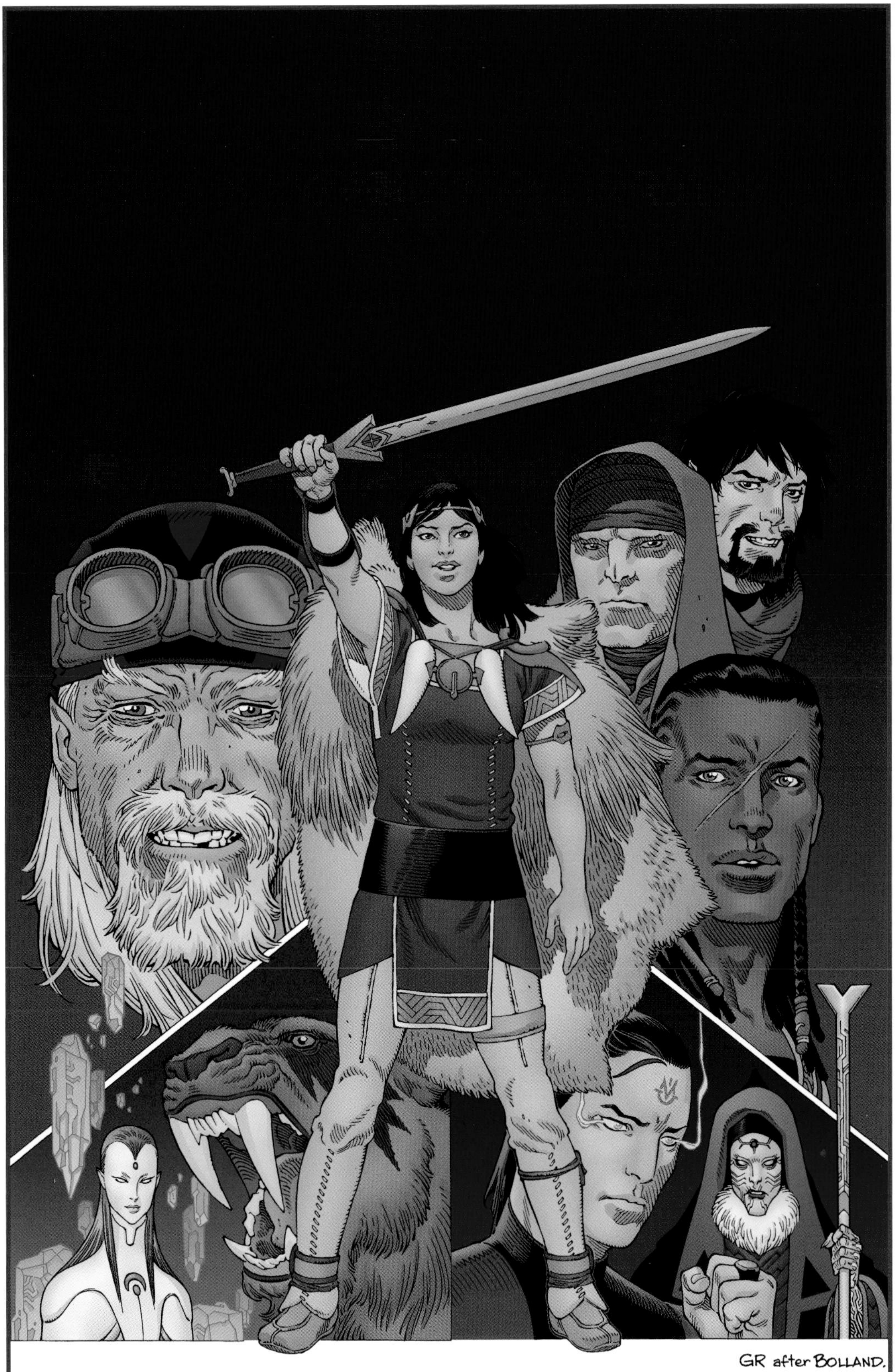
GR after BOLLAND.

COLORS BY LOVERN KINDZIERSKI

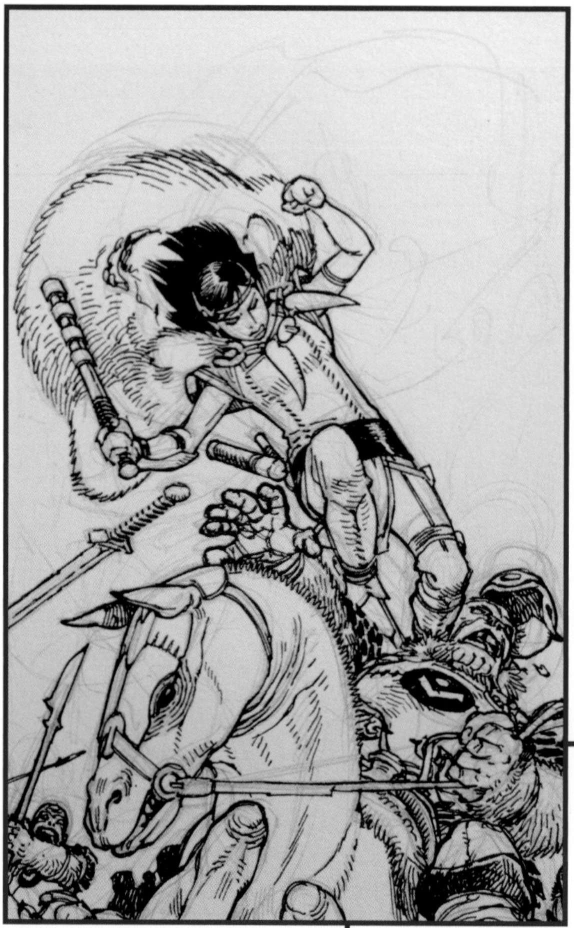

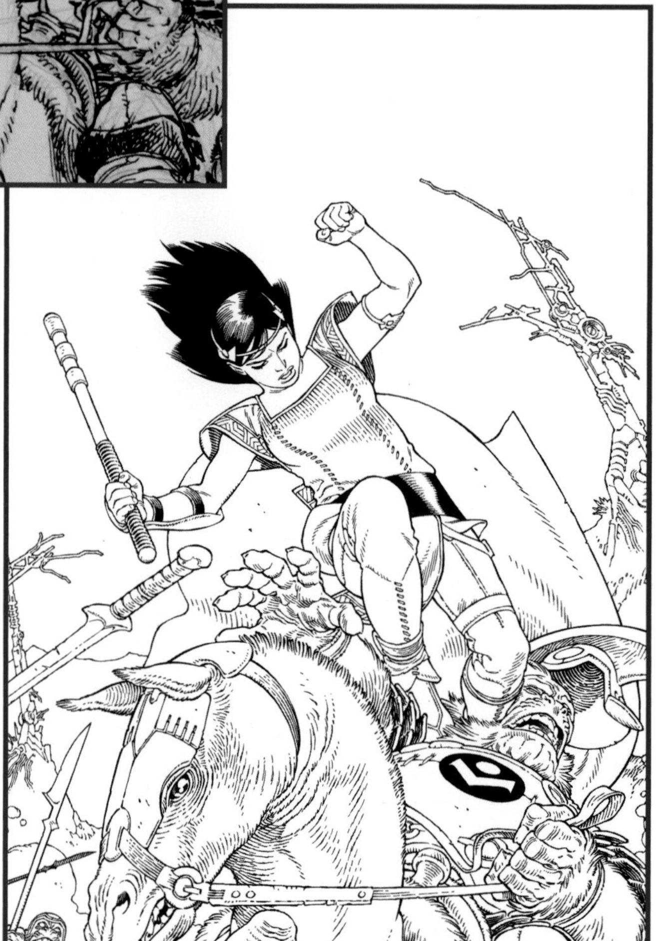

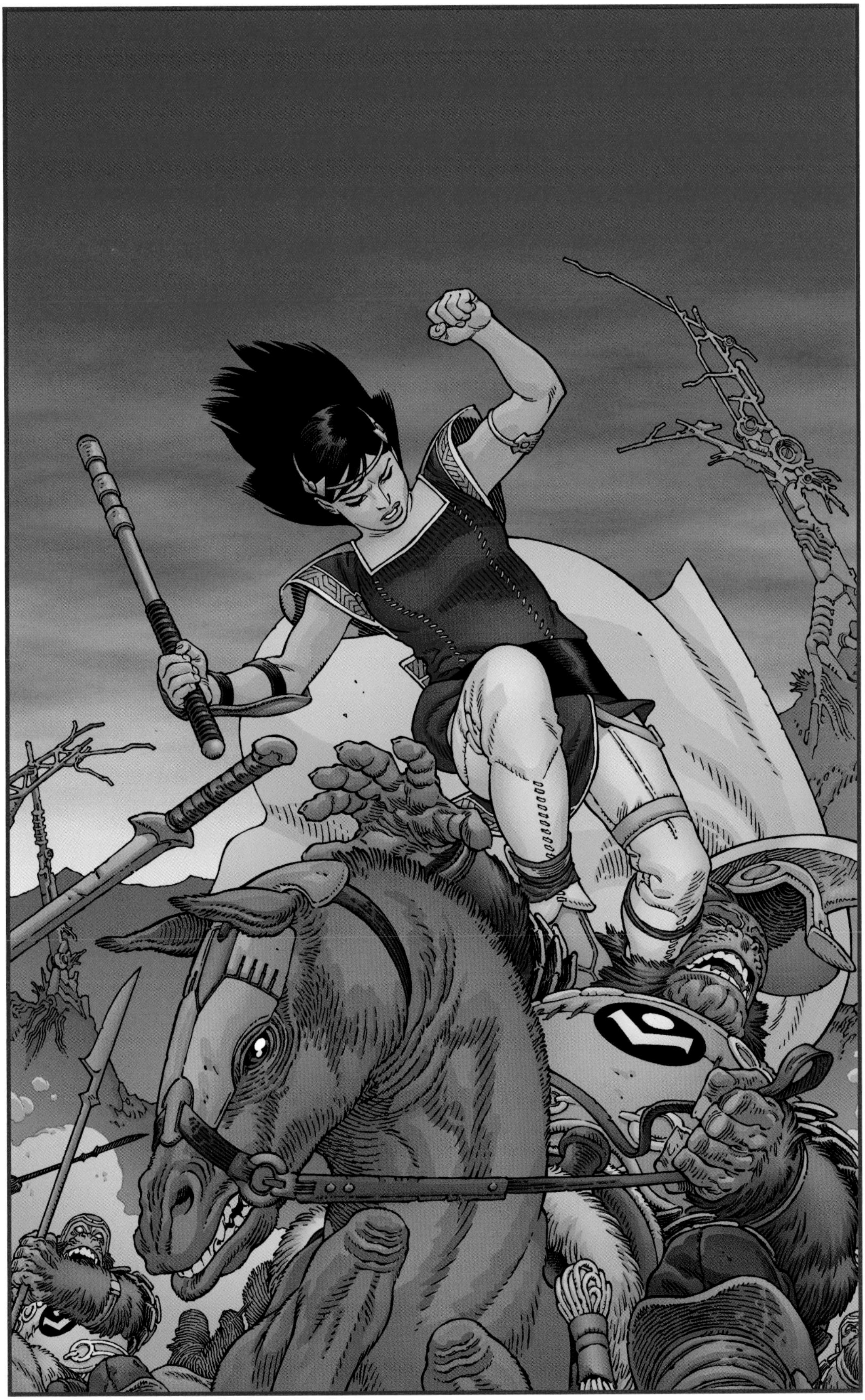

COLORS BY LOVERN KINDZIERSKI

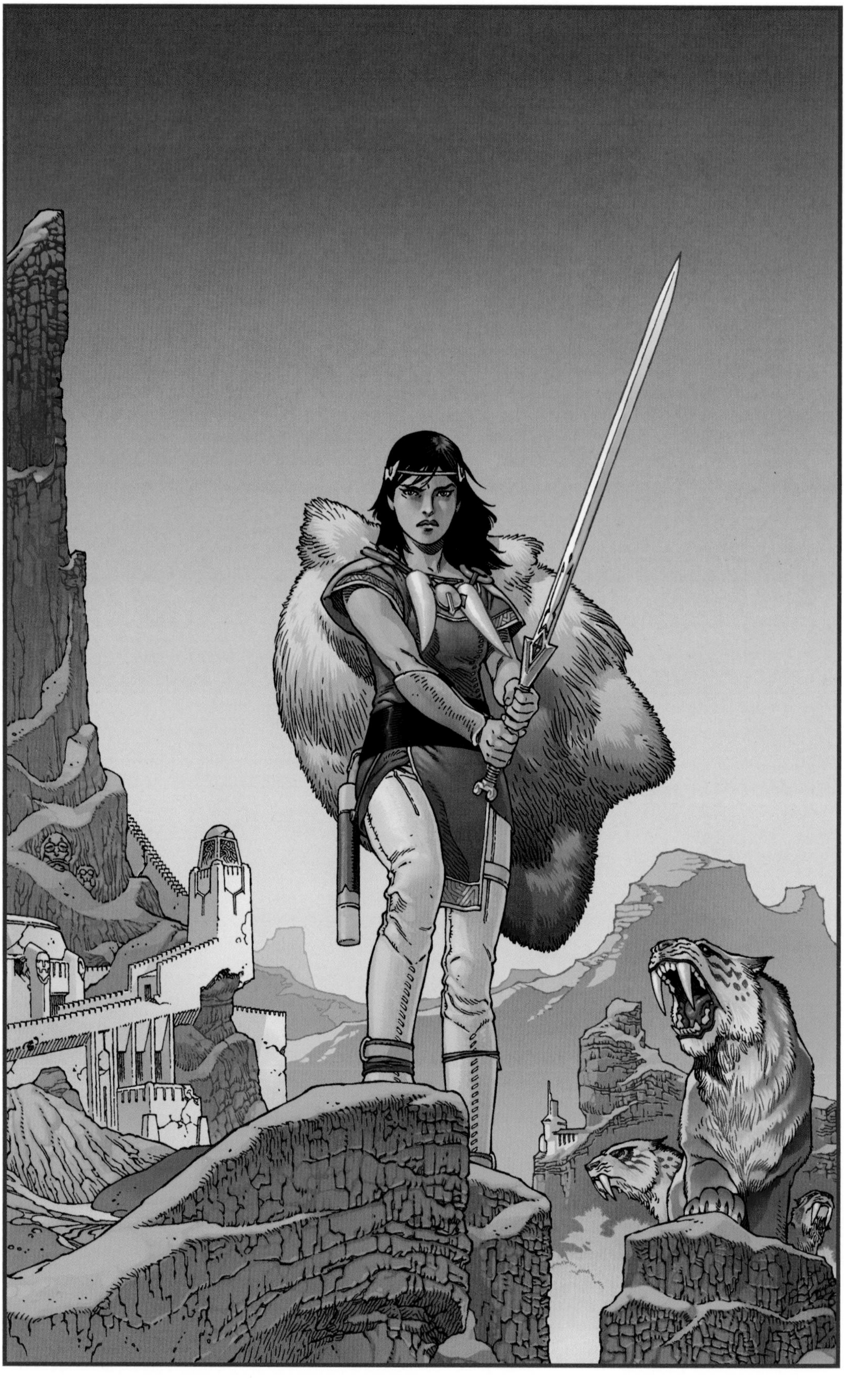

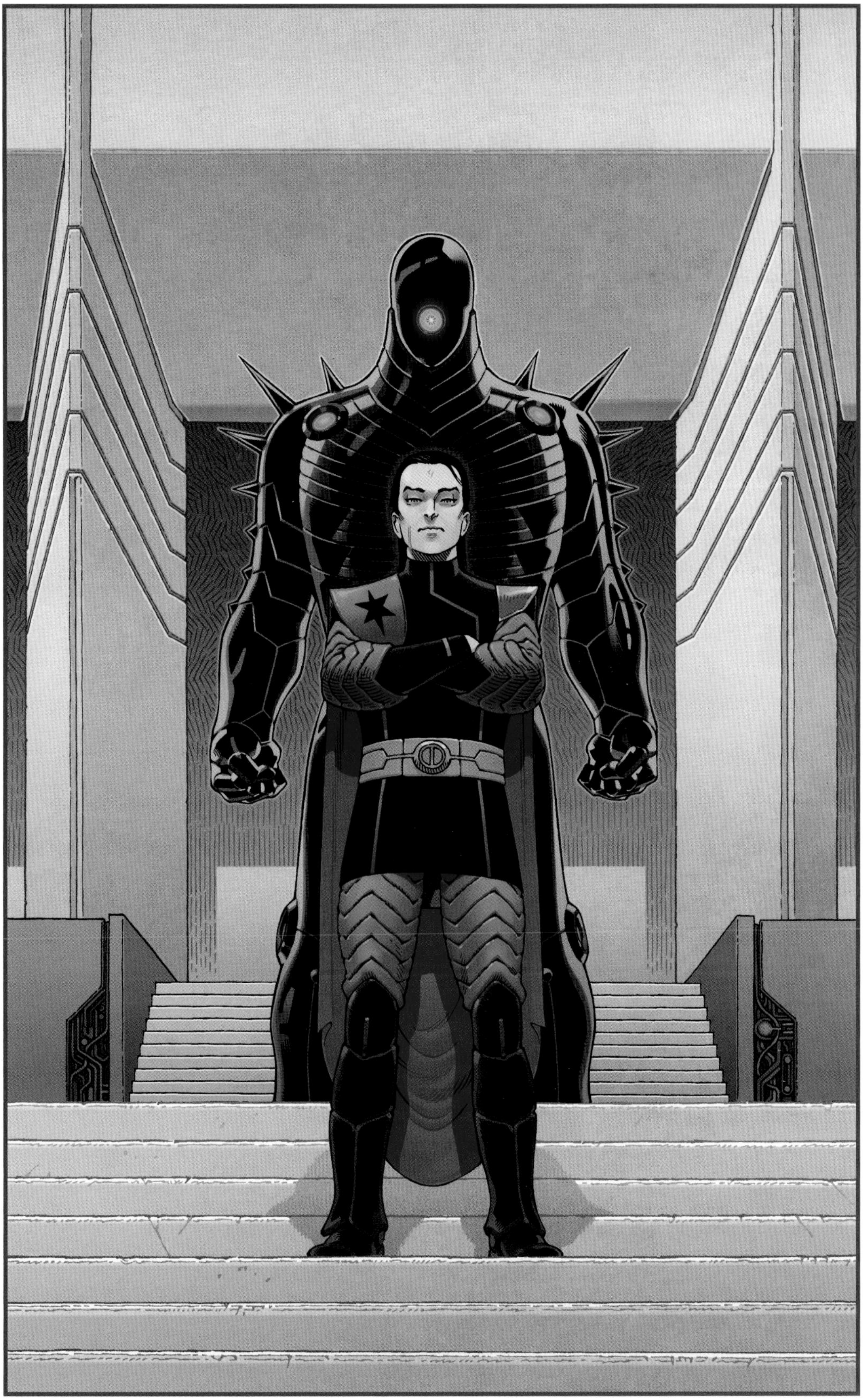

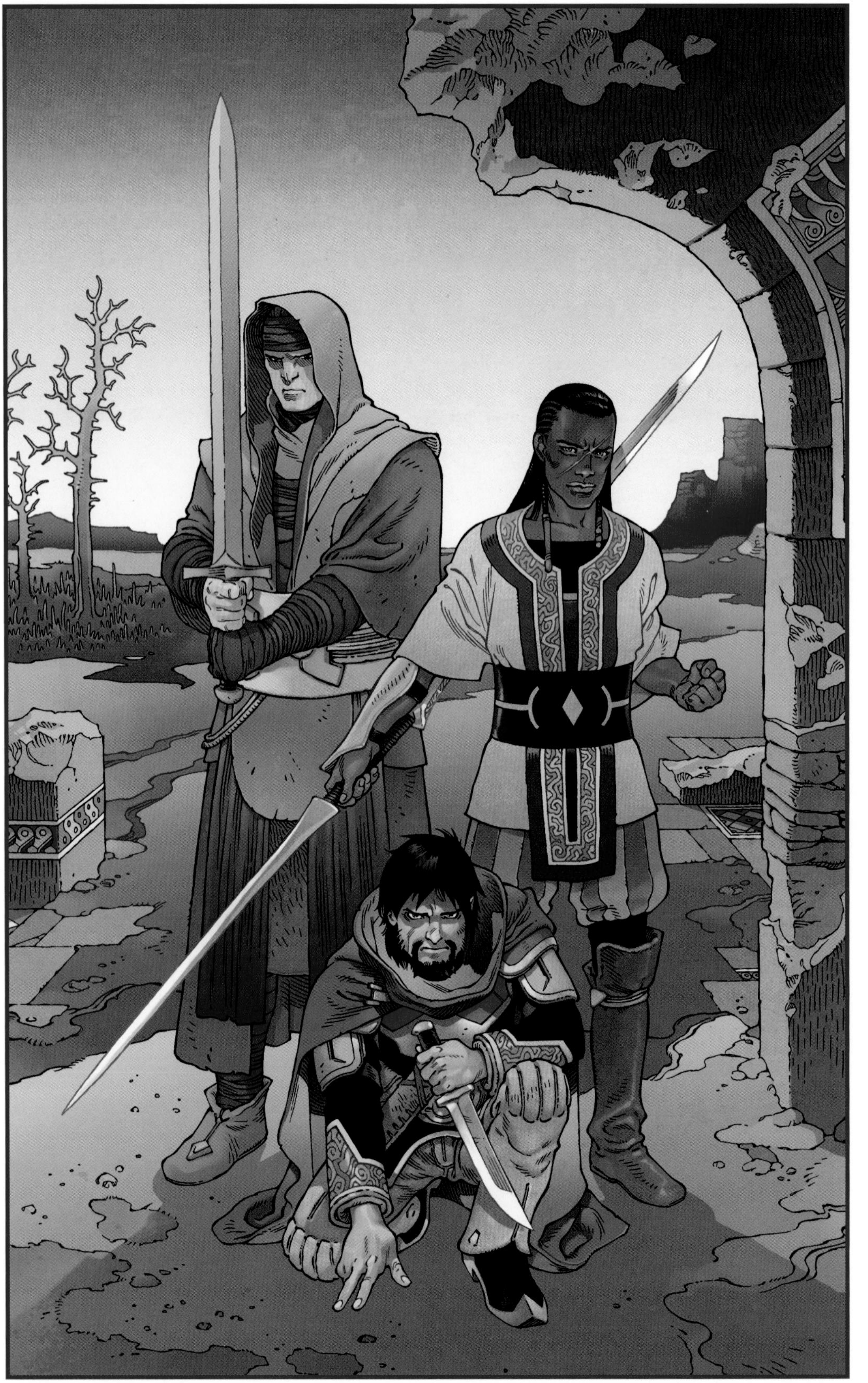

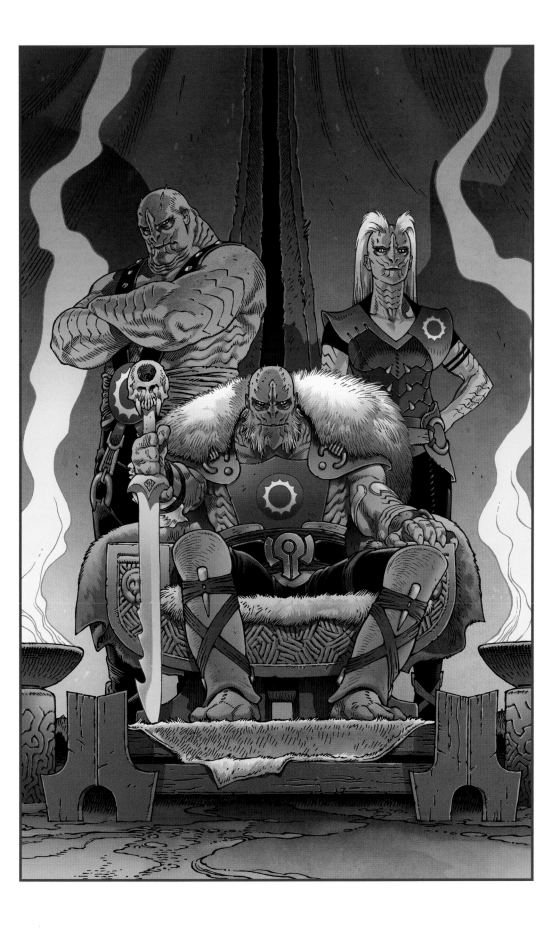

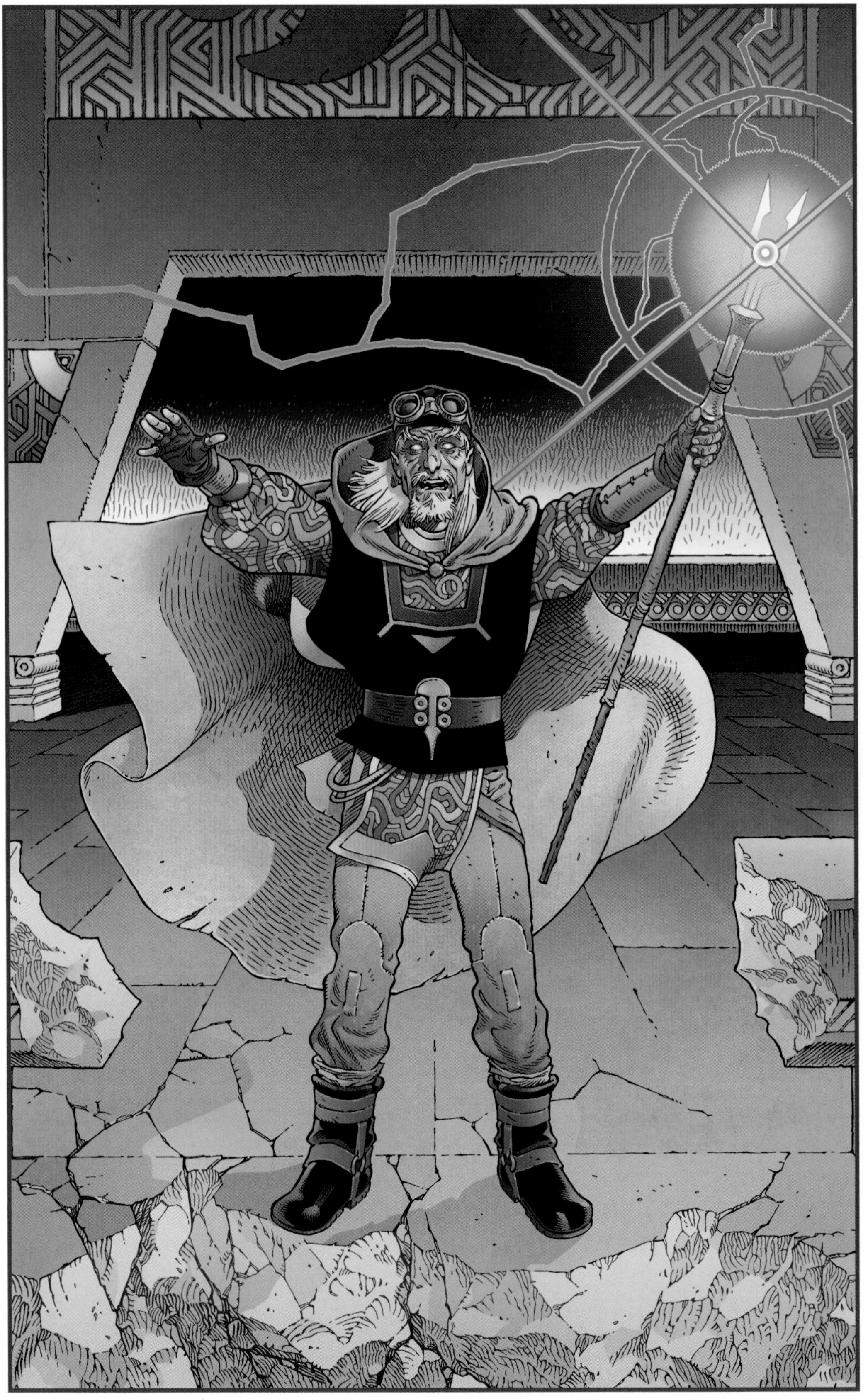

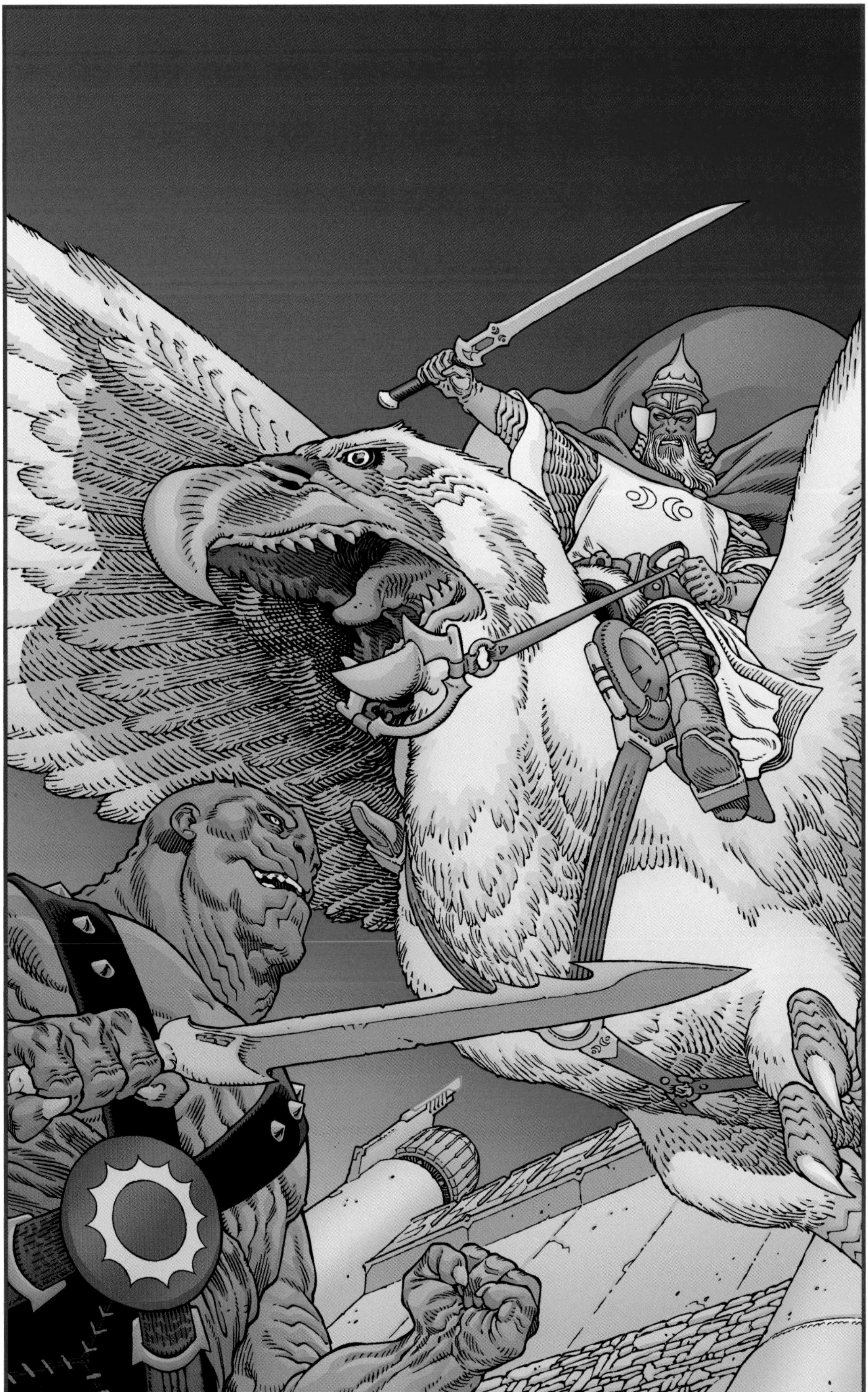

COLORS BY LOVERN KINDZIERSKI

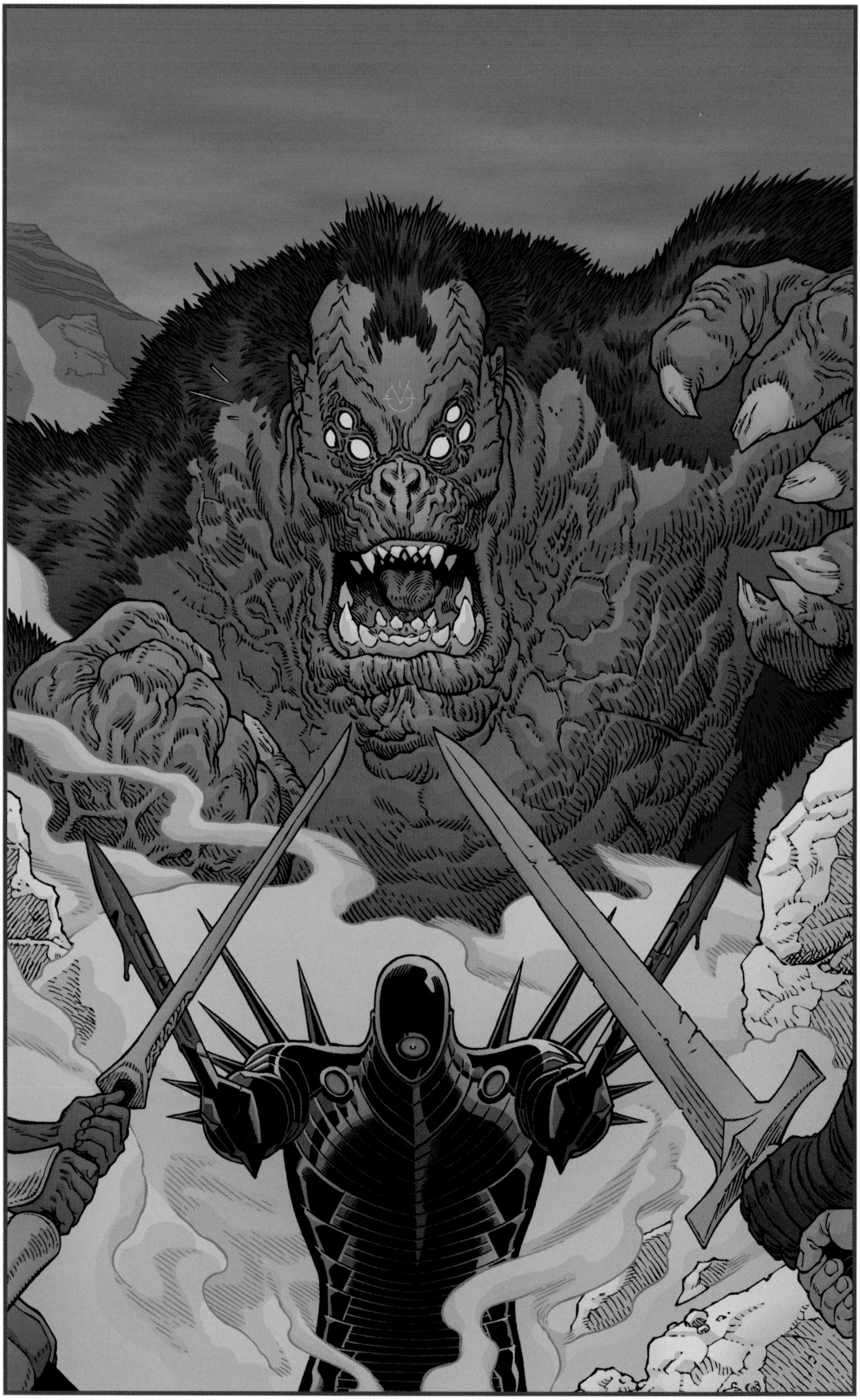

COLORS BY LOVERN KINDZIERSKI

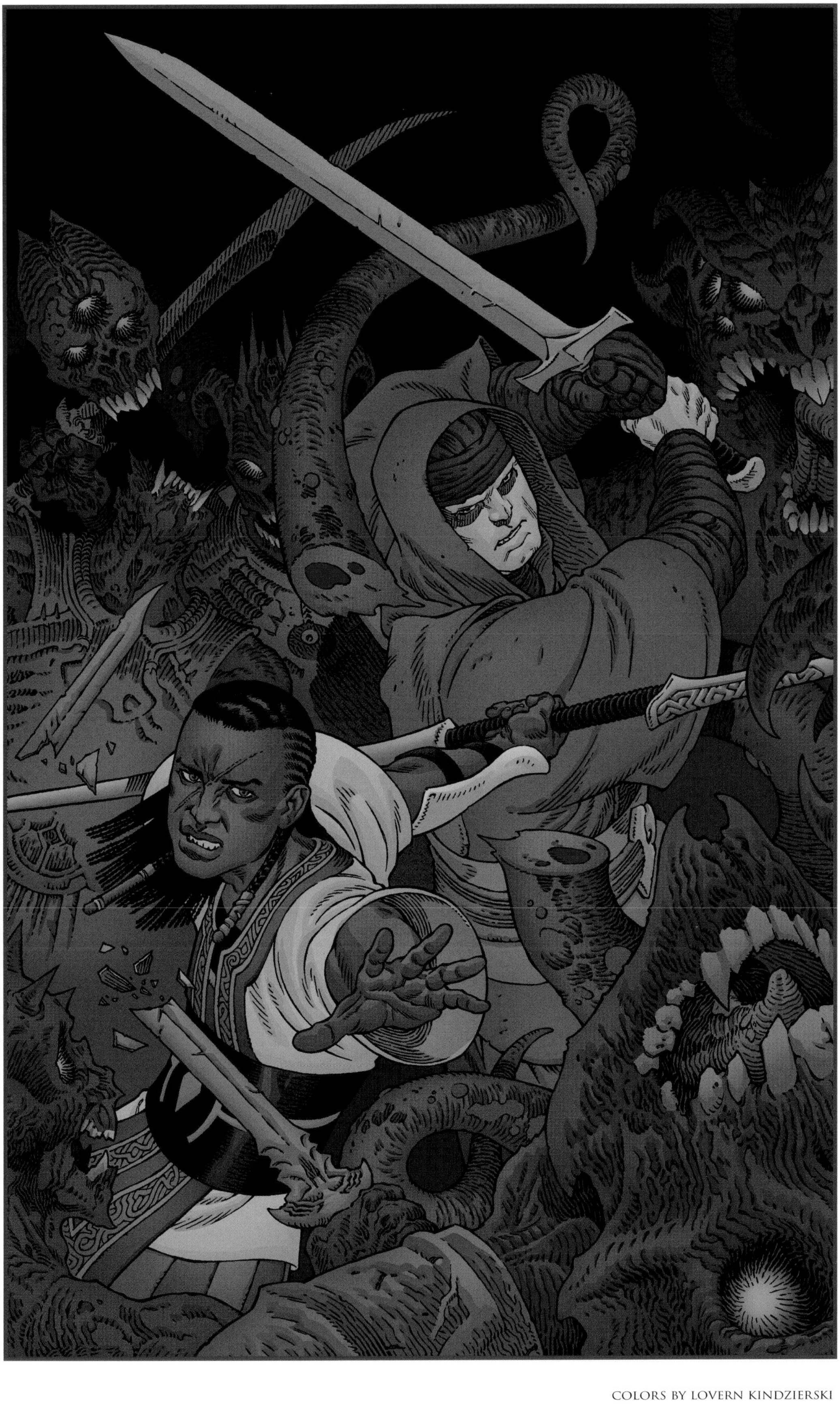

COLORS BY LOVERN KINDZIERSKI

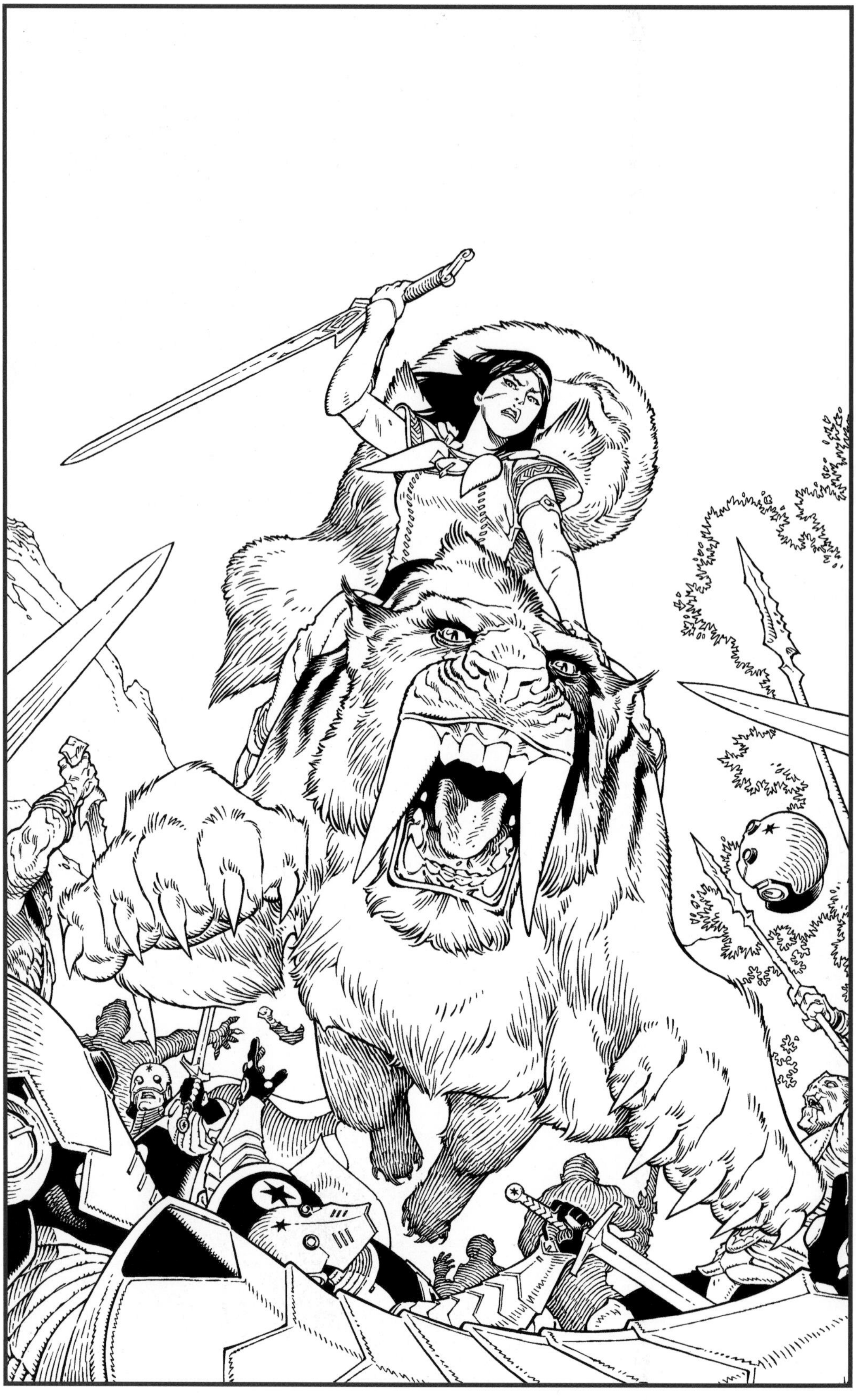

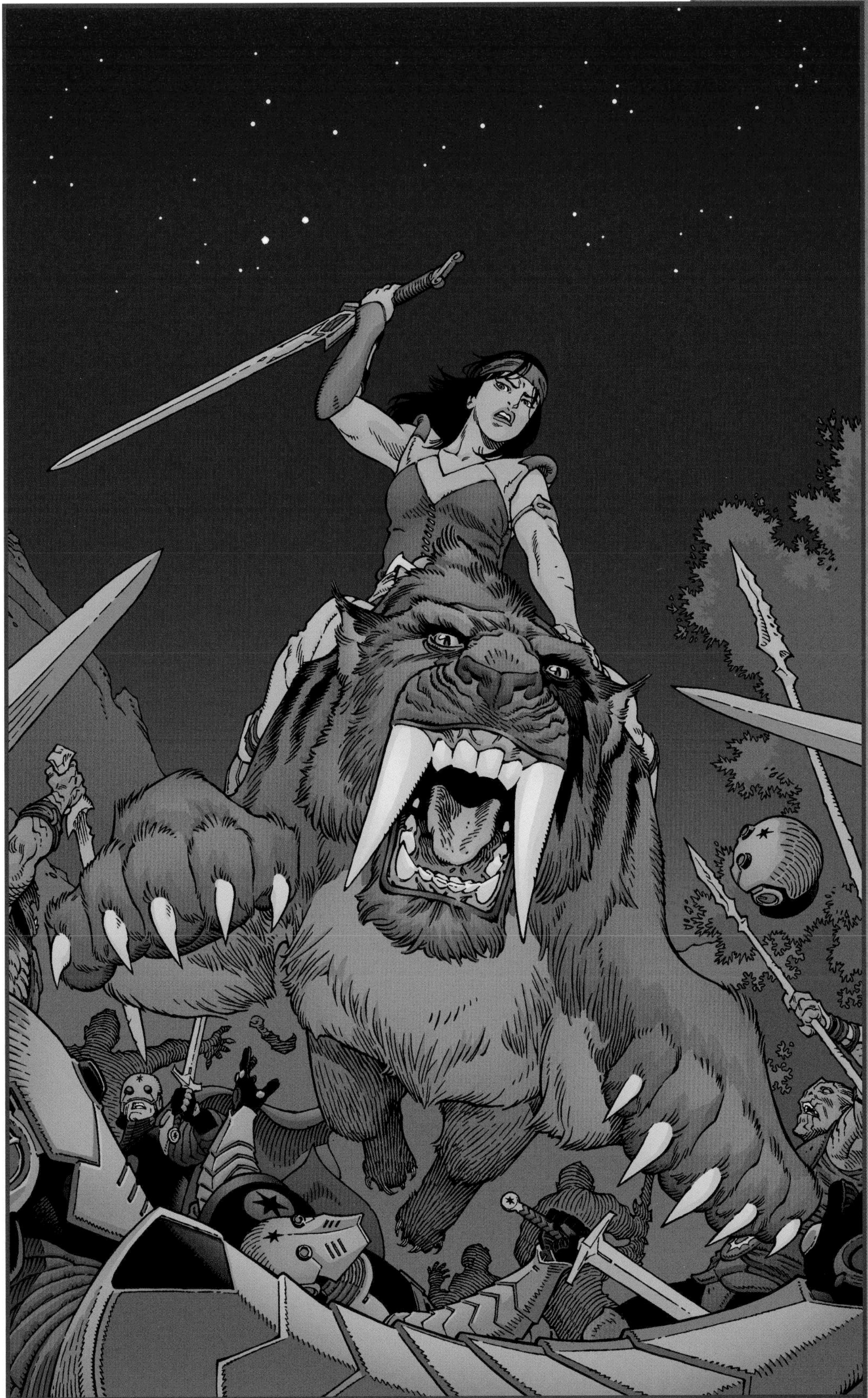

COLORS BY LOVERN KINDZIERSKI

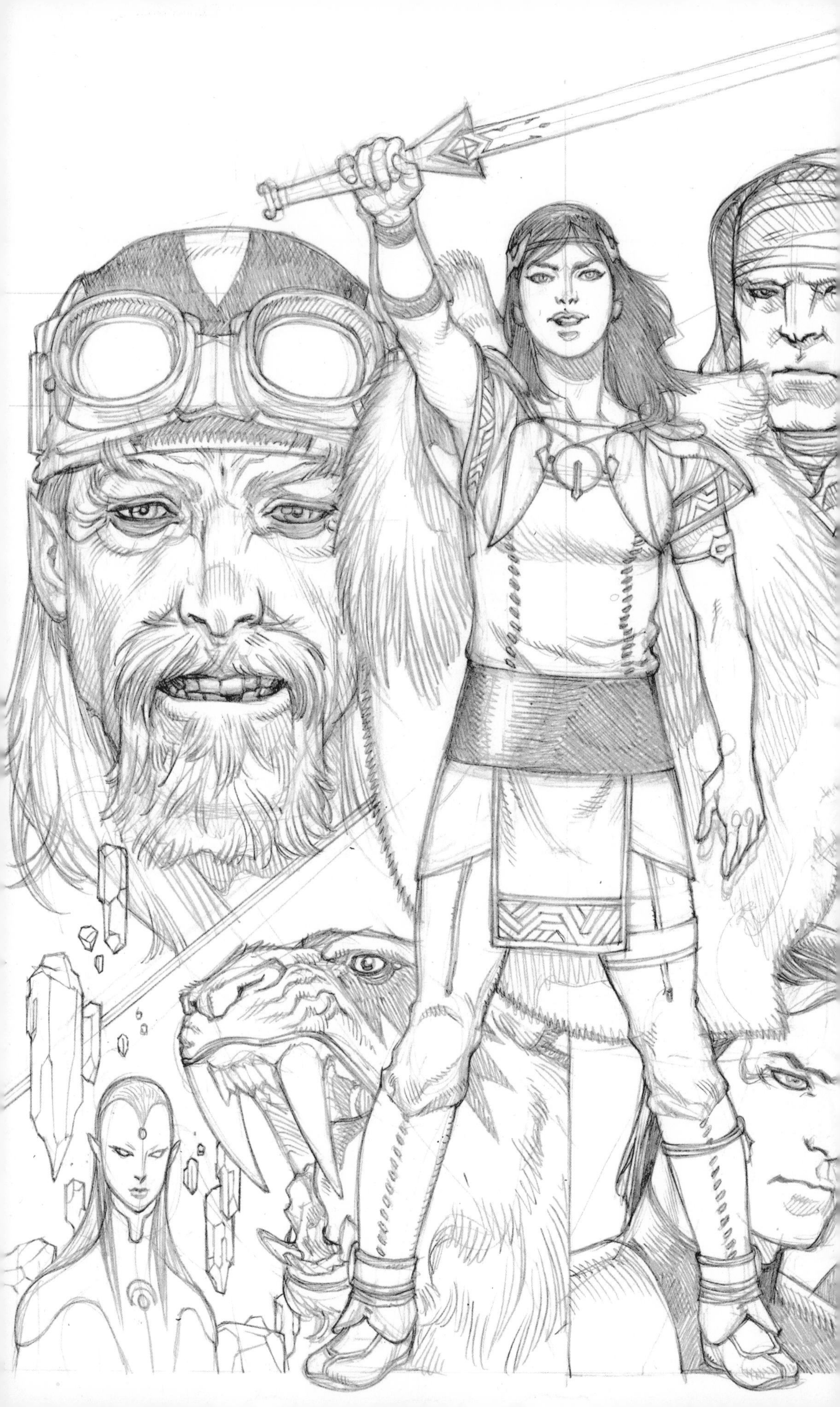

GABRIEL RODRÍGUEZ

INTERVIEW BY
TED ADAMS

TA: *Let's talk about your literary influences for* **Sword of Ages**. *Clearly, the Arthurian myth is a big part of it. I'm curious if there was any particular version of that myth that you looked to when you were developing* Sword of Ages.

GR: Well, I have several influences in the sword-and-sorcery genre, though not necessarily the Arthurian myth. But I do have a deep love for mythology. One of the first books my mom ever gave me was about Greek mythology, from the origin of the universe to the heroes and demagogues.

From that point on, I started studying myths from other parts of the world, including the tale of Arthur. The Arthurian myth has a unique quality, in that it deals with building a better society. This may not necessarily succeed, but having the goal of creating a new world based on the ideals of justice, love, and fairness—and to fight for it—makes it worthy. I've read several versions of the Arthurian myth in short stories. I recently read the T. H. White novels, which I loved.

TA: *Those are great, some of my favorite books.*

GR: Yes, those books are awesome. Not only because of how they capture the magic and the ideals of the Arthurian myth, but also because the characters feel very human. The dialogue between the mythic aspects and the everyday quality of life is so vividly captured.

Another strong influence is John Boorman's *Excalibur*, which captures the humanity of the characters and also manages to capture an incredibly dense and huge universe of concepts and mythology in a very contained story. It's one of the few movies in which you see that every shot and scene is there for a purpose. It builds a lot with very little. For example, the Uther Pendragon

story, which is only a few minutes at the beginning of the movie, fleshes out the entire character in just a couple of scenes. It serves as the basis for how the story develops.

All these things are mixed into the creative pool in which *Sword of Ages* was born. When you want to tell a story in comic-book form, it's always about lack of space. You have to be strategic about what you want to tell and how you want to tell it. That's something I had in mind from the get-go.

TA: I know we've discussed moving to full-length graphic novels. Let's talk about that.

GR: For a while, I've toyed with the idea of working on a comic book project not as a series of monthly issues, but as a graphic novel. I think, in a way, it will allow me to have more freedom in terms of how I manage the pacing and drama of the storytelling, especially considering the massive scope of this tale. These first 100 pages might only be one sixth of the entire story! There will be more room to play with the narrative tone, the speed of events, and the way in which chapters are divided. It's going to be way more fitting for the kind of story that we are building.

Luckily, you and IDW are as excited as I am about giving these books a new way to come to life on the page! It makes sense to me that we would handle this kind of story this way. It will give us more freedom as creators in how to tell our story, and I hope it will be more rewarding for the readers as well, since they will be receiving larger chunks of the story in each new chapter.

Hopefully, it will also make the wait between issues more manageable. With this kind of story and the sheer amount of detail it demands, it's a really slow process to bring them to life. But above all, we're aiming at making it a more rewarding reading experience. We think this is the right way to do it.

TA: Sword of Ages *also has science fiction elements. Were there any particular influences, literary or cinematic, that struck you there?*

GR: One of the things that I wanted to do with this project when I started was to pay tribute to the science fiction and fantasy books that I read during my childhood. For fantasy, Michael Moorcock's and J. R. R. Tolkien's novels stuck with me the most. For sci-fi, probably the *Foundation* series by Isaac Asimov and *Dune* by Frank Herbert. In these books, you have entire

TA: *So much of your storytelling in* Sword of Ages *is exterior rather than interior, with big, panoramic action scenes. The characters are literally in the light, because they're outside, not in.*

GR: My story certainly has a lighter, brighter approach. It's not as dark as much of the fantasy out there. I'm trying to recover a sense of wonder and adventure that used to be in a lot of adventure comics I read when I was younger. I think it's sort of absent in comics and literature right now. I'm trying to bring back this idea of a story with very human and flawed characters, but also with a bright side that will help the reader engage with and enjoy the ride.

I wanted this to be as much about the landscape of the world as the plot that's driving the story. I've been studying European comic book authors as I've been working on the book, so there's a lot of focus on how the landscape and architecture look and how they're shot. One of the earliest decisions I made when laying out *Sword of Ages* was how to approach the width of the page. I basically have widescreen panels in which the background is as present as the characters themselves. Even when the shot is tight on the characters, I always try to have some of the environment showing behind. That sense of a believable world in which the characters are moving is key.

TA: *We should talk about* **Lovern Kindzierski**. *The combination of your art and his coloring, it's extraordinary. I'm curious what led you to choose him and what kind of conversations you've had with him.*

GR: When I was conceiving *Sword of Ages*, one of the things I wanted to pay tribute to was the work Moebius did in *The Incal*, especially the way those books were originally colored. Same

universes, societies, and political conflicts that make the settings vivid, despite how out-of-this-world the imagery can be. It's an engaging way to tell stories that have a big scope and a lot of potential for visual development.

It's weird, because when I was a kid, I didn't like stories in which they mixed science fiction and fantasy, and yet this one evolved into that very easily. I think it's the proper way to tell this story. When I started developing *Sword of Ages*, I imagined it as an apocalyptic retelling of the Arthurian myth. Originally, it was going to be in a futuristic *Mad Max* sort of world where Excalibur reappears and needs a new wielder. But I decided that having this as a sequel to the Arthurian story restricted me too much. So, to have more freedom to play with the characters and drive this story, I decided to make this a prequel, which immediately recalls the opening lines of the *Star Wars* saga: "A long time ago in a galaxy far, far away...." This has become a much more fun way to approach the writing and gives me room to explore parts of the story that haven't been explored before. Like, where does Excalibur come from? What if Excalibur wasn't its original name? Where does the name for the Isle of Avalon come from? It expanded the opportunities for me to explore this myth as an author.

for the work of Alejandro Jodorowsky.

There's a subtle way to approach color palettes, working mostly with flatter coloring. I wanted to get something that, even though it could feel contemporary, would capture some of the appeal of European fantasy comics, particularly since I was going to be drawing with lots of detail and tiny elements. I wanted an artist who could do that kind of coloring.

Lovern immediately said that he was interested. The coloring he did for the *Elric* miniseries with P. Craig Russell was exactly the kind of coloring

I wanted for *Sword of Ages*, so when he jumped in, I knew he was going to be the perfect fit. Then I received the first few pages, and they completely blew my mind. The colors added a new level of depth to the art that helped the story develop and grow. Every time I get a colored page back, it's like Lovern is showing me the possibilities of where the story could go next. It's been a dream. Lovern was probably the first color artist I knew by name when I read comic books as a child. I remember I got a copy of the *Batman: Sword of Azrael* miniseries that was published in the early '90s. It was the first superhero comic where I noticed something special about the coloring. So, being able to work with Lovern on this, my first writing experience as an author in comics, has been incredible. It's been a sort of karmic relationship.

TA: I love to hear that. It's so fun when you get to work with people you admire. You mentioned Moebius, and I can see his influence on this series. What other artists influenced you? I'm particularly interested in European artists that the U.S. audience might not be as familiar with.

GR: In terms of narrative and panel layout, I'm pouring everything I learned from my favorite European authors into this book. Starting with Moebius, that would be *The Incal, Arzach,* or *The Airtight Garage,* but also the work he did as Jean Giraud in the western series *Blueberry.* I think those are the pillars of my approach to the visuals of *Sword of Ages.*

The other European artist who has been a huge influence on this book is Hermann Huppen, who did a couple of series that I read when I was young. One is *Bernard Prince,* which is a series of adventure comics about this smuggler who's always getting into trouble in different parts of the world. Another is the *Jeremaiah* series, a post-apocalyptic saga filled with social commentary and reflection. Huppen is so good with detail and page layout. Especially when there's an establishing shot where he has to present all the elements that are going to be involved in the development of an action sequence. The guy is a master at that.

I also studied a lot of Katsuhiro Otomo's work in *Akira.* I think he's probably the manga artist who's been most influenced by European comics. When you see Otomo's work, you realize that he's using an amount of background detail that's unusual for manga art. Manga tends

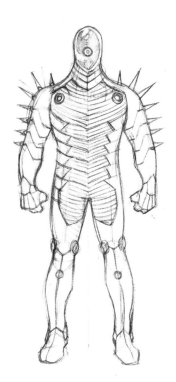

to be like Alex Toth's work—you put exactly what you need for story development into the panel and nothing more. In that regard, Otomo is much more Baroque than the average manga artist. The way he approached the city of Neo Tokyo in *Akira* was a strong influence on my work. He showed me how to use the landscape and environment to develop both the mood and the emotional context for the characters. Those three artists, Moebius, Huppen, and Otomo, were the major influences on this book right from the start.

There's also a very short book called the *The Shadow's Treasure* by Jodorowsky, where he wrote a series of poems and illustrated them. The way in which he handled the lines and the texturing and the shaping of the characters in that book has been an important influence in what I tried to achieve with the graphic development of the art in *Sword of Ages*.

TA: There's a lot of death toward the end of Sword of Ages, *Volume 1 and resolution to the things you've been building on throughout this first story arc. What do you have in mind for the next arc?*

GR: Well, the ending of this first arc of *Sword of Ages* leaves the reader with a major change in the status quo of the relationships of all the forces that have been in conflict. This will form the basis for the society/civilization that these forces will push forward as the story progresses.

We end with Avalon realizing she must take up the torch of leadership for her people and try to figure out what to do now, considering that there is this new enemy force on the planet that plans to conquer everyone.

Future arcs will show how Avalon has to grow in order to become a worthy leader. But she's also a young woman entering adulthood and has to decide what she wants to do with her own life. It's going to be a sort of dialogue between these two aspects of her personality, which will be the driving force of the drama in future installments. And, of course, we've already established the cast of characters who will accompany her on this journey.

TA: Do you have a sense of the timeframe where you'll pick up the story? Will it start right after the events of Volume 1, or will you let some time pass?

GR: The entire story of Avalon is going to be split up into three major timeframes. We're going to have a couple of volumes that will be set in

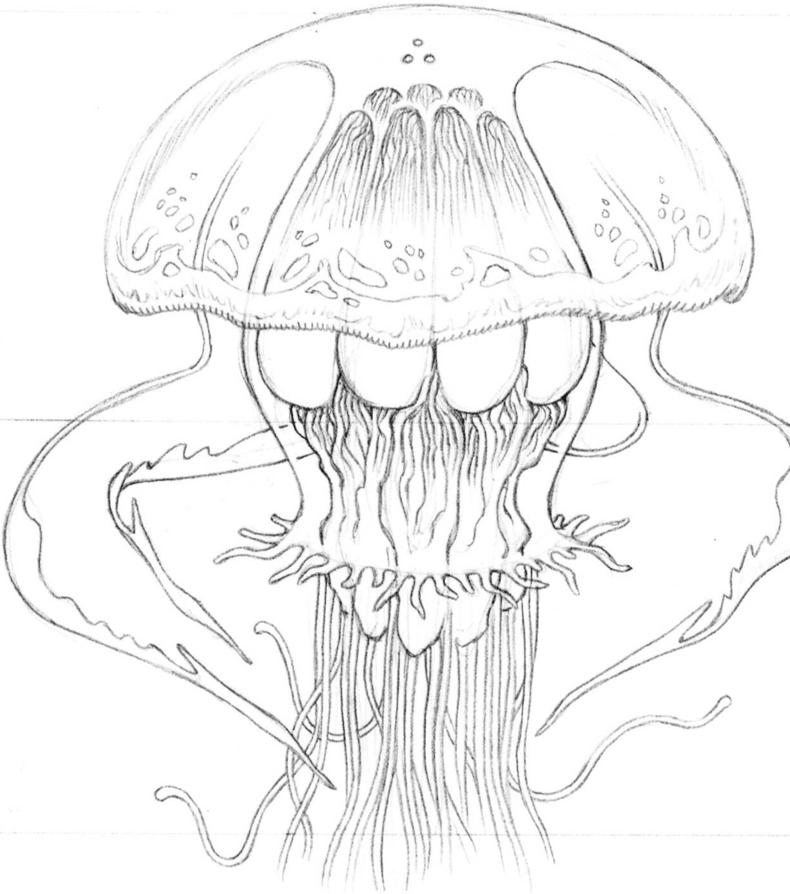

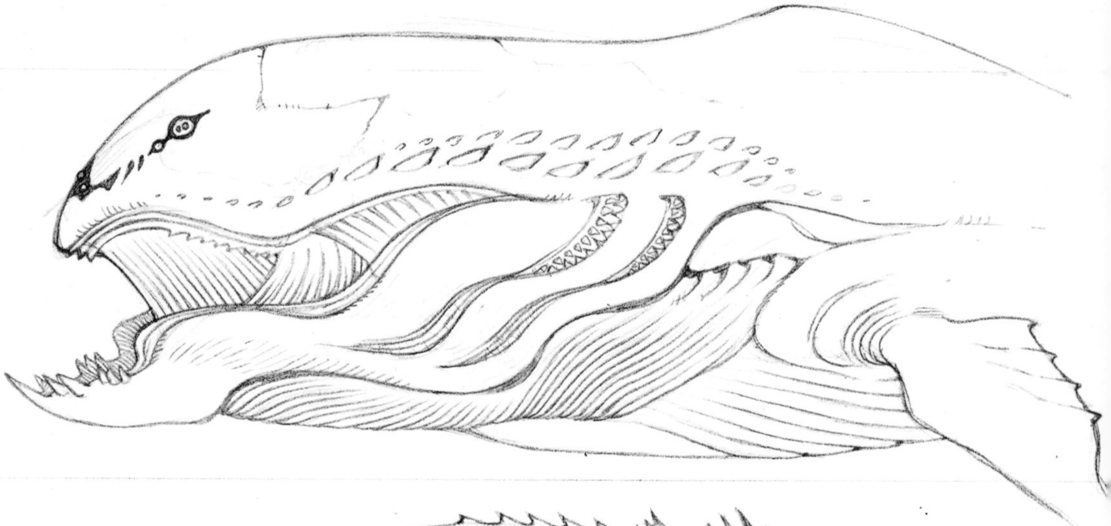

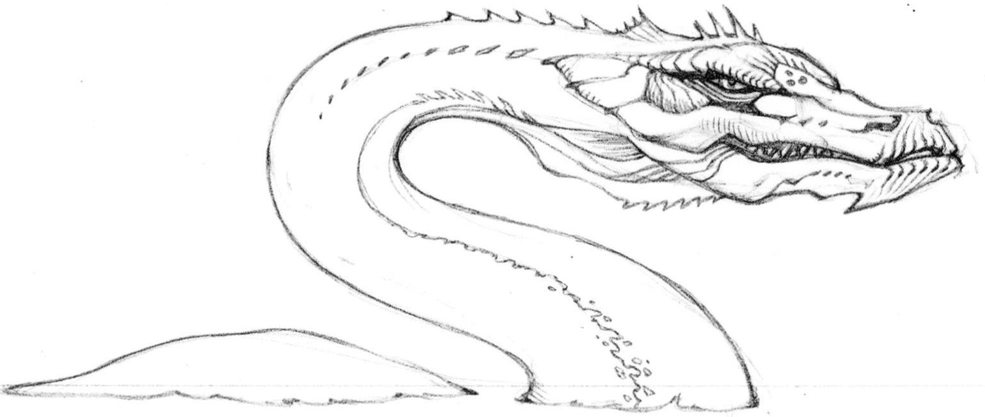

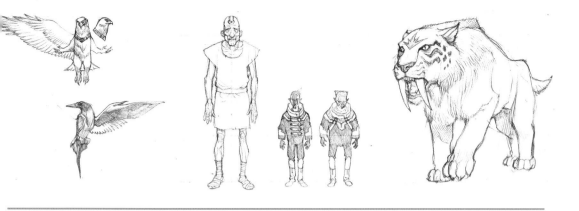

Avalon's youth—this first introductory chapter and then the next volume that will show how she is handling all the situations she ended up clashing with in the first volume.

Then there will be a second chapter equivalent to our own Golden Age, when Avalon becomes the leader of the main culture that is rising in her world.

The third chapter will be the twilight of the origin of the Sacred Sword. Focusing on these three moments will be like visiting the life of Napoleon or Elizabeth I and considering how they got to power, how they managed power, and how that power decayed at the end of their reigns. How their own personal lives changed throughout all three stages—a sort of mirror to the Arthurian legend.

The myth of King Arthur almost always starts with his childhood and how he got the sword. Then, how he became the King who used law and reason to leave the Dark Ages behind, transforming them into a Golden Age. And finally, how his power decayed, leaving behind a legend that would live on in the ages to come, inspiring others to carry the torch of civilization and freedom and fight for the right things. It's that kind of story, but I'm also trying to give it a personal touch by telling it through the eyes and experiences of this young woman who will become what I hope to be a layered, complex, and—at times—contradictory character, as she explores her own maturity through all these events.

TA: Is there anything else we didn't cover that you'd like to mention?

GR: Even though it was incredibly scary to tackle the challenge of writing and drawing my first story in comic-book form, I think, in a way, I got into a story that was more ambitious than what I was originally thinking I would be able to handle. It's been an incredibly freeing experience, incredibly rewarding to me as a creator, and I'm hoping to be able to deliver the readers a story that's worthy of investing their time to experience it. We're only seeing the start of what *Sword of Ages* could be. I'm already thinking about and developing several additions. I have six or eight new characters in mind who will be major players in each of the factions colliding in the story.

To have the chance to explore this world with this amount of freedom and support from my editor and publisher has been amazing. It has allowed me to let the story and characters grow and progress naturally in unexpected ways. This will continue to be part of the adventure of creating *Sword of Ages*, as I discover new characters and situations along the way. Even though I have an idea of the ultimate ending of the story, I keep questioning myself about what the journey to reach that final spot is going to look like. It will be quite a challenge just to follow up this story and create new pages for the upcoming chapters.

TA: You keep creating it, and we'll keep publishing it!

Interview Transcription by Elaine LaRosa • Edits by Gabriel, Ted, & Peter Adrian Behravesh • Art by Gabriel

WORLDBUILDING

When creating a fantasy series like *Sword of Ages*, one of the main challenges of the creative process is to build a believable world where the story can take place. The realer the world that the characters inhabit, the more immersive the storytelling experience will be for the readers.

But "real," in this case, doesn't mean "realistic." Fantasy and sci-fi give writers and artists the chance to get creative—even extravagant—and that's part of the charm. For these worlds to feel real, they must be consistent, properly fleshed out, and charged with history, and they must contain every possible detail that will help drive the story through the panels and pages. They can even contain "unreal" elements, as long as those elements respect the inner logic of the world they are shaping.

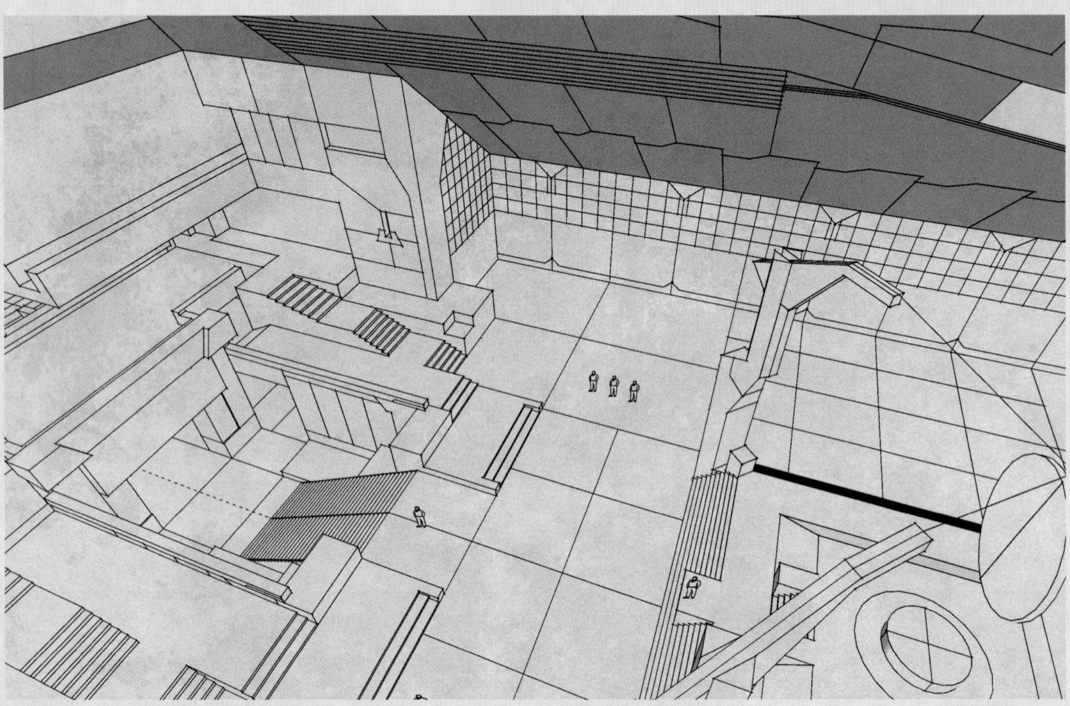

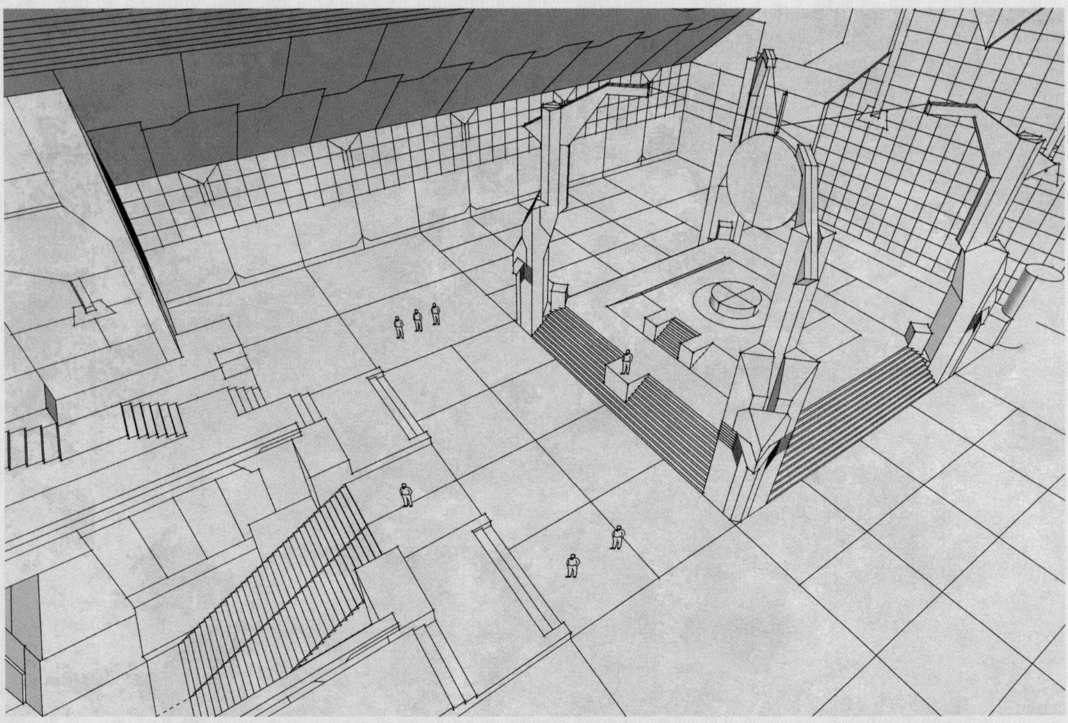

Interior views of the Temple's Inner Sanctum, focusing on the main entrance and staircase (top) and on the Star Crystal altar and the hanging Twin Gods' Sigil (bottom).

THE TWIN MOONS TEMPLE

Early on, as I was writing the five chapters of this first book of Avalon's adventures, and conceiving the world in which the story would develop, I decided (as I did with *Locke & Key*) to take advantage of my architectural training and build a 3D model of the most complex setting of the story. In this case, the Temple of the Twin Moons in Caledia has the responsibility not only to be a testament to the ancient history of the world of *Sword of Ages*, but also to stage the main action sequence of the first act—a massive battle that takes place over more than 30 pages in the last two issues.

So, here you can take a little tour through the 3D model of the main building of the Caledian Temple, including a detailed rendering of its Inner Sanctum, the Chapel, and the balcony that overlooks the valley beyond the city walls. This model was built using Google Sketchup, a tremendously useful digital tool that helps me study layout alternatives to design the action sequences and also pick specific views to use as a guide for drawing believable perspectives of the world surrounding the characters in key panels. Some of these views are presented here, showing 3D renderings next to the hand-drawn final panels.

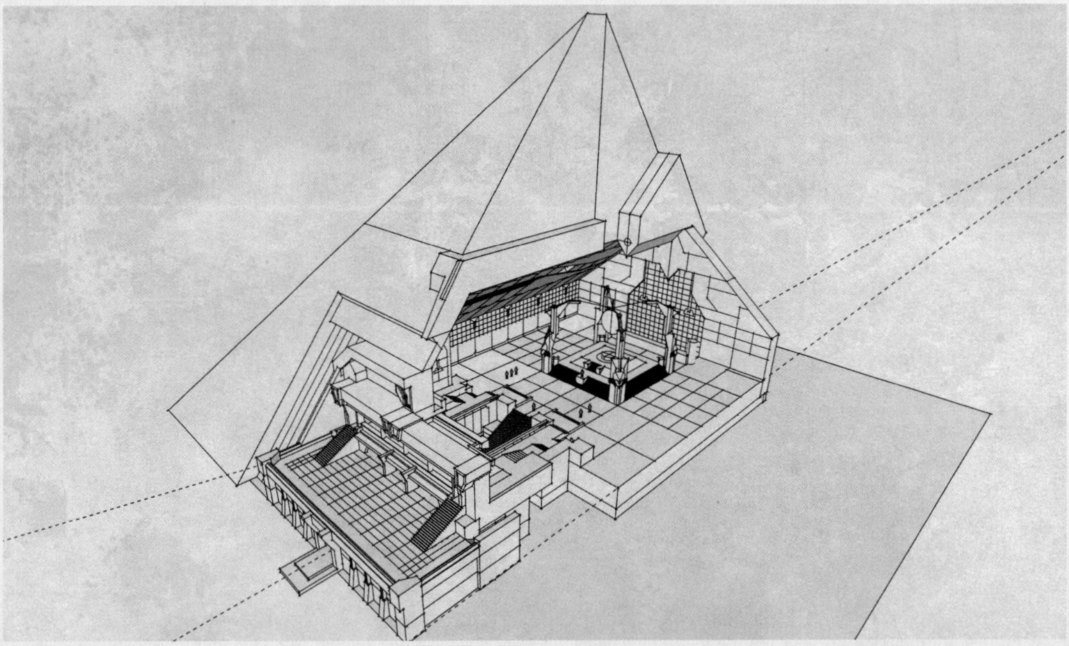

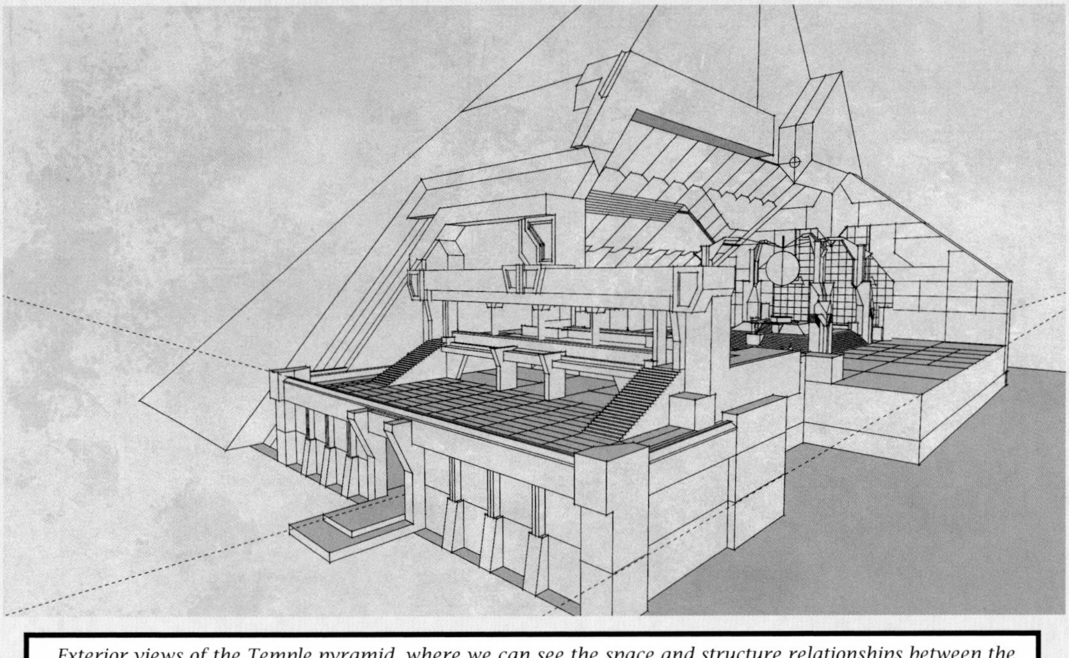

Exterior views of the Temple pyramid, where we can see the space and structure relationships between the Sanctum, the Chapel, the balcony, and the main entrance. This model was designed as a cross section in order to easily allow still shots from the interior rooms for use as perspective and layout references.

Fig. 1: *Introduction to the Temple's Inner Sanctum in a double-page spread. The purpose of this establishing shot is to set the stage for the final act of the first arc.*

Fig. 2: *Closer view of the Sanctum's main entrance. It's very important to have scale reference, like this staircase, in order to understand the size and placement of the characters in the scene.*

Fig. 3: *Shot of the balcony's external staircase. More important than having fully detailed reference is having just the elements you need. In this case, the shape and proportions of the space were the key references.*

Fig. 4: *Shot from the Temple's balcony railing. In the actual panel, the perspective is forced in order to make Merlin's presence more prominent. It's always important to remember that reference is a tool, not a rule. You can bend the rules as much as you need for storytelling purposes.*

Fig. 5: *Another shot of the altar. Here we can see how the reference was forced by the characters' placement in order to enhance the scale relationships and the drama of the action scene displayed.*

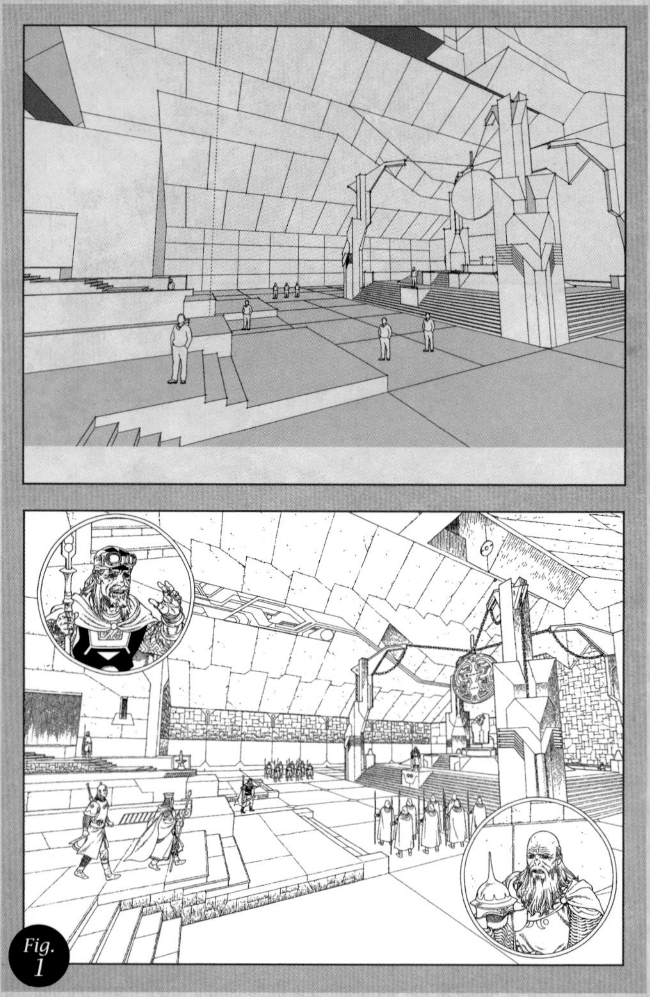

Fig. 1

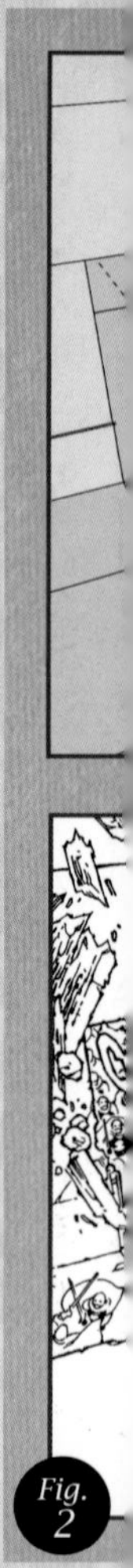

Fig. 2

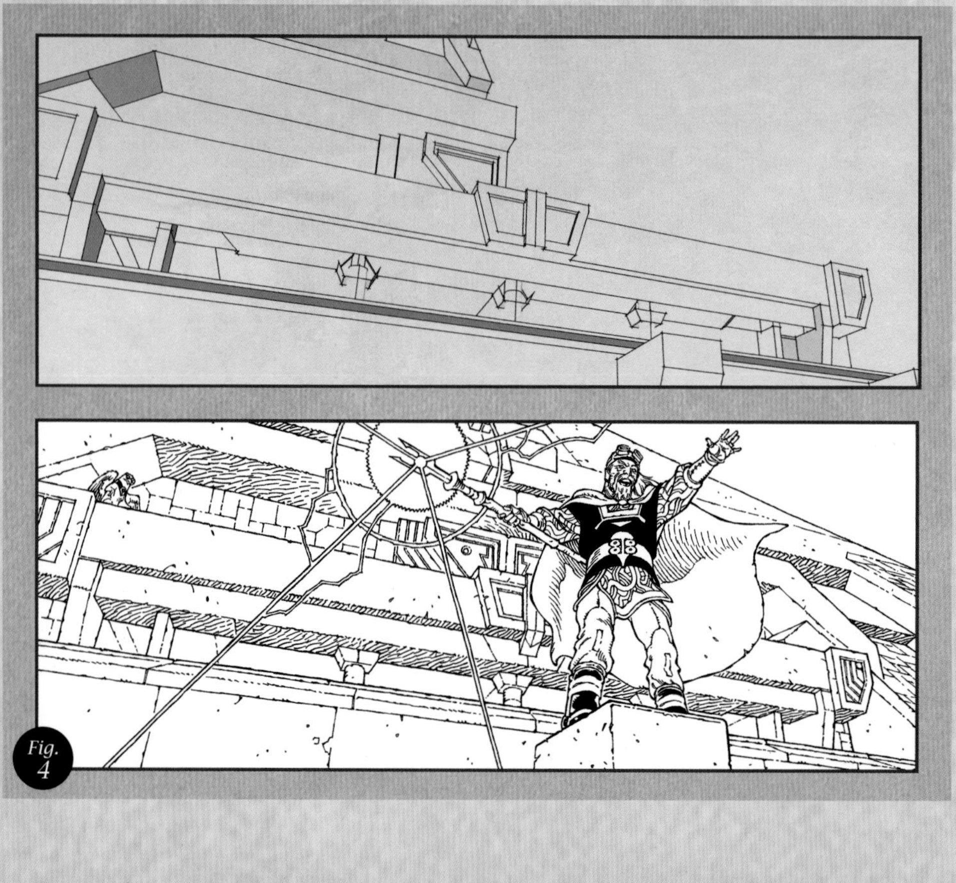

Fig. 4

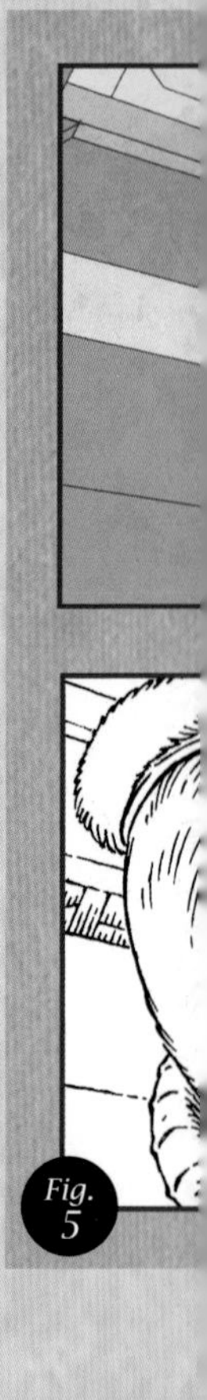

Fig. 5

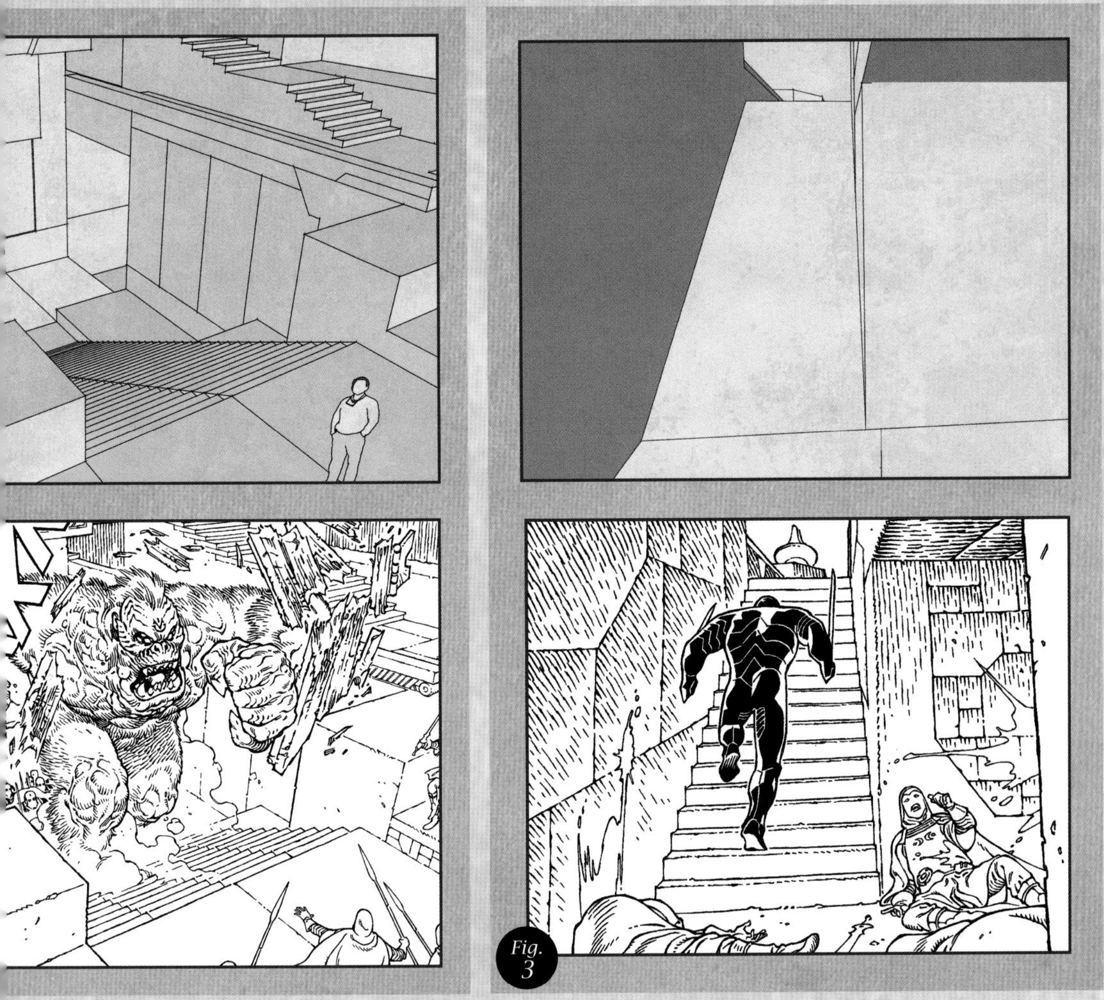

Fig. 3

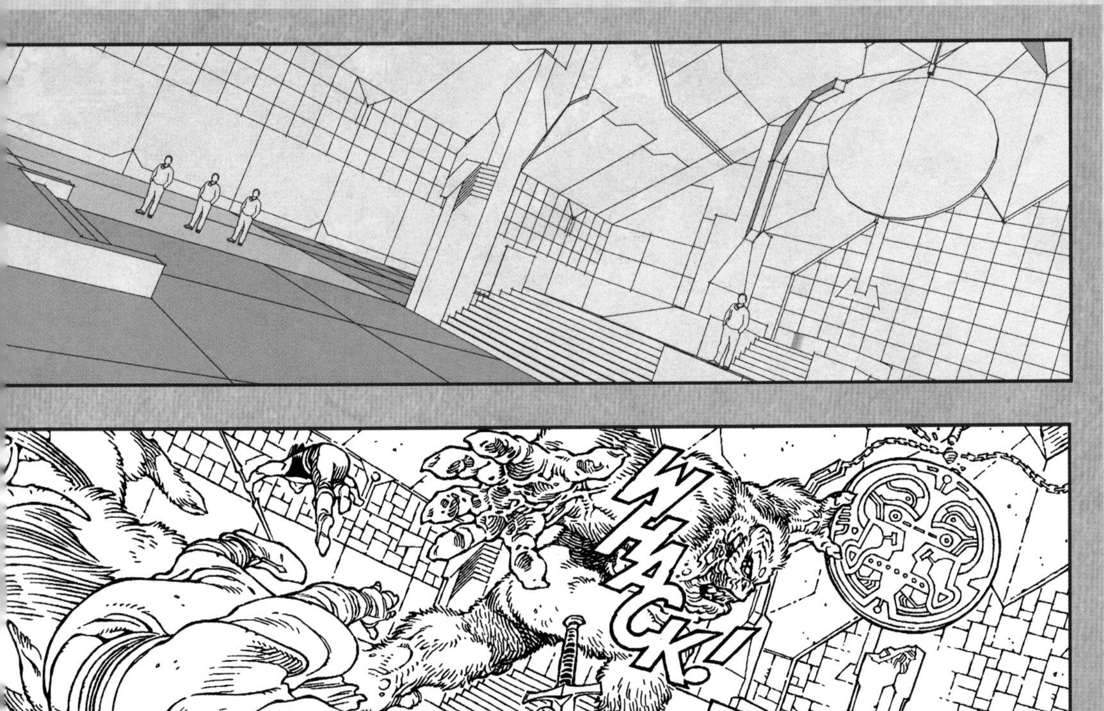
WHACK!

CALEDIA AND THE CITADEL WALL

In the development of the second double-page spread of Issue #4, I used a different approach. In this scene—which was incredibly complex in terms of its narrative content, and also required me to build an entire landscape for a massive action sequence—my strategy was to organize and design the space and elements based on narrative demands, rather than a static model.

Aware that trying to design a model would eventually force me to pick a shot able to contain it all, I worked backwards. The first decision I made was to place all of the elements that would comprise the final shot on the page itself: Lancer in action, Nikola flying toward him, the Red Clan warriors trying to climb the walls, the monks moving into battle positions, the towers, the broken gateway, the bridges between the citadel and the wall, the mutant giants, the armies fighting beyond the wall, and so on. I tried to place them in balanced relationships, with hierarchical relevance. Then, I filled in the setting around them. Using a forced curved perspective, I was able to make the sequence read fluidly while also maintaining the integrity of multiple elements in multiple scales on multiple layers, conveying a more dramatic sense of depth.

All of these decisions were defined as precisely as possible in the first rough sketch, which I did as a small, letter-size paper drawing, first in very loose pencils and then in ink. This gave me a template that I scanned and printed in the size of the final drawing. Then, using a light box tablet, I retraced the entire drawing with a blue lead mechanical pencil, and added all of the details that would be needed in the final inked version. This is something I try to avoid when drawing regular panels, as it usually means extra work and extra time, but in key shots like this one, it helps me test the weight and relationships of the graphic elements in order to properly measure the amount of information I'm feeding to the reader.

Then, I proceeded with the inking, in which I got rid of anything that might be unnecessary: excess textures, extraneous details in the tinier figures, or any extra lines that might make the composition of overlapping elements confusing.

Finally, I scanned the drawing. I used photo editing software to isolate the yellow channel of the CMYK image. Then, by converting it to grayscale, and by modifying its brightness and contrast, I created the final, clean line art. From there, the magic of coloring and lettering completed the creative process, allowing my drawing to become an actual scene charged with life, drama, and narrative purpose— hopefully making the world believable and the characters inhabiting it alive and appealing.

Gabriel Rodríguez
Santiago, April 10th, 2018

Fig.
6

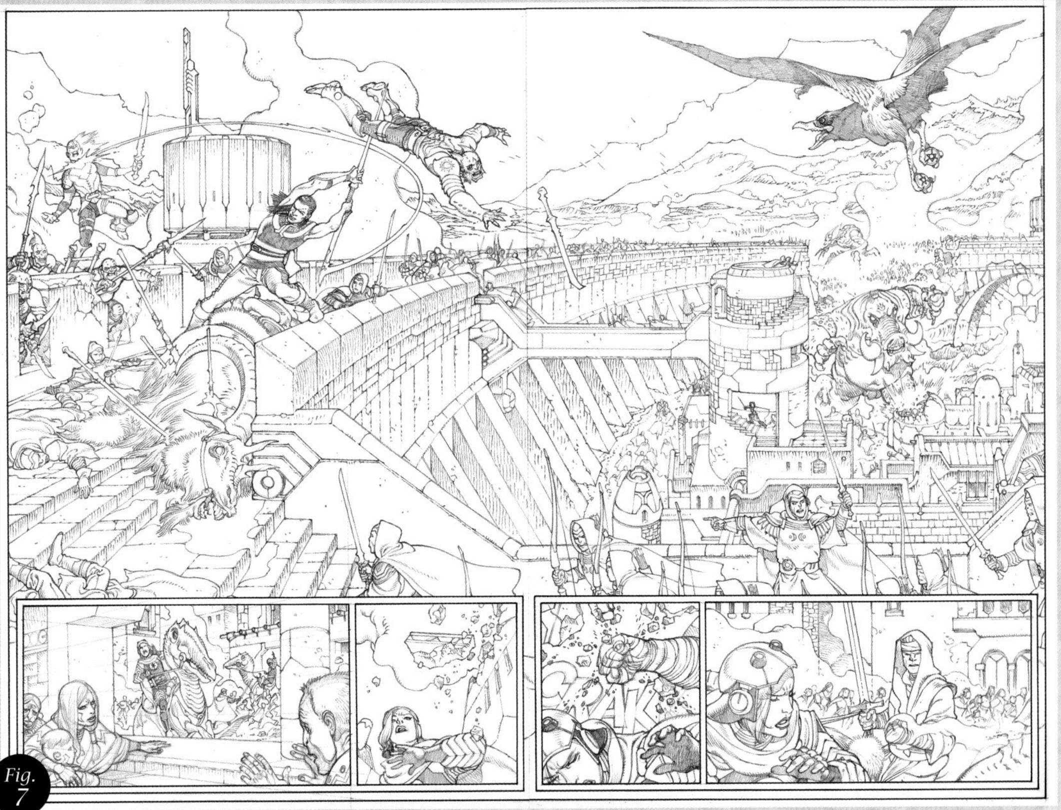

Fig. 7

Fig. 6: *Basic sketch layout. Pencils and ink on paper, done in ¼ scale.*

Fig. 7: *Final pencils. 0.5 mm blue lead mechanical pencil on double A3 paper, full size.*

Fig. 8: *Final inks. Faber-Castell PITT artist ink pens. Tip sizes: B (for full blacks), M, F, S, and XS on double A3 paper, full size.*

Fig. 9: *Final black-and-white file. After scanning, CMYK image reduced to 94%. Yellow channel isolated, making it grayscale, and brightness and contrast adjusted to get the flat black. 300 dpi TIFF.*

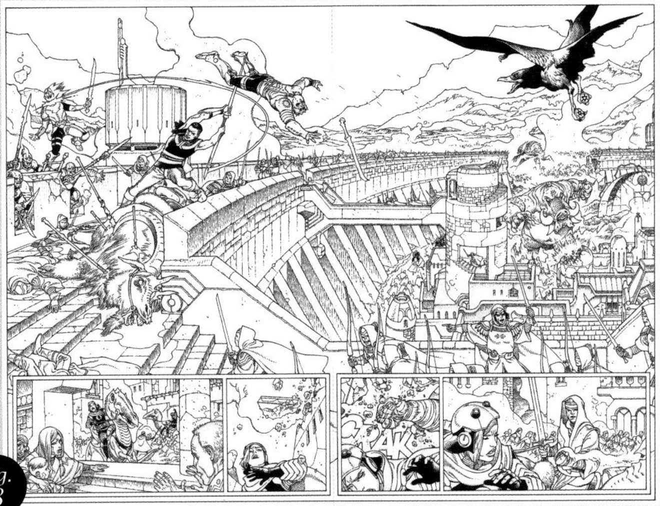

Fig. 8

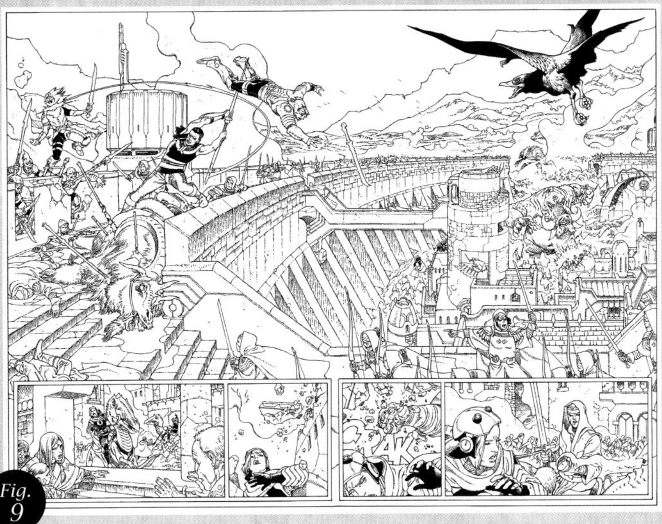

Fig. 9

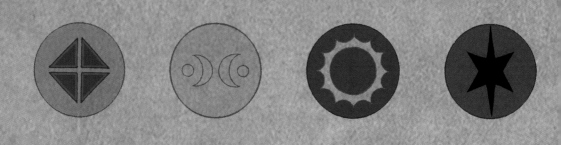

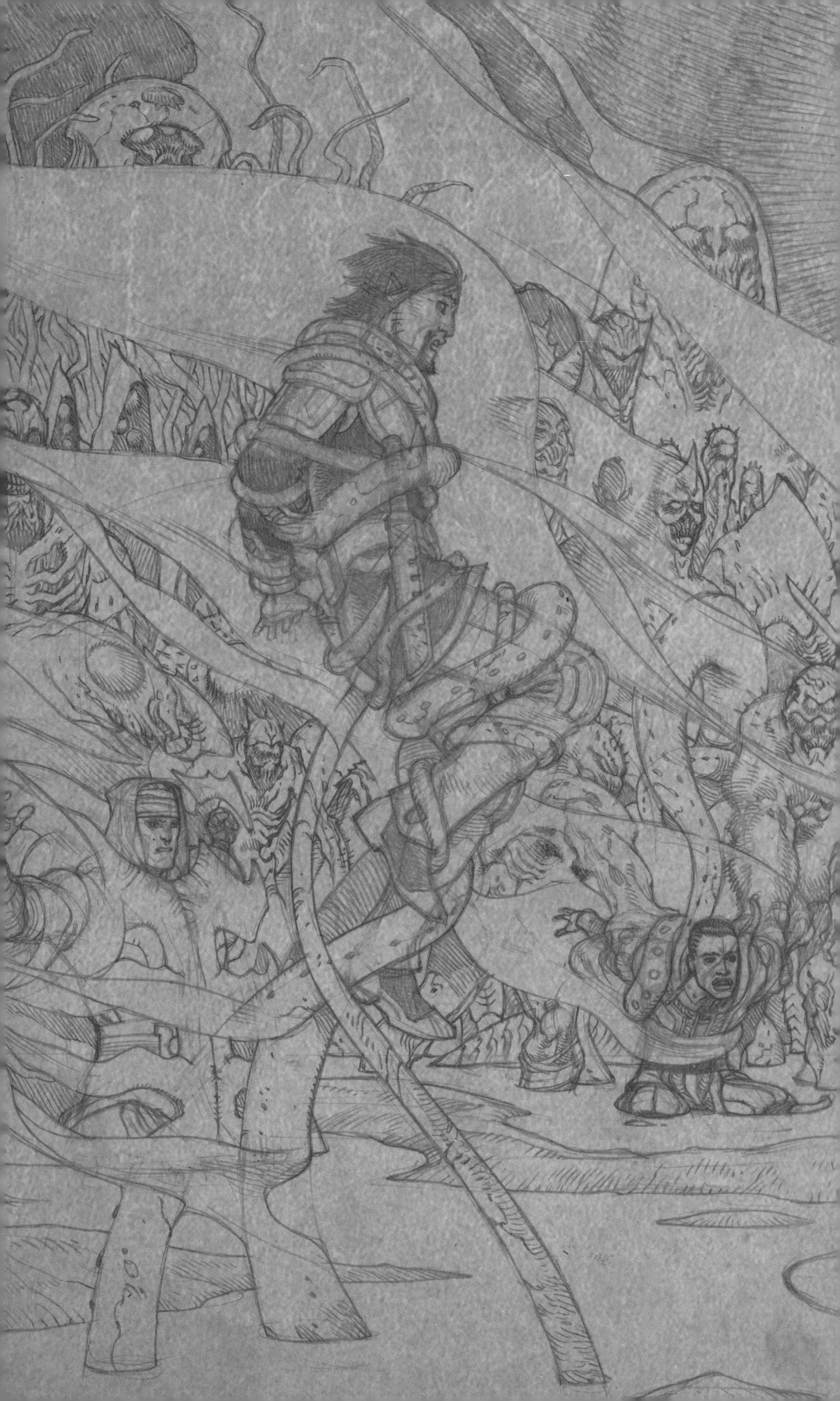